W9-CEW-089

HOW TO HANG A WITCH

HOW

TO HANG

A WITCH

Adriana Mather

ALFRED A. KNOPF
New York

THIS IS A BORZOI BOOK PUBLISHED BY ALFRED A. KNOPF

Text copyright © 2016 by Adriana Mather
Jacket art copyright © 2016 by Sean Freeman

Visit us on the Web! randomhouseteens.com

Educators and librarians, for a variety of teaching tools, visit us at RHTeachersLibrarians.com

Library of Congress Cataloging-in-Publication Data
Names: Mather, Adriana.
Title: How to hang a witch / Adriana Mather.
Description: First edition. | New York : Alfred A. Knopf, [2016] |
Summary: Follows fifteen-year-old Samantha Mather, who has moved to Salem with her stepmother 300 years after her family hanged witches there, to find she is ostracized by the witch descendants at school, as she unravels the lost secrets of the hangings and her family.
Identifiers: LCCN 2015022728 | ISBN 978-0-553-53947-9 (hardcover) | ISBN 978-0-553-53948-6 (lib. bdg.) | ISBN 978-0-553-53949-3 (ebook) | ISBN 978-0-553-53950-9 (pbk.)
Subjects: | CYAC: Witchcraft—Fiction. | Supernatural—Fiction. | Blessing and cursing—Fiction. | Trials (Witchcraft)—Fiction. | Salem (Mass.)—Fiction.
Classification: LCC PZ7.1.M3765 Ho 2016 | DDC [Fic]—dc23
LC record available at http://lccn.loc.gov/2015022728
ISBN 978-1-524-70083-6 (intl. tr. pbk.)

The text of this book is set in 11.5-point Bembo.

Printed in the United States of America
July 2016
10 9 8 7 6 5 4 3 2 1

First Edition

For
Sandra Mather,
whom I love without question

⌐⌐⌐

For
James Bird,
who brightens my every moment

⌐⌐⌐

And for
Claire Mather,
who had the foresight to know I would become a writer

CHAPTER ONE

———————

Too Confident

Like most fast-talking, opinionated New Yorkers, I have an affinity for sarcasm. At fifteen, though, it's hard to convince anyone that sarcasm's a cultural thing and not a bad attitude. Especially when your stepmother can't drive, 'cause she's also from New York, and spills your coffee with maniacal brake pounding.

I wipe a dribble of hazelnut latte off my chin. "It's okay. Don't worry about it. I love wearing my coffee."

Vivian keeps her hand poised over the horn, like a cat waiting to pounce. "All your clothes have holes in them. Coffee isn't your problem."

If it's possible for someone to never have an awkward moment, socially or otherwise, then that someone is my stepmother. When I was little, I admired her ability to charm roomfuls of people. Maybe I thought it would rub off on me—an idea I've since given up on. She's perfectly put together in a way I'll never be, and my vegan leather jacket and torn black jeans drive her crazy. So now I just take joy in wearing them to her dinner parties. Gotta have something, right?

"My problem is, I don't know when I'll see my dad," I say, staring out at the well-worn New England homes, with their widow's walks and dark shutters.

Vivian's lips tighten. "We've been through this a hundred times. They'll transfer him to Mass General sometime this week."

"Which is still an hour from Salem." This is the sentence I've repeated since I found out three weeks ago that we had to sell our New York apartment, the apartment I've spent my entire life in.

"Would you rather live in New York and not be able to pay your father's medical bills? We have no idea how long he'll be in a coma."

Three months, twenty-one days, and ten hours. That's how long it's already been. We pass a row of witch-themed shops with dried herbs and brooms filling their windows.

"They really love their witches here," I say, ignoring Vivian's last question.

"This is one of the most important historical towns in America. Your relatives played a major role in that history."

"My relatives hanged witches in the sixteen hundreds. Not exactly something to be proud of."

But in truth, I'm super curious about this place, with its cobblestone alleys and eerie black houses. We pass a police car with a witch logo on the side. As a kid, I tried every tactic to get my dad to take me here, but he wouldn't hear of it. He'd say that nothing good ever happens in Salem and the conversation would end. There's no pushing my dad.

A bus with a ghost-tour ad pulls in front of us. Vivian

jerks to a stop and then tailgates. She nods at the ad. "There's a nice provincial job for you."

I crack a smile. "I don't believe in ghosts." We make a right onto Blackbird Lane, the street on the return address of the cards my grandmother sent me as a child.

"Well, you're the only one in Salem who feels that way." I don't doubt she's right.

For the first time during this roller coaster of a car ride, my stomach drops in a good way. Number 1131 Blackbird Lane, the house my dad grew up in, the house he met my mother in. It's a massive two-story white building with black shutters and columned doorways. The many peaks of the roof are covered with dark wooden shingles, weathered from the salty air. A wrought-iron fence with pointed spires surrounds the perfectly manicured lawn.

"Just the right size," Vivian says, eyeing our new home.

The redbrick driveway is uneven with age and pushed up by tree roots. Vivian's silver sports car jostles us as we make our way through the black arched gate and roll to a stop.

"Ten people could live here and never see each other," I reply.

"Like I said, just the right size."

I pull my hair into a messy ball on top of my head and grab the heavy duffel bag at my feet. Vivian's already out of the car, and her heels click against the brick. She makes her way toward a side door with an elaborate overhang.

I take a deep breath and open my car door. Before I get a good look at our new home, a neighbor comes out of her blue-on-blue house and waves enthusiastically.

"Hellllooo! Well, hello there!" she says with a smile bigger than I've ever seen on a stranger as she crosses a patch of lawn to get to our driveway.

She has rosy cheeks and a frilly white apron. She could have stepped out of a housekeeping magazine from the 1950s.

"Samantha," she says, and beams. She holds my chin to inspect my face. "Charlie's daughter."

I've never heard anyone call my dad by a nickname. "Uh, Sam. Everyone calls me Sam."

"Nonsense. That's a boy's name. Now, aren't you pretty. Too skinny, though." She steps back to get a proper look. "We'll fix that in no time." She laughs a full, tinkling laugh.

I smile, even though I'm not sure she's complimenting me. There's something infectious about her happiness. She examines me, and I cross my arms self-consciously. My duffel bag falls off my shoulder, jerking me forward. I trip.

"Jaxon!" she bellows toward her blue house without saying a word about my clumsiness. A blond guy who looks seventeenish exits the side door just as I get hold of the duffel strap. "Come take Samantha's bag."

As he gets closer, his sandy hair flops into his eyes. *Blue.* One corner of his mouth tilts in a half smile. I stare at him. *Am I blushing? Ugh, so embarrassing.* He reaches for the bag, now awkwardly hanging from my elbow.

I reposition it onto my shoulder. "No, it's fine."

"This is my son, Jaxon. Isn't he adorable?" She pats him on the cheek.

"Mom, really?" Jaxon protests.

I smile at them. "So, you know my dad?"

"Certainly. And I knew your grandmother. Took care of her and the house when she got older. I know this place inside and out." She puts her hands on her hips.

Vivian approaches, frowning. "Mrs. Meriwether? We spoke on the phone." She pauses. "You have the keys, I assume?"

"Sure do." Mrs. Meriwether reaches into her apron pocket and retrieves a set of skeleton keys rubbed smooth in places from years of use. She glances at her watch. "I've got chocolate croissants coming out of the oven any minute now. Jaxon will give you a tour of—"

"No, that's alright. We can show ourselves around." There's a finality in Vivian's response. Vivian doesn't trust overly friendly people. We had a doorman once who used to bring me treats, and she got him fired.

"Actually," I say, "do you know which room used to be my dad's?"

Mrs. Meriwether lights up. "It's all ready for you. Up the stairs, take a left, all the way down the hall. Jaxon will show you."

Vivian turns around without a goodbye. Jaxon and I follow her to the door.

Jaxon watches me curiously as we go inside. "I've never seen you here before."

"I've never been here before."

"Even when your grandmother was alive?" He closes the door behind us with a click.

"I never met my grandmother." It's weird to admit that.

In the front foyer are piles of boxes—all of our personal belongings from the City. Vivian sold everything heavy when she found out this place was furnished.

We step past the boxes into an open space with glossy wooden floors, a wrought-iron chandelier, and a giant staircase. Vivian's heels click somewhere down the hallway to the left—a sound that follows her around like a shadow. As a child, I could always find her by listening for it, even in a roomful of women in high heels. I wouldn't be surprised if she slept in those shoes.

I take in our home for the first time. Paintings in gold

frames hang on the walls, separated by sconces with bulbs shaped like candles. Everything's antique and made of dark wood, the opposite of our modern apartment in NYC. *This is some fairy-tale storybook business,* I think, looking at the curved staircase with its smooth wooden banisters and Oriental rug running up the middle.

"This way." Jaxon nods toward the staircase. He lifts my bag off my shoulder and starts up the stairs.

"I could've carried that myself."

"I know. But I wouldn't want you to fall again. Stairs do more damage than driveways." So he definitely saw me trip.

He smiles at my expression.

This guy is too confident for his own good. I follow him, holding the banister in case my clumsiness makes a second appearance.

Jaxon turns left at the top of the stairs. We pass a bedroom with a burgundy comforter and a canopy that any little girl would go bonkers over. After the bedroom, there's a bathroom with a giant claw-foot tub and a mirror with a gold-plated frame.

He stops at the end of the hall in front of a small door that looks like it could use a fresh coat of paint. The doorknob's shaped like a flower with shiny brass petals. A daisy, maybe? I twist it, and the wood groans as the door swings open.

I gasp.

"Like it?" Jaxon asks. "My mother was over here all week moving this furniture in and fixing it up for you."

To my right is a dark wooden bed whose four posts are carved with flowers, a matching flower-carved vanity with a marble top, and a delicate nightstand with an old lamp made of yellow glass. Directly in front of me is an armoire. I love armoires. Next to my bed is a small white rug for cold mornings. And overlooking the front lawn is a window seat with white lace cushions.

"It's a real dump," I say.

Jaxon laughs, and an approving smile crosses his face.

I run my hand along the ivory lace bedspread and down comforter. My black duffel bag looks unsophisticated in comparison with these antiques balanced on sloping wooden floors.

Unsure what to say next, I pull my lip gloss from my pocket and pop off the cap. This is the longest conversation I've had with someone my own age in years.

Jaxon lifts my bag off his shoulder. "Where do you want this?"

"I'll take it." I reach out to grab the strap. But I misjudge his movement, and instead of smoothly lifting the bag out of his grip, as I intended, I smear my open lip gloss on his hand.

He stops and smiles. "Pink's not really my color."

"Sorry!" I say quickly. "I don't usually attack people with my lip gloss." *As though some people use lip gloss as a weapon? What am I even saying right now?*

All I can think to do is wipe it off with my hand, which I do awkwardly—more of a swat than a wipe, really. His grin widens. He puts my duffel bag down and grabs a tissue from my vanity.

Jaxon lifts my hand with the strawberry-flavored smear on it. He turns my palm up and lightly runs the tissue over it. My heart gallops. *I don't even like blonds.*

"It's not going to break," I say. "My hand, I mean . . . it's not going to break."

"I'd rather not take any chances."

His confidence is starting to frustrate me. He's hogging it all and should really leave some for the rest of the planet.

He looks from my hand to my face. "Who knows what you'll attack me with next."

I take my hand back. "What? Oh yeah. I mean, no. I mean, I won't touch you." *Shit. Really?*

He nods, barely containing a laugh. "See you in school tomorrow."

Don't laugh at me. You probably never had an awkward moment in your life, with all your floppy blond hair and tanned skin. So shut it! He disappears down the hall lit by small lamps, and for the first time since my dad got sick, I actually feel like myself.

CHAPTER TWO

Pleasant Company

Vivian and I look silly at this long dining room table with our take-out food. *This thing's meant for eight people with crocheted place mats.*

I spear a bite of ravioli from the plastic container and offer Vivian some. She shakes her head. My dad's the chef in the family, which kinda makes sense, since he's a spice importer. Vivian doesn't cook much. And when she does, it's always steak and potatoes, and I'm a vegetarian.

"Your father always used to talk about his childhood here," Vivian says.

"Not to me." He never wanted to talk about Salem, especially in the past year since my grandmother died. I didn't even know we still owned this house until a couple weeks ago.

"I guess he and Meriwether were longtime friends," she continues with a tinge of judgment.

"I think she's sweet." I take a bite of garlic bread.

Vivian crinkles her nose. "Too sweet. I bet she's nosy as anything."

"I don't know." I'm not going to agree with Vivian about Mrs. Meriwether, who seems perfectly nice.

"Watch, she'll be sending her son over to gather information for her." Vivian shakes her head. Then, with an eye roll, she continues, "But I bet you wouldn't mind that."

I stop mid-bite. "I really don't care one way or the other."

"Uh-huh. Well, it wouldn't hurt you to try to make friends here." She dabs the corners of her mouth with her napkin and a small amount of cranberry lipstick marks the linen.

My fingers tighten around my fork. "You know it ends in disaster anyway." It's only a matter of time before someone gets hurt or their parents forbid them to spend time with me.

"People are disappointing. Still, you'll have to curb the attitude a bit. Smile, even."

Vivian's subtle judgments poke at my fears that this place will turn out to be just like the City. "Maybe I'll visit Mrs. Meriwether." I watch for a reaction. "Learn by example."

Vivian raises one perfect eyebrow, trying to assess whether I'm serious. Four months ago, she would have laughed at that, and I would have meant it as a joke.

I close the ravioli container with a sigh. As a child, I used to follow Vivian everywhere. My dad called me her personal fan club. Vivian loved it. She's always her best self while being admired. But since my dad was admitted to the hospital, there's been tension between us. And since I found out we had to move, it's ballooned into something I don't know how to step back from.

I push my chair away from the table and Vivian winces

as it scrapes against the floor. I don't say anything as I exit the dining room, which looks like it was plucked from an old British movie. The only things missing are white-gloved servants and pleasant company.

It's a short walk to the stairway. I pass a bathroom with dark mulberry walls and another room I can only describe as a lady's tearoom, which looks out over a rose garden.

I grab the railing and take two steps at a time. When I reach the top, the only light is the one coming from my room, which glows a soft yellow at the end of the hallway. Vivian's room is at the end of the other hall, probably her way of trying to get as far away from me as possible. Vivian and I were never the cuddly types or people who worked things out with a heart-to-heart. But I can't say this divide doesn't bother me, either.

I wish my dad were here. These old rooms must be filled with his memories. *Maybe being here is good in a way. Distracts me from constantly worrying.* I push open my door.

"Seriously?" My once neatly folded clothes in my armoire are now in a heap on the floor.

I inspect the armoire latch to see if it's broken. It seems fine. Maybe I just didn't close it all the way?

"That's one way to unpack," Vivian says, standing in my doorway.

"These were all put away an hour ago. Must've piled them too high."

"Maybe we have a ghost who doesn't like you." Vivian smiles. I'm sure she's trying to lighten the mood, but this move to Salem has left me a little raw.

"Hilarious," I say, and she turns down the dimly lit hall and away from me.

A pair of black sweatpants rests on top of the pile of

clothes, and I trade my jeans for them. As I straighten the mess, I assess my new room. Pictures of my dad rest on the old trunk under the far window, and my mother's jewelry box is on the vanity. I try to imagine my parents hanging out in this room when they were young.

I put the last folded shirt back in its proper place and close the armoire, tugging on it to make sure it's latched. I pick up the small golden picture frame off my trunk before plopping onto my down- and lace-covered bed.

In the picture, I'm four years old and sitting on my dad's lap outside a café in Paris. His cheek rests on the top of my head as I hold my cream puff with both hands. He's just smeared a bit of cream on my nose, and I'm laughing. This was the trip where we met Vivian, before I started going to school and stopped traveling with him as much.

"How can I start school tomorrow without you here to give me a pep talk?" I ask the picture. I'm really not looking forward to it. "These kids have to be nicer than at my last school, though, right? Sleep tight, Dad. I'll love you for always." I kiss my dad's picture and put it down on my bedside table near a slender vase holding a single daisy-like flower with a dark center. *Looks like my doorknob.* I turn out the light.

CHAPTER THREE

About My Last Name

I double-check the paper in my hand that says "Homeroom—Room #11." I pull the classroom door open. Being the new girl is like having a target on your forehead. People either mess with you or make bets on who will hook up with you first.

I scan the room and bite my lip. Most seats are taken, except for a couple in the first row next to two girls wearing all black. Not in the way I do with ripped jeans, but more gothic chic. Lace blouses, black blazers, and skinny jeans. The rest of the room is pretty predictably preppy, what you would expect from a town bordering Boston—a place my dad calls the khaki capital.

I slip into the seat next to the blond girl in all black.

"That seat's taken," she says.

"Yes, it is. By me." I freeze. I'm so used to having to defend myself that I just picked a fight without meaning to. She and the olive-skinned brunette with curly hair on the other side of her turn toward me.

"Move," the blonde says. Her black eye makeup frames her icy glare.

"It's fine, Alice," says a girl I didn't see approach. Her dark auburn hair is perfectly tucked into a high bun, and she wears a black lace dress that flairs at the waist. "I'll sit here." She gracefully lowers herself into the desk on my right. The bell rings.

"Hello, everyone. I'm Mrs. Hoxley, as many of you know. And, as you also know, I do not accept tardiness. Welcome to your first day of tenth grade," says the stout woman with glasses and a skirt suit from the eighties. *Well, she's a charmer.*

I pull my jacket off as Mrs. Hoxley does roll call. She goes right past the *M*'s without mentioning me.

"Is there anyone I missed?" Mrs. Hoxley scans our faces.

I raise my hand.

"Yes?"

"My name's Sam. I just moved here from New York." I swallow hard. *I hate talking in class.*

"Speak up. I need your full name." Her pencil taps her clipboard.

"Samantha Mather," I say a bit louder. All eyes are on me, and people whisper.

"Mather, is it? I did receive a notice about you. Haven't had a Mather in this school for more than twenty years."

She remembers the last Mather at this school. . . . Who? My dad?

Alice and the girl next to her—Mary, I think—exchange a glance. "When that crazy old lady died, I thought they were gone," Alice whispers to Mary but keeps her cold gaze on me.

I turn toward her. *Don't react. Breathe.*

"But I guess we're just not that lucky," Alice continues.

The challenge in her expression shatters my thin hold over

my temper. "Are you talking about my dead grandmother? Real classy."

"I do not appreciate students speaking out of turn," says Mrs. Hoxley.

How did I just wind up being the one in trouble?

Alice laughs.

"Alice, that goes for you, too," says Mrs. Hoxley. "I expect you to keep your family history out of the classroom."

"Got it," Alice says.

Family history? This can't seriously be about my last name.

For the rest of homeroom, Alice and Mary pass notes and throw sideways looks at me. I don't see this playing out well. Mrs. Hoxley reviews the rules and hands out our schedules. Mine is delivered by someone from the principal's office. I have AP History first period, followed by AP Chem.

When the bell rings, I grab my jacket and black shoulder bag.

In the hallway, I wander, trying to figure out which way the room numbers go. I pass a glass trophy case that has GO WITCHES! written on it. *Of course their mascot is a witch.*

Still staring at the case, I walk smack into someone. A guy with wavy dark hair and high cheekbones stares down at me. Gray eyes take note of my reddening face. He's so attractive that I forget my words and my mouth hangs open. Is there a desk somewhere I can hide under before I make any more blunders? He walks away before I can tell him I'm sorry.

"Sam," Jaxon says, a few feet in front of me. "You lost?"

Yes, and wishing I could press reset on this day. "Just looking for AP History."

"It's right here." He points to the door on his left. "You a sophomore or a junior?"

"Sophomore. You're a junior, though."

"It's that obvious, huh?"

"You've got that upperclassman cock—" *Oh holy hell.* I almost called him cocky. My hands go clammy. Only worse, I just said he has an upperclassman cock. I might die. This might be the end for me.

Jaxon bursts out laughing. "Why, thanks. I didn't think you noticed."

"Oh, no. I didn't mean that. I meant upperclassman cockiness." *Great, now I've said both the things I didn't mean to say.*

My only escape is into the classroom, which I take, but he keeps pace with me. I take a seat in the back, trying to will myself to blink out of existence.

Jaxon takes the seat next to me, still grinning. "That might be the best thing anyone's ever said to me."

I stare at my desk. This would be funny if it wasn't so horrifying. Thankfully, he's being nice about it. "I wish I could say that was the only stupid thing I've done so far."

"Not having a good first day at Salem High?"

I shake my head. "Have you noticed a group of girls in my grade that wear all black—rich goth types?"

"The Descendants?"

I venture a look at Jaxon. "What?"

"Like that?" He nods toward a guy and a girl entering the room. The guy wears an expensive-looking black button-down shirt, black pants, and black loafers. And she has on a floor-length black dress with a tailored black blazer. Her hair is a perfect bob.

"Yeah, exactly like that."

"There are five of them in our school. He's the only dude. They're descended from the original witches. Everyone kinda love-hates them. People think they can curse you if they want to. I think it's total bull."

"You're kidding, right?" But I can tell from his expression that he's not.

"Jaxon." A girl waves from across the room. She's pretty, in that equestrienne sort of way.

He smiles at her. "Hey."

"Sit with us," she says, gesturing to her equally preppy girlfriend.

"Nah, I'm good. I'm waiting for Dillon." She looks from him to me with dagger eyes.

Great. One more person who doesn't like me. I'm on a roll today.

CHAPTER FOUR

I Never Laugh at Cookies

I stand near the curb outside Salem High, scanning the cars pulling into the pick-up area. Across the street, four of the Descendants walk down the sidewalk. I have to admit that together they have something intriguing about them. They're hard not to watch.

As they pass, people step out of their way. Everyone follows them with their eyes, though—even me. Then all together, as if on cue, they turn and stare at me. I bite my lower lip and look away.

I feel a small pinch in the back of my head. I whip around to find Alice holding a couple strands of my hair. She raises one golden eyebrow above her dark-framed eyes. *What the . . . ?*

She walks right past me and into the street, not even acknowledging the cars. *Creepy as hell.* I take a step off the sidewalk, and the guy with dark hair from the hallway watches me.

Just as I'm about to yell at Alice, Vivian's car stops with a screech. Alice catches up with the other Descendants, and they continue down the sidewalk.

"Making friends?" Vivian asks as I get in her car.

I guess she didn't just see Alice pull some of my hair out. "More like enemies." I really wish I hadn't snapped at Alice in homeroom.

Vivian speeds away so fast that there's the scent of burning rubber. "Sam." Her tone suggests I did something wrong.

"Honestly, it isn't entirely my fault. They have some creepy witch social order at this school. My last name isn't helping." I just want someone to hug me and tell me I'm not awful and it will all blow over, but that's not Vivian's way. I need my dad.

"Salem prides itself on its witches. That history is very real to the people who live here."

"Well, that's insane." I can feel the upsets from my day threatening to overtake me.

She sighs. "That attitude won't help you make friends." She turns a corner, and I grip the door. "Maybe try to understand it from their perspective."

"I'm not going to apologize for some dude who wore a curly white wig three hundred years ago and made bad decisions just 'cause we have the same last name."

"It's more complicated than that, and being stubborn is only going to make it worse."

That's it. Breaking point achieved. "I don't want your advice."

Vivian's grip tightens on the wheel as she slams on the brakes. "Then you'll get what you get."

I cross my arms, pulling away from Vivian's comment and away from her in general as we bounce along our driveway.

I beeline it for the door the second the car stops. When I enter the foyer, the fluffy white couches and big fireplace in the room to the right catch my eye. In all my unpacking yesterday, I didn't really explore. I lean my bag against the small wooden mail table and head for the hallway to the right of the stairs, happy for something to distract me.

It's long and lined with doors. Portraits of dead relatives hang on the walls. *I can imagine them walking down here with only a candle.* I peek inside the fireplace room—which is probably the living room. There's a beautiful old rug, and the coffee table is an antique leather trunk.

The next door in the hall is closed, and I push it open. "Whoa."

The room is huge, and on the left is a grand piano. There are a couple of seating areas with white antique couches that I can't imagine sitting on. Crystal decanters containing some sort of drink rest on a silver tray with small crystal glasses. I lift the cover on the piano keys and press an out-of-tune note.

At the far end of the room, between two tall windows, is a painting of a girl about my age. She wears a blue and white silk dress draped with lace and holds a bouquet of yellow flowers. Her expression makes her look at ease, like she knew the artist. I'm intrigued.

Under the painting is a small table with an open book of poetry on it. The pages are yellowed. "'Black-Eyed Susan,'" I say, reading the poem title. *The flower! Right, that's what she's holding. And come to think of it, that's the kind of flower that's in my room, too.*

Something crashes behind me, and I let out a small scream. I whip around to find the keyboard cover on the piano slammed shut. *Not okay.* Vivian calls my name and I sprint out of the fancy room, closing the door behind me. My hands shake.

"Yeah?" I reply.

"Door!"

By the time I get back to the foyer, Jaxon's standing in the middle of it holding a plate of cookies. "Don't laugh, my mother wanted me to bring these."

Vivian gives me a look that can only mean "I told you they were nosy" before she turns to leave. I might agree with her, but after the day I had, I'm grateful for anyone in that school who doesn't think I suck.

I take the offered plate. "I never laugh at cookies."

"Chocolate chip butterscotch."

"Seriously? Your mother's amazing," I say loudly for Vivian's benefit.

"Yeah, if you ever get hungry, stop by. My mother kills it in the cooking department. It's kinda her thing. She grows herbs and all kinds of stuff, even in the winter."

A strand of sun-kissed hair falls out of place and I stare at it for a second longer than I should. "You wanna stay for a bit? I was just looking around the house." I can't remember the last time I invited someone to hang out with me. If my dad were here, he would be grinning foolishly at us, and I would feel super self-conscious. Four months ago, I would have awkwardly avoided eye contact with him. Now I only wish his eyes were here to avoid.

Jaxon pushes the loose hair off his forehead. "Sure."

I remove the plastic wrap on the plate of cookies, and he follows me down the hallway. "I only made it to the piano room," I say with a full mouth as we walk past.

I reach for the handle of the next door at the same time he does, and I almost smack him with the half-bitten cookie. He smiles. No one really talked to me in New York, especially not guys who looked like Jaxon. But the way he's enjoying my awkwardness makes me want to sock him.

He swings the door open to reveal a room covered floor to ceiling with books. Every dark wooden bookshelf is packed, and there are even books on the ground and on the small tables. The only place without books is an old brick fireplace with bare wooden paneling on either side of it. It's not fancy like the fireplace in the living room, but I like it better.

"A library." I forget all about hitting Jaxon.

"Every time I saw your grandmother she was in this room."

"It's strange you know more about my grandmother than I do." I put the cookies down on a table.

"Why didn't you ever come visit her?" Jaxon asks.

I hesitate. I wonder what he knows about my family.

Jaxon's fingers graze the top of an antique reading table surrounded by plush armchairs. A small cloud of dust rises. "It's okay if you don't wanna answer."

"No, it's fine. I just don't really talk about my family that much. I don't have any other relatives besides my dad and my stepmom." I can tell by the expression on his face that Jaxon knows what happened to him. "My dad never wanted to come to Salem. So we never came. And he and my grand-mother were always fighting, so she never came to the City, either." I busy myself by looking through a pile of books.

"Charlotte used to talk about you," Jaxon says.

I put down a book too fast and it slips off the top of the pile, sliding to the floor with a bang. My grandmother talked about me? I didn't even know she knew anything about me.

We're silent for a couple of seconds. He doesn't push the topic, even though I suspect he wants to. I pick up the fallen book and walk to the old fireplace. There are niches built into it, like small brick ovens for pizza. There's no guard separating it from the rest of the room. The wood floor just ends and the bricks begin.

"I bet this was used for cooking," I say.

He laughs. "Yeah."

"That's funny?"

"I mean, it's kinda obvious, but then again, you're a city girl," he says playfully.

I laugh, happy to be off the topic of my family. "Oh yeah? What do *you* know about old fireplaces?"

"Well, we're kinda *really* into our history around here."

"Tell me about it. You guys are obsessed with it."

"And I build furniture," he continues. "So I pay attention to these things."

"Really?" My surprise is genuine. I didn't expect that he did much of anything besides look cool.

"Some of these fireplaces have hooks for hanging kettles and things." He ducks his head under the arched brick to get a better look. "Found one. Give me your hand."

I join him under the arch of the fireplace, and he grabs my right palm. His hands are lightly callused and warm. He directs my fingers to the left side of the arch. Crouched next to me this close, he smells like Christmas trees.

"You're right!" I grab hold of a small iron hook and pull. It moves in my hand.

There is a loud creak and we look at each other. A gust of wind blows past us that smells like old leather and dried flowers. I back out of the fireplace, not entirely convinced bricks won't fall on my head.

"Holy . . . ," I say, looking at the wall to the left of the fireplace. Part of the wood paneling has cracked open a few inches, revealing a door. "You have to see this."

Jaxon stands next to me, eyeing the wall with curiosity.

"I heard some of the older houses have these; I've just never seen one before."

"How are you so calm? We just found a secret freaking door!" My volume surprises me.

I run my fingertips over the edges of the door. They match perfectly with the fireplace and the paneling on the wall. No one would ever suspect. I give it a push and it swings open. Behind it, a narrow hallway leads to an equally narrow spiral staircase. The walls inside are made of the same old brick as the fireplace, and the floor has wide wooden boards like the older parts of the house. I practically shake with excitement as I take a step in. *If there was one thing I always wanted as a kid, it was to find a secret passageway.*

"Sam!" yells Vivian from down the hall.

I jump out of the tiny, intriguing hallway and back into the library, pulling the door behind me.

"Quick, help me."

Jaxon grabs the edge of the door and pulls. But it won't close the last inch.

"Sam, you down here?" Vivian's voice gets closer. I really don't want her to see this. I haven't even investigated it yet.

"Take your fingers out a minute," Jaxon says, reaching into the fireplace. Just as I move my hand, he pushes the hook and the door clicks shut.

"I've been calling you." An annoyed Vivian enters the room. "We have errands to run."

"Okay." I try to act like everything's normal, but I'm pretty sure I'm sweating.

She looks from me to Jaxon, and she notices something's up. At least there's no way she could guess it's a secret door.

CHAPTER FIVE

Let Me Be a Tree

My head smacks the car window as Vivian stops short in front of my school. I rub my neck. *I slept for crap last night.* Not that it's anything new; I haven't slept well since my dad went into a coma.

"Here." Vivian reaches into the backseat. "Bring these to class. They might soften people up a little and help with the friend problem." She hands me a box of pastries.

I realize she's serious. *How can I say no?* This is a big gesture for her. She must be legitimately worried about me. *But seriously . . . pastries?* This isn't one of her luncheons. If I bring these in on day two of school, it's only going to make me look like I'm trying too hard. Those girls will jump all over it. The bell rings.

"Thanks." I try to muster a smile. I grab my stuff and run inside. By the time I turn down my homeroom hallway, there are only a few stragglers in sight. I swing Mrs. Hoxley's door open just as the second bell sounds.

Everyone is already settled, and the only available spot is

next to Susannah—the Descendant whose seat I accidentally took on the first day.

"Just in time, Ms. Mather. With offerings, I see." Mrs. Hoxley greedily eyes the pastries.

I should have dumped these in the garbage can. "These are just a . . . well, I thought . . . um . . . I brought these." *Great, I sound like a complete idiot.* The Descendants laugh as I hand the box to Mrs. Hoxley.

I pull out my strawberry-flavored lip gloss and my notebook with my calendar in it and sit down. Mrs. Hoxley passes around the pastry box. Everyone takes one except for the Descendants. I study my calendar, pretending I'm busy. I can't help but notice that my birthday is next month.

Sweet sixteen, my ass. I hate my birthday. My parties were so awful when I was little that a rumor started that I was cursed. By eleven, I stopped celebrating altogether. Everything is already so crappy, the last thing I need is more bad luck.

I circle October 27 and cross it out. I put my pen down and glance at the clock. One more minute before I can get out of here. My pen rolls toward the edge of my desk and I make an attempt to grab it, but miss. Susannah doesn't, though. She catches it midair before it hits the ground.

We lock eyes. Susannah's dark auburn hair is in another neat bun, and she wears a black lace dress. She reminds me of a ballerina in a weird way. She doesn't have that mean edge the others do, either. She holds the pen out for me. Her nails are painted black.

"Thanks."

The bell rings. I shove my notebook in my bag and stand. The Descendants don't say a word on their way out.

When I'm in the hallway, people watch me. Not in that

new-girl way, but in the they-know-something-I-don't way. So this is what happens when the Descendants don't like you. I really don't get the social structure of this school.

I turn the corner toward history class. Alice's blond ponytail and black blazer peek out from behind an open locker. She moves her hands as she speaks, and I get a glimpse of Susannah's face. I hug the wall and walk toward them. I mean, I'm going that way anyway.

"I told you to drop it," Alice says from behind the locker.

"You don't think it's strange that John's great-grandfather died last night?" Susannah asks as I inch closer, trying to hear them over the crowd of students. I pull my schedule out of my back pocket and lean against the lockers to look less conspicuous.

"He was ninety," Alice says.

"Yeah, but how do you explain—"

"Enough," Alice says.

"I say we talk to her."

Alice shakes her head and her ponytail glides across her shoulders. "Not a chance. And don't think I didn't see you catch her pen this morning."

Me? Are they talking about me? I take a step forward. Why would Susannah want to talk to me about someone's great-grandfather dying?

"So, come on. Out with it," Jaxon says near my ear.

I jump, sending my elbow into the metal lockers. Alice whips around at the loud clang and finds me two feet away from her, staring in her direction with a guilty look on my face. She narrows her eyes and I quickly walk away from the wall, shifting my gaze to Jaxon. I don't know why I thought that was a good idea. Stealth is not my thing. And I'm positive Alice is only going to like me less now.

"Out with what?" I reply, walking toward history class and away from Alice at a fast pace.

Jaxon holds the classroom door open for me. "The secret door. What'd you find in there?"

"Truthfully, I didn't go in."

"Scared?" His blue eyes light up.

I smile and slide into my seat. "No, we came home late 'cause Vivian dragged me all over town doing errands. And ten minutes after we got home, our lights went out and wouldn't go back on."

"So, basically, you were waiting for me to go in with you."

I feign annoyance at his amused expression.

"Settle, everyone," says Mr. Wardwell, taking off his blazer and hanging it over his chair. "As many of you probably expect, our AP History class will play an active role in Salem's annual history fair by doing a historical reenactment. I'll assign you each a role today."

Oh no! I can't even talk in front of my homeroom class of twenty people.

"Also," continues Mr. Wardwell, "you will write an essay on a specific aspect of the Witch Trials. This is a group assignment; you'll work in pairs. Your homework tonight is to find a partner and a topic." He lifts a stack of papers to distribute. "These are the format guidelines."

This is not my day. *Please just let me be a tree, or something else with no lines.*

"We are pairing with Ms. Edelson's honors class for the performance, and the jobs will be distributed equally among you. Don't argue with me about your specific assignment; this isn't up for a vote.

"Now, this class is special," Mr. Wardwell continues, "because we have actual descendants of the main players in the

Witch Trials. I think it only apropos they are given the opportunity to play them."

Halfway through his sentence, my stomach jumps into my throat. *No, no, no! This is a horrible idea!* My relatives played a big part in those Trials. I can't do that.

His eyes land on me. "Samantha, I'm not wrong in assuming you're related to Cotton Mather, am I?" Everyone turns to get a good look at me.

I slide down a few inches in my seat. "Yeah. Um, actually, maybe someone else wants to play him?" The two Descendants in the class take a particular interest in me.

Mr. Wardwell's forehead wrinkles. "As I said, this isn't up for debate, Samantha."

"Sam," I correct him. "I'm just . . . *really* not a performer."

"This isn't about winning an acting award, *Sam*. It's about celebrating our history. And you will participate if you hope to pass this class."

Well, that sucked.

"John and Lizzie, you'll also play your ancestors," Mr. Wardwell says to the Descendants.

"Great," says John. He shoots me a nasty look.

Wait. *John* . . . was that whose great-grandfather died? I shift uncomfortably in my seat.

"Mr. Wardwell," says a girl from my homeroom in the front row. Her voice is high-pitched and she grips her stomach. "I need to use the bathroom. It's an emergency."

Before he can reply, she runs out of the room with her hand covering her mouth.

"Read your guidelines, and I'll be back in a moment." Mr. Wardwell exits the room, following the girl.

"Yo, Jax," says the guy with the lacrosse jacket sitting in front of me. "You wanna partner on this essay or what?"

"Do you mean, do I wanna write the whole thing while you eat all my food and pass out covered in crumbs on my couch?" Jaxon asks. It's clear they're good friends.

"I mean, if you're offering," says the guy.

"No, man, I already told Sam I'd be her partner."

"Lies," says the guy. "But I don't blame you. She's way cuter than me." He reaches out his hand and I take it. "I'm Dillon."

"Sam," I say, and he kisses my hand. I pull it back and he grins. Jaxon shakes his head. Lizzie's bob swishes in my direction, and she whispers something to John. I'm suddenly regretting listening to Alice's conversation. I kinda wish I wasn't on their radar at all.

Mr. Wardwell steps back into the classroom. "Everything's under control." He doesn't make it more than two feet before a guy, also from my homeroom, pushes past him. "Or, apparently not."

Oh, crap! What are the chances two people from my homeroom are sick? Please let this be a coincidence. Whatever it is, do not let it be those pastries.

CHAPTER SIX

The Strangest Girl

I enter the hall after my last class, and the suspicious looks have escalated. I overhear snippets of conversations as I walk. "Poisoning . . . She did it on purpose. . . . At least fifteen people, maybe more . . . How messed up do you have to be?"

I turn left, toward my locker, and readjust my bag on my shoulder. The other students avoid me. Did fifteen people from my homeroom really get sick? I feel awful.

There's a group surrounding my locker and laughing. When they see me, they pretend they have somewhere to go.

You've got to be kidding me. PSYCHO is written in big black letters across the front of my locker. I scan the hallway. Just my luck, John and Susannah are headed in my direction. Susannah pushes a loose auburn wisp back into place and opens a locker a few feet away. She won't meet my eyes.

John steps around Susannah and leans so close to me that I can almost taste his cologne. "Sometimes the truth hurts."

I know I should just walk away, but how is this fair? I

haven't even said a word to him, much less done anything. He snickers, and my words erupt from me like soda from a shaken can. "Believe me, if I was trying to get people sick, I would've started with you." I slam my locker shut and turn away from him.

"Hey, Sam," he says loudly once I'm a good fifteen feet away. "You put your father in the hospital, too? I hear he might die."

That's it. I drop my bag and lunge at his perfectly proportioned face. *I'll kill him! I'll tear his grin off!* Jaxon, who I didn't even know was there, catches me right before I make impact.

"Not cool, man," Jaxon says to John.

We've gathered a crowd of onlookers. I flail, but Jaxon has me secured, his arm tight around my waist.

John flashes a cocky smile and gives me the finger. Susannah pulls John's hand down and attempts to lead him away.

"This isn't over," I say to John. I'm not even sure what I'm threatening him with, but somehow it doesn't matter.

"Next time I'll let her get you, dude. In fact, I'll help her," Jaxon adds.

John holds out his arms, inviting me to come and get him as he walks away with Susannah. *How the hell did they find out about my dad?*

"What's going on here?" asks Principal Brennan, a tall man with a shirt one size too small and a comb-over. Everyone disperses.

Jaxon removes his arm from my waist. "Someone tagged Sam's locker."

Principal Brennan examines the writing. "I've read the reports from your school in New York. This is a bad start to the year, Samantha."

My defensive bristles go up. "You think it's my fault? How can I control this?"

"You can start by controlling your temper," he says in an authoritarian voice.

I clench my teeth.

Brennan puffs out his chest and I fear for his buttons. "Now go. I'll handle this." He makes a shooing motion with his hand.

I open my mouth but close it again when Jaxon gives me a warning look. I pick my bag up off the floor and storm down the hall toward the exit. Jaxon follows.

"You okay?" he asks as we leave the building.

"Fine."

"You want me to hit that clown? I'll hit him."

"No. I can hit him myself."

"Yeah, I saw that. Come on, we'll both hit him. You take his fat head, I'll get the rest of him." He turns back toward the school.

I can't help but appreciate Jaxon's effort. I crack a smile. "Stop! It's fine, I promise."

He pauses. "Well, can I walk you home at least?"

I nod. "Lemme text Vivian." I pull out my cell phone and start typing. Within ten seconds, I get a response.

Vivian: *I'll be home in a few hours.*

Obviously she's in a real rush to pick me up. "Let's go."

Rounding the corner and leaving the school behind makes it easier to breathe. I kinda want to be alone right now, but Jaxon's the only person who's nice to me in the whole school and I feel bad telling him to go away. Can this really all be because of my last name? Even the teachers are judgy. "Jaxon, I gotta ask you something."

"Go for it."

"You didn't make a bet that you'd hook up with me, did you?"

His eyes smile. "Would I win if I did?"

A hearse followed by a line of cars makes its way down the street. We watch it pass. "I'm the most hated person in that school, and you're still nice to me. It doesn't make sense."

"Honestly, jokes aside, my mom told me what happened to your father. My father died a few years ago." He looks down at his hands.

"My dad isn't dying," I say reflexively, and try to block the image of the hearse out of my thoughts.

"Yeah, I know." He gives me a half smile. "I just get that this is really hard for you. I was messed up for over a year."

Maybe Jaxon is actually a nice guy. "I'm sorry. I didn't know."

"If you ever want to talk about it or whatever . . . I mean, I know you have your stepmom, but I've been told that I'm an *excellent* listener."

I look at him. He has an amazing ability to lighten any subject. I wish I could be like that. "Is that a fact?"

"Fact. And I love that you tried to kick John's ass, by the way. That guy's a dick." He stops on the cobblestone sidewalk in front of the black iron fence and freshly cut grass of my house.

"I would have messed him up, too, if you hadn't stopped me."

"Obviously." He heads up my driveway toward my house. "Let's go check out that library."

I consider saying no, but I don't have a reason besides having had a bad day. Plus, he's been doing his best to make it easier on me. Jaxon and I drop our bags in the front foyer and head down the hallway to the library. The wooden boards creak lightly under our feet.

"Let's lock it," I say, stepping into the library and flicking the light switch on.

Jaxon shuts the door and turns the brass latch. Vivian said she wouldn't be home for a few hours, but I'd rather not chance it. Once she knows, it'll no longer be my secret.

My fingers feel around for the hook, and a rush of excitement elbows out my stress. I'm actually glad Jaxon stayed. If he hadn't, I'd probably be in my room right now with my face buried in a pillow. I pull the hook and the hinge clicks, popping open the dark brown panel to reveal the hidden door. Jaxon pushes the panel all the way open, and we enter the secret hallway.

There's a lantern hanging just inside the narrow passage. I pull it down. "Think this thing works?" It's heavier than I expect.

Jaxon inspects it in the dim lighting. "It's an antique for sure, but more like seventy years old than three hundred."

I flip the little knob on the metal base and a small flame shoots up, throwing dancing shadows along the old brick. "If this thing is from the nineteen hundreds, I guess we're not the only ones who've discovered this passageway."

Jaxon closes the door behind us with the handle on the inside. "Yeah, but for now this place is just ours."

Something about the way he says "ours" makes me very aware how long it's been since I've had a friend. "You know, I don't really talk to my stepmom about my dad. You said before that I had her to talk to. Anyway, I don't know why I'm telling you this." I take the first steps of the spiral staircase at the end of the hallway with caution. They were clearly meant for people with tiny feet.

"'Cause of my listening skills," he says from behind me, and I can almost hear his grin. "So what's the thing? You guys don't get along?"

"Actually, before my dad got sick, we used to. We're alike

in strange ways—bad-tempered, independent, maybe too straightforward. It just got weird when my dad went into the hospital. I stopped talking for a while, and when I did talk again it felt like she was mad at me. I don't know."

I reach the top of the stairs, and Jaxon's right behind me. It's everything I imagined a secret room might be. It isn't big, and it has a cozy feel, like an old dusty bookshop in London. There's a heavy antique desk covered in papers and books in front of a tiny square window.

"Okay, this is awesome." Jaxon runs his hand along the sloped wall. "This must be one of the gables you can see from the street."

"Gables?" I pick up a book on top of an old leather trunk, and the thrill of finding this place washes away my feelings about school. It's like the library; stacks of books line the room.

"The place where the roof comes to a peak. That's why the walls are sloped."

"How do you know it's called a gable, though?"

"One of Salem's most popular tourist sites is the House of Seven Gables. I've been there like ten times between field trips and visiting family."

"Oh," I say. "It looks as if a lot of these books are about the Witch Trials."

"Yeah." Jaxon blows dust off the stack near him. "And your relatives."

On the desk rests a faded photograph of a beautiful woman with her hair tied loosely in a bun. She grips a little boy's hand. I catch my breath. My dad's smile still looks exactly like that. I run my finger along the gold frame. "This must have been my grandmother's study. She was stunning. I've never seen a picture of her before."

Jaxon joins me at the desk and peers at the picture. "Your father?"

I nod without looking at him and pick up a leather-bound journal. I open it to the satin ribbon marker. The page is filled with beautiful cursive. I read out loud.

It was a good day of research. I'm delighted by a letter I found in one of Perley's books. Good and thorough historian, Perley was. The letter was written by Dr. Holyoke on Nov. 25, 1791, and read: "In the last month, there died a man in this town, by the name of John Symonds, aged a hundred years lacking about six months, having been born in the famous '92. He has told me that his nurse had often told him ... she saw, from the chamber windows, those unhappy people hanging on Gallows' Hill, who were executed for witches by the delusion of the times."

Finding Symonds' house in Salem will once and for all clear up the mystery of the hanging spot. I will look for it first thing in the morning. I must go now, however, my teakettle is whistling.

I wrinkle my face. "What do you think this means?" I peer at Jaxon, whose cheek is now close to mine. I breathe in his woodsy smell. "Is she saying people don't know where the witches were hanged?"

"Sounds like it," says Jaxon. "I always learned it was at Gallows Hill Park. It's possible it's not. I never questioned it."

The next page is blank. "This was her last entry." I flip back to the beginning of the journal. Again, I read out loud.

I spoke to the mayor today. Nice and all, but a complete imbecile. He has no idea if the hanging spot is correct. And, he freely admits Upham willy-nilly named the current spot in Gallows Hill Park. Then everyone in this town blindly followed. Upham even admits that he has no evidence for naming that place. Ridiculous.

I've asked the mayor to look into it and he politely brushed me off. Disgraceful, if you ask me, that Salem does not know the most historically important spot in its own town. Mable and I will sort this. My biggest hope is that this will bring me closer to getting my Charles and my Samantha back home to me.

I close the journal, not sure how to process that last line. My grandmother wanted a relationship with me? My dad always said that she was the reclusive eccentric type, which I assumed was a euphemism for grumpy and crazy. I knew they fought, but if she really wanted to see me, she would have, right?

"My mom's name is Mable," Jaxon says.

"Really?" I pause, looking at my grandmother's picture on the desk. "What do you think she meant by that last line? I don't see how the hanging spot's related to me." I wonder what his mom knows about this.

"Yeah, it's pretty mysterious. I think we found our paper topic for class, though."

"The location of the hangings? That's actually a really good idea. It'll be like a treasure hunt, trying to find the place."

Jaxon's phone rings and he glances at it. "It's my mom. I kinda forgot about a dentist appointment today."

"Forgot?"

"Or, maybe wanted to come here more." He turns his body to face mine.

I'm suddenly very aware that my grandmother's journal is between us. "Thanks for being nice to me when no one else is. I can't promise I won't screw it up, though."

Jaxon smiles. "You're the strangest girl I've ever met."

I realize I'm smiling, too. "Well I'm not sure what that means about you, since you want to spend time with me."

"It means—" He leans forward a little. His phone rings again, and I take a step backward. *Was he going to kiss me? Do I want him to kiss me?*

He looks disappointed. "Gotta go," he says, looking at his phone.

CHAPTER SEVEN

Watching and Whispering

I head straight to the public library, excitement about the secret study fueling my steps. After a useless search online for that house my grandmother wrote about, I figure my only shot at finding it *and* the hanging location is to look in the old archives.

The air's crisp with the smell of autumn, and the first few leaves have started to change color. The streets have that family-friendly feel. Store windows already have pumpkins and witches' hats in them. I pass an old brick-walled pub called Mather's Maleficence and trip on a tree root jutting out of the sidewalk. Fantastic—so everyone in this town knows my relatives.

I stop in front of the library, marked by a handmade wooden sign hanging from a post. It's a brick and brownstone building with columns supporting the doorway. Apparently, it used to be the home of Captain John Bertram, a successful merchant and shipowner. He had bad luck, and most of his family died off in the mid-1800s, probably in this very building. I read all about it when I was looking up the address.

I push open one of the heavy wooden doors and make my way to the woman at the front desk. She's a small, white-haired creature with reading glasses balanced on the end of her nose.

"I'm looking for some old records of Salem from the seventeen hundreds," I say quietly.

She inspects me over her glasses in a way that makes me conscious of my posture. "I haven't seen you here before."

Great. I get to be the new girl in Salem High *and* in the town. "I just moved here."

"You'll be needing a library card. What's your full name?"

"Samantha Mather," I whisper.

"What was that, now? Speak up, girl," she says, and leans a little closer.

"Samantha Mather," I say a little louder, more conscious of my own last name than I've ever been.

"Mather, is it?" she replies at full volume. She raises a disapproving eyebrow at me. "Lots of history here. Not all of it good."

I nod, and can feel eyes staring at my back. I bet there are at least a couple of people here who know about my locker incident today.

"Do you know where I could find information about where people lived in the late sixteen and early seventeen hundreds? And maybe a map?" I ask, anxious to leave the onlookers.

"Upstairs to your left, in the back, small room on your right. Have copies of all the original town documents from around the time of the Witch Trials. Come back when you're done and we'll see about that card."

"Thanks." I dart for the stairs without making eye contact with anyone. *You can judge me, but I don't have to look at you while you're doing it.*

Two hours with a stack of dusty old books at a small wooden table in a cramped room and I'm finally getting some useful information. I found the address for Symonds's house that Perley referenced in his essay "Where the Salem 'Witches' Were Hanged." But it's unclear if it exists anymore. It doesn't line up with the current streets.

I run my hand along a pile of books about my relatives Cotton Mather and Increase Mather. If my last name is gonna be such an issue here, I want to know why. I mean, they *were* highly respected members of society. Increase even brought over the charter from England saying that Massachusetts was a province.

Unfortunately, Cotton was kinda the thorn. He was crazy smart, graduated Harvard at sixteen, and wrote seven languages, including Iroquois, by the time he was twenty-five. Some historians say he was good and honest, but more think he was the main instigator of the Witch Trials. He was so concerned with uprooting "evil" that he was willing to let people hang to do it. I can't help but think how the tables have turned for the Mathers in Salem.

A shadow falls on the page I'm reading. I look up to find Lizzie standing just outside the doorway of the reference room. I notice she has two different-colored eyes—one golden brown and one green—that seem more dramatic because of her black hair.

"So it's true," she says, and inspects her black nails with glittery skulls painted on them.

"'Scuse me?" I fold the paper with the information I was collecting and push it into my pocket.

"They told me you were here."

What's her angle? "They, who?"

"You can't hide in a town like this, Mather."

I can't help but think about the witch accusations. And the fact that she's addressing me by my last name doesn't escape me. "Are you saying you followed me here?"

"What I'm saying is that I know where you are." She lifts her gaze from her nails, and her two-toned eyes assess me.

Goose bumps sprint down my arms. I'm not even going to pretend I'm not creeped out by this. She clearly doesn't mean just now. She means always. I try to play it off. "So, what, you spend your free time tracking me? Your life sounds like it sucks."

For the briefest of seconds her eyes narrow. "You'll find that there're only a few things that matter in Salem and that you're not one of them. No one cares what happens to you here."

Was that a threat? If there is one thing I learned in the City, it's that I can't show her this bothers me. "I'm not sure I care if you know where I am. You found me reading a book. Congratulations on your discovery."

She actually smiles. "Give it time. You will."

That's it. I'm done with this conversation. I kick the door with my black boot and it slams in her face. By some highly unfortunate coincidence, as the door booms shut the lights turn off. From outside the tiny sliver of a window in the door, which is now my only source of light, she laughs.

You've got to be kidding me. I stand up and bang my knee into one of the wooden chairs. "Ow!"

I push the chair aside and more slowly make my way to the wall. *This cannot be happening right now.* I swat the wall with my hands and land on a small switch. Up, down, up, down. Nothing.

I grab the door handle and pull, but it doesn't budge. I pull harder. Nothing. I throw my weight back, and with all my might I pull again. Still nothing. Lizzie walks away, leaving me stuck and all alone.

Did she lock me in somehow? As far as I can tell, there's no manual lock. She would need a key. How'd she do it? Maybe it's an old lock and it jammed when I slammed the door? But that still doesn't explain why the lights went out. I reach for my cell phone, but there's no signal.

That only leaves banging and yelling. "Help!"

What if no one hears me? I'm in an unpopular part of the library. Not so unpopular that Lizzie and her spies couldn't find me, but still. What's that girl planning, anyway? I find it hard to believe that this and the locker stunt are unrelated.

Twenty minutes pass before a scraggly-looking janitor finds me.

"Please help me get out of here!" I yell. It's starting to smell really musty, and it's dark. Plus, I'm not a huge fan of spiders, which I'm sure have taken up permanent residence in this rarely used room. I can almost hear them crawling toward me over the old manuscripts. Above all, I don't like being trapped.

He fidgets with a ring of keys but doesn't seem to have the right one. He puts his hand up as if to say "Hold on" and walks off.

Another ten minutes pass, and I'm getting jumpy. In fact,

I'm sweating pretty badly. I press against the window. *Please, someone come back . . . anyone.*

My face is fogging up the glass when the librarian from downstairs appears in front of me. My heart jumps into my throat. *Holy moly, she scared the crap out of me!* And she didn't come alone; there's a small group of spectators forming behind her.

"Don't panic. It only makes it worse!" she yells.

"I'm not!" I lie.

"Good. They can feel it, you know," she warns.

"Who can feel what?" I ask.

"The ghosts," she says loudly.

Involuntarily, I look over my shoulder. Nothing's there. Of course nothing's there. What's wrong with this town? I want to yell that I don't believe in ghosts, that it was probably Lizzie's fault the door locked. But by this point I've already made enough of a spectacle of myself.

There's a low buzzing noise. *A drill?*

"Stand back!" yells the janitor.

The door vibrates, and within seconds a small metal bit falls near my feet. The door swings open, almost hitting me. I jump out of the way and crash backward into the table, my feet lifting six inches off the ground. I flail my arms wildly to regain my balance. There are gasps from the crowd.

"Are you all right?" asks the librarian with a bit of drama in her tone.

"Yeah. Thanks," I say to her and the janitor. I must look crazy. With all these eyes on me, I half wish I could stay in the dark room until everyone loses interest. I'm slick with sweat, there are little tendrils of hair stuck to my face, and I just threw myself into a table. Much to my disappointment, the watching and whispering crowd has doubled in size.

I step into the light and I spot John near one of the back rows of people, leaning against a bookshelf. We make eye contact, and my abused nerves go haywire. I don't think. I just run.

CHAPTER EIGHT

Something Is Off Here

"I got a call from the principal today," says Vivian from the living room doorway.

I sit cross-legged on the big white couch. Papers and books surround me in disarray.

I fidget. "Did he tell you about the locker?"

"Yes." Judgment's written in her eyebrows. "I just don't understand how you could garner that kind of reaction so quickly."

I tense. "As though it would make more sense if it happened later on? When people knew me better?"

"You know I don't mean it that way. You snap at people unnecessarily. What's going on with you lately? You don't tell me anything anymore."

I steady myself. She's right. Before my dad got sick, I would have told her what happened and she would have made some biting comment about the kids who did it. Which of course would make me laugh and make the whole thing easier somehow. Now it feels like I'm always on the defensive. I sigh. "There was something wrong with those pastries this morning. More than fifteen kids went home puking. Everyone blames me. That's why they wrote PSYCHO on my locker."

Her lips tighten. She places a small pizza box down on the couch next to me. "I'll handle this." She walks out of the room.

She's calling the bakery. Her voice gets progressively louder and she's using her you-are-obviously-an-idiot tone. We both have short tempers, and being on the receiving end of hers is terrifying. There were only two times when I was little that we lost our tempers at each other. But those fights were so bad, our neighbors called the police on us, once because she threw a vase at our connecting wall and another time because she screamed so loud and so long that they were afraid someone was being murdered.

Of course, my dad wasn't home for those fights, and I never told him. They were about me going to therapy because I didn't have friends, and she thought I was too attached to my dad. There was always some part of me that was afraid she was right, that I was the problem.

I open the box and take a bite of the cheese pizza—not New York standard. I check my phone for the hundredth time to see if Jaxon texted me. Nothing. All the stuff he told me today seemed real. It is a little odd, though, that he's really nice when no one else in school is. *Great, Vivian's suspicion of nice people has rubbed off on me.*

I stop mid-bite and put the half-eaten pizza back in the box. Jaxon admitted today that he knew about my dad. No one else in school knew. How could they? That's the only way John could have found out. I feel sick.

I gather my books and papers and head for my room. I can't believe I almost trusted him. It's easy to trick someone who's lonely with pretty words. *I'm so stupid.*

"That doesn't change the fact that I'm going to talk to Mable about this." Vivian has steel in her voice. "Sorry isn't good enough."

Mrs. Meriwether? I plod up the stairs. What does she have to do with the bakery? Suddenly what Jaxon said about his mother's cooking makes sense. The sick feeling I have spreads. Maybe Vivian was right about them.

"It's handled," says Vivian from the bottom of the staircase.

She'll fight for me, but right now I really need comfort more than anything. "Great." My tone reflects my disappointment.

"You're welcome," she says, and I walk down the hall toward my room.

There's a light creaking of old wood as I approach the burgundy bedroom. I peek inside and flip on the light. The rocking chair moves back and forth. I grab the arm and it stops. I scan the room, but everything's still.

Stepping back into the hallway, I look both ways before heading to my room, wishing the hallway sconces were brighter and didn't cast so many shadows.

I stick my hand in my room and flip the lights on before I enter. I slowly push the door open to find my clothes are once again in a pile on my floor.

"What the hell," I say to the empty bedroom.

Okay, that's it. Either someone's messing with me or there's something wrong with this armoire. I press the old latch a couple of times, and it squeaks. I lift what remains of the folded clothes in the upper part of the armoire and place them on the floor next to the pile. In the center of the back panel is a delicately carved black-eyed Susan, matching the rest of the furniture in my bedroom. I check all the edges of the wood and the hinges, to see if anything is faulty.

As a last resort, I knock on the wood itself—the doors, the sides, and the back panel. *Wait, this part sounds different.* I tap near the flower. Definitely hollow. I pull my head out of the armoire and give it a push to move it from the wall. It doesn't budge. The thing weighs like five hundred pounds.

I return to the flower and grab the edges of it. There's a small noise, and one of the petals appears to have tilted. *Did it just move or did I imagine that?* I brace the flower with the tips of my fingers and pull. It pops off easily and lands in my palm.

I reach my hand into the hole where the flower was, and the edge of something silky brushes my fingertips. I lean forward and manage to pinch it. Carefully, I pull out a bundle of old letters tied with blue ribbon. They're yellowed with age and have a musty perfume smell. I now couldn't care less about my clothes being all over the floor.

I sit at my vanity and untie the bow that holds them together. Gently, I open the flap of the first envelope and unfold the thick stationery inside. The writing is small and so elaborately curled, it's difficult to make out.

My dearest Abigail,

Nothing wouldst give me more joye than to once againe see your smile. I verily believe mother's illness is nigh finished and that I maye return to you. Have patience, my love, for I am over a barrel with these unfortunate times.

Forever yours,
William

Old love letters. How romantic. *I bet they belonged to the girl in the portrait by the piano.* Was this her room? And for some reason, I have a strong feeling it was. She loved black-eyed Susans. That's why they're all over this furniture.

The lights go off, and I jump. *You have got to be kidding me! Not now!* I put the delicate letters down and feel around for the flashlight on my nightstand. My hands shake.

"Vivian!" I yell as I run through the dark hallway, but no one responds. When I get to the top of the stairs, lights glow in the foyer. "Vivian!"

"What?" Her voice comes faintly from down the hallway.

I run all the way to the kitchen, knowing that's where I'll find her. She always makes loose-leaf tea at night. I push the swinging door at the end of the hallway. She's next to the stove, lighting a flame beneath an antique kettle.

"My lights went out again," I say.

"The repairman fixed the lights."

After the weird things that have already happened to me today, I'm definitely not excited about my room being dark. "Well, they're out in my bedroom."

She puts her empty mug down with a clang on the marble countertop and walks out the back door to the patio. I follow, and hold the flashlight as she opens the breaker box filled with switches.

"You're right; one of them is off." She flips it back into position. "Let's go take a look." She enters the house, moving quickly.

I don't want her to see those letters. "It's fine." I keep pace with her. "I'll let you know if they're back on."

"I'll look myself. If there's still a problem, I'll call that idiot and make him come back. I have no interest in spending another evening bumping into my own furniture because I can't see ten feet in front of my face."

There is no arguing with her, especially when she's feeling snippy. We walk toward my room. Did I close my door? I don't remember doing that. The back of my neck tingles. I grab the handle before Vivian does, hoping I can hide those letters. "The light's on," I say quickly.

"You're acting like a nervous wreck. Are you okay?" She eyes me and pushes my door open.

I immediately look at my vanity, but the letters are gone. *Gone! What the . . . ?* I walk to it and pull the chair out to see if they fell.

"This room's a disaster." Vivian wrinkles her nose. "Sam, are you sure everything's okay?"

My heart sinks. I can't understand where they could have gone. "Yes. And I didn't do this."

"The lights?"

"This!" I point at the clothes. "It was like this when I got here. And now something's disappeared, and I think someone's messing with me."

"Are you trying to tell me you think someone was in the house? All the doors were locked."

"Something is missing from my room, and this is the second time my clothes are all over the floor." I'm having trouble keeping my cool.

"Slow down. What's missing?"

"Just something."

Her eyes land on the hole in the back of my armoire. "If you're not going to tell me, then how can I help?"

"Fine. Letters. I found them in the back of my armoire."

"So you're telling me that someone threw your clothes on the floor. You somehow found letters in your armoire. And then the lights went out and they disappeared?"

"And the rocking chair in the burgundy bedroom was rocking by itself."

She frowns. "Are you sleeping well? You know I was kidding when I said the ghost didn't like you, right?"

"I don't *think* it was a ghost. I *think* it was a person."

Her kettle starts whistling. "I need to get that. Then we can talk more about this."

"No." I close the door behind her as she leaves.

This is only going to start the therapy conversation again. I'm not crazy. And my sleep has nothing to do with this. I'm being deliberately toyed with. *Would those witch lunatics from my school go so far as to mess with my house? Yes, I think they would. Maybe even Jaxon's in on it. I bet they're all having a good laugh over this.*

My cell phone buzzes on my nightstand. It's a text.

Jaxon: *Find anything?*

For some reason this makes my blood boil. *He's playing me for sure.*

Me: *A liar.*

Jaxon: *???*

I throw my phone on my bed and grab my metal flashlight—a light source or a potential weapon. I resist stamping down the staircase only because I have no desire for Vivian to know where I am.

I go into the piano room and stand in front of Abigail's painting, examining every detail. She's calm, with her dark brown hair and happy gray eyes. Behind her, everything is heavily shadowed. But I'm pretty sure she's standing next to the fireplace in the library, right in front of the hidden door.

"Somehow I've stepped into your world of secrets," I say to her painting.

I look for a painter's signature, but there's none. Carefully, I shine my flashlight behind the portrait. *Bingo*—there's an index card taped to the back, with some writing in my grandmother's cursive. Thank you, Charlotte. It reads *Abigail Roe ~1691.*

The year before the Witch Trials? I look at her lace and silk dress again. This seems way too fancy for Colonial America. I've seen drawings of Puritans from that time in my history textbook and they wore super-plain clothes and bonnets. Black and earth tones, not these cheery blues and whites. From what I read, children didn't play or have toys because those things were considered frivolous and sinful. There's no way she could have walked around in this thing in seventeenth-century Salem. *Something is off here.*

Behind me, a crystal glass falls to the floor.

CHAPTER NINE

Cursed

I slow my pace in the hallway to leave no time for Jaxon to talk to me before class. It's only my third day, and no one will make eye contact with me. Where I'd normally have to squeeze between people, they just step out of my way. It's not like how they move out of respect for the Descendants; it's like they're afraid to touch me. I overhear snippets of conversations about my library fiasco, which is already common knowledge.

The bell rings as I reach AP History, and I try to ignore the tightness in my chest. I steel my face and open the door. Wardwell gives me a disapproving look but can't say anything since I'm technically on time.

I take my seat next to Jaxon but keep my gaze straight ahead.

"We'll begin with your paper assignment." Mr. Wardwell wears a tweed blazer with suede elbow patches.

"Sam?" Jaxon whispers. I ignore him, and the tightness spreads.

"Jaxon," says Mr. Wardwell, "if you're so eager to talk in my class, then maybe you'd like to tell me your paper topic."

"Sure." Jaxon isn't fazed. "I'm working with Sam, and we're doing our paper on the location of the witch hangings." He leaves out the bit where we think the current location is wrong.

The pretty girl who saved Jaxon a seat the other day doesn't turn around to look at us, but everyone else does. *Don't worry,* I think in the pretty girl's direction, *you can have him.*

"Wonderful choice." Wardwell nods. "We're visiting Gallows Hill Park on Friday. You can do some research then."

I raise my hand, and Mr. Wardwell nods. "Yes?"

"Can I do the paper by myself?"

"No. It's a group assignment." He moves on to another student, and Jaxon stares at me. I don't dare look at him or I might cry.

Lizzie turns toward me from a few rows up, her hair hiding her awful smile from Mr. Wardwell. Behind her desk, she pulls out a little handmade doll with MATHER embroidered on it and a noose around its neck. Jaxon grabs my arm, as if to tell me not to react. I shake it off.

John, from the desk next to Lizzie, mouths "cursed" at me.

I freeze. This was the word that tore apart my friendships as a child. It started not that long after my friend Kara fell into the lion's cage at my seventh birthday party.

"She's not well enough to see you," Kara's mother said, holding the door only halfway open.

"We'll come back in a couple of days," my dad said, and put his hand on my shoulder.

"Sam?" Kara's voice came from down the hallway.

"I'm so sorry, Kara!" I yelled, trying to peer around her mother. I didn't know what I was apologizing for, but I knew I was sorry.

As Kara reached the door, her mother yanked her backward. "Kara, you're not going to be seeing Sam anymore. They were just leaving."

My eyes began to fill with tears, and my dad stiffened next to me. "Of course you're upset about what happened. But it's not Sam's fault. Keeping the girls apart is an over—"

I reached out for Kara, but her mother blocked me.

The door slammed in my face. I didn't really understand what it all meant. All I knew was that I didn't have Kara anymore because there was something wrong with me, and I wasn't sure I could take that.

John grins at the shocked look on my face. Is there some way they could know about all the bad luck I had when I was a kid? Or is this just some awful coincidence?

"I'm not cursed. And if you say it again, I'll smack that smile off you!" I yell. The room goes silent and everyone stares.

Mr. Wardwell stands straighter. "Miss Mather, I will *not* have that kind of threatening outburst in my classroom. If you cannot control yourself, you'll leave. Is that clear?"

Lizzie tightens the noose around the little doll's neck.

I clench my fist. "So it's totally fine that she has some sick voodoo doll with a *noose*? Are you kidding me? They took my freaking hair the other day!"

Mr. Wardwell looks at Lizzie, but the doll is nowhere in sight.

"Out!" Mr. Wardwell points toward the door. I yank my bag up and storm off.

"Mr. Wardwell," Jaxon says, "it's not—"

"I don't want to hear it, Jaxon." Mr. Wardwell follows me into the hallway.

"I want you to go into that room there." Mr. Wardwell shakes his finger at me. "And calm yourself down. I'll be in to talk to you when I'm ready."

I cross the hall, enter the empty classroom, and throw my bag on the floor. I know I shouldn't let my temper get the better of me like that, but those Descendants are completely insane. Who does that? I don't believe in witchcraft or whatever that crap was, but still. And was Jaxon defending me? I don't need his help. I've always been just fine on my own. I don't know why I got it into my head I might make friends here.

I pace around the room until I wear myself out. I kick the desk near the window before I sit in it. I want my dad back. I need to talk to him. I need to hear that eventually things will get better. Right now everything is so very wrong. And it seems to be slipping further out of my control by the minute. I put my head in my hands, and my hair falls in my face.

My dad knelt down beside me. "It's not your fault. You know that, right, Sam? That woman is a . . . She's scared about what happened to Kara and she wants to blame someone." He pushed my hair back from my wet cheeks. "You're one of the most kind and beautiful people I've ever known, and I promise you I'll do everything I can to fix this."

I nodded. "Okay, Daddy." But somewhere inside me, I knew things would never be the same.

After some minutes of closing my eyes, my breath slows. When I sit up again, the dark-haired guy I collided with the other day stands just inside the doorway. For a few seconds, we're both silent.

"You will leave." His voice is flat, but his face is intense.

"The classroom? I can't."

"Salem," he says, and for the first time I notice that he, too, wears all black.

CHAPTER TEN

Under All That Bravado

The bell rings at the end of my sixth-period literature class, and I'm the first person out of the classroom. I can't wait to get out of this place. If I hear one more person whisper that the Descendants cursed me, I'll scream.

I rush to my locker. Good, Susannah isn't there yet. I spin the numbers on my combination lock and quickly open the latch. As I grab my notebooks, Jaxon heads straight for me. I slam my locker shut and walk toward the exit. But by the time I reach the door, he catches up.

"Sam, what the hell's going on?"

"Go away."

"Not until you tell me why you're so angry." He keeps pace with my speed-walking. "You've been avoiding me all day."

"You know why." I turn down the sidewalk away from the school.

"No, I really don't."

"Please, I don't need to feel any more ridiculous than I

already do." I watch the cracks in the sidewalk pass under my feet, trying to steer my mind away from how hurt I feel.

"I've been nothing but nice to you. Am I missing something here?"

I look at him for the first time since we started talking. "How did the Descendants find out about my dad being in the hospital?"

"I don't . . . Oh, shit."

"Shit is right." I adjust my gaze downward again and walk faster than before. There had been some part of me that still hoped it wasn't him. I shouldn't have trusted him.

"It's not what you think."

"I don't want to have this conversation."

"Sam, you weren't there. You don't know what I said."

"I don't care." *I'm better off alone.*

"Well, I do," he says. "By lunchtime of your first day, I heard the Descendants were going to make your life hell. There were rumors all over about you. I talked to Susannah, told her to get the group to back off, that you were going through some tough things. I had no idea they were going to use it against you."

The weight of the day settles behind my eyes and I want to get away from him before I embarrass myself more. I make my way onto the sidewalk near my house. He steps in front of me before I reach my driveway.

"Move," I say.

"No. Not until you say you believe me."

"Jaxon, come on." I make eye contact with him. "You're a junior with a ton of friends. People like you. I don't believe for a second that you want to spend all this time with me." My voice shakes a little. "I just want you to stop making fun of me."

"I'm not making fun of you." He's so sincere, I'm not sure

whether to hit him for being such a good liar or to believe him.

"You already won. I feel like crap. Job done."

"Come over and talk to my mom."

I stop. *What's he up to?*

"I'll make a deal with you. Come talk to my mom, and if you're not convinced I'm telling the truth, then I'll leave you alone." He watches me consider it. "*And* I'll do our history paper. You won't even have to talk to me."

I eye him suspiciously. "Fine. But you better not suck at history."

I follow him to his house, with its blue shutters and nautical star. The moment he opens the screen door, delicious scents of warm dough and apple-cinnamon fill my nose.

The house is surprising. Its interior is reminiscent of the inside of a boat, one with high masts, used for adventures. Rustic raw-wood beams stripe the white ceilings. The shelves are made from driftwood, and so is the banister.

"Mom!" Jaxon yells, and heads down the hallway to the left. He leads me through an arched wooden doorway.

The kitchen counters are covered with cookies, pies, and every wonderful thing. Models of ships decorate the walls, and glass jars of spices line the windowsills.

"Samantha!" Mrs. Meriwether beams from behind her mixing bowl. "You've finally come to visit."

"Hi, Mrs. Meriwether." I approach the island filled with sweets.

"My mom owns Sugar Spells Bakery in town," Jaxon explains. "But she spends most of her time here, making new recipes."

So she *owns* the bakery. I nod, hoping that Vivian didn't yell at Mrs. Meriwether over those pastries.

Mrs. Meriwether smiles. "Have anything you like."

I choose a heart-shaped tart with fresh raspberries and bite into it. "It's delicious."

"Mom, tell Sam what I told you when I came home after the first day of school," Jaxon says.

She tilts her head. "He told me the students were turning on you."

"And?"

She eyes Jaxon curiously. "And that he knew what it was like to have that happen and would try to stop it."

"See."

I look back and forth between them.

Mrs. Meriwether puts down her mixing bowl. "Jaxon, leave us a minute."

"Mom—"

"Jaxon."

He huffs, but walks out of the room.

"Take a seat," she says, and I pull out one of the high-backed chairs at the island. She adds brown sugar to her bowl before continuing. "Did you know I grew up in this house?"

I shake my head.

"Your father and I were practically inseparable. We were born one month apart. Did everything together. He was the best at thinking up pranks but a total cheat at running races." She laughs. "Used to make me look the wrong way and would take off."

I try to imagine my dad acting silly with a young Mrs. Meriwether. After everything started going downhill for me socially, my dad lost a lot of his playfulness. He took it hard that he couldn't change things for me. I sigh. "I always wanted to know about this place, but he wouldn't talk about it. I didn't know about you." I worry I've said the wrong thing, but she only looks thoughtful.

"Yes." She stirs her bowl. "He divorced this place after

your mother died. He was devastated. We all were. But he didn't let it interfere with being a father. You should have seen the way he wouldn't put you down as a baby."

I look at my hands. "I miss him." *Every day without him feels empty.*

"I know you do." Her voice is kind. "My heart breaks for you, thinking how you must be suffering. But it won't help to shut people out. I see Charlie's stubbornness written all over you. You know, he sprained his ankle one year while we were ice-skating down at the river. Dragged himself home the whole mile and a half. Wouldn't even let me carry his shoes. Charlotte nearly had a fit."

"I'm not trying to shut people out. It's just, no one really likes me here."

"Jaxon does. And if you let him in, you might find something worth knowing under all that bravado."

"I don't have any bravado," Jaxon says from the hallway. "I'm just naturally awesome."

"Jaxon, eavesdropping is a terrible habit," she says, "made common by swindlers and little old ladies."

He appears in the doorway with his confident grin. "Don't worry. I just came back to see if you were done."

"That's up to Samantha," she says.

"Yeah, I think so," I say. "Can I come back at some point? I'd love to hear some of those stories about my dad."

"There's nothing I'd like more." She scoops out a mound of batter that smells like eggnog and warm butter.

Jaxon gestures for me to follow him.

CHAPTER ELEVEN

The Friendship

"How are you not fat?" I ask, gripping the warm cup of hot chocolate with a hint of chili and cinnamon from Mrs. Meriwether's Sugar Spells Bakery.

Jaxon pats his flat stomach. "Good genes."

We cross the street toward the harbor, and I get my first view of the enormous ship. "Whoa."

"You haven't seen *The Friendship* yet?" He's all smiles.

"Is that what this pirate ship's called?"

He laughs. "It's actually a reconstruction of an East India trading ship, built in 1797."

I look at him sideways. "You know the exact date?"

"My father used to take me down here as a kid. He built boats, and he loved this one in particular."

Suddenly his house makes a lot more sense. I sip my hot cocoa.

"It traveled the globe over a dozen times and returned to Salem after each trip, bringing things from all over the world." He looks out at the masts with their complex wooden tiers.

"Really?" I'm charmed by Jaxon's love for this old boat.

"Unfortunately, the British took the original in the War of 1812 and sold it for parts."

"That's sad. It's beautiful."

There's an openness about him when he talks about this ship. "Yeah, I hate when people tear apart beautiful things."

My cheeks warm. "So you used to come here with your dad?"

"Yeah, he'd explain all the parts of a ship and how they worked. That's why I like to build furniture. I built a lot of things with my dad."

The sky has started to turn from orange to pink. "What was he like?"

Jaxon smiles. "He always wore suspenders, and he had a deep laugh, one of those ones where your whole body shakes. And he carried this old pipe around with him that drove my mom nuts. She used to say he was stinking up the place. But more than anything, he loved my mother. He had the biggest sweet tooth. He used to sneak into the kitchen late at night and eat the new pastries she made for the shop. She would complain, but secretly she loved it."

His love for his father is so relatable that my breath catches in my throat. "He sounds wonderful."

He puts his arm around my shoulder and pulls me closer. I tense at his touch. *Maybe Mrs. Meriwether was right about Jaxon. I haven't even really given him a chance.* I'm just not used to people being nice to me. The couple of times someone from school sought me out like this, it was to play a trick on me, which didn't exactly help me in the trusting department. I relax my muscles and lean gently against him, getting a whiff of pine needles.

"I didn't have any friends in the City." We watch the colorful sky reflected in the water, and I wonder about his arm, which hasn't released me.

"You always say what you think, don't you?" He says this like it's a good thing.

I shrug. "Vivian says I have no filter. Funny thing is, I think I get it from her. But really, I just don't see a need to sugarcoat things."

"So then I guess you don't miss New York?"

"Not exactly. But I miss being able to go to the hospital every day. This is the longest I've gone without seeing my dad since he went into a coma. The apartment sold way faster than Vivian thought it would, and we had to move before we could get him transferred to Boston."

Jaxon holds me a little tighter, and I don't resist snuggling into the warmth of his body. My chest rises and falls a little faster against his side. Jaxon looks down at me. "If you don't mind my asking, what happened?"

I pause. Jaxon's the first person to ask me to tell this story. "Four months ago, my dad was cooking breakfast. It was Saturday morning, and before he got sick I had a talent for sleeping till noon. I'd sleep through car alarms, fire trucks, basically anything. But that morning, somewhere in my unconscious brain, Vivian's panicked voice registered and I shot straight out of bed. I didn't know it then, but what I was reacting to was her on the phone with nine-one-one.

"I just remember running into the kitchen and seeing my dad lying on the black tiles. The weirdest thing is, in that exact moment I realized that he had been in the middle of making me my favorite breakfast—chocolate chip banana pancakes. His eyes closed just before I reached him.

"The doctors said there was a small tear in the lining of

his heart. They fixed it with surgery, but he's been in a coma ever since. They don't know why."

Jaxon shakes his head. "I'm incredibly sorry."

"I wake up feeling panicked a lot now. I . . . I think it might be my fault. My dad's getting sick, I mean." I've never admitted that to anyone.

"Sam, it's definitely not your fault."

Suddenly I feel exposed and have a desperate need to hide. I pull away from Jaxon's side. "You don't know me that well. People always get hurt around me. I'm like a magnet for disaster."

"You can't blame yourself for—"

"Let's just drop it." I bite my lower lip. "I better get home. I never told Vivian where I was going."

"Sure."

We walk off the dock and back toward the street. It's colder without Jaxon's arm, but I'm not sure I'm comfortable being that close to anyone. Mostly people don't touch me.

"Is there anything else to see on the way home?" I ask, hoping to push out my own dark thoughts. "Historical landmarks or anything?"

"Yeah, they're everywhere," he says as we walk. "Down that way a couple of blocks is Old Burying Point, the oldest graveyard in Salem. One of the Mathers is buried there. I'll take you one day when it's not dark."

"Who's scared now?" I ask.

He grins as we walk through a small street lined with beautiful old houses. "And down that way, Judge Corwin lived. A lot of people from Salem went there to discuss witchcraft accusations."

His hand grazes mine, and I pull it away before I consider if I want to. "You really do know a lot of history. I'm impressed."

"Is that a compliment?"

"I give them when they're deserved."

"Can you repeat it? I wanna remember it."

"No." I try not to smile, but fail.

He stops in front of a ginormous mansion with big glass windows and a roof dotted with cupolas. It reminds me of a New England–style castle. The greens are beautifully laid out, and an imposing fence surrounds the property.

"What is this place?" I ask.

"It used to be a jail."

"Fancy jail."

"It held prisoners from the War of 1812," he explains. "A lot of people died here, most of them hanged. Home to the Boston Strangler."

He points past the building to a graveyard. "Howard Street Cemetery."

"You guys have cemeteries everywhere."

"I guess there are just a lotta dead people in Salem."

"That's not creepy at all," I say.

"Giles Corey was pressed to death here." His voice has a dramatic edge. "It happened in this very alley."

"What? Why would anyone do that?"

"Well, when he was accused of committing witchcraft as a very old dude, he refused to plead guilty or not guilty. Giles was stripped naked, put in a pit, and two heavy boards were laid on his chest with heavier and heavier rocks placed on top."

"That's seriously barbaric. Why didn't he just plead not guilty?"

Jaxon shrugs. "All I know is that over two days he was asked to plead three times. And all he said was, 'More weight!' At some point people say his tongue came out of his mouth and the sheriff pushed it back in with his cane. Then right before he died, he cursed the sheriff."

"That's one of the most horrible things I've ever heard." *I wish I wasn't visualizing it.*

"Apparently, every sheriff since then has died of a heart attack or contracted some blood disease."

"Oh man. So what's this place used for now?"

"Eventually the town bought it and turned it into apartments and a restaurant."

"Huh. People live in an old jail." *I wonder if I could ever do that.*

"People say that Giles Corey haunts this place and that sometimes you'll feel a cold hand on your shoulder." He lifts his eyebrows.

"I don't believe in ghosts."

"Yeah, me neither. But we might be the only ones."

The wind picks up and I cross my arms. At which point, something lightly grazes my shoulder. I jump. Jaxon laughs.

"That's not funny."

"I thought you didn't believe in ghosts?"

"I don't! Doesn't mean I don't jump when people poke me unexpectedly."

"Got it. No unexpected pokings." He smirks. "Only expected ones."

"For a moment there, I was *almost* thinking how mature and knowledgeable you are. Then you act like a total ass."

"What was that? I heard everything up to the knowledgeable part."

"Unbelievable." I shake my head, and we turn around the corner as the sun sets behind the old houses and tall trees.

CHAPTER TWELVE

The Right Time to Leave

The floorboards creak under my feet in the long hallway that leads to the library. A painting of a particularly surly-looking old man with a large dog catches my eye and I stop short. My dad told me about this painting.

"Tell me again how you met Mom," I said as I slid under my covers.

My dad sat on the side of my bed and tucked in the blankets around my feet. "I was fifteen at the time, six years older than you are now. And I was the most handsome thing you'd ever seen."

I giggled. I'd seen pictures of my dad at fifteen, and he was skinny, with hair that stuck off his head in patches like a half-bald porcupine.

"Your mom was delivering some books to your gram. Your mom's family owned the local bookshop. And I was walking down the hall-way toward her. She stepped to her right to let me pass, but I stepped the same way at the same time. We went back and forth like this five or six times. I admit that in the end I was doing it on purpose just to look at her a little longer." He winked at me.

"Your mom demanded that I stop moving altogether, and when I did, she pushed me with both hands into the wall. I knew in that moment that I loved her, with her wild curly hair. Above me, my great-grandfather's painting scowled down disapprovingly. I couldn't help but grin at the cranky old man and his basset hound."

I sigh and walk into the library, toward the fireplace. There is so much about my family I don't know. I don't even really know the story of how my mom died. My dad always said that she died happier than he'd ever seen her because I was in her arms. That for a few short minutes after I was born, we were the perfect family. Then he would shut himself in his office for the rest of the night.

I pull the hook, flick on the lantern, and push the secret door closed behind me. The bricks and old wooden beams light up. I go to the spiral staircase and take the steps slowly, enjoying the thrill of this hidden place. I wonder if my dad ever knew about this passageway or if it was something my grandmother kept to herself.

I smile at the little room filled with books and make my way to my grandmother's desk, strewn with papers that she must have expected to return to. I set down the lantern and situate myself. I open the journal and read.

I received a letter from Charles today containing pictures of my darling Samantha. I simply cannot bear this wall he constructed between us. He won't even let me visit New York. I understand why Charles fears this family. He fears the curse, even though his stubbornness prevents him from saying so.

I am more determined than ever these days to solve this mystery. Mable is a great help and a dear comfort. Although, I'm not sure I haven't gained a few pounds from her cooking.

My breath catches on the word "curse," and my hand shakes as I turn the page.

I spoke with some of the descendants of the accused witches and asked them about their death records. It's obvious they think I'm mental. But to be frank, I'm too busy to care. After a few hours of nonsense conversations, I went directly to town hall and compiled a list of deaths of Witch Trials descendants.

I will spend my day tomorrow mapping them out, but I can already tell there is a pattern. Every hundred years or so, for unknown reasons, members of those families and my own seem to die within a very short time period. I don't know the cause yet, but I must break this curse before it gets to my Charles or my Samantha. Period.

If she wanted to know me, why did Dad keep us separated? It's not like him. There are two possibilities. One, my grandmother was nuts. Or two, my grandmother was right, and my family is literally cursed. In which case, my dad's illness is probably connected. Maybe he really is sick because of me. A dull ache pounds in my chest. I put pressure over my heart with my hand to keep the ache from spreading. *Please, no.*

There's a faint shuffling noise downstairs. Vivian must be home. I snap the journal closed and pick up the lantern. Quietly, I make my way down the twisty staircase and listen at the door. I open it, leaving just enough room for my left eye to peer through. Nothing. I yank the door open, slip through, and close it behind me in one fluid motion. My heart drums in my ears.

I tiptoe through the library and my foot catches on a book. I stumble forward and put my hand out before my face connects with the wall. *Where the hell did that come from?* Before I toss it on the shelf, I catch the title—*The Right Time to Leave.* I stiffen, remembering what the dark-haired guy said about leaving Salem. I grip the book and open the door.

"Vivian!" I yell, but there's no response.

I look both ways down the hall. "I know I locked the doors," I tell myself. It's a habit every New Yorker's neurotic about. I walk to the front foyer and scan the room.

"Vivian!" I yell.

Still holding the book, I bolt upstairs. I reach my room in seconds and lock the door behind me. How would anyone know I was in the library? Was someone watching me?

Glass shatters, and I jump backward, hitting the locked door with a thud. A pane of my bedroom window lies in shards on my floor. For a few seconds, I don't move. I focus on a pinkie-sized black rock nearly camouflaged against the dark floorboards.

My right hand curls into a fist. *I will* not *be harassed in my own house!* I lunge forward and grab the rock. It's cold and smooth. I turn it over in my palm. Scratched into one side is the word DIE.

The front door slams, and I freeze.

"Sam!" Vivian's voice echoes in the foyer. I release my breath.

"Vivian!" I yell back and swing open my door. "Come up here! Someone just threw a rock through my window!"

Her heels are muffled by the rug on the stairs but click in a hurried pace once she reaches the wooden floorboards of the hallway.

She studies the broken window and then the glass. "Outrageous," she says angrily.

"Here." I hand her the rock.

The muscles around her eyes tighten. "What's this about, Sam?"

I pause, not sure how to begin. "Today in school, this guy said 'You'll leave Salem.' Almost like a threat. And then, I find this book in the doorway of the library." I hold out the book. "I was creeped out, so I came up here. I wasn't in the room for more than a minute before this rock came crashing through."

"You're sure this book wasn't already there? That whole room's bursting with books."

"Positive."

"I'm going to check all the windows and doors," she says, and exits.

"I'm fine. Thanks for asking," I say to myself, and peer through the shattered glass to the dark yard below.

CHAPTER THIRTEEN

You'll Regret Every Word

"Nineteen people and two dogs were hanged, one person was pressed to death, and, at the very least, four people died in prison." Mr. Wardwell sits on the edge of his desk scanning our faces. "These are the deaths directly associated with the Salem Witch Trials. But, as many of you know, the repercussions had a far greater reach. Many families suffered for generations, lost their property, went into debt from their stay in jail, and were emotionally shattered.

"I ask this question every year to my students, and I will ask you. What was the cause of the Salem Witch Trials? Were the factors complex and entangled? Or was there one major factor that drove them forward? Was it politics, religion, culture, or just plain hysteria? As we navigate these essays you're writing, and as we prepare for the reenactment, we'll continue to examine these questions. Any preliminary answers are welcome."

Lizzie raises her manicured hand, sporting a diamond-studded skull ring.

Mr. Wardwell nods. "Lizzie."

"Cotton Mather," she replies. "The main cause was Cotton Mather."

Jaxon rolls his eyes. I appreciate that he knows how ridiculous she is.

"He was an expert in witchcraft," she says, "which he studied for many years prior to the Salem Witch Trials, waiting for his opportunity to discover some. Then he consulted on a witchcraft case in Boston and arrogantly wrote a book about it. This book became a bestseller and provided the map for what happened three years later in Salem." She pauses, then adds, "Some people don't know when to quit. And their actions get people killed."

Talk about arrogance. *I know she had something to do with that rock.*

"Well-thought-out answer, Lizzie," says Mr. Wardwell.

Lizzie turns toward me, wearing a dangerous look. I stare back at her, not willing to concede that I'm bothered. The hair on my arms stands up, and she raises an eyebrow before she turns away.

"Great." Mr. Wardwell looks around the room. "Any other theories?" The class is silent. No one dares answer after Lizzie. "If not, we'll take five minutes to discuss with your partners."

There's a two-second pause, and then everyone erupts into chatter.

"Sam—" Jaxon starts in a consoling tone.

"It's fine, Jaxon, really. Let's not talk about it."

"I forgot. . . . You're a tough city girl."

I smile. "Would you expect anything else?"

"Absolutely not."

"Oh, by the way, I found the house, or at least the general location," I say.

"What house?"

"The one my grandmother said you can see the hanging site from. I read up on it at the public library."

Jaxon's face flickers in recognition when I say "library." So, the whole world does know. At least he has the decency not to bring it up.

"Wanna go check out my map after school today?" I continue.

"Are you asking me on a date?"

I laugh.

"I'll take that as a yes," he says. The bell rings.

We grab our bags and head for the door.

"Meet you after classes," I say.

"Yeah, pick me up at my locker. I like red roses and European chocolates. None of the cheap stuff."

I shake my head as we part ways.

People recoil from me as I navigate the hallway. Not the freshmen so much—they don't know jack about social dynamics. But all the upperclassmen avoid me. I can distinctly hear the word "cursed" being whispered. The Descendants either know how I was made fun of with that word at my old school, which means they're really putting effort into making my life difficult, or it's a coincidence, which is creepy in its own way. I honestly don't know which scenario is worse.

I round the corner toward chemistry and collide with Lizzie's back while she's talking to Susannah. Lizzie turns and stares.

People around us notice. Susannah fidgets with her hands and avoids looking at me.

"This is where you say you're sorry, hope like hell I forgive you, and walk away," Lizzie says slowly and deliberately, like I'm an idiot.

My nails press into my palms. "Or this is where *you* apologize for throwing a goddamn rock through my window. Then you can walk away and go play with your little dolls."

Lizzie's different-colored eyes narrow and she takes a step toward me. She smells like bonfire and mint gum. Susannah grabs Lizzie's hand, but she shakes Susannah off.

"You'll regret every word of that," Lizzie says just as the dark-haired guy walks past us.

"And you!" I yell at him. Lizzie looks confused as I redirect the conversation. The guy pauses for a second to give me a disapproving glare, and keeps going like I've offended his sensibilities.

This only frustrates me more, and I make a fast attempt to grab his arm. My fingers make contact with his black shirt, but he pulls away and I lose my hold. I take a step forward, trying to recover my footing, but it only gets worse. I fall toward the metal lockers.

I put my hand out, but it's too late; my clumsiness is in full swing. My forehead collides with a lock, creating a reverberating bang. The hallway blurs momentarily and I slide to the floor. Everyone turns to watch. I try to get up, but there's a sharp pain radiating from my forehead and I'm super dizzy.

Lizzie stands over me, amused. Around me, people whisper that Lizzie used a spell on me, that she cursed me. I want to scream at them, but my head pounds.

"Okay, back up." Principal Brennan pushes through the crowd. "What happened here?"

"She threw herself into the lockers," Lizzie says, and the whispers continue.

"I tripped." I wince.

"Everyone, disperse. Now!" says Principal Brennan. "Let's get you to the nurse. Can you stand?"

"I think so," I say, but when blood drips onto my hand, I faint.

CHAPTER FOURTEEN

Death Is Like That

I pull one of my legs out from under the down comforter and readjust the pillow under my head. The sun sets through my taped-up window. I grab the water on my bedside table and take another Advil just in case my head decides to pound again. On the whole, though, my head is not my problem. My overwhelming sense of embarrassment is.

Vivian pops her head inside my bedroom door. "Jaxon and his mother dropped by. I told them you were resting." I never asked her if she yelled at Mrs. Meriwether about those pastries, but I'm not sure I want to know.

"Oh, okay." I attempt a smile. "You know, Mrs. Meriwether is actually a nice person. You might like her."

Vivian wrinkles her nose. "I'm going out to pick up some food. What would you like?"

"Grilled cheese and tomato soup."

She nods. "I'll be back soon."

I close my eyes as she leaves. Between this and that weird

locked door in Salem Library, it's like I went out of my way to make Lizzie look powerful. I'm sure the rumors are flying by now.

A smooth, cold hand covers my mouth and pushes down on my lips. My eyes snap open. The guy with the dark hair sits on my bed, his black waves falling onto his cheeks as he leans over me. His fingers increase their pressure as I struggle. I scream, but only a muffled moan escapes his fingers.

"Stop," he says flatly, as though nothing out of the ordinary is happening.

I pull at his hand, but he's too strong. He looks at me with such intensity that goose bumps sprint along my skin.

"I am not going to hurt you."

That's what every psycho says right before he eats you! I swipe at him with my right hand, but he catches it midair. I reach toward his face with my left hand. He blocks with his elbow. *I'm trapped!*

"I said I am not going to hurt you." He has a slight British accent, and the formality of it seems out of place. "I will release your mouth if you do not scream. But if you continue to fight, I will continue to hold you down."

I lock eyes with him and stop pushing. Anything is better than being held down. I nod. *Please let Vivian still be here.* She would definitely kick the crap out of this guy for me. She once tripped a businessman crossing the street just for looking at me inappropriately. The dark-haired guy assesses me for a few seconds and then pulls his hand off my mouth.

I push myself up and back so fast that I slam into my headboard. Even so, there is only one foot of space between us. I absolutely do regret saying those things to Lizzie. I had no idea she would go so far as to send this guy to my house. I consider screaming, but from this close distance, he could do some real damage before anyone would hear. I look at my door.

"It is locked," he says.

I turn to the window. The sun hangs low in the sky, and there isn't much light left.

He follows my gaze. "She is gone."

My heart sinks. I didn't hear her engine start.

He examines the bandage on my forehead. "You are injured."

"Yes." The word sticks in my mouth.

He frowns.

"What do you want?" My voice has become a whisper, which only makes me angry. I should be punching him and fighting instead of whispering questions at him.

"I want you to know that I regret what happened today."

Wait, what? I search his face for some hidden meaning and find none.

"But you had no right to open those letters." There's a calmness about him that's unnerving.

I can't be hearing this correctly. "The letters in my armoire?"

"It is rude to read someone else's private correspondence."

"Rude?" My brain fights through the fog of fear. "Rude!" I say a little louder. "You broke into my room. You have no right to talk about rude." I shut my mouth tightly, aware of his proximity and my hair-trigger temper. His dark gray eyes don't react.

"I can see your manners do not improve upon closer inspection."

"Are you insulting me?"

"And you are not very clever."

It takes everything in my power not to push him off my

bed. "Listen, creep, I do *not* have to defend myself to you. *You* have to defend yourself to *me*! Now you better explain why you broke in."

"I have already explained."

"If you wanted those letters, why didn't you knock on the door and ask for them?"

"Because you were reading them."

"Tough! They were in my room." I fail to match his calm. "And what? You followed me, watched me through windows?"

"I have been watching you since you arrived in Salem."

This is worse than I thought. *He's crazy.* I look at the door again and bite my lip.

"I told you it was locked."

"Just tell me what you want and go away."

He sighs. "I used to live in this house. And I do not trust you."

His explanation doesn't make me feel better. "So you stalked me? You're a lunatic!" Is this where Lizzie's getting her information?

His gray eyes narrow. "Then you should leave Salem before I do something crazy."

For a second I wonder if I've pushed him too far. "Get out of my room."

"No."

"Then I hope you like jail," I say with force. He almost laughs. I almost punch him. "That book in my library—that was you, wasn't it?"

He nods.

"Why? Because I'm a Mather?"

"That is one piece of it, yes."

"What's the rest?"

"You seem to enjoy repetition in conversation. Once again, I did not want you reading those letters."

He's the most infuriating person I've ever talked to. "So they're yours?"

"More than yours."

"Those letters are really old. They can't be yours." I'm positive they belong to the Abigail in the painting downstairs.

He pauses. "They belonged to my sister." There is a slight waver in his voice.

"Then, your sister shouldn't have left them here!"

"She is dead." He sounds so sad that for a moment, I not only feel bad about yelling at him, I want to reach out and comfort him.

I shake it off. "Well, they were in my armoire."

"They do not belong to you. And neither does the armoire, for that matter," he says with finality.

"This is my grandmother's house. Everything in it belongs to my family."

"Not necessarily."

Is there some situation where my grandmother could have his sister's furniture? "Why would anyone leave their furniture in someone else's house?"

"Because they could not help it."

"Why wouldn't someone be able to help it?"

"Death is like that."

I examine his face, with its proud expression. "Did your sister know my grandmother?"

"I should not think so."

"When was she here?"

"For the last time, on the day she died in 1692." There is no hint of sarcasm in his delivery.

I take a hard look at him. He wears all black like before,

—84—

black dress pants, black dress shoes, and a thin black cashmere sweater. The clothes match his formal accent. His hair hangs in waves around his face, and he smells of freshly washed linen. I shake my head, annoyed at myself for even considering believing that he's telling the truth.

"Seriously, what is this? Either you're crazy or you're messing with me. And besides, you touched me. You held my mouth down. You can't be a ghost. This must be Lizzie's idea of a sick joke."

"I can see it was a mistake to come here." He stands and walks toward my door.

I swing my legs out of bed and land on the soft white rug. "Don't think . . ." Black spots form in my vision. I shouldn't have gotten up so fast. I stumble.

"Samantha?"

I reach out for my bedpost, but he grabs my arm and steadies me. "Lie back down. You are ill."

"Don't tell me what to do." I scowl at him and his accent as he helps lower me into the bed. "I'm calling the police."

"I would not suggest it." He walks to my door but does not reach for the lock or the doorknob. He just keeps going and disappears right through the wood.

CHAPTER FIFTEEN

Manic Hummingbird

I slide into the navy blue pleather bus seat, and Jaxon slides in after me. Everyone talks excitedly as they arrange themselves in pairs. A field trip on a Friday—what could be better? It takes more than a few tries for Mr. Wardwell to get a word in.

When the class is somewhat settled, the bus lurches forward. I touch the small bandage on the right side of my forehead.

"Does it hurt?" Jaxon asks.

I pull out my strawberry lip gloss and put it on. "Not really. More humiliating than painful."

"Everyone's saying Lizzie cast some spell on you and that you literally flew across the hall, smashing into the lockers. So, basically, Salem's crazy, which we already knew." He offers me a butterscotch candy and I decline.

I agree that it sounds nuts, and a week ago I would've laughed. But I can't deny that every time I get near her, weird things happen. "I sorta had an epic fall."

"Yeah, I'm not gonna lie, that was some bad luck."

"Story of my life."

"Seriously, though, I've seen the Descendants gang up on people before. Don't worry; they lose interest. They just get off on people thinking they know magic. You're the perfect target for that."

"Maybe. It's just that the stuff with my house freaks me out," I say before I catch myself. I'm just starting to accept this friend thing, but I'm not ready to tell him about the rock or what happened last night. I haven't even figured it out myself yet. And it all makes me sound nuts.

Jaxon's smile disappears. "What stuff with your house?"

"Okay, everyone," Mr. Wardwell says from the front of the bus. "We are pulling into Gallows Hill Park. And before we get out, I want to make one thing clear: You must stay in the designated areas. If you don't, you'll spend the entire field trip on this bus."

He ushers us out of our seats and into the parking lot.

"What stuff with your house?" Jaxon repeats as we walk onto the circular grassy field surrounded by small hills and bushy trees.

I glance at Lizzie and John in the front of the group. "I'll explain later."

"As all of you know," says Mr. Wardwell, "when citizens of Salem were convicted of witchcraft in 1692, they were sentenced to hang. Witchcraft was a capital crime, and people believed that if they killed the individuals practicing it, they could keep the devil from taking root in their communities.

"The court set group hanging dates, and Sheriff Corwin was charged with picking the execution site. He was instructed that it must be outside the town limits. This location at the time was outside Salem proper, believe it or not. On their assigned hanging day, the convicted witches were bound with their hands behind their backs, placed in the back of carts, and pulled up this hill to my left. Shall we go up?"

We follow him onto a dirt trail and up a hill covered in tall trees. The path gets steeper, and my breath quickens. Through the branches to my right, the dark-haired guy watches me. I stop so fast, I almost lose my balance. A surprised yelp escapes my lips before I steady myself.

"They're just trying to mess with your head. Don't let it get to you," Jaxon says, kicking the ground. I shift my gaze to our feet and to the last bit of a stick drawing in the dirt of someone hanging. *Mather* is written above it before Jaxon destroys it all with his shoe. He obviously thinks it was Lizzie and John. Maybe it was.

I look back to the trees, but the dark-haired guy's gone. Did I actually see him, or am I so on edge that my mind's playing tricks on me?

"Keep up, everyone!" Mr. Wardwell bellows.

After another minute of climbing a practically vertical trail, we come out on the top of the hill. *How did a cart get up here, much less one carrying people?*

"This is the exact spot where the convicted witches were hanged," Mr. Wardwell says and scans our group. "Bridget Bishop, Sarah Good, Samuel Wardwell, and many more."

I lean toward Jaxon and whisper, "Wait, Mr. Wardwell is descended from a witch?" *No wonder he doesn't like me.*

Jaxon shakes his head. "I think his name is just a coincidence. There was some scandal about it years ago, but I don't really remember."

Mr. Wardwell looks pointedly at me and Jaxon, and we pretend we weren't talking. "Don't let the name of this park fool you. They didn't use gallows in the late sixteen hundreds. Instead, they threw a rope over a high tree branch. The convicted would stand on the back of the cart with nooses around their necks and the cart would roll away."

That's disgusting.

"I'm going to give you all time to look around. Don't wander off this hill. We'll meet back here in ten minutes."

Jaxon grabs my hand. It's warm and feels solid against my own. Heat shoots up my arm and into my cheeks. We follow a small offshoot of the trail to the left and into a patch of trees.

"It's kinda creepy to think about this stuff," I say, trying to pull my attention from his thumb gently rubbing against the back of my hand.

Jaxon shrugs. "I don't even notice it anymore. I've been hearing it my whole life."

Jaxon stops and leans his back against a tree. My hand slips out of his. "So, now tell me what happened in your house."

Me and my big mouth. "A rock came through my bedroom window with the word DIE scratched into it." Between the sighting, the drawing, and Jaxon's hand, I'm too frazzled to argue about not telling him.

Jaxon's face hardens. "Are you serious? Why didn't you tell me?"

"I mean, what were you going to do about it?"

"Help you find the people who did it and beat their asses." He says this like it's obvious.

Even if one of them might be a figment of my imagination? "I don't know."

"Is that it?" he presses. "Was there anything else that happened?"

I bite my lip and look down.

"You're obviously not telling me something."

"I'm just not good at trusting people, or telling people my problems, or talking in general. Really, the list goes on," I say. Little does he know that this is the most I've opened up in years.

"Try."

"I wasn't kidding when I said people get hurt around me."

"I'm willing to take that chance."

Are you? "You might think I'm crazy."

"I already do."

I smile. "It's not your problem, though."

"Don't you get it?"

"Get what?"

His face softens. "That I like you." He pulls me close to him and my stomach bottoms out. He puts his hands on my hips, and I can feel his fingers guide me.

I place my hands on his chest, trying to concentrate. My body's acting like a lost, manic hummingbird. "It's kinda weird."

"I still wanna know."

My thoughts are too cloudy to protest. "Fine. You win. I'll tell you."

He smiles. "If I was winning, you'd be kissing me right now." He leans close, and his breath is warm on my face. I consider walking away, but my body won't budge. In fact, it's betraying me by moving closer to him. His lips lightly graze mine.

"You taste like strawberries," he says.

His lips press into mine again, only not so softly this time, and everything inside me lights up. He pulls me closer, and I open my mouth.

"Best to leave the letters out of it," a voice says next to me.

I push off Jaxon's chest so hard and so fast that I slam him into the tree he's leaning against. The dark-haired guy stands next to us. I shake my head, hoping he'll disappear.

"I'm sorry, I just thought . . . ," Jaxon says.

"He cannot see me," the dark-haired guy says, as calm as ever.

I look wide-eyed at Jaxon. He doesn't even glance toward the guy standing a foot away from us. *Ghost.* This is just bad. I'm so embarrassed, that I'm angry.

"You need to go away, *now*," I say through clenched teeth.

"Shit. Sorry," Jaxon says. "But you did kiss me back."

The dark-haired guy raises an eyebrow and turns back into the trees. I stand there for a few seconds, trying to make sense of what just happened. He just ruined my first kiss. "Not you. I didn't mean you should go away."

"Well, you said it."

"Ten minutes is just about up!" Mr. Wardwell yells.

I can't do this. It's all too much. From friends to kissing in one day, and now this dead guy who's stalking me. I'll figure out all this stuff about a family curse by myself. I don't need anyone's help. "Jaxon, seriously. I'm not good for anyone. I'm not so sure I'm not cursed." My bottom lip trembles. I turn away and walk toward the class.

Jaxon grabs my arm. "I don't believe in curses."

I brush him off and keep walking. "Just stay away from me before I get you hurt, too." I wish I could crawl in a hole and disappear.

"I don't want to stay away from you," he says.

"Well, I want you to." I fight back tears as I rejoin the group.

"Great, you're all here! Quiet down, everyone. Now, did you all know that it can take more than an hour to die by hanging?" Mr. Wardwell asks cheerfully.

CHAPTER SIXTEEN

Salem Isn't Like Other Places

I make a left onto Blackbird Lane, dreading the idea of going home. It's Friday night, and the only thing waiting for me is a ghost who hates me. And Jaxon . . . I can't even think about him without getting sick with embarrassment. The only thing I have to look forward to is finally visiting my dad on Sunday, when they transfer him to Boston.

I stare at my door without opening it. "Screw this," I say to the house.

I drop my shoulder bag by the side door and turn toward town. I don't know where I'm going, but I'm sick of feeling like someone's going to attack me all the time. I need some space.

I plod down the sidewalk, looking at the pretty houses and quaint shops. People have already started to put out Halloween decorations even though it's mid-September. *Coffee sounds perfect,* I think as I stop in front of a little café named The Brew.

I open the door and a bell chimes. Freshly ground beans and holiday spices fill the honey-colored shop. No one is in line.

"Pumpkin latte," I say to a girl with a high ponytail behind the counter.

"Yup," says the girl, and grabs a cup. "Last name?" she asks with a marker in hand.

You've got to be kidding me. I go into the one freaking coffee shop that writes your last name on the cup instead of your first? This is just not my day.

"Mather," I say quickly, and hand her my credit card.

The recognition clicks. *Great.* Usually when I have a bad day like this, I put on my jams, get in bed with some mint chocolate chip ice cream, and watch funny movies until I feel better. But the last place I want to be is in my room.

"Pumpkin for Mather!" announces the girl.

Really? You need to yell that? I snatch my latte and give her the stink eye. The cup holder has a coffee stain on it that looks remarkably like a noose. I glance around the shop suspiciously. A few of the customers eye me with thinly veiled judgment. Is it gonna be like this every time I leave the house?

"Why, yes," I say to the judgy starers with a dramatic accent. "I'm one of *those* Mathers." The few people not watching now turn toward me. "We do eat babies, but only on Fridays. Oh, wait. It *is* Friday." One woman grabs her boyfriend's hand and walks out.

"Afraid my curse is going to rub off on you? Ooooooh!" I wave my hands, latte included, in the air. Then I stick my tongue out at the lot of them and stamp out. I know there was nothing mature about it, but it did make me feel a little better.

I zigzag through the streets until the sun goes down,

counting black houses and how many shop names allude to witches or witchcraft. By one of the antique iron lampposts on the edge of town rest a bouquet of roses and an unlit black candle. Someone must have died here. Probably a car accident. For a moment, I think the roses are black, too, but when I get closer, I realize they're dark purple.

A few kids from my school walk past me on the sidewalk, headed for the lit-up shops. They point and whisper. I pull up my hood, hoping to disappear in its shadow, and keep walking. This blows.

I cut through an alley and wind up at the entrance of Old Burying Point. It's surrounded by trees and the backs of old wooden buildings, oddly tucked away in the center of town.

It's cold, now that I'm not speed-walking. Also, it's way darker. Where did the lampposts go? Large gray stones line the ground before the cemetery. I step onto them, leaving the brick of the sidewalk behind, and realize there are words engraved under my feet. I bend down.

"'I am wholly innocent of such wickedness,'" I read out loud.

"Mary Bradbury said that at her trial," says a girl's voice. I turn to find Susannah standing behind me, wearing a black ballerina dress. How did she know it was me with my hood up? Was she following me?

"Oh" is all I say, expecting to see the other Descendants pop up at any moment.

"This is the Witch Trials Memorial." She inspects me for a reaction. "Each of those stone benches has the name of someone who hanged. My ancestor Susannah Martin is over there." She points into the darkness.

"You were named after her?" *That's super creepy.*

"We all were. It's tradition. Our families have done it for generations."

Her casual conversation sets me on edge. *What does she want?* "I'm glad my parents didn't name me Cotton. I don't think it would suit me."

She laughs, and the wind blows a few pieces of her hair around her face. "No, probably not."

"Why are you talking to me?"

She ignores my question. "There's a Mather gravestone in here. Want to see it?"

Now I feel like I'm being set up. I look around, but there's no one in sight. "I guess."

"You don't have to."

"I know I don't have to."

At that, she walks toward a small iron gate. I follow but continue to look over my shoulder. She points to the shadowed stone slab benches in the Witch Trials Memorial as we pass. "Alice Parker and Mary Parker. Not blood related. Just a lot of Parkers in old Salem."

There is something heavy and dark about her pointing out the hanged relatives who share names with her best friends. I zip up my hoodie the last inch. "Might as well be family, the way you all stick together."

"We've always been that way."

Does she mean her and her friends or all their ancestors for the past three hundred years? We make our way through the first few gravestones. They're discolored, the letters worn with age.

I wonder why she only mentions Mary and Alice. "What about Lizzie and John?"

Susannah opens her mouth but closes it again. After a few seconds, she asks, "Why did you fall into those lockers?"

"I just did."

"It wasn't Lizzie," she says, as though it's a fact.

"There, we agree." Although, I never did figure out that thing in the public library.

"I was there. You yelled 'And you!' to someone, but there was no one there." She twists a black beaded bracelet on her wrist, the kind elementary school kids make for friendship.

We walk toward the far right corner of the graveyard. I try to avoid the headstones in the dark. Even so, I worry that I'm standing on someone's face. Susannah, on the other hand, glides gracefully along.

"I don't know," I say.

"I think you do."

"It's hard to explain." What is it about this girl? I shouldn't tell her things. Her friends hate me. Until ten minutes ago, I thought she hated me. Maybe she does.

"Here." She points at a small old gravestone.

I shine my cell phone on it. It reads: MR NATHANAEL MATHER DEC^D OCTOBER Y^e 17, 1688. AN AGED PERSON THAT HAD SEEN BUT NINETEEN WINTERS IN THE WORLD.

"Did you see someone in the hallway?" she asks.

I hesitate.

"You did, didn't you?"

"Yes."

She furrows her brow. "I thought so," she says, and after a pause, "I have to go."

She got what she wanted, and now she's leaving. I shouldn't have told her. She heads for the graveyard exit at a much faster pace than we came in.

I struggle to keep up. "Wait, that's it?"

"Yes."

"Why do you care that I saw something in the hallway,

anyway? And what was that you were saying about John's great-grandfather dying the other day?"

She stops abruptly on the brick sidewalk by the entrance to the graveyard. *Oops. I just openly admitted to eavesdropping. Maybe I need to work on this filter thing a little more.*

She turns toward me. "Be careful, Sam."

Is that a warning or a threat? "What do I need to be careful of?"

She looks over her shoulder and back at me. "Salem isn't like other places."

"Well, that I know." I hate this. I can't continue to live with horrible anxiety that some dark-haired lunatic will pop in or goth nutjobs will terrorize me at school.

"No, you don't know," she says, and turns toward town without another word.

CHAPTER SEVENTEEN

Common and Uncouth

Mr. Wardwell gets in his car, parked on the sidewalk near my gate. He doesn't see me in the dark and pulls away from the curb by the time I get to the driveway.

I run for my house, anger propelling me forward. "Vivian!" I yell as I open the door, but there is no need. She is standing fifteen feet away from me at the small table covered in mail. "What was Mr. Wardwell doing here?"

"He was helping to fix the window."

"In my bedroom?" I ask, getting louder.

"Yes."

"How did that happen? That is *not* okay." My world is spinning out of control.

She stiffens. "I met him at the hardware store, and he brought over his repair guy. Really, Sam, I don't appreciate being grilled on this subject."

I narrow my eyes. "My dad is in the hospital."

She puts down the mail. "I know exactly where your

father is. Don't you dare ever make an insinuation like that again."

I march straight to my room and slam the door. I glare at the new glass in my window and pace around in circles.

"Ghost?" I say out loud. "Hellllo? Where are you?"

Silence.

"Go ahead. Ignore me. I'll just go straight downstairs and destroy that painting of Abigail."

I head for my door, but before I get there, he blocks my path. I almost walk smack into him. His hands wrap around my arms. He squeezes so hard it hurts.

"The arrogance." His gray eyes fix on mine. "Summoning me like a dog." His accent's more pronounced when he's annoyed.

"I don't care if you don't like me," I say. "I don't like you, either."

"Keep my sister's name off your lips."

I lift my chin and use the voice my dad uses when doing business with difficult people. "I want to make a deal with you." He relaxes his grip a little, and I can tell I've surprised him. "Help me figure out if I'm cursed and how to break it, and I'll leave this house."

He lets go of me. "I have no reason to trust you."

"Then we're even."

"I could make you leave without the bargain."

"Yeah, but I could do a lot of damage before I go. There's all kinds of stuff around here covered in black-eyed Susans."

There is a long pause. "Yes."

I let out the breath I didn't know I was holding. "Good. Where do we start?"

"That is not something I know."

"But you've been around for three hundred years, watching people. You have to know something."

"I have not been in Salem since the late sixteen hundreds."

"At all?"

"No."

"Where were you?"

"Other places."

Could he be more vague? "Why?"

"That is my business."

"Okay, fine. What do you know about my family?"

"Very little. I know that Increase Mather was well respected in the seventeenth century and quite influential in Boston, that his son Cotton Mather followed in his footsteps, and that his tenth or eleventh great-granddaughter, Samantha Mather, is common."

"Did you just call me common?"

"I believe I did."

I clench my teeth. "You're a jackass."

"Common and uncouth."

"I wasn't born in the sixteen hundreds! Girls curse. Get used to it."

"I would rather not."

I grab my head in frustration. "Fine. Don't. Let's go to my grandmother's secret study and I'll show you what I found."

"The study is mine. I designed it."

"I don't care whose study it is. Just meet me there."

He disappears. I kick my boots off to avoid making noise in the hallways and close my door gently behind me. I hope he's not a figment of my imagination. Who in their right mind would create an imaginary person who insults them?

There's no sign of Vivian as I creep through the hallways and enter the library, but I don't turn on the lights, just to be safe. Instead, I navigate the tables and books with the light from my phone. I run my fingers along the arch of the brick fireplace and pull the hook.

The door pops open, and a soft glow illuminates the end of the hallway. *Great. The ghost took the lantern?* It must be convenient to disappear from one place and appear in another.

When I reach the top of the stairs, he's standing in the middle of the room on a faded rug. For a second, I realize how out of place I am compared to him. These antiques match him, make him more attractive and proud than he already is.

"What's your name? I can't keep calling you dark-haired dude in my head."

He frowns. "I would rather you did not call me that, as well. My name is Elijah Roe."

Odd name, but it suits him. I walk to my grandmother's desk and sit down, thumbing through her journal.

"Here." I show him the entry referencing the curse, and he moves close to me.

While he reads, I sift through papers for the deaths of the descendants my grandmother mapped out. I don't have to look far; the folder rests on the top of a nearby pile.

There are fifty or so pages of death statistics in the folder. I flip through and find that she circled three years in red. And in those years, all the descendants she was tracking died in a very short time frame. My stomach drops. This doesn't bode well for my dad. I shake my head and try to concentrate on the numbers. I don't understand the pattern, but I can see there is one.

Elijah hands me the journal. "An old woman's diary does not constitute evidence of a curse."

If I didn't want to figure this out so badly, I would tell him what he could do with his comment. "Look, this is where she mapped out the deaths of the descendants. It includes all the main families involved with the Witch Trials." I hand him the folder. "My life is falling apart, and if my grandmother's right and it's because of some stupid curse, then I want to know."

He takes the death records.

"I know this whole thing sounds ridiculous," I say. "No one knows that more than me. I don't even believe in ghosts. Salem has warped my mind."

"Spirits," he replies.

"What?"

"We are called spirits. 'Ghost' is a vulgar term."

"Well, *pardonnez-moi*." I can't help myself.

He raises an eyebrow. "This will take careful consideration. The records are incomplete in recent years. I will amend them."

"Great." Before the word leaves my mouth, he's gone.

I sit back in my grandmother's chair and push my hair away from my face. I hope I didn't just make a very stupid deal.

CHAPTER EIGHTEEN

Delicate Things

I stare at the picture of me and my dad in Paris.

My dad held a glossy pastry in his hands, with cream billowing from the top. "Sam, you're about to eat the most delicious thing you've ever tasted. And I'm the lucky one that gets to be here to witness it. If you pass out from delight, don't say I didn't warn you first."

I grinned foolishly at my dad as he hoisted me up onto his lap. He placed the large cream puff into my small hands.

"Now, hold on. Before you bite it, we should document this moment." My dad waved at a pretty woman about to enter the café we were sitting outside of. "Mademoiselle, pardon. Pouvez-vous prendre une photo de nous?"

She smiled at my dad as he handed her his camera. She had a loose braid, long legs, and high heels. "Of course I will."

"Now, wait a second, something can be improved here," my dad said as he pulled me closer. "And I know just what it is." He swiped a piece of cream from the pastry and put it on my nose. "That's it. Perfection."

I laughed, and my dad wrapped his arms around me. He was right. In that moment, everything was perfect.

I put down the picture. *One more day until I see you.* My cell phone is next to the frame and I notice a missed call from Jaxon from late last night. I cringe, remembering our botched kiss.

I push back the covers and slide my feet into black flip-flops. The black-eyed Susan in the slender vase on my bedside table catches my eye and I touch its silky petals. There's no way this is the same flower as when I got here. Elijah must replace it. He must have really loved his sister. I wonder what happened to her.

I listen for heels clicking as I walk down the hallway, but everything's silent.

"Elijah?" I whisper in the front foyer. No response.

I should've asked him about the hanging location. He just left too fast. *Whatever.* I'll find the house my grandmother talked about myself. I'm curious about it anyway, and I'll need it for that history paper. I can't write "The ghost in my house told me" in my footnote and expect it to go over as hard evidence.

I push the kitchen door open. A faint smell of coffee lingers. Vivian left some in the pot for me. I grab a white mug from the cupboard and see the #1 DAD mug behind it. I gave it to my dad on his birthday when I was in fourth grade. He used it every morning since. He said he's proud of the title and wants everyone to know. It's one of the few things I brought from the NYC apartment.

I mix a generous amount of cream and sugar into my coffee and make my way to the back door. I step onto the patio and sit at the white cast-iron table. It smells like the beginning of fall.

"Samantha!" booms Mrs. Meriwether from her enormous garden. She waves with a handful of herbs.

I look around. No Jaxon in sight. "Good morning, Mrs. Meriwether!"

"Have you had breakfast?"

"No." Then I quickly add, "But I'm alright."

"Nonsense. Come over and have some with me. Jaxon usually sleeps for a few more hours, and I'm just about to sit down."

"Don't worry. I'm okay."

"I don't see Vivian's car in the driveway, and I would hate to think you're hungry over there when I have so much food."

"I'm in my pajamas." I glance at my black plaid jams.

"Best clothes in a person's wardrobe," she replies, and I give up. There's no resisting this cheerful woman.

I walk off the patio into the damp grass. I might seriously regret this decision if Jaxon wakes up and finds me at his kitchen table. But she did say he sleeps late. Maybe I can find out something about my grandmother.

Mrs. Meriwether opens the back door. "Come on in."

She leads me toward the dining room table, which is made from weathered wood and has the same rustic edges as everything else in the house. Eggs, strawberry waffles, and hash browns are laid out in an impressive display.

I sit. "This looks amazing."

"You'll have to come over more often. I never have enough people to cook for. Should've had a dozen children."

I smile at her and pile food on my plate. "Mrs. Meriwether, you were close with my grandmother, right?"

"Charlotte was a second mother to me. Took care of her right up until the end."

"What was she like? I mean, was she . . ." I want to say "sane," but that sounds so rude. "Clear-minded when she got older?"

"Charlotte had a mind of her own. People didn't always understand her." She pauses. "Her eccentricities were more pronounced with age, especially her belief in the unseen. But yes, she had a perfectly sound mind until the day she passed."

"Do you believe in things you can't see?" I ask, not really sure how to address the curse or the grumpy ghost.

"Almost everything worth believing in cannot be seen. Love, for instance."

"I never really thought about that."

"Sam?" Jaxon says behind me. *Shitballs.*

Mrs. Meriwether notices my reaction. "Jaxon, you're awake before noon. Isn't this a lovely surprise."

"I heard voices," he says. *Join the club.*

"Take a seat. I'll get you a plate."

He sits at the end of the table, between me and Mrs. Meriwether. She heads toward the kitchen, and I stare at my food.

"I'll go," I say as soon as she's out of earshot.

"Why?"

"You know why, because of . . . well, yesterday."

"So you're mad at me?" He frowns.

"What? No. I'm just . . . I don't know what I am."

Mrs. Meriwether returns with a plate and a glass of freshly squeezed orange juice. She looks at us. "Need to go check on my macarons. Delicate things, you know."

When she's out of the room, I get up.

"Sam, stop. I won't kiss you anymore. I just don't wanna fight."

"Believe me. It's not that."

He looks relieved. "So you do want me to kiss you?"

My face turns bright red. "Sometimes I seriously want to knock you out."

"I'm not afraid of some stupid curse, or whatever you think is wrong with you."

I sit back down and lower my voice. I'm not thrilled about Mrs. Meriwether overhearing this. "I know you don't believe me. But I'm not lying. One of my best friends fell down the stairs in my apartment building. Another got hit by a car when we were crossing the street. I attract disaster."

He ignores my warning. "You wouldn't have come here if you were trying to avoid me. You're at my house in your pajamas."

"I came because your mom invited me."

He looks at me like I can't possibly be serious.

"Okay, fine." I pick my fork back up. "So what?"

"So, you like me." He smiles, shoveling eggs onto his plate.

I can't help it. I laugh. *I do like you, more than you know.* What if something does happen to Jaxon and it's my fault? I couldn't live with that.

"You still taking me on a date to that house today?" Jaxon asks.

I smile. "Not if you put it like that."

CHAPTER NINETEEN

Black House

I study the map I made of the house's location.

"It's definitely in those woods. I'm telling you," Jaxon says.

I frown at the large trees, not willing to accept that truth. I'm not an off-roader. "I didn't bring a flashlight."

He laughs. "It's the middle of the afternoon."

Woods always make me nervous. I grew up on concrete.

"If your map's right, then I know the house you're talking about . . . know *of,* anyway. It's one of those things that everyone dares each other to find on Halloween. There's an old tale about it."

"Oh, that makes me feel much better."

"It's just a bunch of ghost stories. Nothing to worry about. None of it's true."

He doesn't know it, but that's the worst thing he could have said. "What if we get lost?"

"We won't. I have a compass on my phone."

Cell phones. That's right. At least there's that. "Okay, but who lives in the middle of the woods? It doesn't seem natural."

I walk reluctantly. The moment we hit the shade of the trees, I shiver.

"It looks like there's an old trail headed in the right direction. See how the growth is younger over there?" Jaxon points ahead and to the right at some short brush. "Also, I'm sure it wasn't weird to live this way when the house was built. It's not like they had paved roads then."

The idea of no paved roads only makes me feel more out of control. A bird caws, and I grab Jaxon's arm. He slips his hand into mine, and I'm too consumed with nerves to analyze my feelings about it.

He stops to look at the ground around us. "If your map's right, I think it's up this hill."

"You're paying attention to which way we walked, right?"

"You know, it's pretty cute the way you're ready to punch John out in the middle of a hallway like it's nothing, but trees scare you."

"I'm not scared." Neither of us believes me.

"Then maybe I should tell you the story about this place."

My stomach twists. "Wouldn't bother me at all."

He puts on the dramatic voice he used to tell me that Giles Corey was pressed to death. "Legend has it, an old woman lived out here for hundreds of years. She wasn't ugly like in storybooks, but she had mean eyes. And she could kill you just by looking at you. She ate birds, and her house was filled with their dead bodies. Most of all, she hated people who were in love. Once in a while a young couple would wander too far out and would never be seen again."

Strangely, that made me feel better. "That's ridiculous."

"Yup. Told you it was."

"People actually believe that crap?"

"People believe a lot of weird stuff in Salem."

Through the trees ahead of us, a rundown two-story black

house becomes visible. The windows are made up of tiny panes, half of which are broken. The trees press close to the sides and vines overgrow parts of the walls.

Every instinct I have tells me to turn around and go home. "You guys really like your black houses here."

"Yeah." Jaxon scratches his neck with his free hand. "That's weird. It's not more than a mile into the forest."

"Why is that weird?"

"I've just never heard of anyone actually seeing it before. I mean, if it's only a mile in, it should be totally findable. I considered telling you before we started that it was most likely made up. But I didn't want to ruin the adventure of searching for it."

I have to force my body to continue toward the house. "So what are you saying?"

Jaxon grins. "You must be good luck."

"Well, that would be a first."

"Wanna go in?"

"Not really. But we need to go to the second floor to look out the bedroom window to see the hanging location." My palm sweats against Jaxon's.

"If you want, I'll go in and take a look, and you can wait here," Jaxon offers.

"Yeah, that's definitely not happening."

We approach the front door, and he grabs the door handle. Very unfortunately, it unlatches. Why isn't this thing boarded up?

The door opens into a large, empty room with a fireplace at one end, like the one in my library. There is barely any light, and I step tentatively onto the creaky floorboards. It smells like decaying leaves. The strange thing is, it's too clean.

"I don't get it. This place has been abandoned for a long

time, right? Shouldn't there be graffiti or garbage or something?"

"Maybe we're the first people to find it."

I don't buy it. "Let's just go upstairs and get this over with."

There is a narrow hallway to the left of the room. And in it, the bottom steps of a staircase are shadowed in dim light. Jaxon heads for it and I stay close behind him, gripping his hand and trying to steady myself. The stairs groan under our feet. Jaxon stops.

"What?" I ask reflexively.

"Nothing—just a broken stair. Be careful."

Behind me, a step creaks. "Did you hear that?" I ask as we maneuver around the broken stair. "The steps creaking when we were standing still?"

"Sam, it's an old house. They make noises."

I'm not convinced. I look over my shoulder every two seconds. I don't know what I'm expecting to see, but whatever it is, I don't want to see it.

Reaching the top of the staircase, we find ourselves in another small hallway. There are two doors to choose from. Jaxon drops my hand and heads for the one on the left. He opens it.

"It's too small for the master bedroom," I say from the hallway, not wanting to go in if I don't have to.

Jaxon walks past me and toward the second door. The wood whines as he opens it, and I wrinkle my nose at the dusty, stagnant air. It's larger than the first room and has a broken rope bed frame and a few pieces of decrepit furniture.

Jaxon smiles optimistically. "At least there's only one window in here. Makes it easy to figure out where to look."

I approach the shattered diamond-shaped panes. "And it also makes it dark."

"Look." Jaxon points to the wall behind the rope bed. "Your name."

My muscles tighten. *What did he just say?* I leave the window. As I get closer to him, I notice the walls are covered floor to ceiling with writing, blurred under a layer of dirt. Near Jaxon's finger are written *Charles* and *Samantha*. All the blood drains from my face.

"That's not funny. Charles is my dad's name." I knew I shouldn't have come here.

Jaxon gestures at the room. "Sam, did you see these walls? They're covered with names and crazy stuff. I'm sure it's just a coincidence."

"How do you explain that our names are together?"

"They're both really common names. I thought it'd make you feel better. This is the graffiti you were missing downstairs."

I look at the writing more closely. "No, this looks like the rants of a psychotic person who was locked in here for years. Let's find that hanging spot and get outta here."

I walk back to the window, my skin crawling. *I want out of this place.* The windowsill has carvings that look like bird feathers. I can't help but think about Jaxon's ridiculous story.

Jaxon joins me. "Okay, definitely wasn't expecting that," he says as he takes in the view. Over the tops of the trees there's a small hill way in the distance just behind the Walgreens.

Walgreens? "No. No way. That's crazy."

He nods. "It's the only hill in sight. Everything else's flat. If the letter you found was right and you can see the hill from this window, that's the place."

I lean forward to get a better view of the forest, and place my hand against the weathered frame. A woman sobs, a deep rib-cracking wail. I whip around. My heartbeat pounds in my ears. "What was that? Did you hear that?"

"Hear what?"

"A woman crying."

Jaxon puts his hand on my lower back, and I jump. The walls with their writing feel claustrophobic. I can't stay here. I head for the exit, not waiting for him. As my feet hit the hallway, the door at the end of it slams shut. I lunge for the staircase.

"Sam, it's just the wind," Jaxon says as he tries to keep up with me. I can hear him grinning.

I jump over the broken stair. "So not okay."

I'm moving so fast, I'm positive I'm going to trip. I sprint through the room with the fireplace and swing the front door open. An amused Jaxon follows me out. I shake my hands in front of me, trying to get the feeling of the house off me.

"Honestly," I say, speed-walking away from the awful place, "you didn't hear that?"

"Sam, it was a bird."

I slow down a little and look at him. "Maybe."

"Definitely."

"Let's just get out of these woods. Worst place ever," I say.

"Yeah, you're officially off date location duty."

CHAPTER TWENTY

Death Records

Jaxon and I walk up my redbrick driveway as the last bit of light leaves the horizon. Under the overhang of the doorway stands Elijah. *Did he find something?*

"I'm gonna go over to Dillon's house in a bit. He's having a couple of people over. You should come," says Jaxon.

I stop a few feet away from the overhang.

"She will be otherwise engaged," says Elijah.

I glare at him before I catch myself. "Actually, I need to get up early in the morning. We're driving to Boston to see my dad."

Jaxon moves closer to me. "I'll text you tomorrow, then."

"Say farewell or I will for you," says Elijah.

In any other circumstance I would tell him where to stick it, but I just made up with Jaxon and I don't need to look crazy again.

"Sounds good," I say, and turn toward my door just as Jaxon leans forward.

Jaxon lingers for a few seconds before turning toward his

house. I push my door open and close it before Elijah can follow. It doesn't matter, though, because he walks right through the wall.

"What the hell, Elijah? Are you trying to embarrass me?"

"Who's Elijah?" Vivian asks, entering the foyer. She's in a particularly good mood.

I look down at the mail on the table, trying to act casual.

"You succeed artfully in embarrassment without any help from me," Elijah says.

"No one important," I say to Vivian. "A boy at school."

Vivian's eyebrows push together. "Then why were you talking to him in our foyer?"

"I wasn't. I was talking to myself."

"Right." Her look of worry turns to a smile. "Are you hungry? I thought we might go out for a change. Celebrate your father's transfer."

"No thanks. I grabbed some food with Jaxon on my way home."

"Suit yourself," she says.

I walk past her and up to my room, Elijah by my side.

"Don't do that!" I whisper, and close my bedroom door behind me.

"I do not enjoy waiting," he says flatly, his wavy hair brushing against his cheek.

"Then why didn't you come find me?"

"I have no intention of searching all of Salem for you."

I scowl. "I was trying to find the hanging location. Which I could've just asked you for and saved myself a lot of trouble, if you didn't disappear last night."

"It is behind the Walgreens."

"I know!" I snap, although I wasn't convinced until he confirmed it.

"I have made sense of the death records."

"Really?" Curiosity replaces my annoyance.

He picks up a few sheets of paper from my window seat and sits down. The handwriting on them is in old-fashioned cursive. I sit down next to him, and for just a second I swear he smells like freshly cut grass.

"At first glance, the clustering of death tolls follows no discernible pattern."

He speaks with his old-world accent. His eyelashes are long, longer than mine, and his eyebrows are perfectly shaped. It seems unfair that they're on a guy, especially a dead one.

"I looked for medical causes, but there was nothing out of the ordinary during the years your grandmother dog-eared. In fact, the rest of Salem's population was birthing and dying at a perfectly consistent rate."

"Is there something different about the Witch Trials' families?"

"Kindly do not interrupt me," he says with anything but kindness.

Kindly I will smack you in your perfect face.

"After a few false starts, I mapped out the approximate population size of the Witch Trials' families. My efforts showed that there was a significant increase in the number of descendants living in Salem around years with more deaths. And, more important, there were members from each of the major families in Salem itself. In years when there were not, everything was status quo."

"So it has to do with the number of descendants in Salem? I'm not following."

"The deaths appear to start when critical mass is reached," he says.

"Elijah! What does that mean?"

"Stay in school, Samantha."

You arrogant SOB.

"At least one descendant from each major family must be present in Salem. The moment they are, the deaths start."

My thoughts go straight to my dad. "What about now? Are there descendants from all the families in Salem?"

"Yes."

My stomach drops. "Are you sure?"

"By the proportionately largest number to date."

My mouth is dry. I know the answer to this question, but like a moth drawn to a flame, I feel compelled to ask it. "Have there been any descendant deaths?"

"Seven. All since you moved here. You were the only missing lineage."

And John's great-grandfather was one of them. "Seven? Maybe it's over?"

"Unlikely, if you compare the numbers to previous years. If I had to guess, I would say there are a lot more coming."

It's hard to breathe. I look at his papers to make sense of the figures he's written out. But when I see the death count at twenty-five for a previous year, I wish I hadn't. *Please don't let my dad be one of them. Please.*

"So there is definitely a curse. You see that, right?" I start pacing. *We actually moved my dad closer to Salem from New York. Does that make it worse? Can we transfer him back?*

"I do not know."

"But you admit that it's more than a coincidence?"

"It is unusual, yes."

"How are you so calm?"

"I am already dead."

CHAPTER TWENTY-ONE

You'll Never Be Alone

"Room ten-twenty-seven is that way," says the nurse, and points down the hospital corridor.

I don't wait for her to finish her sentence before I take off running. A surprised visitor jumps out of my way as my feet pound down the hall. I swing my dad's door open and let out my breath. His face is covered with tubes, but I'm used to that.

His blankets are neatly tucked around him. They're a different shade of blue from the last hospital's. I touch his arm, the one without the IV and heart monitor.

Vivian clicks into the room and shuts the door behind her. "You almost knocked that man over."

"Uh-huh," I say, without paying attention.

I sit on my dad's bed and hold his hand. Without thinking, I trace the cooking scar on his pointer finger. *He looks the same.* I examine the streaks of white around his temples. Maybe a little thinner than last time I saw him, but not too different.

"We moved to Salem," I say. "After all those times I bugged you to take me there, we're living in Grandma's house. It's enormous. I can't believe you grew up in that place. I get lost trying to find the bathroom. . . . I'm using your bedroom. The one you had as a kid, with different furniture, though.

"Mrs. Meriwether fixed it up for me. She told me you guys were best friends when you were little." I laugh. "You never told me about her. She's kinda great. And, holy moly, her cooking is out of control."

I examine his palm. "When you wake up, maybe you can tell me about Grandma—" I stop short. His heart monitor alarm wails.

"Why is it doing that?" I ask Vivian.

She steps forward, examining the display of his vitals, and shakes her head. "Did you knock the monitor off his finger?"

"No." I run to the door. But by the time I get there, a nurse comes in.

She feels his pulse, and presses a button on the intercom. "I need two nurses in ten-twenty-seven now."

My hands shake. "What's wrong? What happened?"

Two men in scrubs enter. "I'm gonna need you to leave the room," the first one says.

"Let's give them some room to work, Sam," says Vivian, heading for the door.

"No!" I yell. My dad's heartbeat flatlines. "Dad! Please. You can't. I don't know. . . . Please, Dad. I need you!"

One of the male nurses catches me before I reach the hospital bed. The first nurse pulls out a set of defibrillators. They open my dad's gown.

"It's okay," the male nurse tells me. "I'm gonna take you out of here."

I can't get my breath. I try, but there's only wheezing. The room spins.

The nurse guides me toward a chair in the hallway.

"Breathe, Sam," says Vivian.

I can barely hear her. This isn't happening. My dad isn't dying. Minutes pass. I don't know how many. I close my eyes and attempt to breathe.

I pulled my knees closer and my back pressed into the cold steps outside my apartment building as my dad's town car pulled up.

"Sam?" He didn't say his usual goodbye and thank you to his driver. He knew why I was perched outside in the dark against the railing.

I held up a few jagged pieces of hair hanging above my shoulder. "They cut my braid off."

He sat down next to me and forced a smile. "That's just because they knew how pretty you'd look with short hair."

My lip trembled as I held up my one remaining long braid to show him how bad my situation was. "They laughed." A few tears fell onto my cheeks.

He grabbed my hand and easily hoisted me from my sitting position. "Come on."

I let him lead me into our well-lit lobby, with its big chandelier. He headed straight for the doorman's desk and grabbed a pair of scissors. Without any hesitation, he cut off a big chunk of his own black hair right from the front.

I was so shocked that I stopped crying.

"There. Now we're the same. You'll never be alone, Samantha. As long as I am in this world, I'll be there with you. What do I always tell you?"

"Fall down seven times, stand up eight."

"And what are you going to do?"

"Stand up."

"That's my girl. Now, should we go show Vivian our new haircuts? Maybe she'll want one."

I couldn't help but laugh. The thought of Vivian cutting her own hair was too ridiculous. I leaned into my dad's side, and he held me while we waited for the elevator.

The first nurse comes out of my dad's room. She approaches Vivian. "He's stable," she says, and my chest releases its grip on my lungs. "He may have had a heart attack, but it's hard to tell until the doctor sees him."

"Will he be alright?" Vivian asks, and I stand.

"For now, yes," says the nurse. "I would wait a couple of days before visiting again. He just transferred here, and sometimes patients have a bad reaction to moving. I would give us a few days to monitor him. We'll be in touch if anything changes."

"Can I see him?" I ask.

"I would let him rest, Sam," says Vivian. "We'll come back when he's more stable."

"Why don't we just wait here until he's more stable?"

The nurse interjects. "I really think it best you go home."

"Thank you. We'll do that," says Vivian.

"Please, can I say goodbye?" I ask.

The nurse looks unsure. "Just be quick."

I run into his room before anyone can object. His tubes are back in place, and except for his disrupted bedsheets, you would never know anything happened. I kiss him on the forehead.

"I promise I'll fix this," I whisper. "I won't let anything happen to you. I love you."

The nurse opens the door, and I back away, taking a mental picture of him as I go.

CHAPTER TWENTY-TWO

Way to Say Goodbye

"We should transfer him back to New York," I say to Vivian as we turn down our street. This is the most I've spoken since we left the hospital.

"Don't be ridiculous. You heard what that nurse said about travel being hard on patients. It could be bad for him."

"I don't trust it here. He'd be better off in New York."

"Where you couldn't see him?"

"I'd take the bus."

Vivian shakes her head. "We'll talk about this when you've calmed down."

"I am calm," I say as we bounce into our driveway.

"Sam, you seem really unsettled lately. Agitated, even. I know this move has been stressful. Maybe it's best if you talk to someone about it." She puts the car in park and turns toward me, dropping her jeweled wrist from the steering wheel.

"You mean therapy."

"Well, you haven't been sleeping, and you've been seeing things. I just think it's worth thinking about. I have a few errands to run, but maybe we can chat about it when I get home."

I get out of the car, shaking. "I'm *not* going to therapy and I'm *not* seeing things. My dad is in a coma. Just because *you* can sleep doesn't mean I can."

"Well, that's more than a little unfair."

I slam the car door.

She speeds away in reverse. The back bumper of her car scratches against the dip at the mouth of the driveway. How did we wind up like this, where we fight more than not? I unlock the side door, and the heaviness of my situation presses down on me with a steel hand.

I only make it to the middle of the foyer before I sit on the floor. I fold over and put my forehead on the wood. My back shakes and tears fall down my cheeks.

"Elijah?" I say through my sobs. I lift my head off the floor. "I know you don't like to be summoned, but I need your help. Please."

He appears. "Let me help you up, Samantha."

"I don't care about me." I wipe my tears with the back of my sleeve. "I only care about my dad. I don't want him to die. I'll do anything. Help me break the curse."

He sighs. "I am helping; I made that confounded deal with you."

"I mean really help, like you care, like you would if it were Abigail."

His eyes get a faraway look.

"What if I leave Salem and transfer my dad back to New York? Then all the families won't be here—"

"An elderly descendant died in her sleep while you were

in Boston today. I don't believe it will make any difference if you leave now."

My heart sinks.

"Please, you must get off the floor." Elijah offers me his hand, and I take it. His palm is cold the way it was when it was pressed against my mouth. He pulls me into a standing position and tucks my hand into the crook of his arm.

We walk into the living room, and he gestures toward the white couches. "Sit."

"You're the bossiest person I've ever met," I say, but plop down onto a cushion anyway. I wipe the remaining dampness from under my eyes. He grabs some wood to start a fire.

"I am a lot older than you. I know better."

"You don't look a lot older."

"That is beside the point."

"How old were you when you died?"

He lights the kindling and closes the screen around the fire. "Eighteen."

"You loved Abigail a lot, didn't you?"

Looking at him standing next to the mantel, flames lighting up his face, I can't help but think how attractive he is. "Yes. Our parents died when I was fifteen and Abigail was thirteen. It became my responsibility to take over my father's business. I dedicated myself to caring for her so she would not have to endure living with our relatives. We were as close as any two people could be."

"What happened to her?"

"I am not going to discuss that, Samantha. I have said too much already."

"You haven't said anything. I barely know anything about you except that you want me to leave."

"That is enough."

I sigh. "Fine. Don't talk to me. But will you help me?"

He sits down in one of the white armchairs. "Yes, if I can. But you may not like everything I have to suggest."

"Like what?"

His movements are elegant as he adjusts his posture. "I do not think you will disrupt this pattern by yourself."

"I have Jaxon and Mrs. Meriwether . . . and you. Who else do I need?"

"I believe it will require the assistance of the Descendants."

"Those nuts?" My face falls. "You're right. I don't like that suggestion."

"Considering that these deaths do not affect your family alone, I think it prudent to inform the potentially injured parties. They may be able to help with information."

"Of all the things you could've said, you had to say that? Now I feel guilty if I don't tell them. I don't know. Maybe they can help. We don't even know how the curse started."

"If there is such a curse, I imagine it started with the Trials."

"Well, what was the cause of the Salem Witch Trials?" As soon as the question leaves my mouth, I remember Lizzie's answer from class. "It was Cotton Mather, wasn't it?"

He looks like he's reliving unpleasant memories. "He was a main player but not the only one. Give me time to think about it."

"Can I borrow your notes on the descendants' deaths?"

"If you want them."

"If I have to convince a group of people who hate me to help solve a curse that could be killing our families . . . I can't even say this without thinking I sound one hundred percent crazy. Anyway, I just need those notes, otherwise I have no chance with the Descendants."

He nods and disappears.

"Way to say goodbye."

CHAPTER TWENTY-THREE

People Are Dying

I slip into my seat next to Susannah in homeroom before the bell. It's Monday morning of week two at Salem High, and my situation has only gotten more anxiety-inducing.

"Alice," I say. Might as well go straight to the difficult one.

Alice, Mary, and Susannah turn—black clothes and dark expressions. There's something undeniably beautiful about them. If they weren't so mean, I'd feel the same awe other people do.

"Look, I know you hate me. But I know something important about your families that you'll wanna hear."

"I doubt you have anything to say that I want to hear," says Alice. "Unless it's the sound of you shutting the hell up."

"Talking to you is basically the last thing that I want to do. But, again, it's important."

"Well, what is it?" asks Mary.

Alice glares at her. "Mary, stop."

"What if it's actually important, Alice? She said it was about our families."

Alice rolls her eyes before facing me. "You have thirty seconds."

Man, I so wish I didn't have to be nice to you. "It can't be explained in thirty seconds."

"That took ten. Twenty seconds left." Alice waits to see if I'll challenge her.

It takes all my willpower to smother my frustration. "The simplest way to say it is . . . we're cursed."

Mary laughs. "You mean, *you're* cursed."

I can't help but wince. "I mean *we,* as in all of us. As in people are dying."

Mary laughs again, but Alice and Susannah don't. The bell rings.

"Welcome to Monday morning," says Mrs. Hoxley. "Fresh start to the week. We only have one announcement. This Wednesday, school's canceled for Remembrance Day—the official start to Salem's History Month." People hoot. "Now I'll give you time to sort your schedules and finish your homework. There will be *no* talking."

Mrs. Hoxley scans the room, looking for dissent. And even though I never talk, she glares at me. She's hated me since the pastry incident, when she threw up in the middle of the hallway.

I pull out my agenda. I honestly don't know how I'm gonna get these girls to talk to me long enough to convince them. I'd think I was crazy, too. What a nightmare.

Susannah slips a note onto my desk. It reads *Explain.*

I stare at the small piece of paper without a clue what to write. I make three failed attempts, which sound equivalent to "my gut told me something was wrong and then—bingo—I figured out people were dying."

With one minute left to homeroom, I write *read these,* and

pass the note back with Elijah's handwritten papers. Mrs. Hoxley looks ready to comment, but the bell cuts her off.

The Descendants leave without a glance. At least Susannah takes the papers with her. I shove my stuff in my bag and rush to history. I didn't return Jaxon's texts yesterday, and I'd like to explain before class starts.

I barely step one foot inside the door when Mr. Wardwell says, "Sam, you've been called to the principal's office."

"But—"

"No buts. Head over there."

I glance at Jaxon's empty seat and leave. What's this all about? Susannah wouldn't give those papers to a teacher, would she? I would look like a total psychopath.

When I open the heavy glass door to the principal's office, the secretary's eyes are glued to a book. I walk right past him, and I turn the handle of the door that says PRINCIPAL BRENNAN in a large font. Vivian sits in a chair facing Brennan's desk. I freeze.

"Is Dad okay? What happened?"

"Your father's fine. Jimmy here just wanted to have a chat with us," Vivian says in her I'm-the-nicest-person voice. *Gross, did she just call him Jimmy?*

I look between them and take the seat next to Vivian. Am I in trouble?

"Now, Sam," Brennan says, "I know you've struggled to adjust in your first week at Salem High. Which is perfectly understandable given your father's illness and all. But it's come to my attention that the problem is larger than I imagined."

At least this isn't about those papers I gave to Susannah. "Okay?"

"I think it best you visit the school counselor once a week for the next couple of months, to monitor your progress," Brennan continues.

"Monitor my progress? Like therapy?" I glare at Vivian. I'll give her one thing; she's persistent.

"Not therapy. Just an informal check-in. Jimmy—'scuse me, *Principal Brennan*—thought it would make your transition easier. That way you could discuss anything that's bothering you."

"No."

"Sam." Principal Brennan runs his hand through his thinning hair. "It's not a request. I want you to go to the counseling office and set a schedule with Mrs. Lippy before you return to class."

"You want me to go talk to someone named Mrs. Lippy? If you—"

"Let's discuss this outside." Vivian cuts me off. "Don't worry, Principal Brennan. I'll handle it."

He looks at me sharply, but Vivian stands, and her long legs distract him. "It was a pleasure meeting you, Vivian. Sam, I look forward to good progress reports."

I get up and walk straight through the waiting room and into the hallway.

"Sam." Vivian catches up with me. "It was the best I could do. Apparently, a lot of students complain about you. I know how it sounds, but the principal called all concerned about you not fitting in with the school. This seemed like the best-case scenario. That is, if you want to continue going to high school."

"Whatever."

"Do not give me attitude when I just saved you in there."

"I can't talk. Mrs. Lippy is waiting."

CHAPTER TWENTY-FOUR

Ropes Mansion

I unfold a small piece of white paper shoved into the edge of my locker. It reads: *Meet us at Ropes Mansion garden on Essex at 3:15 ~Susannah*. I look at my cell phone. It's 3:05. I speed-walk through the crowded hall and out the door.

I text Jaxon not to wait for me, and search Ropes Mansion on my phone. It's not far. Either they plan on jumping me in a garden or they think Elijah's notes have credibility.

A few blocks from the school, I pass a funeral home with a young woman outside it struggling to keep her composure as she greets people. Who did she lose, I wonder? A friend, her husband, her father? I shake my head to clear the thought, but look right at the placard that says the name of the deceased . . . *Proctor. Another descendant death.* I bite my lip and pick up my pace.

It only takes me a few minutes to get to Essex. It's an old street lined with brambly trees and redbrick sidewalks.

I approach the tall tower of a Gothic church and check my phone again. The map says it's right here, but I don't see a garden or Susannah.

I follow the spiked iron fence around the church. FIRST CHURCH IN SALEM, FOUNDED IN 1629, a sign reads. The fence ends, and there's a big wooden trellis covered in vines. *Should I go through?* I look around, and step onto the path that leads toward the archway.

Passing under the thick vines, the small dirt walkway opens into a labyrinth of trails, all lined with blooming flowers. In the center of the buzzing garden is a sundial, and around it, Susannah, Mary, and Alice.

I can tell they're arguing by their hushed voices and hard expressions.

"Samantha," Susannah says, and they all turn. With their black clothes and the Gothic tower in the background, they look more intense than usual.

"You're late," says Alice.

I look at my phone. "By two minutes."

"Exactly," Alice says to Susannah as though it proves a point.

What were they talking about before I arrived? "Did you read the papers I gave you?"

"Yes," says Susannah, handing them back to me.

Alice fixes me with her gaze. "Who gave them to you?"

"There's no way that's your handwriting," adds Mary, and Alice pinches her in the arm.

"Ow." Mary pulls her arm away. "That hurt, you know."

"Don't worry about where I got them. What did you think?"

"Are you incapable of answering a simple question?" Alice squints at me like I'm dim-witted.

"We were surprised that you knew so much about the local families," says Susannah.

"You knew about these deaths, didn't you?" I ask, reading into the diplomacy of Susannah's answer. Was that why she wanted to talk to me about John's great-grandfather and why she told me to be careful in the graveyard? What are these girls up to?

Mary sulks. "It's news to me."

Susannah looks at Alice before continuing. "Those papers contain decades of records. How'd you track them all down?"

I guess that's what they were fighting about when I came. Alice and Susannah know something they didn't tell Mary. Hmmm. Mary pulls at her springy brown curls and frowns. She's not as closed off as Alice or as poised as Susannah. If there's one of them that's likely to speak freely, it's her. That's why Alice always tells her to shut up. "Mary, what do you think?"

"I think you're right. I think we're cursed. And I, for one, wanna figure it out. I have zero interest in dying or watching my family die. Lizzie's brother—"

"Mary." Alice cuts her off. "Enough."

So they know I'm right about these deaths being more than a coincidence. Thank you, Mary. "Okay, Alice, if you don't think there's anything weird about this, then I'll just go."

"That handwriting is old cursive, and that information would take you months to compile. You're clearly up to something. And I want to know what."

"And you three are in a hidden garden without Lizzie and John. Plus, Mary didn't even know any of this until today. You're up to something yourself."

"I'm not playing games with you."

-133-

"You could just ask me nicely, and I *might* consider telling you," I say.

Alice gives me the finger.

I walk away. Alice either accepts me as an equal and we work together on this or I'll figure it out with Elijah. I'm not going to put up with her crap every day. I'm done.

"Don't go, Samantha," says Susannah. For some reason, I can't bring myself to hate her. "Please tell us what you know."

I stop.

"Let her go," says Alice.

"You don't like your family, Alice, but I'm really close with mine. What if these numbers are right?" Susannah presses.

"Yeah, really, Alice," adds Mary. "I'm not cool with gambling on this."

"Fine. But this is between us. Lizzie and John are out of it for now." Alice looks at me. "Well?"

Not that I ever want to talk to Lizzie or John again, but I don't get why Alice is excluding them. Makes me wonder what else she's hiding. I rejoin them at the sundial. There is an inscription on it that reads HOURS FLY. FLOWERS BLOOM AND DIE. OLD DAYS OLD WAYS PASS BY. LOVE STAYS. *And so does a curse.*

"Let's go to your house, Mary. It's only a block away from here," Susannah suggests.

"Not gonna happen," Alice says before Mary can answer.

I can't help but notice that together we look like a friggin' coven. I clear my throat. "Okay, here's what I know. These deaths aren't random. They occur in a pattern. And they're triggered when at least one member of each of the major

Witch Trials' families is in Salem. Unfortunately, there's a complete list of major families here right now."

The shock is obvious in Alice's expression. She quickly glances over her shoulder. "We need to discuss this somewhere more private."

CHAPTER TWENTY-FIVE

She's Not One of Us

"You expect me to believe that?" Alice asks, cracking her knuckles and leaning back on the burgundy pillows on Mary's couch. Mary's house has a much more homey feel than mine does. Nothing is terribly fancy or breakable, and everything looks lived-in. The coffee table has light scratches, and there is a small chip in the platter holding the veggies and dip that we've been munching on.

"Look." I lean forward in my armchair and hand Alice my phone displaying an old map of Salem. "Mr. Wardwell said the main requirement for the hanging location was that it had to be outside of town. The *only* way out of town at the time was over Town Bridge. That Walgreens is right on the other side of where that bridge used to be. It would have been the closest and easiest place to choose."

"We should go check it out," says Mary, sitting cross-legged on the floor, wrapping a curl around her finger.

Alice examines the map. "Being in a convenient location

and visible from some window you say you found doesn't mean you're right."

"Okay, well, look. There's an old cart road on that map right behind where the Walgreens is now. And *no* cart road or any road at all where everyone thinks the hangings happened. I mean, I went to the place you guys call Gallows Hill and there's no way they got carts full of people up that steep thing easily. They definitely didn't do it without a cleared road," I say.

Susannah and Alice share a knowing look.

Susannah nods. "Then it's settled. We go."

My recent woods experience comes to mind. "Now? In the dark?"

Alice smirks. "If you're scared, you should stay here. You won't be missed."

I shift in my chair. "I'm just not sure what we'll get out of seeing it in the dark."

"Clarity," says Susannah, and looks at me. "Your grandmother thought the real hanging location was important, Samantha, because it holds an imprint of that event. Like a memory."

I'm not following.

Alice shakes her head. "No way, Susannah. We're not doing that with her."

"I think we should," says Mary.

Okay, seriously, what's going on?

"How can we expect her to tell us what she finds, if we don't include her in what we know?" Susannah asks.

"She's not one of us," says Alice. "Don't forget that."

"She *is* one of the descendant families," says Mary.

"On the wrong effing side of history, Mary."

"Well, she wears black," Mary says as though that means

anything. I crack a smile. There is something endearing about her.

"Alice, it's too important." Susannah plays with the fringe of the pillow on her lap.

Alice points her finger at me. "If you say one word of this to Jaxon or anyone else at school, I will burn you to the ground."

"Uh, okay," I say. Her threat doesn't really make sense, but it sounds morbid.

Mary stands up, practically bouncing. "I'll get the candles."

Candles? I do *not* want to be in those woods with candles. But if I don't go, I might break this thing we have going, and they might never include me again.

Mary opens the coat closet near the front door and digs around in the bottom of it. She returns with a cloth bag and four black hooded capes and tosses one to each of us. *My life is getting more ridiculous by the minute.*

The front door opens, and someone who is unmistakably Mary's mother comes through with a bag of groceries. Her hair is more tightly curled than Mary's and she wears it pinned high up on her head, but her eyes and mouth are almost exactly the same.

"I see I've arrived just as you girls are leaving," Mary's mom says, clearly noticing our black capes.

My instinct is to hide mine under my butt. I can only imagine the questions that would pour out of Vivian if she walked in on a similar scene.

Mary throws her arms around her mother with enthusiasm, almost knocking the groceries out of her hands. For a second Mary looks more like a little girl than she does a gothic chic, secretive Descendant.

Mary's mother kisses the top of Mary's head. "Come back home soon—we're going to have dinner in a few hours. You girls are welcome to stay."

"My mom is expecting me," Susannah says. "But thanks, Mrs. P."

"I'll be here," Alice says.

"I don't doubt that," Mrs. P says, and winks at Alice.

These girls must spend an awful lot of time together. I can't even imagine what it must be like to have a routine like that with a group of friends. I awkwardly stare at Mary's mom, unsure if the invitation extends to me.

"This is Sam." Mary gestures toward me, and I'm grateful for the well-timed introduction.

Mrs. P's eyes widen ever so slightly and I'm positive she knows who I am. "Don't let these girls make you dance naked in the moonlight."

I appreciate that someone else finds the whole witch thing silly, but her nonreaction to the black capes and that comment make me seriously wonder what it is these girls do in their spare time.

Mary laughs. "But it's such a fun initiation."

"Yeah," Susannah says. "And it beats the heck out of the sacrificial one we used to have."

Alice rolls her eyes. I don't think she likes that her friends are joking with me, however twisted the jokes might be.

"You should see your face," Mary says, grinning at me. She kisses her mom on the cheek. "Be back soon."

I follow the girls out the front door and into the long driveway. Mary pulls out car keys.

"You have a car?" The New Yorker in me is surprised.

Alice and Susannah smile. "Yup," says Mary. "I only have a learner's permit, but Alice just got her junior operator license."

I don't even want to know which level of inexperienced that is. Mary throws the keys to Alice and we all climb into a black Jeep Wrangler. The moment my door closes, I grab my seat belt.

"Have you guys always lived in Salem?" I ask.

Susannah turns toward me in the backseat. "Always. For generations. As far as I know, most of the witch descendants never left."

"I'm leaving," Alice says. Alice drives like a City taxi driver, fast and aggressive. Vivian's maneuvering seems tame next to hers. Thankfully, the Walgreens is only a half mile away.

Mary pouts. "You can't. The circle will break if you do."

"Here," says Alice as the Jeep screeches to a stop in a parking space. We all fly forward. What circle? They act like they're in a secret society. If it's possible, I think they might be more distrustful than I am.

The parking lot is U-shaped and there's a fifteen-foot cliff of rocks and dirt running along the back of the property. We walk toward it, Susannah and Mary carrying bags of spider legs or whatever nonsense they packed.

"It looks like we can get up the hill over there," says Mary, and points toward the dark corner of the lot where the slope is less steep.

Alice steps onto the slanted earth and we follow. I grab a couple of tree branches to keep from sliding. *This is really not my thing.*

"Let's walk to a more secluded spot," suggests Susannah.

Let's not. The light from the streetlamps fades as we make our way deeper into the trees, and I can't see more than a couple feet ahead of me. Low-hanging branches threaten to take my eyes out, or at least disturb the tiny sense of security I have left. I walk with my hands in front of me.

"This'll work," says Alice when we reach a small circular clearing.

I look in all directions, but I can't place where we are. The trees are thick, and as far as I can tell there's no moon. Mary pulls out a dark blanket, and we help her spread it out. The clearing's just big enough for it.

I sit down and pull on the hooded cape, mainly to minimize my peripheral vision. If I can see Elijah, does that mean I can see other ghosts? *Quick, think about something else. Kittens, puppies, daisies . . . black-eyed Susans, Abigail, ghosts. Shit.*

Susannah and Mary light candles and arrange them on the blanket. The trees flicker in the flames and the branches look like they're moving. I have a strong urge to look over my shoulder. Why didn't I back out when I had the chance? If someone says "Let's contact the dead," I don't care how stupid I look, I'm running full speed outta here.

Alice ties little bundles of I don't know what . . . herbs? This silent ritual thing is killing me. *Someone say something so I can get out of my own freakin' head!* "So, what ex—" I start.

"I'll tell you when to speak. Until then, shut up," Alice snaps, her long blond hair shining in the candlelight.

"Don't worry," says Susannah. "You'll catch on."

Susannah lights four candles in the middle of the blanket, and everyone's faces glow. *So not comfortable.* Alice looks at Susannah and she nods.

"I call upon the power of water. That it may wash away my doubts and calm my spirit. Only through stillness may I see clearly." Susannah finishes her words by dripping water from a small glass bottle onto her fingers and flicking it over the candles. They sizzle but don't go out.

Susannah looks to her left at Mary. "I call upon the power of earth. That it may guide my path and ground my spirit. Only through balance may I see clearly." Mary picks up some dirt from the edge of the blanket and sprinkles it over the candles.

Mary looks at Alice. "I call upon the power of air. That it may elevate my thoughts and lift my spirit. Only through breath may I see clearly." Alice waves her hands around the flames and they leap into the air.

They all look at me. *Fire? Am I supposed to say 'fire'? What are the words again?* "I call," I say uncomfortably. "I call upon . . . the, um, fire . . . power of fire."

"That it may light my way and impassion my spirit. Only through purification may I see clearly," they all continue in unison.

Alice hands each of us one of the bundles she made. I mimic them and stick the end of mine in the fire. Alice holds out a bowl, and we drop in the burning herbs. There's a strong musky smell and a lot of smoke.

They all say together, "I mean what I say, and I say what I intend. Know my desire and give me clarity."

"Repeat," Susannah whispers.

"I mean what I say . . . and I say what I intend. Know my desire and give me clarity?"

Susannah and Alice offer me their hands. I take them. Through the smoke, their faces waver slightly, like bad reception on a TV. *Wait, what is that?* A moment passes and their faces flicker more violently. Then they blur completely with the faces of other women. It's as if I'm seeing two sets of people at once, the Descendants and some unknown older women.

I open my mouth, but everything goes black. Even the noise of the crackling flames stops. For a split second, a picture flashes through the darkness—the back of a boy's head bleeding on the ground, his body crushed under a large piece of metal.

Mary's scream breaks my vision and the blackness, and I once again see the girls as they normally are, without the blurred faces. It takes me a second to figure out what's happening. Everyone's panicking, blowing out candles and scooping up the spell ingredients.

"Samantha, come on," says Susannah, and I get up.

Alice snatches the blanket, and I follow them at a fast clip through the trees. With each step I become more aware of the blackness and the nagging sense that something was in the woods with us. I run so fast that I slide down the slope of the hill and land back in the parking lot with scratched hands. Mary paces by the Jeep.

"What was that?" Mary demands.

I grab my head, trying to stop the nausea. My skin pulses with the impossible rhythm of my heart. Maybe there were hallucinogens in those herbs? Was I wrong all along? Do they actually know magic? I mean, I see ghosts. This isn't that different.

"I don't know," says Alice. "Those faces . . ."

Mary pulls her cape off. "You saw that, right, Susannah?"

"I did."

And who was that crushed guy? *There was so much blood.* "Did you—"

"Everyone just stop talking for a minute," says Alice.

"I wanna go home," says Mary.

Alice pulls out the keys and unlocks the Jeep. No one hesitates; we all jump in. *I so wish I hadn't come to this,* I think as I climb in the backseat. From the side mirrors, I can see that everyone has the same disturbed expression. We ride home in silence.

CHAPTER TWENTY-SIX

Something in Common

I don't get three steps into my foyer before Vivian yells, "How dare you come home this late and not call!"

I haven't had time to process what I saw, and Vivian's yelling only agitates me further.

"You're filthy. Where were you?" She's talking at me, not to me.

"I was with some girls from school." I don't apologize, not after what she did today.

"Why didn't you answer your phone? I called at least five times."

Ignoring her never gets a good reaction, but it's not like I can tell her what I was doing. "I didn't want to talk to you."

She stiffens, and I know I've gone too far. "I'm surprised you have any friends with the way your principal says you behave. But we both know they won't last long."

"Really? You had to say that? I bet you feel awesome

about yourself for finally getting me into counseling. Maybe I can use my time to talk about what a crap parent you are."

"You just bought yourself a week before you see your father."

"You can't keep me from seeing my dad!"

"I can and I will until you learn how to behave."

I head for the staircase.

"You don't want me as your enemy, Samantha. You won't like it."

I don't bother to turn around.

I open the door to my room, and Elijah's sitting on my window seat. He takes one look at my expression and my clothes and stands. "I will leave you."

"Why would she say that?" I demand.

He shakes his head. "I cannot say."

"Why would anyone do that? It's just mean."

"Yes."

"Am I really that awful?" My bottom lip trembles.

His brow furrows.

"If I don't have my dad, I don't have anyone. I'm all alone."

He turns toward my window and doesn't answer. I just need someone to be nice to me right now. I've hit my limit. "Forget it. You can't stand me, either." I kick off my muddy boots.

He stares out my window. "I was just remembering that I once had a very similar conversation with Abigail."

His comment surprises me. "Really? About what?"

"It is a long story."

Does that mean he might tell me? I wouldn't mind hearing about someone else's life right now. "That's okay."

For a moment he hesitates. Then he turns, his face etched with emotion. "Sit."

I look down at my legs. "My jeans are muddy. Turn around." I don't care if he's been dead for three hundred years. He's the closest thing I have to a friend besides Jaxon.

He looks at my legs, and seeing that I'm right, turns to the window again. I slip off my clothes and into my sweats.

I look back up at him and realize my reflection is visible in the windowpane. Was he watching me? I sit cross-legged on my bed. "You can turn around."

He grips his hands behind his back. "You already know that Abigail loved black-eyed Susans. She thought them the beauty of New England, said we were lucky to have them. She used to pick them during the late summer, and I would find them the rest of the year pressed in books and journals, and even in my accounting paperwork."

I wrap a blanket around my legs. "That's sweet."

He nods. "That bed you are sitting on. I had it made for her, along with all the furniture in this room. I rode to Ipswich to have it designed and surprised her with it on her sixteenth birthday. You should have seen her face when she first saw it. She ran her fingers over the flowers and cried."

"So you're the one that had the secret compartment put in the back of the armoire? And the secret door in the library? You really like hidden things, don't you?" What I want to ask is, What were you hiding? But I know better. He's always just out of reach even without any instigation.

He almost looks amused by my observation. "Those letters you found, they were love letters between Abigail and a boy we grew up with. He was a few years older than her—my classmate and my friend. I always knew there was something between them, but I never let on. I did not want to cause her any embarrassment."

His respect for his sister makes me feel self-conscious about trying to read her letters.

"One day, she confided in me that she was in love. She asked that I carry a letter to him in secret. I agreed but was nervous for her, knowing his family was pushing for him to marry the governor's daughter. If their love became public, they would have been kept apart. Or Abigail's propriety would be questioned. Pretty soon, I became their direct line of communication." He looks at the armoire in a nostalgic way. "The hidden compartment was intended to give her a place to keep her private things."

"Did they wind up together?" William's words in the letter I read sounded apologetic.

"No," he says.

I wait, but he doesn't continue. "Thank you for sharing that with me. When I found those letters, I knew they were special. Now I know why."

His face softens. "I have not spoken about her in hundreds of years. It is not entirely comfortable."

"I get that. Not the hundreds of years part, but I don't share personal things, either. I don't have friends long enough. And when I do, they tend to use the things I say against me. It's just easier not to talk."

"I hate to think that we have something in common." He sits next to me, and for the first time, I think he's joking.

"Yeah, that would be terrible."

The corners of his mouth move ever so slightly in the direction of a smile.

"Are you smiling?" I ask.

"Absolutely not." His mouth lifts a tad higher.

"Be careful. I might actually think you like me."

"I will be sure to leave you another book, then."

"Or another rock," I reply.

His smile disappears. "I did not throw that rock through your window."

"Really?" I pause. "Do you know who did?"

He shakes his head. "Did you speak with the Descendants today?"

The events of my night rush back to me. "Yeah, they agreed to help. But . . . we went to the hanging location and, um . . ." *How do I say this?* "And we performed a ritual or a spell or something?"

His face turns serious. "You practiced witchcraft?"

I can't help it. I laugh. It sounds crazy. And now that I'm not in those terrifying woods, I'm starting to think I imagined it. "I guess."

"What happened?"

His tone worries me. I trace the lace pattern on my bedspread with my fingers. I thought if anyone would say witchcraft doesn't exist, it'd be him. "The girls' faces blurred and became other faces. Then everything went black and I saw a guy crushed under a piece of metal."

He stands. "Whose faces?"

"I honestly don't know. They were older, though."

"You must return to the hanging location with the Descendants. I will observe this for myself."

"No way! I'm not doing that again. I almost threw up, I was so scared."

"Unless you can think of another way to see those faces, we are returning to that hill." His tone indicates that I'm not going to get anywhere by arguing.

"There's obviously something you're not telling me. What is it?"

"I took it upon myself to read some journals belonging

to descendants in the years with more deaths. Most of what I found was useless, mundane musings. But there was one thing that stood out. One hundred years apart, two individuals saw faces like you are describing."

"And then what?"

His forehead wrinkles. "They died shortly after."

CHAPTER TWENTY-SEVEN

I'm on Display

I scan the lunchroom tables. Alice, Mary, and Susannah are at their usual place near the window. I so wish I had asked them to go to the hanging spot in homeroom. And if I don't do it now, school will be over, and tomorrow's Wednesday—Remembrance Day. I just need to do this, even if Alice embarrasses me in front of everyone.

As I close in on their table, people's heads turn in my direction. I've never seen anyone approach them during lunch. It's like walking up to the throne without an invitation. I stop at the edge of their round table. This is much worse than in the garden. I'm on display here.

"Take a seat, Samantha," says Susannah.

I look at Alice. "Stop standing there like an idiot," she says.

Usually someone calling me an idiot would not inspire feelings of relief. But in this case, it does. I pull out a chair and sit down. "I really don't know how to say this, other than to just say it. We need to go back to the hanging location."

"That's your big announcement?" Alice exudes confidence. "We know. We'll go after the witches and warlocks party tonight."

"I wasn't invited to the party." Why did I say that?

They all pause. Then Susannah says, "Come to the party, and we'll go together after."

"Okay, but this is on you," Alice warns Susannah.

I'm not sure if I should say thanks for the invitation or ask Alice what the risk is. Is it because Lizzie hates me? Alice definitely isn't my biggest fan, either. Also, why were they keeping yesterday a secret from Lizzie and John? Whatever. This is about my dad, not about being friends.

Alice breaks the momentary silence. "Are you done? Or did you have any other brilliant ideas?"

"I think other descendants might have seen those blurred faces we saw in the woods. In previous years where a lotta people died, I mean."

Mary shifts uncomfortably. "You're just full of good news."

"You think or you know?" asks Alice.

"I know."

"How could you know that, Samantha?" Susannah asks.

"I can't explain that. But there's something you should know about it. The descendants who saw those blurred faces—"

"I don't know whether to be embarrassed for you or disgusted by you," says Lizzie's voice behind me. *Oh, crap.* What is she doing in the freshman-sophomore lunch period?

Alice gives me a look that says *It's your own fault, for trying to sit with us.* I stand and face Lizzie, but she looks past me to the Descendants. There are about twenty juniors in the lunchroom, including Jaxon.

"This better be a joke," Lizzie says to the girls.

"Well if it is, the punch line sucks," says Alice.

Lizzie looks unsure. I'm confused, too. Was that directed at Lizzie or me? I try to exit the group, but Lizzie grabs my arm and her nails dig into my skin.

"I can break you if I want to," she says before she lets go, her brown and green eyes issuing a warning.

Jaxon watches me from a table across the room, and I decide to just walk away from her. I really don't wanna cause a scene in the middle of the cafeteria when half the school is watching.

"What was that?" Jaxon asks as I walk toward him. He pulls an impressively large lunch out of a bag.

I take the seat next to him. "Nothing, don't worry about it."

"Didn't look like nothing."

"I was just talking to the Descendants, and Lizzie got mad." I try to act casual about it.

"No one talks to them at lunch. Believe me, I've seen people try. They're just met with blank stares until they feel so self-conscious they walk away."

"I believe that."

"You wanna tell me what's going on?" Jaxon offers me a peanut butter, banana, and honey sandwich.

"You sure?" I ask.

"I have two."

I laugh and take the sandwich. "What're you doing in my lunch period?"

"Teacher was sick and the sub never showed. You weren't

handing out pastries again, were you?" He grins. Does he not know they came from his mother's bakery? Maybe Vivian didn't bring it up to Mrs. Meriwether after all. That's a relief.

I smile and bite the delicious sandwich. "Do you know something about a witches and warlocks party tonight?"

"Yup."

"Is that all you're gonna say?"

"Depends. Is that all *you're* gonna say about the Descendants?"

I shake my head at him, amused. But in reality, I don't know what to say. I don't want to lie, but I can't tell him the truth. If I do, I might compromise the civility I have going with the Descendants and then they won't go back to the hanging location with me. "Susannah left her notebook in homeroom, and I was just returning it." Weak, but not the worst.

"Kinda looked like you were sitting at their table. Like you were friends with them."

"Come on. No way." I *was* sitting there. I *was* being friendly with them. But that doesn't mean we're friends. Right?

He's not convinced, but lets it go. "Costume party. Alice's house. Descendants throw it every year right before Remembrance Day. It's a tradition."

Costume party? Hosted by Descendants? Not my idea of a good time. But if I don't go, they might not wait for me to go back to the hanging location. "Are you going?"

"I look very good in a warlock costume. Wouldn't seem right to deprive people of that."

"Yeah, the school might never forgive you."

Jaxon gives me a choice of pastries from a small box tied

with string. I wonder if I can somehow convince Mrs. Meri-wether to pack my lunches.

"I'll pick you up at nine, nine-thirty?" asks Jaxon.

"Uh, yeah. Sure. Do I have to wear a costume?"

"You won't be let in without it."

CHAPTER TWENTY-EIGHT

You Bit Everyone

Line dancing, costume parties, and public speaking are at the top of my slow-death-through-embarrassment list. My clothes are spread out on every available piece of furniture in my room. I so wish I didn't have to go to this thing.

"Sam! Door!" yells Vivian from downstairs.

I glance at my cell phone. It's 8:17 p.m. Could Jaxon be that early? I scoop up some clothes and shove them back into Abigail's armoire in a messy pile. "Coming!"

I make it down the first couple of stairs before I stop dead in my tracks. Vivian's talking to Susannah in the foyer.

"Hey," I say, and they look up.

"I didn't know you girls were going to a theme party," Vivian says in a friendly tone as I make my way down the rest of the stairs.

That's because we haven't spoken a word to each other since last night. I shrug.

"I might have something in my closet for you," Vivian

says. This is a perfect example of our current relationship. Fight, and then ignore the fact that the fight ever happened.

"I'll be fine."

"Let me know if you change your mind," she says, and clicks down the hall.

Susannah is wearing a flattering black Victorian dress with a full skirt and a high neck. Her hair is fashioned in an elaborate version of her usual bun.

"Whoa. You look awesome." There's no way I'm going to be able to match that.

"Thanks." She smiles.

"I was just getting ready. You want to come up?" She obviously came for some specific reason, and I don't want Vivian overhearing whatever that reason is. She already thinks I'm unstable; all I need is for her to hear I'm inadvertently practicing witchcraft.

"Sure. This is a beautiful old house. I always wondered what it looked like inside."

We walk up the stairs together. "I spent about three days getting lost in it."

"I can imagine." She takes note of the dimly lit sconces in the hallway.

"Here we are," I say, opening the door to my room.

"It's like stepping back in time." She repeats my exact thoughts when I saw this place.

"So what's up? I know you didn't just happen to be in the neighborhood."

"No, I didn't." She looks down at the antique silk purse at her side and pulls out an envelope. "This is a letter from your grandmother to mine. I found it when I was helping my mother go through some old boxes this summer. It talks about the mysterious deaths."

"So you did know about them?" I was right in the garden. There was definitely something they knew and didn't tell me.

"Sort of. To be honest, I thought your grandmother was, well, unbalanced. It was *my* grandmother's response that worried me. It was shoved into the same envelope. She never sent it."

"Okay," I say, unsure.

"Samantha, how did you know other descendants saw blurred faces?"

"Is that what that letter says? The one from your grandmother?"

"Yes. I showed it to Alice, and she agreed that there might be something to it. Then you come into school saying that other descendants saw blurred faces."

I'm beginning to see why Alice is so suspicious of me. The information I have would seem weird to me, too, if I were in her position.

"My grandmother never sent the letter. So how'd you find out?"

"I can't tell you."

"I know we haven't given you any reason to trust us, with writing on your locker and the hair pulling and all the rumors—"

"And the rock," I say.

"Rock?"

"The rock you guys threw through my window that said DIE on it?"

She scrunches her delicate features. "I don't know anything about that. That's horrible."

Maybe Lizzie and John did it and she didn't know? "Yeah, well. You can see why I'm not exactly jumping at the chance to trust you."

"I get that. What can I do to change your mind?"

"I don't know. I guess to start you can tell me why Lizzie's been following me around."

She glances toward my window, which doesn't lessen my suspicions or comfort me one bit. "It's complicated."

"Does it have anything to do with why you didn't invite her or John that day you met me in the garden?"

She touches the lace around her collar. "Yes."

I wait, but she doesn't continue. "Susannah, if you won't even tell me why Lizzie's doing all these awful things to me or why you guys are hiding the fact that you're hanging out with me, how am I ever supposed to change my mind about trusting you?" This comes out more forcefully than I intend. But really, I feel like I'm being attacked from all sides here. And if Lizzie has some master plan, I wanna know what it is.

She nods. "You're right. We shouldn't hide it. That's wrong."

We stand in awkward silence for a few seconds, but she doesn't explain further. "Okay, then I guess we can just go to the hanging location tonight and then go our separate ways." Saying this out loud hurts. I didn't realize how much I was hoping things might be different.

She grips her thin fingers together. "My little sister has cancer, Samantha. She was in and out of hospitals a lot last year. For a while we thought she was getting better. Just recently, though, they found more malignant cells. Now you understand why I'm so worried about this pattern of deaths. We both have so much to lose."

The weight of her words takes me by surprise. "I'm so sorry." That's why Jaxon approached her about my dad. He thought she would be sympathetic.

"I don't expect you to trust me right away, especially with

everything that's happened. Just, please, think about it. We can't go our separate ways, because then . . ."

She doesn't need to finish for me to understand the fear at the end of that sentence. I know it all too well. "Okay. I'll think about it."

She nods. "I'll let you get ready. I can show myself out." She walks out my bedroom door, and part of me wants to tell her that everything's going to be okay. But the truth is that I have no idea if it is.

Instinctively, I let my gaze fall on the pictures of my dad, resting on my trunk. "I'm gonna figure this out, Dad. I'm doing everything I can. I'm falling down seven times, and standing up eight." Which means I now need to go to this party so that I can figure out what those blurred faces were all about. Even if all I want to do is camp out in the hospital.

I check my cell. It's 8:39. I swing open my armoire and examine the mess inside. On top of the pile is a neatly folded black lace dress. *What's this doing here?* I carefully pull it out, and it swishes to the floor. It's the prettiest thing I've ever seen.

"Elijah?" No response. "Thank you. Thank you so much." I wait, but there's no answer.

I pull off my ripped jeans and shirt. Did he do this because he wants to make sure I go to the hanging location with the girls? Or was he just being nice?

I examine myself in my vanity mirror and feel self-conscious. I slip on a pair of lace-up boots and shove my wallet into one of them. Somehow that detail makes me feel more like myself.

"That's a beautiful dress. I don't remember it," says Vivian from my doorway.

I turn around, but don't answer.

"Looks like an antique," she continues.

"Maybe." I pull out my jacket and put it on my bed, avoiding eye contact.

"You can't wear a leather jacket with that dress. Especially a fake leather jacket. It won't look right."

I want to yell at her to get out of my room, but I'm afraid she won't let me go out if I do.

"Sam, take my black cape. It'll match perfectly. Consider it a peace offering."

That's the closest Vivian ever gets to an apology. "Can we go see my dad tomorrow?"

She sighs. "Don't you think I want to see him, too? I was just worried about you last night. We can definitely visit him tomorrow."

Some of the tension leaves my chest. "Okay," I say. "Let's see that cape."

She smiles, and clicks toward her room at the opposite end of the house. I follow as she talks about clothing eras and how the cape's from such and such a time period. She goes straight into her bedroom and then to her closet.

I have no idea what she means by all of it. I'm just relieved that I'll see my dad. I punctuate her fashion talk with a "Great" occasionally. On her dresser, I spot the corner of a medical bill. Note to self: come back when she's not home.

"Here," she says, and hands me a heavy silk cape. It's actually quite beautiful.

She always dressed me up as a kid, like I was her personal doll. Funny thing is, I used to like it. The attention made me feel special.

Vivian sat down on my bed and placed a shiny black box in front of me.

"What is it?" I asked, sitting up against my pillows.

"The only way to find out is to open it."

Vivian used the same tone of voice with me as she did with adults. She never treated me any differently because of my age. I liked her for that.

I lifted the lid and pulled aside the tissue paper. Inside was a cream dress with intricate beading patterns. "Whoa. It looks like yours."

"It's exactly like mine. I had it made. You know why?"

I could not believe that I was holding a replica of my very favorite thing in Vivian's wardrobe. And that was saying a lot, considering the size of her closet. "For my fifth-grade graduation?"

She nodded. "A twenties-style dress will match your short hair perfectly. And when everyone is admiring your bold fashion choices, you can give those girls who chopped your hair off the finger."

I laughed.

I put on the cape and she inspects me. "Hmmm," she says to herself, and digs through a jewelry box. She slips a silver necklace over my head. It has a pendant made of silver loops entwined to form a knot. "Much better."

She straightens the cape on my shoulders, and I suddenly feel the heavy awfulness of the fights we've been having lately. Maybe I've made the wrong decision, keeping what's happening in Salem from her. If Elijah was right, and my dad is in serious danger, doesn't she deserve to know? At least some piece of it?

"V, do you remember when you had that twenties dress made for me?"

She smiles. She always likes it when I call her V. I haven't done it in months. "Back when you had the brains to follow my fashion sense."

I laugh. "Yeah. I was really scared to go to my graduation that year and face everyone. That dress made it a lot better."

"It didn't hurt that one of those punks fell on her way up to the stage, either."

I grin. "Nope. That didn't hurt one bit. Anyway, thanks for all this."

She tilts her head slightly. "You're welcome."

The tension in the air is thinner, at least for the moment. I can't help but think how nice it is. "I was just thinking that maybe we could spend a little time together, like we used to. I know I've been weird lately . . . and difficult. I've just been overwhelmed."

The grandfather clock chimes downstairs. It's 9:00. Jaxon will be here any minute.

Vivian's expression softens. "You want to talk about it?"

"Yeah, I think maybe I do. I have to leave in a minute, but could we talk tomorrow?"

"Dinner. I'll make it a good one, after we visit your father."

"Deal," I say. If we were the hugging types, we probably would right now. Instead, I smile and she nods and I walk quickly down the hallway toward my room.

I examine myself in my vanity mirror. I'm too dressed up to be a witch. Green face paint would help. Wait, I'll make a wart. At least that gives me something witchy. I draw a dot in the middle of my cheek with my eyeliner. *Better.*

"Sam, Jaxon's here!" Vivian yells.

I turn my light off and head into the hall. I stop at the top of the stairs and look down at Jaxon. He smiles. I take the steps cautiously, to not step on my dress. Reaching the bottom, I turn to face him.

"What?" I say after a few seconds of silence.

"You're beautiful."

My cheeks get hot. "Thanks."

"I like the whole Marilyn Monroe mole thing."

"What? No, it's a wart," I say. Jaxon laughs.

We cross the foyer and Jaxon holds the door open for me. He wears a black vest with gold buttons, black pants, and a floor-length black coat. "I have to say, I'm impressed."

"That I opened the door for you? Or that I was right about looking good as a warlock?" Jaxon walks toward his drive-way and offers me his hand. I take it.

I shake my head. "With your costume, stupid."

He opens the passenger door of a pickup truck and helps me in. "There are a lotta costume parties here. I'd start preparing, if I were you." He walks around the truck.

"I'm sure I won't have to worry about it. I highly doubt I'm at the top of everyone's invite list. You got your mom to lend you her truck?"

"It's actually mine." He starts his engine and backs out of the driveway.

Come to think of it, I did wonder why Mrs. Meriwether had two trucks in her driveway. "Why don't you ever drive to school, then?"

He grins. "Because I was doing donuts late at night with my friends and she caught me. I only convinced Mom to let me drive because you're wearing heels."

"What made you think I was gonna wear heels?"

"Just a good guess."

"Well, I'm not."

"Whoops." His grin widens.

"You're the worst," I say, smiling.

"You mean I'm the awesomest, because now you don't have to walk in a dress."

" 'Awesomest' isn't a word."

"It is now." He reaches into the glove compartment and

pulls out a small box. "Oh, and my mom sent this for you." He places it on my lap.

It's a tiny pink pastry box from her bakery, tied up with black and gold ribbons. I pull at the bows and open the small lid. Inside is a bunch of black and purple violets sparkling with sugar.

"It's a corsage," he explains as we pass a large house with white columns wrapped in white lights. Each window has a candle in it. Must be Alice's. Jaxon parks his truck in the first available spot on the crowded street.

"No one's ever given me a corsage before," I say in a quieter voice than normal, lifting the delicate flower arrangement out of the box.

He turns toward me and takes it from my hands. "She says it's edible. So when the party's over, you can eat it." He carefully pins it to my dress. "I told her this wasn't prom, but you know my mom. There's no telling her no."

I smile at him. "It's beautiful." Maybe this party won't be so bad after all.

"Let me get your door," he offers.

But before he makes it to my side of the truck, I open it myself. I step tentatively onto the uneven sidewalk so that I don't catch my dress on anything.

Jaxon laughs. "Sam, you're the most stubborn girl I've ever met."

"And just think, this is me in a good mood."

He puts his hands on either side of my waist and pulls me close to him. His woodsy smell encompasses me. "Good thing I find stubbornness hot." His face is inches away from mine.

I lean forward, and the edge of my boot slides into one of the sidewalk cracks. I take a step to keep from falling. "Do you also like girls who can trip standing still?" I ask. *That's the closest he's come to kissing me since the woods, and I trip?*

He laughs and grabs my hand. We walk up the lawn to the front door.

"Welcome to the Parker residence," says a butler at the entrance. "May I take your coats?" I give him my cape.

My stomach drops when I realize this party's like Vivian's dinners on steroids. It's a high school party. Why's it so fancy? Everyone stares at us in an obvious way. "Let's get something to drink."

"Sure," Jaxon says.

"Hey!" calls a familiar voice as we make our way toward a beautifully arranged table covered with autumn treats. It's Dillon. And he's standing with the pretty girl from our history class who always flirts with Jaxon.

"Hey," Jaxon says. He nods at Dillon and gives the girl a hug. She wears a lace-up corset and a skintight short black skirt. I don't get the as-close-to-naked-as-possible costume thing. Dillon, on the other hand, threw on every black item of clothing he owns with no real thought. If he wasn't clean-shaven, with coiffed hair, he'd look homeless.

"You know Dillon, and this is Niki." Jaxon gestures to them. "This is Sam."

"Nice to meet you," I say to Niki, but she keeps her attention on Jaxon. *Well, this is gonna be fun.* I glance at the costumed people. The whispers and stares are blatant.

Dillon hands us hot apple cider from the table and pulls out a flask. He dumps a shot in each of our cups, and tucks it back into his many layers. "We have a real Mather at a party full of witches. I'll drink to that!" He lifts his cup.

He's dopey, but I kinda like him. I take a sip of my cider, and it's delicious.

"You'll drink to anything," Jaxon says.

Niki looks at me for the first time. "You have something on your face."

It takes me a second to figure out what she means. "It's a wart."

"Oh." She sounds skeptical.

I scan the crowd but don't see the Descendants. Strangely, I notice I'm also looking for Elijah.

"That's what I like to see," Dillon comments as I take a big sip of my drink, and I realize I've just about finished it. "We'll do shots later, Sam."

I'm already starting to feel a little light-headed.

"Or maybe we won't," Jaxon says. "I'm gonna show Sam around. I'll find you guys in a bit."

"Okay, man," Dillon says.

Niki says nothing, but her disappointment is clear.

"Samantha!" Dillon yells as we walk away. "He likes you!"

My cheeks flush. I'm sure Niki wants to kill me.

"Shut up, dude!" Jaxon yells over his shoulder.

"Don't break his heart!" Dillon yells, but we're already making our way through the crowd.

Jaxon grins. "Don't listen to that clown. He's obviously drunk."

"So you talk about me to your friends?"

"Maaaybe I said something about liking you." Jaxon blushes, and we step into a formal sitting room decorated with a copious amount of black candles.

"It's hard to believe anyone likes you," Lizzie says from the chaise longue, and I stop short. "Get out."

Please don't let this happen right now. I can't leave until I come up with a plan with the girls.

"Shut up, Lizzie. It's not your house," Jaxon says.

Lizzie gets up. Her skintight dress brushes the floor. It has a lace collar that stands high in the air behind her head and makes her more terrifying. "It's my party, Jaxon. Why don't you just step aside and let me deal with her. Unless you want me to start on your crazy mother."

Mrs. Meriwether? That's so mean. For the first time since I've met him, Jaxon gets really mad. If she were a dude, I'm pretty sure he would punch her.

Before Jaxon has time to respond, John interrupts. "What the hell?" He holds out his arms for Lizzie to see. A severe rash of red ovals covers his hands.

We all stare. "It looks like bite marks," he says, his voice unsure. A girl screams and we turn. She has the same rash on her face. Dread drops an anchor in the pit of my stomach.

Lizzie points at me. "Did you do this? No one's forgotten about that pastry stunt you pulled." Her voice is loud enough that all the people within twenty feet of us start whispering.

I glance at Jaxon, mortified. But he's looking at his own hands, which also have red marks on them. Oh no.

Lizzie chews on the side of her mouth. I try to focus on a possible out, but can't. I wish I didn't drink that alcohol. I take a step backward. Lizzie grins, and she mutters something under her breath.

Susannah, who I didn't know was in the room with us, interjects, "Lizzie, don't."

Is she standing up for me?

"Walk away, Susannah. *I'm* going to deal with this problem because you clearly can't."

Susannah grabs Lizzie's arm. "No, Lizzie. I want her here."

All the amusement on Lizzie's face drains away. Only anger remains. "You disrespectful little shit. You have no loyalty!"

I don't know what Lizzie planned to do, but I'm pretty

sure Susannah just saved me from it. "Susannah, you don't have to do this," I say, feeling bad that Lizzie's anger is now focused on her.

Lizzie glares at me and throws her drink at my face. I try to step to the side, but I'm not fast enough and the cider splashes on my hair and cheek. I look at Jaxon. He's scanning the hysterical crowd, not paying attention to the Descendants. His rash is worse and the house is in chaos. Everyone's screaming.

Lizzie walks toward Susannah, who steadily backs away. Lizzie raises her hand, and Susannah's eyes widen. Glasses crash against the floor and people run.

"Sam, let's get out of here," Jaxon says.

"I can't leave Susannah like that." But really, I can't leave. I have to go to the hanging location.

"She'll work it out on her own."

I look at poor Susannah, who's now backed against a wall by Lizzie. Alice pushes past a group of screaming people to get to her. I break away from Jaxon and move toward the girls. Jaxon grabs my arm.

"Stop—I have to tell them something," I say.

"No, you have to get out of here right now."

Alice pushes Lizzie away from Susannah. "Alice!" I yell, but she can't hear me.

"Sam, people think it's you," Jaxon says.

I pause, realizing I'm the only one without bite marks. And Jaxon's right; my name is being flung around. "I just have to say one thing." I try to push past some hysterical girls.

"Leave, Samantha," Elijah says, appearing by my side. "It is not safe."

Alice and Lizzie are yelling at each other. Jaxon pulls on my arm.

"I will follow the Descendants," Elijah says.

More people push in around me. The wedge between me and the Descendants widens.

"You did this!" a girl I've never seen before yells. She lunges at my face with her marked hands. She misses but manages to rip off my corsage. I don't resist anymore. I run.

Tables are knocked over, and the floor is strewn with broken glass. Jaxon and I move quickly through a formal dining room, into the kitchen, and out a door.

He sidesteps a crying girl on the ground.

"Jaxon, it's on your neck," I say as we loop around the house to the front yard. I hold my dress in my hand so I don't trip. "The rash."

"There she is!" yells a guy from my homeroom, and he points at me.

A group turns toward me. Jaxon and I sprint to the truck. My breathing's heavy. Someone shouts my name as we get in. Jaxon turns his key in the ignition, and the yelling guy pounds on my window with the side of his fist. I smack the lock button, and Jaxon's truck screeches away from the curb.

"What was that?" I ask, not sure how to process the wild scene.

"I've never seen anything like it in my life."

I look at the bite marks on his neck as he drives. "Does it hurt? The rash?"

"No, not really. Just looks gross."

"Jaxon, come on. People were screaming and throwing themselves on the ground. There is no way it doesn't hurt."

"Yeah, I guess it stings a little."

"Or a lot."

"I don't know how you avoided it."

"I swear I didn't do that," I say, touching my dress where the corsage used to be.

"That's so weird, 'cause I totally thought you bit everyone at the party."

I smile despite all the stress. Still, I'm not sure it wasn't my fault. What if it's part of the curse? We sit in silence for a few blocks.

Jaxon pulls into his driveway and parks. We both jump out fast, like we can somehow get away from the experience we just had.

He flips his hands over, and the red marks look a little less angry. "It's so weird that you didn't get this. I mean, I'm glad you didn't."

"I told you people around me get hurt." I can't erase this guilty feeling I have.

"Just don't start telling me to stay away from you again."

I can't stay here, though. I have to go change, and wait to hear what Elijah says about the Descendants. There's still a chance we can go to the woods. "I gotta go."

"Sam—"

"It's not about that. I just gotta go."

Seconds pass. "Fine." He turns around and walks toward his house.

My heart tightens. I want to say thanks. I can only imagine what they might have done to me if he hadn't pushed to leave when he did. But instead, I watch him walk away.

I turn toward my house, and Vivian is standing in the doorway. "Where's my cape?"

I pull the necklace off and hand it to her. "I left it." I walk toward the stairs.

"Real nice attitude, Sam."

CHAPTER TWENTY-NINE

Puritan Rebel

I run my hands through my wet hair to make sure all the cider's out. I lock my bedroom door and pull out my phone. Nothing. There's no way that rash was coincidental. Either someone set me up or I caused it in some weird way.

Elijah appears in front of me.

"Good. You're here." I grab my boots. "Let me get a jacket and we can go."

"You are not going into the woods tonight, Samantha. At least not with the Descendants."

"But we have to! We don't know how much time we have left," I almost yell.

"The police are at Alice's house now, and a good number of parents. A lot of people are blaming you. They are already nervous about all the recent deaths in Salem, and this only makes them more anxious. They are not thinking clearly."

The hearse I saw with Jaxon, the purple roses by the lamp-post, the woman outside the funeral hall, and John's great-grandfather all flood my thoughts.

"It would not be wise to go back there. You will have to go tomorrow."

My voice wavers. "But my dad . . ."

"You have to calm yourself. You cannot solve this without a clear mind."

I take a deep breath and try to stop myself from crying.

Elijah takes my hands. "I will help you, Samantha. In whatever way I can."

His gray eyes are kind. I take my hands back and wrap my arms around him. I bury my face in his chest. For a moment he's still. Then slowly he returns my hug. He smells subtly of burning logs in a fireplace.

"Will you stay for a little while?"

"If you like."

"Will you tell me about Abigail?" I want to talk about something other than my fear.

"Yes," he says into my wet hair, his cheek resting on my head. "What would you like to hear?"

I'd really like to know what happened to her, but I know better than to ask. "Who painted the portrait of her downstairs?"

"I did."

I pull away to look at his face and I realize he has a tiny freckle on his bottom lip. "You're a painter?"

His eyes smile. "There were no Puritan painters. Idle action was discouraged in all forms."

"Then how?"

He releases his arms from my body. "It started as drawings for Abigail when she was little. But after our parents died, she did not speak for a long time. I was looking for ways to make her happy."

I sit down on my bed and scooch up to the pillows. "But that painting is beautiful. No one does that on their first try."

He appears embarrassed. "Lots of time in the evenings. Not much to do then. I practiced. No sports or dancing or music. People believed they led to laziness and to sin. Poor Abigail. She loved to make up songs but could only do it at home."

I motion for him to sit next to me, and after a moment of hesitation, he does. "I've seen drawings of that time, and everyone wore bonnets and ugly black dresses. Where did she get the blue silk gown in the painting?"

"A merchant by the harbor made frequent trips to Europe. Same way I got my paints and canvases and the extra candles by which to paint."

"So you were a Puritan rebel?"

"Earning that title took minimal effort. Laughing too loudly would probably suffice."

I smile at him. "Did anyone ever find out what you were doing?"

"One person, yes."

"Who?"

"My fiancée."

My eyes widen. "You were engaged?"

He looks away for a moment and the happiness in his expression disappears.

"What?" I ask gently, hoping he'll let me in a little.

"I told you my sister was in love with William. She was happy, Samantha. I have never seen anyone so happy. I also told you that William's family wanted him to marry the governor's daughter. They were stupid, snobbish people. William assured Abigail, however, that she had nothing to worry about."

Reliving this memory makes his eyes heavy and his voice strained.

"This was concurrent with the time when people became hysterical about witchcraft. As you know, it escalated and they arrested many townspeople. By July, Salem was dangerous and untrusting. People looked suspiciously at their neighbors and closest friends. I was most fearful for Abigail's safety, so I arranged passage for us on a ship to Europe. But she refused to leave William."

My stomach tightens. "Please tell me they didn't accuse her."

"There were rumors about Abigail over the next couple of months, about her singing to the devil. William came to me, nervous about the gossip. I begged him to elope with her and get her out before any official accusations were made. But his mother had fallen ill, and he did not want to leave his family. As time went on, the rumors got worse. Officials showed up at our door and questioned her."

"You must have panicked."

"I was sick with it. But my sweet sister was calm. She was confident that good would prevail. Then, somehow word of their relationship got out and William stopped talking to her. He denied all of it."

"He abandoned her?" My voice rises.

"I went to talk some sense into him. He said the stress was bad for his mother, and he could not tie his family to an orphan suspected of witchcraft. That he had to protect his good name. I wanted to kill him. But I knew that if I took action it would be worse for Abigail. It was all too much for her, first the town turning against her, and then William. She would not talk or eat. She just lay in her room, drawing black-eyed Susans. Doctors came, but they had no solutions. So I sat by her bed, watching her day after day.

"Then the officials came back." He pauses. "They would

have arrested her, Samantha. They had every plan to, but I dissuaded them on account of her being so ill. I told them that if they took her and she died from their lack of care, they would be sure to rot in hell. For everyone knew my sister would not hurt a soul. I never told her that."

The extraordinary weight he had carried. "Did William at least check up on her?"

"No." For a second his fist clenches. "She did not give up hope, though, not until we got the news. He was engaged."

"To the governor's daughter?"

"Yes. When my sister heard, she let out a single scream. Two weeks later she died of a broken heart."

"I would've killed him," I say.

"At first I was angry. But more than retribution, I wanted answers. It did not take me long to track the rumors back to my fiancée. The worst betrayal of my life. I had told her things that led to my own sister's death. I confronted her. She admitted it. Said she was jealous of my relationship with Abigail, and she did not mean for everything to escalate. After that, I was furious with everyone. Most of all with myself."

My heart hurts for him. I'm not sure if I could stand something like that. "How did you ever get through it?"

His eyes look haunted. "I hanged myself from the balcony of the general store in town in the middle of the night. The townspeople found my body with a note that read 'It is the greatest evil of all, to separate people who love each other. I blame all of you.'"

I cover my mouth with my hand. "I never heard that story."

"That is because no one wanted to remember it."

No wonder he's heartbroken and furious. I would be, too. "What can I do?"

"You can save your father. I failed to protect Abigail, and I have never forgiven myself."

I wish I could make his sadness disappear. It seems so unfair that he had to go through all of that. I gently slip my fingers into his. He looks from my hand to my face. "Samantha." We lock eyes. For a second, his expression softens, and I want to pull him close. But he lets go of my hand and walks to the window.

The hold he had on my body dissipates, and I examine my hands. Why am I feeling this strong connection? And why am I embarrassed? "Why did you bring me that dress tonight?"

"I could see you were badly in need of assistance."

"You were watching me?"

He doesn't respond. He just stares out the window.

"Thank you. That was one of the nicest things anyone has ever done for me."

He almost smiles. "Yes. It looked well on you."

My body warms with the compliment. My phone buzzes. It's a text from Jaxon. "Rash is better. Sleep tight and don't let the zombies bite." Elijah disappears.

CHAPTER THIRTY

I Can See You

Twigs snap under my feet as I run through the dark trees. There's a man standing in a patch of light just ahead. A branch scrapes my cheek. I grab my face but don't stop. I need to get to him. He's young-ish, maybe late twenties, and he wears antiquated clothes. His hands fold behind his back the same way Elijah's do.

He looks up when I enter the clearing and I follow his gaze. A crow sits on a large branch. And below it hangs a noose. I try to scream, but the sound is muffled.

I sit straight up as the rest of the scream leaves my mouth. My phone says it's 7:27 a.m. I slip out of my bed, trying to shake the anxiety of my dream as I head into the hall.

It's Wednesday, and there's no school. I walk straight to Vivian's room, hoping she's awake and we can go to Boston. Her door is cracked open, and I push it. Her bed is made and I don't hear her in the bathroom. I eye the medical bill on her dresser. Just a quick look.

Carefully, I lift the papers on top of it. It reads *Explanation of Benefits—This is not a bill.* I guess it's a summary of Dad's insurance coverage? There are columns of numbers. The amount-billed column is high—many thousands of dollars high. I scan the deductible and copayment columns. They're all zeros. I turn to the next page, same thing.

I scan ahead to the bottom of the last page, where the totals are. It reads *Patient responsibility (amount you paid or owe to provider): $0.* I look at the date. It was sent less than two weeks ago. My heart stutters as I arrange the papers in their original positions.

What does this mean, exactly? Does this mean she lied this whole time about my dad's medical bills being high? The thought terrifies me. Not because she lied, but because of the scale of the lie.

I make my way to the stairs and grip the banister. Unless I'm completely missing something, there was no reason to sell the New York apartment. Why do it? Money. But my dad makes a really good living. Vivian wants more money? That's the only answer. So, what, is she waiting for my dad to die to get a huge inheritance? I feel ill. How could she do this?

"You look like you saw a ghost," says Vivian from the bottom of the stairs.

I'm afraid to look at her. I don't know what I'll say. I can't believe I almost opened up to her last night. "I had a nightmare."

"Well, I just got off the phone with the hospital, and the doctor scheduled tests for your father throughout the afternoon. I think we should shoot for visiting this weekend."

Now I look at her. I want to tell her she has no right to even talk about my dad.

She frowns. "I know you're disappointed, but don't be mad at *me* about it. I didn't schedule those tests."

I walk past her on the stairs and don't say a word. I just

head straight to the kitchen. Normally, I would scream. But I can't. What if she really is waiting for my dad to die, to get his money? And then I yell at her and push her to do something crazy? She's controlling his medical treatment. I need to think about this. I can't let her know that I found that statement.

I mix my coffee, barely looking at it. I need to solve this curse. That's my only avenue to helping Dad, my best chance at his waking up. It's a long shot, but I have to believe in something.

"Is all well?" Elijah asks in his proper English-inspired accent.

"How does it work, being a spirit?" I ask, without answering his question. I sip my coffee.

"I am not sure what you are asking."

"You said you followed me a lot when I first got here. What did you mean?"

"If I know where you are, and I focus on you in that space, I can see you. It is like having a window into your world, much like your television. If you know what channel to go to and what time to tune in, you can see your show."

Well, that explains how he knew I was in danger at the party. "And if you don't know where I am?"

"Then I must search for you. It can take quite a while."

"And what about physical things? If you carry my coffee cup, for instance, would other people be able to see it?"

"That is more complex. Small things I can make disappear from view. Large things I cannot. It is akin to physical strength. Some things I am strong enough to lift, while others I cannot move. And blinking, the act of appearing and disappearing . . . blinking physical items from one space to another is even more difficult. It takes a lot of practice and concentration."

"What about me? What if you lift me up?"

He looks amused. "You would appear to float. I do not have any ability to make the living disappear, only inanimate objects."

"I don't think I understand these rules."

"You will."

"Could you do me a favor?" I ask.

"I was wondering how long it would take for you to say that sentence. I have already retrieved the cape."

"Oh! Thanks." I'm embarrassed by how easy I am to read. "Actually, could you check on my dad? Vivian said they're running tests on him today. I'm just not sure I believe her. And I had my heart set on visiting him."

"Yes, they are running tests today."

I slump down in a chair at the small breakfast table near the window. "How do you know? Did you focus on him or something?" If he knows where my dad is, does that mean he watched when I went to the hospital?

"No. I checked on him earlier."

He checks on my dad? "How was he?"

"The hospital is taking good care of him."

I relax a little. I desperately want to see him, but I'm glad he's okay. And the thought of going to the hospital with Vivian is awful. I couldn't stand watching her pretend she cares.

If I can't go to the hospital . . . "We need to find out more about the curse and whatever that chaos was last night."

"Figuring out last night may take a while. Everyone is still recovering."

"Did all of the Descendants get the rash?"

"Yes, Susannah worst of all."

"So I really was the only one who didn't get it?"

"I am afraid so."

I was hanging on to the hope that maybe I wasn't. I sigh.

"I spent my night going through more of your grandmother's research. I have not finished, however."

"I'll help you." I get up and head for the kitchen door. I'm grateful he doesn't sleep and can work on this stuff at night. I already feel the intense pressure that I'm not figuring this out fast enough and that at any moment my world could fall apart.

He doesn't blink out, or whatever he calls it, this time. Instead, he walks by my side through the house and toward the library.

"Why am I the only one who sees you? Is it because you choose not to let other people know you're around?" I keep my voice hushed. I like that idea.

He closes the library door behind us. "I have nothing to do with your seeing me."

So much for that theory. "Then, why do I?"

"That is not something I know."

I pull the hook in the fireplace and we step into the narrow hallway. "But you're dead."

"I am aware."

"Shouldn't you know these things?"

He almost laughs. "I know little more than when I was living. I just move around faster."

The idea that death brings clarity is blown. "Have you met other people who could see you?"

"Yes, a few. They are rare."

As I reach the top of the stairs, I notice Elijah has rearranged the piles of books into organized stacks. The dust's gone. Spirits clean?

I'm not sure I wanna ask this next question, but my curiosity is running the show. "If I see you, then do I see other spirits?"

"Yes."

Visiting graveyards just shot to the top of my never-again list. Was I walking around all this time seeing spirits and thinking they were living people? "So what's in these piles of books?" Let's just think about something more cheery, like curses, for instance.

"Most of this is research on the Trials and the Mathers. I left Salem before the Trials concluded; I needed to educate myself."

"Why did you leave Salem?"

"No one kills themselves because they are happy where they are."

Well, that makes perfect sense. I can only imagine his surprise when he died and found himself back in Salem for some indefinite period of time. I'd leave, too. And now he's back here researching the Trials. I guess you can't avoid your life, even in death.

CHAPTER THIRTY-ONE

Love and Arrows

I turn to the last page of my grandmother's research note-book. "Nothing new in this one, either," I say to Elijah, who has a stack of diaries in front of him from historical collections and people's attics.

"Research is not instantaneous and must be built piece by piece. Quick does not mean good. That perspective will impair your perception. You will miss something."

Easier said than done when my dad's life is at risk. "What about Mrs. Meriwether? She knew my grandmother really well. Better than anyone. Maybe there's something that my grandmother didn't write down? Something that Mrs. Meriwether knows?"

"Possibly. However, speaking with her will only yield results if you are direct."

"Were you listening when I went to her house the other day?"

He looks disapproving. *Great.* That means he heard me

with Jaxon. How embarrassing. I'm already awkward enough without some attractive dead dude overhearing everything I say. I may never toot again.

I flip through a journal I've already read to see if there's something I missed. "Do you think my grandmother's drawings could be of any significance? They're in the margins, and she doesn't say anything specific about them."

"Perhaps. Let me see."

I hand the notebook to Elijah.

He studies it, and his brow furrows. "Are there more?"

"Yes, but they're all similar versions of a woman with long wavy hair seen from behind."

He turns the pages of the notebook. "None that show a face?"

"No, why?"

"You should ask Mrs. Meriwether."

"Is there something strange about it?"

"It is better to ask too many questions than not enough."

I agree, but I think he might be omitting some detail. "Okay. I'm gonna go over there."

He nods, and continues reading. I pull my hair up into a ponytail as I make my way through the passage. When I enter the library, the light outside is already dimming. I need to find the Descendants once the sun goes down.

"Well, there you are. Where've you been all day?" Vivian asks as I walk to the side door.

"Here."

"I looked for you earlier and couldn't find you."

I did hear her calling, but had no desire to answer. "Must've been on a walk."

She looks unsure. "Must have."

"I'm going next door."

"Okay." She checks her gold watch. "Just be back by seven for dinner. I've ordered a ridiculous amount of French food."

"Oh." The word catches in my throat. An image of a younger Vivian snapping that picture at the Parisian café flashes through my mind. Since my dad and I met her, French cuisine has been a bonding food for the three of us, something that is just ours. We always have it on special nights, like when my dad comes home from a long trip, or for the first snowfall in winter.

"I know you were sad about not seeing your dad today. I thought this might cheer you up. And we can have our chat. You might faint when you see how many desserts I got."

It's painful to watch her be nice after seeing that bill this morning. "Gotta go," I say, swallowing my sadness.

I walk out the door and make my way to Mrs. Meriwether's porch, struggling to push Vivian out of my mind. I raise my hand to knock, but Jaxon steps out of the door.

"Hey. I didn't think you were home. I came over earlier, but no one answered."

"Really? I guess I didn't hear the door. Is your mom here?"

"And here I got excited you were looking for me."

I smile. "I wanted to ask her about some of my grandmother's things I found."

"I'm going to see her. She's at the Remembrance Day Fair down at Salem Common. Her bakery has a booth. Come with me."

"I don't know." I look at the barely visible sun. I need to find the Descendants.

"Sam, it's your first fall in Salem. The fair won't come around again for another year."

"Uh . . . I was supposed to maybe do something with Susannah."

"She's down there. She showed up right before I ran home

to grab twine for my mom's pastry boxes. Come on. The whole town is there. It's fun."

I relax slightly. This saves me from going to the Descendants' houses. Who knows what their parents think of me after last night. "Let's do it."

Jaxon and I head down the sidewalk. "If you're nice to me, I might even give you one of my mom's famous funnel cakes."

"And if you're nice to me, I'll refrain from giving you that zombie rash again."

We share an amused look. "Glad you got your sense of humor back instead of all that doom and gloom."

I still think that doom and gloom stuff. It's just not fair to unload it on Jaxon.

"You're pretty cute for a witch."

He's joking, but it hits too close to the weird stuff I've been doing recently. "Do you think there's any way that rash could be witchcraft?"

Jaxon laughs. "Definitely. Strong theory. Right up there with fairies and ghosts."

Worst answer ever. "I hope you don't mind my asking, but why would Lizzie say your mom was crazy?"

Jaxon's jaw tenses. "My mom had a rough patch after my father died. She got really depressed, and for a while she'd still talk to him. She didn't care who overheard. There were other things, too. But the gist of it is that people in town thought she'd lost it. They even stopped going to her bakery for a bit. It took a couple of years to get everything back in order. We almost lost the house. And Lizzie sort of instigated those rumors. She wasn't a fan of your grandmother, either."

I'm getting the sense not many people were. "Wow, Jaxon. I don't know what to say." No wonder Jaxon's so nice even though the school hates me. He knows what it feels like to have awful rumors spread about his family. "I could kill Lizzie for saying that to you."

His grin returns. "Don't let me stand in your way."

We approach the edge of Salem Common, a large park in the center of town packed with people and lights. Music plays, and the air is thick with the aroma of carnival food. There's the distinct roar of excited conversation.

Jaxon leads me through the crowd to his mother's booth. "Hey, Mom. Look who I found on our porch. She was coming to talk to you."

"Oh, Samantha! What a wonderful surprise. Have a funnel cake."

I don't resist as she hands me a plate of delicious fried dough covered with powdered sugar.

"Mom, you just killed my whole strategy."

She looks from one of us to the other. "Samantha's no fool. You'll have to do better than bargaining my funnel cakes, Jaxon." I laugh. She knows him so well. "Now, my darling girl, what did you want to see me about?"

She reads the hesitation on my face. "Jaxon, make yourself useful and help out in the booth while Samantha and I have a word."

Jaxon walks toward the booth, and I wipe the powdered sugar from my shirt before I begin. "I know this is a weird question. But I was going through my grandmother's things and I noticed that she had drawings in her notebooks of a woman with dark wavy hair. Does that mean anything to you?"

Mrs. Meriwether's cheer fades. "Charlotte had a lot of nightmares, poor thing. Especially near the end. This woman was in most of them. She never saw her face, but she used to call her 'the crow woman' because there were always crows with her."

I stop mid-bite. There was a crow in my dream this morning.

"She thought the woman was somehow connected to the Mather curse. Which I suspect you know all about, since you are reading Charlotte's journals." She raises her eyebrows.

She just saved me from my next awkward question. "Do you believe there is a curse?"

Mrs. Meriwether purses her lips. "I don't know. But Charlotte did. She never figured out what it all meant, though. And Charlotte was very special to me, as I've said before. Sometimes you do things because you believe in a person, and not because you believe in everything they do."

I guess the whole idea of a curse is a bit out there. I'm just glad my grandmother had Mrs. Meriwether. "That makes sense. Thanks."

"Anytime. Now I imagine you'll want to enjoy this lovely fair. Jaxon!"

Jaxon doesn't need to be called twice. He hurries back. "Find out what you needed to know?"

I nod. Jaxon pulls me into the crowd. Could there be a connection between my dream and the crow woman? I want to ask Elijah. I scan the crowd for the Descendants, but no luck. I get a few nasty looks, though.

"Basketball?" Jaxon asks as we approach one of those carnival games where you need to make a basket in a hoop that is one inch wider than the ball itself.

An older woman is walking next to us, holding her husband's arm. "I just have a bad feeling about it. There have been too many accidents and deaths recently. It's not natural," she says. They continue walking and are drowned out by carnival noise.

"Can we find Susannah first?" I ask, feeling even more urgency than I did before.

"Sam, unless there's some pressing issue, I'm going to insist that you have some fun."

I need an angle fast if I'm not going to explain myself.

"Archery?" I ask as we approach targets lined up against hay bales.

"Abso-friggin-lutely."

We stop at one of the stations and wait for the guy with the bows. "There's one condition," I say, hoping I don't regret this. "If I win, you help me find Susannah. If I lose, you choose the next game."

"Deal." His grin widens. When it doesn't disappear after a second, I get uncomfortable.

"What?"

"You have powdered sugar on your face."

"What! Why didn't you tell me?"

He grabs my hand before I can wipe it off. "Leave it."

"Are you nuts? I'm not leaving powdered sugar on my face."

"I think it's cute."

"Well, it's not." I'm trying to sound annoyed, but fail.

He leans in and kisses the sugar off of me. My skin turns warm where his lips were.

"Are you trying to distract me so I don't beat you at archery?" I ask.

He lands a kiss on my lips, and all the sensors in my body go off at once.

"Nothing like young love and arrows," says the robust man with a full beard holding out our two bows.

We back away from each other, and I'm positive I'm beet red.

He chuckles. "How many arrows would ya like?"

"Three each," I say.

I pull out my wallet and give him the money. Jaxon opens his mouth to protest as we grab our bows. "My challenge, my treat."

"Have ya shot a bow before?" the man asks.

"Nope," says Jaxon, and I shake my head. *Good.* At least my chances of winning are fair. There was no way I was going to beat him at that basketball game.

"Ya grip the bow here. Straight arm, solid hold. Put yer arrow in at the notch. Then ya pull back the string all the way to yer chin. Don't pinch the arrow, 'cause it won't go nowhere ya want it to. Got that?" We nod. He looses one arrow, and it hits a small *x* on the wall behind the target.

"Thanks," Jaxon says, and the man steps back.

"You go first," I say.

Jaxon approaches the short hay barricade and stands in the position the bearded man demonstrated. He lets one arrow go, and it hits the bottom ring of the target. His second hits the same area but slightly to the left. The third lands securely in the small ring around the bull's-eye. *Crapola.*

"Looks like I'll be choosing the next game," Jaxon says. "I'm thinkin' pie-eating contest."

"Shut it." I step up to the barricade. My first try, I pinch the arrow. And to my intense disappointment, it wobbles to the ground two feet in front of the target. Jaxon chuckles. Thankfully, my second one lands nicely in the middle ring.

"Nervous?" I ask.

"Not even a little."

I take aim, and my arm shakes. As I release my last arrow, Elijah appears, and it goes right through his body. I scream and stumble backward into Jaxon. He wraps his arms around me, and the instructor takes my bow.

Jaxon squeezes me. "I have to admit that was one of the

more dramatic approaches I've seen, but considering you just made a bull's-eye, I can't say much. In fact, I think I got conned."

My heart rate slows as I realize that I won and everything is alright. What was that, a joke? Elijah looks too pleased for it to be accidental. *Dark friggin' humor.* He's dead, but *come on.* I suddenly become very conscious that Jaxon's arm is around me, and I break contact. I shouldn't care if Elijah sees that. The thought tugs at me uncomfortably.

Before I can gloat about my win, Susannah, Mary, and Alice walk up.

"Let's go," says Alice. I couldn't be happier to see her.

Jaxon's smile disappears. "Nice attitude."

"I don't have time for small talk."

I hate to agree, but Alice is right, even though her attitude sucks. I turn toward Jaxon. He's about to respond, but I put my hand on his chest. "It's okay. I'll give you a call later."

"I don't get you, Sam. Why are you jumping to Alice's commands?"

"Because she's less of an idiot than most people," Alice says.

"Believe it or not," I say to Jaxon, "I think that was a compliment."

Jaxon shakes his head. "What could be so important?"

"I just gotta go." I walk toward the Descendants.

He looks disappointed. "You say that a lot."

Before I can tell him I'm sorry, Mary grabs my arm and pulls me into the crowd. "We gotta move. My parents only agreed to let me out for a few hours."

"And we lost a damn half hour going to your house looking for you. No one figured you'd come out into public," Alice continues as we approach the edge of the Common.

"Is everyone really blaming me for that rash?"

Susannah nods. "I told the police it wasn't your fault, but there are a lot of rumors." I hope Lizzie didn't come down on her too hard last night.

Alice pulls out Mary's keys and unlocks the Jeep. "And the irony of this situation is that people are calling *you* a witch. I bet Cotton's rolling in his grave."

I would laugh, but the whole thing sucks. "Did you guys find anything that might explain what happened?"

"Alice's house was a wreck. But nothing out of the ordinary. If you ask me, it was a spell," says Mary. "The way it came and went so fast was eerie."

"Bull. Who do you know who could make a spell that strong?" Alice demands.

"Well, Lizzie—"

"No." Alice swerves around a car and my stomach drops.

I don't like the idea that someone could wave a wand and everyone gets a rash. Feels too unpredictable. Speaking of which, where's Elijah? "Wait, so Lizzie can or can't do magic?"

"Well," Susannah says, "it's not that she can't. We're all a little inclined. But I, personally, think it was the curse that caused it."

It's not comforting to know there's someone out to get you who has an *inclination* toward magic. "If it was the curse, then why didn't I get the rash?"

"That's the part we can't figure out," says Mary.

Susannah pinches her bottom lip between her fingers. "We will, though."

I know I'm lucky they're talking to me at all, but something about this Lizzie thing gnaws at me. "Why aren't Lizzie and John with you guys?"

"Because Lizzie—" Mary starts.

"Hates you," Alice cuts her off.

Susannah turns toward me in the backseat. "Lizzie thinks you're responsible for certain things that have been going wrong in Salem. She links them to your arrival."

"And she's dating John, so there's that," Mary chimes in.

Well, Lizzie's not wrong, exactly. And I'm not surprised they're dating. I could have figured that out myself if I wasn't so preoccupied with the curse and my dad. "That's why she's been following me?"

"Enough," Alice says, and Susannah breaks eye contact.

"Did something happen I don't know about?"

Alice jerks us to a halt in the Walgreens parking lot. "That rash wasn't enough for you?"

Seeing the dark trees, and remembering that dream I had, makes me sick. "You know what I meant," I say.

Mary hands me a hooded cape and I put it on.

CHAPTER THIRTY-TWO

The Markings of Witchcraft

Alice takes the first step onto the slope and we follow. The silence between us is thick with secrets. I try to forget my surroundings, but as we lose the light of the parking lot to the overgrown forest, my anxiety tries to crush me.

My cape catches on a branch and I jolt to a stop. The other girls keep moving. I yank at the cape, but it's stuck. Everything looks the same in the dark—faint, crooked shadows, black on black.

"Wait!" I yell to the girls, and my voice cracks.

The wind howls in the trees, and it sounds eerily similar to the woman's wail I heard in that awful house. I pull at the branch my cape is attached to with force, and the rough bark scratches my palm.

"I am here, Samantha," says Elijah.

I suck in air and put my hand on my forehead to steady myself. My shaky legs become steadier as Elijah untangles my cape from the branch. I grab his hand tightly, probably too tightly. He doesn't say anything, but curls his cold fingers around my own. When we catch up with the girls, they start walking again.

We come to the little clearing, and Mary pulls out the blanket. I'm impressed that Alice found this place a second time. I'm not sure I could do the same. The girls unpack the herbs.

"This bears all the markings of witchcraft," Elijah says, releasing my hand. I almost respond before I catch myself.

Susannah lights the candles, and I scan the trees for a noose. I wish I could delete that dream from my memory. In the candlelight, Mary looks as nervous as I feel, Susannah seems only slightly on edge, and Alice doesn't seem bothered at all. I don't get that girl.

Susannah starts the words of the . . . chant? Expectation hangs heavily like a cloud before a downpour.

"I call upon the power of fire," I say clearly when it's my turn. Elijah raises an eyebrow.

"That it may light my way and impassion my spirit. Only through purification may I see clearly," they all continue.

We light the bundles of herbs and drop them into the wooden bowl.

"I mean what I say, and I say what I intend. Know my desire and give me clarity," they say slowly, so that I can follow along. The strong scent of the burning herbs fills the air between us.

We join hands, and my muscles tense. For a moment, there's nothing. Then, as before, their faces flicker—slowly and faintly at first, then building to a rapid blur. There's a strange, ethereal layer to each of the girls, as though other people share the same physical space with them. The flickering faces are the same older women as before, and there's something desperately sad about them.

The older woman now occupying Mary's face looks around her and settles her gaze on me. She says, "These trees were locust once. This growth is new."

"The water used to come right up to this hill," says the old woman sharing Susannah's body, also turning toward me. "It was called Bickford's Pond. It is how Benjamin Nurse came to retrieve his dead mother."

"From the crevasse where they *threw* our bodies," says the older Alice with a toughness that reminds me of her young counterpart. My eyes follow her pointing finger to barely visible rocks that steeply drop off.

My skin goes cold, and sweat forms on my palms. *What is this?*

"July nineteenth, sixteen ninety-two. I was in the first group to hang," continues the old Susannah.

I'm not seeing this. Am I? *These women . . . I don't know how to process this.* My heart punches me inwardly. I try to stand, to end the vision or whatever it is, but my body won't move. I can't even lift a finger.

"The first time I walked into that court"—the old Susannah says "court" with severe distaste—"the young girls started having fits. One even threw her glove at me."

Are the Descendants using a spell on me?

The old Susannah's wrinkled face frowns. "I laughed at them. I knew immediately by the astonishment of the magistrate that I had deeply misjudged the situation. 'Do you laugh at this?' he asked. 'Well I may at such folly' is what I told him. But the magistrate was serious. 'Is this folly? The hurt of persons?' he asked. I declared that 'I never hurt man, woman, or child.' I even recited passages from the Bible to prove my faith. But they only claimed that the Devil's servants could imitate the innocent." She sighs.

"The worst part was that jail," says the old Mary, shivering at the memory.

"No," says the old Alice. "The worst was that we were denied counsel and sentenced to death because children said they had visions of us hurting them. When that girl had a fit in the courtroom and accused me of being the cause of it, I told her plainly—"

The older women's faces flicker. Mary gasps and wheezes, breaking the circle. The hold on my body shatters like ice hitting concrete and my hands fly to my chest, pulling at my clothes to get more air.

"It felt like the life was being sucked out of me," Mary says between pants.

"We were getting somewhere," says Susannah, leaning forward with both hands on the ground in front of her.

"We should try to continue," says Alice.

Mary shakes her head. "No way. That was terrifying! And for what? For stories we already know?"

They know these stories?

"We didn't know about the trees or the water," Susannah says between staggered breaths.

Elijah kneels beside me. "You appeared as Cotton Mather."

My head snaps up. "Cotton!"

Alice doesn't miss a beat. "How'd you know your face looked male?"

"I didn't. It was a guess."

"Bull. You were the only one who didn't speak."

Mary, gaining control over her breathing, pulls her knees into her chest. "Let's discuss this in the car."

"I'm not leaving until Sam tells us the truth."

It suddenly occurs to me that they must have known last

time that my face blurred with Cotton's. And they said nothing. What game are these girls playing? "You know what? I'm done answering your questions. You *knew* I looked like Cotton last time we were here."

Alice regains control of her breathing. "Well, now you know, too."

The confirmation that they hid it from me really bothers me. I look at Susannah. "And you wanted me to trust you?"

Alice looks at Susannah, too. "You talked to her without us?" Alice asks. "So Lizzie was right. You were disloyal."

Okay, now I'm lost.

Susannah folds her small hands in her lap. "I told you I think it's a bad idea not to tell Samantha everything we know. You think we're being careful, but what we're doing is shutting out the one person who could help us."

"Or hurt us," says Alice.

"I'm sure we can solve this in the Jeep," Mary says.

Alice and Susannah turn to her. "No!" they say in unison.

I can't help but feel bad for Mary. Elijah's being here is the only reason I'm not running out of these woods. And even with him here, I catch myself peering into the blackness suspiciously.

"I think you're making a mistake about Samantha, and people could die because of it. My sister could die because of it," Susannah says.

Alice takes a breath. "And what if you're wrong?"

"Then I'll take responsibility for that."

"Lizzie won't forgive you," Alice says.

Susannah nods. "I know."

Elijah paces next to me.

"Fine," Alice says, and gestures toward Susannah.

"Alice reads bones the same way some people read tarot

cards," Susannah says, as though that is even a quasi-normal thing. "And about four months ago, she got a reading that something really bad was about to happen."

"My dad went into a coma four months ago," I say before I have a chance to think about it.

Alice and Susannah exchange a look. "The readings Alice did after that showed sadness and loss and the same warning that something bad was coming."

Mary hugs her knees a little tighter. "Alice's readings are always right."

Alice nods. "Then you showed up. And every reading since then has just been you."

"Wait, what do you mean, just been me?" My practical self is struggling with this. Bones and spells and ghosts. I want my simple reality back.

"Just your name," Alice says. "Over and over."

Their strong reactions to me the first day of school don't seem so weird anymore.

"Lizzie and I think it means *you* are the bad thing that was coming, but Susannah isn't convinced."

"Is that why Lizzie's been stalking me?"

"Lizzie's been affected strongly by this awful chain of events," Susannah says. "And she blames you. If she knew we were talking to you openly, she might do something."

I would ask how Lizzie was affected, but I know Alice would shut the conversation down. "Do what?"

"A spell," Mary says.

Elijah stiffens beside me.

"You have to understand that strange things have been happening all over town," Susannah says before Mary can continue. "It's not just the descendant deaths. Alice's uncle owns a coffee shop. And when he opened up yesterday, each table had a noose on it. There were no signs of a break-in, just nooses."

"Was it The Brew?" I ask.

"You shouldn't know about this," Alice says. "Only a few people were told."

They all stare at me, even Elijah. "I went there the other day and my latte had a coffee stain on it that looked exactly like a noose. I thought maybe the girl that worked there was messing with me." I'm starting to regret my little outburst.

"See, even when we have information, you have it right after us. The blurred faces, Cotton, the pattern of deaths," Susannah says.

They all wait.

I look at Elijah. "Just leave my personal details out of it," he says. He doesn't seem bothered, just resolute.

"I . . . I see spirits. Well, one, at least." No one reacts, and I wonder if they heard me.

"I knew it," Susannah says.

"You're a witch," says Mary.

"I'm not a witch."

"And this ghost is here now?" Alice seems skeptical.

"Yes."

"Prove it."

"No." I don't have to look at Elijah to know he's not going to perform some trick.

Alice raises an eyebrow.

Mary scans the trees nervously for Elijah. "Can we please go? I need to get home."

Alice stands in answer and Mary shoots up like she can't get out fast enough. There are still so many questions I need to ask them. And some part of me worries that I *am* the cause of these awful things. Maybe the curse is part of me?

We blow out the candles and pack everything into Mary's and Susannah's bags. The woods become even darker.

Alice turns to me. "If you're lying to us about that ghost and I find out you were somehow involved in these deaths, you won't like the consequences."

"I have just as much to lose as you do if we don't figure this out." I can tell she accepts this, because she turns around and walks into the trees without another word.

"Alice," I say, and she stops, her blond head the most visible thing in the blackness. "The vision we just had. What did Alice Parker say when that girl accused her of witchcraft?" Mary said they knew these stories, but I don't. And whether they're messing with me or not, those women were trying to tell us something.

Alice turns. "In response to the accusations, she said, 'I wish God would open the earth and swallow me up presently, if one word of this is true.'"

CHAPTER THIRTY-THREE

Angry, Not Sad

"Get in here." Vivian's words are barbed.

I read the grandfather clock in the foyer before I enter the living room. It's 9:27. I know I missed her dinner, but I can barely look at her right now without wanting to cry and scream all at once.

"Apologize and I'll consider not grounding you."

I should just do it and walk away. "No." *You apologize. You don't care about my father . . . about our family.*

She puts her glass of wine down and stands. "You're not sorry at all, are you?"

"Samantha, leave her," Elijah says, standing next to a cluster of empty wine bottles.

"Maybe you should be worrying about visiting my dad instead of running around town shopping all the time and getting drunk."

Her eyes harden. I know that look. We've hit the point of no return. "You seem awfully social yourself for someone who says she only wants to be by her father's side."

"You have no idea what I've been doing."

"Did I upset you, *mon chou*?" Vivian taunts, using the pet name my dad called me when I was a little girl. It means "my little cream puff."

My fingers curl into my palms. "Screw you."

Vivian's hand whips across my cheek so hard and so fast that everything goes black for a second. I raise my chin and stare at her. I don't massage my face, even though it hurts like hell. I want to tell her I found the insurance summary and call her every name I can think of, but before I can open my mouth her wineglass shatters on the floor.

Vivian jolts. "You're grounded." She shifts her attention to the broken glass.

Elijah, who I'm pretty sure was the cause of it, gently touches my arm. "Do not give her the satisfaction of seeing you upset."

I nod and run to my room with Elijah by my side. My whole body trembles. I slam my door and slide the lock into place. I stand there fuming. Elijah lifts my chin. He brushes a tear away with his cold thumb.

"I'm angry, not sad," I say with a voice that's sad and not angry.

"I need no explanation."

I'm grateful for that. I don't want to talk about how I feel. What I want is my dad back.

"I will bring you ice." He blinks out of the room.

"Don't cry," I say to myself, and dab my eyes with the sleeves of my black hoodie. I take a few deep breaths, and Elijah blinks in with a small ice pack. I take it from him. "Thanks."

He nods. "May I bring you some tea?"

The formality of his question catches me by surprise.

"Actually, yeah. I'd really like some tea. Will you have some with me?"

"Certainly."

He blinks out, and I take my boots off. I pace with my ice pack, trying to clear Vivian from my thoughts and decide what to do next. *What does it mean that Cotton's face blurred with mine?* I don't like the idea that I'm connected to him. And if I am, does it mean he's trapped here like Elijah . . . or worse, he's trapped inside of me?

Elijah blinks in with a large silver tray full of tea. A wicker basket hangs from his arm, and a fluffy rug is over his shoulder. For the first time ever, he looks uncertain. "Will you hold this tray a moment, Samantha?" I swear he'd be blushing if he had blood.

I pull the ice pack off my cheek and take the tray. "What is all this?"

He unfolds the fluffy rug and spreads it out on my floor. "A room picnic."

I almost fumble the tray. *Why is he doing this?* He takes it and places it in the middle of the rug. He offers his hand, and when our fingers touch I light up. My body temperature steadily rises and I break eye contact. We sit. He opens the basket and pulls out delicious-looking foods.

"Where'd you get all this?" I ask, still flustered.

"The tea and scones are from London. The finger sandwiches and pastries are from Paris. And the Devonshire cream is from Devonshire."

He went all over Europe picking out food for me? How's this happening right now? "This is the best cheering-up present I've ever gotten."

He smiles, and all his uncertainty drains away. It's a real smile. The first one I've ever seen on him. *He has dimples!*

Everything in me wants to touch them. I need to change the subject before I embarrass myself. "Do you think Cotton's trapped inside me?"

He offers me a finger sandwich. "The thought did occur to me."

I crinkle my face. "That makes me want to vom."

"Please refrain from murdering the English language while we eat."

I laugh. His humor always comes as a surprise. I wonder what he was like before Abigail died. "After tonight, I feel like I don't know nearly enough about Cotton."

"Well, I know he was born in 1663 into a prominent family of ministers and followed that path himself. He was prolific and wrote nearly four hundred books and pamphlets."

I glance at the stack of books I brought down from my grandmother's secret study. One of them was written by Cotton. I'll read that one first. "My grandmother's notebooks said he had a difficult relationship with his father. And that his need to impress him may have driven some of the things he did?"

"Increase Mather was an influential figure in the Puritan community. Cotton was determined to match his success. But Increase did not agree with the Trials using spectral evidence—the testimonies where people claimed the specter or spirit of the witch was trying to harm them."

I watch his lips as he speaks. *Are they cold like his hands?* "In history class we learned they would strip people naked and search them for witches' teats. Gross word, by the way. Something that a 'demon familiar,' I think my teacher called it, could suck from. And they poked the witches with pins, right? To see if they could feel them? I mean, that's some nutty stuff."

"Indeed. Often, they would show bite marks as proof. Or they would fall into fits in the presence of the witch."

The rash suddenly doesn't seem out of left field. "How did anyone believe these accusations?"

He looks thoughtful as he chews. "They were very convincing. My fiancée was one of the primary accusers."

"How'd you feel about that?"

"Initially, I imagined her claim to illness legitimate. I worried terribly for her. She would stiffen and stop speaking, or suddenly become frightened by a sight that was not there. I spent many a wakeful hour walking her floors determined to find a medical solution."

"And she was just jealous of your relationship with Abigail?" He must have felt so betrayed.

"Yes. That is where it started, certainly. Then it became about old insults and family grudges. She was consumed with the power of it. And her accusations took the lives of good people. By the time I left, she was a shadow of the girl I had loved. Dark and distorted."

It sounds like a scarier version of high school. "How could people push each other to death like that? It seems so cruel."

"She did it because she felt important. People got away with it because no one stood up for the accused. The first people accused of witchcraft in Salem were an invalid, a homeless woman, and a servant. Who would speak for them?"

Those poor people.

"It is not dissimilar to your own situation. Do you believe the Descendants could torment you without the consent of the other students and teachers?"

"It's not like they exactly agreed. They're just kinda silent about the whole thing," I say.

"Group silence can be a death sentence. It was in Salem," he says.

"Those accusations went to court, though."

Elijah nods. "Court was different then. The accused witches had no way to defend themselves."

That sounds awful. "So, once you went to trial, you were found guilty."

"You went in through the door and out hanging from the nearest tree," Elijah says.

"What role did Cotton play, exactly?"

"It's complex. He wrote a book about a witchcraft case in Boston. Reading material was scarce at the time, and Cotton's book read like a gossip magazine. As you might imagine, it was extremely popular. When the witchcraft scare broke out in Salem Village, the afflicted exhibited the exact symptoms as the people in his book. A copy of that book was present on their bookshelves."

"Oh man. So he unknowingly wrote a guidebook for accusing witches?" Maybe Lizzie's answer in class wasn't so far off.

"Also, understand that Puritan society was oppressively austere. Everyone worked and prayed and that was it."

I shake my head. "So when these accusations began, it was like crazy reality TV and everyone got consumed by them?"

"Completely consumed. It happened faster than one would imagine," he says, and pauses. "You never know in life when something unpredictable will happen." He looks away quickly and lifts the china pot. "How do you take your tea?"

"Cream and sugar, please." These words feel oddly proper. "Elijah, why did you come back to Salem?"

"I missed Abigail. I wanted to see something that reminded me of her."

"But you didn't leave again?"

"No."

"Why not?"

"Troublesome houseguests." He almost smiles.

"Do you still want me to leave?" I ask, terrified of his answer.

He thinks for a moment, and his boyish nervousness returns. "Samantha, you are the bravest person I have met in three hundred years."

My eyes well up. I carry so much weight every day, and no one cares. Having someone acknowledge it is almost overwhelming.

"I am honored to know you," he continues. "I only wish that Abigail could have had the same pleasure."

I wipe away a tear.

He smiles. "I must remember to compliment you more so that you get used to it."

He's right. No one ever compliments me except my dad. I stare at him, and the fluttering around my heart starts again. Why do I feel this way? And more important, why can't I breathe?

He slides his hand into mine and lifts it up. He gently kisses my fingers with almost warm lips. Goose bumps rise all over my body in the best way. My phone buzzes in my pocket. I jump, pulling my hand out of his grip. Unsure how to recover, I take my phone out. Jaxon's calling.

There's a muffled scream of frustration down the hall. "What was that?" I ask.

"Hard to say. Possibly, she discovered the wine on the back of her dress. I dare wonder how she will react when she gets to her new pair of shoes."

"Sam?" says a muffled voice, and we both look down at my phone. I bite my lip. I must have pressed Answer. Guilt ripples through my body—guilt that I interrupted our room picnic and guilt that I considered not taking Jaxon's call.

"Hey, Jaxon," I say into my phone, and stare at Elijah.

He nods knowingly and disappears.

CHAPTER THIRTY-FOUR

Now It's Too Late

My hands are folded in my lap. The sleeves of my black dress cover my wrists and make my arms itch. I hate wool.

"It should next be proved that witchcraft is!" booms a voice at the pulpit in the front of an old-fashioned church. It's the man from the woods. He looks too young to have that voice.

"The being of such a thing is denied by many. . . . Their chief argument is, that they never saw any witches, therefore there are none. Just as if you or I should say, we never met with any robbers on the road, therefore there never was any padding there."

I glance side to side, to see if anyone else thinks this sounds crazy. I discover the pew is full of people wearing essentially the same crap clothes I am, and bonnets, too.

"What the hell?" I say.

All eyes turn toward me.

"Do not call for things you do not desire," says the man, his eyes boring into mine.

He takes a few steps toward me. I push past the people in the pew and back down the aisle. A rope grazes my shoulder. I jerk away from it and look up. A noose hangs from the ceiling. When my gaze falls back on the man, he's only inches from my face.

My eyes fly open and I grip the sides of my desk.

"Nice of you to join us," says Mrs. Hoxley, her lips pushed together like a cranky fish's.

To my left, Susannah looks concerned. *School. Right, it's Thursday morning.* I rub my eyes.

"Sorry," I say, and look down at Cotton Mather's book on my desk. I don't remember taking it out of my bag. I'm really not getting enough sleep.

"As I was saying, those of you who are participating in the historical reenactment will report to the auditorium for first period. Mr. Wardwell and Ms. Edelson asked me to remind you. It will be the same every Thursday for the next two weeks."

This is so not good news. A breeze blows in through the cracked window, bringing with it crisp fall-scented air. The bell rings.

I rub my eyes again and put on my jacket. The Descendants are out of the room without a word. So much for civility.

I enter the hallway, walking at a slow pace toward the auditorium. As soon as people see me, they recoil, like they don't want to chance touching me. *Damn that rash.*

"Sam," says Mrs. Lippy, waving at me right outside the auditorium door. Her hair falls limply around her face and she has lipstick on her teeth.

Not this. "Is everything okay?"

"Peachy. But I will need you to come to my office after classes today."

"I thought our meeting wasn't until Monday." I don't really have time for this.

"Just the same. I've had a few calls. Not all of them

pleasant." She straightens her duck brooch. "Parents worry. As we all do. Some of us more than others."

Great. This is only going to make things worse. What happens next time Vivian is called to the principal's office? If Vivian was telling the truth, they could expel me. And with the way our relationship has been going lately, I wouldn't be surprised if she lets them.

The bell rings. "Okay, well, I gotta go to class."

I open the heavy door and walk the long center aisle to Mr. Wardwell.

"You're late," he says, and hands me what looks like a play.

Everyone is on stage already. And with Ms. Edelson's class, there are twice as many people to watch me stutter through my lines. My mouth goes dry.

I'm getting some pretty nasty looks. Except from Jaxon, of course. I walk up the stairs and stand near him on the stage. He smiles.

"The packets I gave you contain the entire performance with stage directions. I'd like us to read it all out loud. That way if there are any questions we can address them immediately," says Mr. Wardwell in an overly enthusiastic voice that suggests he's likely the playwright.

Ms. Edelson joins him. Not far from me and Jaxon, Alice, Mary, and Susannah stand with Lizzie and John. I didn't know they were in Ms. Edelson's class, but I'm willing to bet they knew I was in Wardwell's. Is that why they left homeroom without a word, because they didn't want to walk with me? I chew on my lip. Alice and Lizzie appear to be arguing about something, but their voices are too quiet for me to make out their words.

"Everyone not directly involved in a given scene will stand against the curtains and wait their turn," Ms. Edelson says in a voice that's gratingly high-pitched. "The restrooms are in the back. If anyone needs to use them, feel free, just don't hold up a scene you're in."

My hands shake as I flip through the first few pages, looking for Cotton's name. It's not there. "Who are you again?" I whisper to Jaxon.

"Reverend Parris. I'm up first," he says with fake enthusiasm.

I sympathize even though he's perfectly calm. We arrange ourselves against the curtain, with Jaxon and a few others center stage. There's ten feet between me and the next person. This is so unfair. They're treating me like I have leprosy, and I was the only one *without* the rash.

In my peripheral vision I see Lizzie staring at me. I can't help it; I look at her. She holds the little Mather doll against her side and is wrapping something that looks like hair around its neck. I can only assume it's *my* hair. The other girls don't seem to notice, or maybe they don't care. Maybe everything Susannah told me last night was to get information out of me. My stomach tenses, and I turn toward the restroom.

I slip through an opening in the curtain and into the backstage area. It's dimly lit and smells like an attic. There are pulleys that control the curtains and large metal shelves. I head for the hallway in the back right corner.

A warm hand slips over my mouth, jerking my head back against a male chest. I struggle, but the grip is too strong.

"It's easy to hurt you," John's voice says in my ear, my neck straining. "You should never have come to Salem, Mather. We know all about you. I owe you one for that rash. And for Lizzie's—"

I slam my elbow into his ribs. He grunts and loosens his hand on my mouth enough for me to bite down, hard. There's a moment before he reacts, and I worry he might not care. His arm tightens around my rib cage, making me gasp for breath. I keep my teeth clamped onto his hand.

All at once he releases me. I fling myself forward and away from him. In the dim lighting, I stumble into the pulleys. I get caught in the ropes and struggle to untangle my legs. I grab on to one to steady myself.

Just before I turn to face John, terrified he might be ready to pounce on me again, everything goes black. I look around frantically, but I can't see the room at all. All I can see is the rope in my hand—every detail of it and nothing else.

Panic creeps along my skin. At the top of the rope there's a girl's body hanging. She rotates slowly in my direction, but her hair covers her face.

After a few seconds of forever, I release my grip on the rope. The moment I let go, the blackness dissipates and the backstage area comes back into view.

What's in front of me is just as gruesome as the image of the girl hanging, though. One of the huge metal shelves is on the floor with its contents scattered around it. Under the shelf is John, facedown, blood oozing from his head.

I freeze. It's the vision I had in the woods with the Descendants.

Students rush back to where we are. Screams erupt. Mr. Wardwell pushes through the crowd. "Ms. Edelson, call nine-one-one!" he yells. Then, to a couple of the frightened students, "Help me pick up this shelf!"

It takes five of them to lift it. Jaxon's one of them. Meanwhile, the blood around John's head forms a pool. Lizzie screams, and rushes to him. Susannah, Mary, and Alice comfort her. I can't make out their words.

"Everyone, move!" yells Ms. Edelson. Some of the students back away, and the Descendants pull Lizzie from John.

"Sam. Samantha!" Jaxon walks up to me.

Ms. Edelson tries to remove the traumatized students from backstage. My vision blurs in and out. Time passes, but I couldn't say how much. Someone is sobbing. More teachers show up, and Brennan is with them.

Then come the EMTs. "No pulse," one says. Jaxon steps between me and John's body, breaking my view of the blood for the first time. I blink.

Jaxon grabs my hand and pulls me gently. My feet move. He asks me if I'm okay, but my mouth refuses to answer. I just keep thinking about my vision in the woods. I didn't even try to figure out who was in that vision. Now it's too late.

How many seconds did I miss while having that vision of the hanging girl? I didn't hear the shelf fall. I don't understand how a shelf falls by itself. The only things I'm sure of are that I have to figure out who was hanging and I need to tell the Descendants about what I saw.

I snap my head up and scan the room for them, seeing the chaos for the first time. I'm sitting in a chair in the front of the auditorium. When did I sit down?

"I think she's in shock," Jaxon explains to a policeman with a bushy gray mustache who takes the seat next to me.

"Can ya hear me, Sam?" says the policeman with a husky voice.

I meet his eyes. "Yes." Jaxon seems relieved.

"Do you feel up to answering a few questions about what happened back there?"

"I guess so," I respond.

"I'm Captain Bradbury. I'll go nice and slow. You let me know if you need a break," he says, and Jaxon sits down on the other side of me.

"Okay." The room's full of policemen, and other students are being questioned, too.

"As I understand it, you were the only person backstage with John when the shelf fell. You wanna tell me what you remember?" He licks his thumb and flips the page of his notepad.

"I went backstage to go to the bathroom." My voice shakes. "I felt a hand over my mouth and another one holding my stomach." Jaxon tenses. "He whispered in my ear, 'It's easy to hurt you.' I managed to get my elbow into his ribs and I bit his hand. He let go and I went flying forward into the ropes. I got tangled in them."

Bradbury furrows his brow. "You're saying this young man attacked you?"

"In a way."

"Have you had any altercations with him before?" Bradbury asks.

I hesitate. "Well, not exactly. He doesn't like me."

"Had he ever physically assaulted you before today?"

"No." I can't tell him about the locker or the rock because I can't prove those.

"And how did the shelf fall?" Bradbury asks.

"I'm not sure. I blacked out when I hit the ropes." *Hanging girl.* "And then he was just lying there."

"It's not likely you're strong enough to knock over one of them shelves. . . . It would take two of my bigger officers to push one of those over. I'd imagine something else musta happened. Did you hear anything or see anyone?"

He already checked out the shelves? I must've been sitting here for a while. "No. I blacked out."

"Shock, most likely. It's common." He really is trying to be nice. "If you remember anything more, even in a few days, I want you to give me a call." He hands me a business card. "We might have you down to the station to give a more formal statement."

"Okay," I say, examining the card with a witch logo on it and tucking it into my wallet.

Bradbury stands and pats me on the shoulder.

"Sam, he attacked you?" Jaxon seems conflicted.

"He's dead, isn't he?" I already know the answer, and the weight of it is more than I can bear.

Jaxon nods. "I'll call my mother to pick us up."

I scan the room again. "Where are the Descendants? I have to tell them something."

"They left. Lizzie was pretty hysterical."

I can't let this vision, or whatever it was, go. The last time I did that, someone died. Next it'll be a girl, possibly someone I know. I need to find Elijah. I stand, and Jaxon stands with me. My legs feel weak and my head spins. I reach out for Jaxon. I feel his hand on my arm before the room blurs.

CHAPTER THIRTY-FIVE

I Saw His Death

"There she is," says Mrs. Meriwether, placing a cool towel on my forehead.

I squint at her. Judging by the blue-and-white-striped couch and the ships on the walls, I realize I'm in her living room. Jaxon paces next to her.

"What happened?" I ask before the events of the afternoon come barreling back. I sit straight up, and the wet towel plops onto my lap. I remember coming over here after school, but I have no memory of falling asleep. How long have I been out? "I gotta go."

"Calm yourself." Mrs. Meriwether takes the towel. "Vivian knows you're here. You've been out for quite a while. You must be starving. I've got soup all ready for you."

I want to argue, but I feel dizzy. I haven't eaten anything all day.

Mrs. Meriwether heads to the kitchen, and Jaxon sits next to me. He touches my forehead. "How do you feel?"

"Okay, I think. Sorry I fainted. I feel stupid."

His eyes are gentle. "No way. It was like a movie. You fell into my arms, and I carried you to the nurse's office."

"Yeah, that's how all romantic movies end. The dude carries the girl to the school nurse."

He laughs, and Mrs. Meriwether comes in with a tray of delicious-smelling food. She places it on my lap. Corn chowder, warm corn bread with butter, freshly squeezed orange juice, and an éclair.

"Vivian won't be home for some time." I can tell by her delivery, she disapproves. "So please, stay as long as you like."

I smile as she leaves. "Any update on what happened today?" I ask between spoonfuls of chowder.

"Not really." He looks uncomfortable, and I can guess why.

"They're blaming me, aren't they?" He doesn't answer. "I feel sick over it. I feel like I should have prevented it."

He shakes his head. "There's no way you could've prevented that. He attacked you."

"You don't know the whole story."

The muscles around his eyes tense. "What do you mean?"

I pause, considering how I would even explain it. "You'll think I'm nuts."

"Sam, try and trust me. Even a little. I'm not the enemy." He's incredibly hard to resist when he's not being pompous.

I sigh. "Well . . ." *How do I start?* "I saw his death a few days ago. I just didn't see his face."

Jaxon looks confused. "What do you mean *saw*?"

I study my corn bread for answers. "Like in a vision."

"As in a dream?" He's skeptical.

I should never have opened my mouth. "A vision. Everything went black, and I saw a guy crushed under a piece of metal. Wait. What's the date?"

Jaxon thinks for a second. "September nineteenth."

I drop my spoon. "Today's the day Giles Corey was pressed to death." I read about it right after Jaxon took me to that jail. My thoughts move a mile a minute. I need to find Elijah.

"Sam, maybe you should lie back down."

I lift the tray off my lap. "I'm fine. I'm just trying to tell you that I saw John die in a vision. You can choose not to believe me. But I gotta go right now."

"You sound, well . . . really stressed. I think you might still be in shock." By "stressed," he means crazy.

I scoop up my bag and walk past him. He reaches out and grabs my arm. "Jaxon, I can't let someone else die." I'm angry at myself for letting my guard down. *He thinks I'm nuts.*

"You didn't let anyone die. It was an accident. You heard Bradbury. There's no way you could've knocked that shelf over."

"I don't mean like that. I can't explain it. You wouldn't believe me if I did." I remove Jaxon's hand from my arm, trying to escape his questioning eyes.

"Just 'cause I don't believe in visions doesn't mean I don't believe you. I'd be freaked out, too, if I saw someone get crushed in front of me." Jaxon follows me to the door.

The sun is almost down when I step outside. The word "crushed" grates on my nerves. Giles Corey and John were crushed. Who's next? "Tell your mom I say thanks."

Jaxon still follows me. "Can I help?"

I want help. But if he's uncomfortable with the idea of a vision, there is no way I could tell him the other stuff. There's a piece of me that hoped he'd believe me.

"Why don't you come back in and lie down and we can talk about all of this when you're fully rested."

"No," I snap. "I don't need to be patronized. People are *dying.*"

He looks hurt. "That's so not fair, Sam."

"Nothing's fair right now. Everything's a mess."

I walk to my house and close the door behind me. "Elijah!" I yell.

"Samantha," he says in a worried tone of voice in the foyer. I must look as frazzled as I feel.

"How's my dad?"

"Well."

I nod. "Did you see what happened? To John, I mean?"

"No, I was doing research. I heard some of the aftermath while you were resting."

I pace in the foyer. "*John* is the guy I saw in my vision. And when he got crushed in front of me today, I had another vision, or whatever. Am I going crazy?"

"You had a vision without performing a ritual?"

"Yeah, well . . ." I remember my dream. "I dozed off in homeroom and dreamed of a guy giving a sermon about witchcraft. He made some analogy, saying how people assume there are no witches because they've never seen one. And would you think there are no robbers just because nothing was ever stolen from you? Or something—"

Elijah cuts me off. "Where is your copy of Cotton Mather's *Memorable Providences Relating to Witchcrafts and Possessions?*"

"Here." I reach into my shoulder bag. "What is it?"

Elijah skims through the pages and points to a paragraph. I read the words and a chill runs through me. "These are the exact words from my dream. But I didn't read this far. I never saw this paragraph." It was a young Cotton in my dream. I just didn't recognize him. "That means it wasn't exactly a dream, was it?"

"I would guess not. Tell me what happened."

"We were in a church, sort of a plain room with wooden pews. I was scared and walking backward. A rope touched my shoulder. I looked up and saw a noose hanging above my head. Then I woke up." Knowing that it wasn't some fantasy my brain invented makes retelling it awful.

"And how did that relate to John's death?"

"John grabbed me and I fell into the ropes behind the stage." Elijah's face hardens. It's obvious he didn't know that part. "My vision went black and I couldn't see anything but the rope I grabbed on to. Then I saw a noose over my head, like I did in my dream, only now there was a girl hanging from it. I don't know who, because her hair was in her face."

"We need to find out." Elijah's tone confirms my fear.

"If we can prevent it, maybe that's a step in the direction of breaking the curse."

Elijah nods.

"Is Cotton trying to warn me or scare me?" The thought of sleeping is now perfectly horrifying. "If only I could talk to him like I do with you, without it being so awful."

"I am confident his spirit is not here the way mine is. There is no scenario where my face would blend with someone's the way his did with yours. He is part of you or bound to you."

I want to puke. "So what? Try to sleep and hope he . . . Shit, I have to call him, don't I." It's not a question. How have I come to a point in my life where I see things that aren't there while I'm awake and I see things that might be there while I'm asleep?

"I do not believe the Descendants will assist you this time.

−223−

The town is in an uproar over John's death. There have been too many fatal accidents since you arrived, and the townspeople are searching for an explanation. The word 'murder' is being used liberally, and the Descendants' families are suspicious of you. They are not letting their children out of sight."

The truth of that sinks in. I wouldn't let my kids out of my sight, either. I show up in a prominent and unexplainable way in relation to the rash and John's death and, now that I think about it, to the nooses in the coffee shop, too. "Okay. I guess I have to try without them. Do you think I can do it somewhere other than those woods?"

Elijah's thoughtful. "Is it fair to say that every time he appeared, you were afraid?"

I don't like where this is going. "Yeah."

"You were also in the woods where the witches hanged, a place that related to him personally," Elijah continues.

"So I have to go someplace scary that relates to him personally?"

"Sometimes extreme circumstances or emotions can break the barrier between the living and the dead." I immediately think of Jaxon's story about his mother talking to his dead father.

This makes sense. The majority of the time I've been in Salem, I was under duress of some kind. "His brother Nathanael has a gravestone in Old Burying Point." The moment the words leave my mouth I regret them.

"Interesting. Nathanael was his younger brother. And you know how important prestige was to Cotton. Nathanael bested Cotton in learning and attended Harvard at a younger age. I would venture a guess that Cotton had mixed emotions about that. The year after he died, Cotton wrote *Memorable Providences*."

"So, what, am I supposed to antagonize him to make him show up?" I like the idea less and less.

"It worked with me when you read Abigail's letters."

"Great. I'm going to get a flashlight." *No way I'm making that mistake again.*

CHAPTER THIRTY-SIX

Default to Sarcasm

"Do dead people usually hang out in graveyards?" I ask Elijah as I step through the iron gate into Old Burying Point.

"Are you asking me if spirits spend their free time roaming graveyards with the occasional hope of scaring someone?"

"Point taken." I shine my flashlight, trying not to walk into any headstones. "Where are you buried?"

He pauses a moment. "My body is gone."

My eyes widen. "What do you mean *gone*?"

"I should not have told you. It is nothing you need to concern yourself about. But I believe it was dug up." He sounds calmer than I am, and it's *his* body.

"Dug up! Who would do that?"

"Perhaps grave robbers."

I shudder. I picture it before I can stop myself. I shine my flashlight on Nathanael Mather's headstone in the corner of the graveyard under a big tree. I prefer the Cotton conversation to this one. "So this is Cotton's exceptional brother."

He nods. I pull out a small blanket from my bag and sit next to the headstone. My skin crawls. I light a candle, and the light flickers across Nathanael's headstone—which has a flying skull on it. If someone tapped my shoulder right now, I would launch in the air like a cartoon character.

"If you remember it, it might be worth trying the spell you used with the Descendants."

In some ways, I'm more scared that this'll work than that it won't. I close my eyes. "Cotton . . . I don't know if you can hear me. Or if you're bound to me. But I need to know a few things. Namely, who was hanging." I speak slowly, unsure what words to use. I peek at Elijah.

He nods.

I take a deep breath. *I can do this. I have to do this. People will continue dying. My dad could be one of those people.* "Cotton, I need you to show me the face of the girl who was hanging. Show me something I can stop. Something I can understand." I wait.

"Show me what you know about this curse. I mean what I say. I say what I intend. Know my desire and give me clarity." For a second, everything's still. The wind stops rustling through the leaves, and my body vibrates. Then, nothing.

Crap. "Listen, Minister. I know you were trying to get Daddy's approval. It must've pissed you off when your little brother turned out to be smarter than you. The year after he died you wrote your book. And then you sit back while people spin lies in Salem, just happy about your fame. Disgusting." My body vibrates again and the air whooshes out of my lungs.

The force throws me backward, and my eyes open. The graveyard is gone, and I'm in the woods. They're different from when I was there with the Descendants. The trees are bigger, wilder. There's a large crowd of people in a clearing. I run toward them, tripping over branches.

A male voice recites a prayer. Nearing the edge of the clearing, I can now see that the voice belongs to a man with a noose around his neck. Young Cotton is on horseback in front of the crowd. I push the people to get through, but they ignore me. Cotton yells to the spectators, "Even the most wicked of creatures can feign the semblance of good. Do not let this man's words deceive you. For it is his actions you must examine. I ask you. Is he guilty?"

The crowd roars in agreement, and the cart is rolled away. The man falls, struggling against the rope. I push the spectators harder. The moment I break through, the crowd disappears. There's no one left besides Cotton and the strangled man.

I can't pull my eyes from the rope. As I watch, the hanging man transforms into the girl I saw at school, her hair obscuring her face. She turns her strained eyes toward me, and her hair moves. It's Susannah. Cotton dismounts from his horse and lands in front of me. I try to get past him, but he blocks my path.

"Susannah!" I yell as she chokes.

Cotton grabs me by the neck, his strong hand making it impossible to speak.

"You are behind the horse. Focusing on the wrong things," he spits. The pressure on my neck increases.

I start to lose consciousness and can't hold on to the vision. I try to pry his hand away, but it's no use. My eyes shoot open, and Elijah's shaking me. "Breathe, Samantha!"

I gasp. "Susannah," I manage. "It was Susannah hanging." I stand, panting. "We have to go to her house. Do you know where it is?"

"Yes. What did you see, exactly?"

I want to get out of the graveyard. I gather my things and walk as quickly as my body allows. I explain the man's prayer and the crowd as Elijah and I make our way onto the street. I describe every detail and every word I can remember. He's particularly interested in the face of the man on the cart.

"George Burroughs," he concludes as we plod along. "He was the only minister convicted of witchcraft. He was accused of being the ringleader of all the witches in Salem. People said he recited a prayer before he hanged. Witches were thought unable to do such things."

I trip on the uneven sidewalk. "The crowd seemed affected. I mean, until Cotton convinced them he was guilty, anyway. So what I saw really happened during the Trials?"

"I do not know. I need to locate the story's origin."

"What do you think he meant by I'm focusing on the wrong things?" I ask.

"Probably just that. But it begs the question, what are the right things?" Elijah stops walking. "Susannah's house." He points up a small stone walkway to a forest green door.

I walk toward her stoop. Why was Cotton so angry? Was it what I said about him, or is he really mad that I'm missing something? I raise my hand to knock, but the door opens before my hand touches the wood. Susannah stands on the other side, looking worried.

"Sus—"

"Shhh. Keep your voice down," she warns. "It's not a good time, Samantha." Her eyes are puffy from tears.

"I know. I'm sorry. I wouldn't have come, but it's important. Remember when we were in the woods the first time?"

She nods and glances over her shoulder.

"That guy we saw crushed under the piece of metal must've been John."

"I didn't see anyone get crushed." Her frown deepens.

Wait, she didn't see that? We talked about it. Actually, no, Alice told everyone to shut up, and then we only discussed the blurred faces. I just assumed the other girls saw it, too. "Oh man. Well, I *did* see that. I didn't know what it meant, until after John died."

"Why didn't you say anything? We could have stopped it." Her voice is now full volume.

Susannah's mother comes to the door just as she finishes her sentence. "Susannah, no visitors." Apparently, she knows who I am.

"I didn't know this was gonna happen. I swear. I didn't know it would be John," I say before Susannah's mother pulls her away. "But I had another vision—"

At the mention of John's name, Susannah's mother turns angry. "Get off my property, or I will call the police!"

I have to tell her. "Please, Susannah, you've got to listen. I saw you hanging in my vision. I think you're next!" I yell. The door slams in my face.

That was *really* bad. "I'm an idiot."

Elijah follows me toward my house. "You told the truth. You would never have forgiven yourself if you did not warn her." He's trying to be nice, but we both know I screwed up.

"I highly doubt Susannah's mother will let her anywhere near me now."

"Well, that is fairly certain."

"I'll try to explain in school tomorrow." I sigh. "Do you think she believed me about the vision?"

"It is difficult to tell. I think it best you explain it when your emotions have calmed."

I agree. "Elijah, what am I missing? What's the thing I'm not looking at that Cotton was talking about? We need to find that story about George Burroughs and see if there's a clue in it."

"Yes."

"Susannah's ancestor recited prayers like Burroughs, didn't she? Also, you said Susannah got the rash the worst, right? And now I saw her hanging. They must be related."

Elijah pauses. "I will do some digging."

"Great." Now I need to make sense of that passage Cotton quoted in my dream. He said people don't believe in witches because they've never seen one. Could he mean me not really believing in all of these things I'm seeing?

We walk to my house, deep in thought. If that's what he's saying, then I need to stop being skeptical and embrace this weirdness. Resisting it has gotten me exactly nowhere. My dad always says that you don't get to choose what happens in the world, only how you react to it.

There isn't much time left. But if Cotton's bound to me, the answer is here. I should be able to figure out whatever he knows. I open the door to my house and lock it behind me.

"I *just* got off the phone with Susannah's mother," Vivian says, waving the phone in her hand. "She said you threatened her daughter. What were you thinking, Sam, after what happened today?"

I don't acknowledge her, and she doesn't try to stop me as I go upstairs. I shake Vivian's comment off and close the door to my bedroom. Things were never easy socially in NYC. There were times I begged my dad to let me change schools. But this is by far the worst situation I've ever been in.

I take off my jacket and slump down on my bed. "I'm scared, Elijah. I'm scared I won't figure this out in time. That I'm not strong enough. Tomorrow's Friday, four days from when we first saw the blurred faces, and I don't feel like I'm any closer to solving this curse."

"There is something I want to show you. It may help in that regard."

"What?"

"I was not certain until yesterday."

I sit up. "Certain of what?"

He walks to my armoire and pulls Abigail's letters down from the recess in the top. He removes one letter from the bundle and puts the rest back. I perk up.

"One of Abigail's letters?" *They were in my room the whole time.*

Elijah sits down on my bed. "This is not one of her letters from William. This one, she wrote to me. I found it the morning she passed away."

I take the envelope from him and touch it lightly with my fingertips. It's yellowed with age and has his name beautifully written in calligraphy on the front. It smells like old books, musty and comforting.

With great care, I pull out the heavy stationery. The crease in the middle suggests it has been folded and unfolded many times. There is a hand-drawn black-eyed Susan in the corner.

My dearest Elijah,

I know the great unhappiness you beare, and I am truely sorry. I do not mean for you to worry about me. Please understand that it is not William I grieve for these past days. He hath created a crack in my heart, but it is all those families upon which it broke. Those men and women ripped away from the ones they love and who love them in turn. It is the greatest evil of all, to separate people who love each other. I weep for all of us. Their barnish fear has kept them from compassion.

Most important, I do not want you thinking that you could have saved me, because you could not. It is my time. There is nothing you could have done to change this. Change the world, sweet brother. They need you, just as I have needed you all these years. It will be a long time before you understand this, but please let me go now with love.

When change cometh, she will bring peace at her back. She will not bend to your will; you must bend to hers. Help her.

With love and fare thee well,
Abigail

I read it slowly, working out the elaborate handwriting and the sentence structure as I go. "She was wonderful, wasn't she?"

"More than you know."

I stare at the letter, imagining how he felt reading this. My heart aches for him.

"I spent a great deal of time considering that last paragraph," he says. "She means you."

He's so intently focused on me that I almost forget how to speak. "What do you mean?"

"We were meant to meet. You are change, Samantha."

I'm not convinced, but I want to be. "She wrote this three hundred years ago."

"My sister was special like you are. She did not see spirits, but she had premonitions. Our parents forbade her to speak of it. But, I assure you, Samantha, she was always right."

Was I really meant to meet Elijah? "What makes you think

this is about me, though? I'm not change. I can't even change my own situation."

"You changed me."

"How could I possibly change you? You're so stubborn."

He smiles. "You are the first person I have wanted to talk to in three centuries."

I want that to be true.

"And I believe that you can break this curse, that you can change your fate and those of the Descendants. You are the true reason I came back to Salem. I was unconsciously seeking you."

I don't know if I'm what Abigail meant when she left this goodbye letter. I don't know how to be change or even how to have a civil conversation sometimes. But I want to break the curse more than I've ever wanted anything in my life.

Overwhelmed, I default to sarcasm. "Abigail was right about one thing, though. I'm definitely everyone's first pick at peace."

I steal a glance at my dad's picture. *I promise you, if there is a way to stop this, I will. I'll do whatever it takes, however nutty.*

"You have more power than you know, Samantha. You just have to be brave enough to realize it."

"Easy for you to say. All you have to do is bend to my will."

He smiles, and his dimples reappear. "Do not get ahead of yourself."

I smile now, too. "But that was my favorite part."

CHAPTER THIRTY-SEVEN

How to Hang a Witch

I step into the chilly morning air and close the door behind me, happy to avoid an awkward conversation with Vivian about her driving me to school. This isn't the longest we've gone without speaking, but it's the worst fight we've ever had. It's not even a fight; it's something more. It's like my world is collapsing. For as long as I can remember, my dad and Vivian were my only people.

I can barely keep my eyes open as I jiggle the key in the lock. I got three hours of sleep, and my drowsiness is giving me a sick feeling. I turn around and almost collide with a male chest. I scream and look up to see Jaxon's worried face.

After all the effort to get out quietly, I'm screaming, "Don't do that!" I speed-walk toward school.

"Sorry, didn't mean to scare you." Jaxon slips my bag off my shoulder, and I'm too tired to protest. "I thought I might walk with you."

He's walked me home, but never *to* school before. "You're checking up on me?"

"Maybe." He doesn't make eye contact. I've never seen Jaxon unsure of himself, and it doesn't feel natural.

He probably thinks I'm still a mess from yesterday. Which I am. But his treating me like I'm unstable only reminds me of how messed up things are and agitates me more. "I don't need you to."

Jaxon keeps up with my pace. He pushes his hair out of his face. "Sam, I wanted to talk—"

"Sick people need to be checked on. I'm not sick." Whatever he wants to talk about, I'm not sure I can handle it right now. I'm not in the best control of myself.

"You saw someone die in front of you. It's not like you're going to be normal, either." His tone is serious, and I tense.

My whole life, people have told me I'm not normal and need help, and Jaxon's joining them makes me feel like I'm drowning. "I don't want to talk right now, Jaxon."

"Why? Because I won't say that I believe you had a vision about John? Or that I think people are going to die?"

My cheeks redden, and I move faster. We're almost to school. "I don't want to defend myself to you. I already have to do that with everyone else." I take my bag back from him, and he catches the strap before I can put it on my shoulder.

He searches my face. "Since when do I make you defend yourself? All I want is for you to talk to me. I want—"

"Let go." I pull on my bag, and his lips tighten. He nods and releases his grip. I push through the door to the school, but he doesn't follow. The second I'm inside, I regret my words. I *do* want to talk to Jaxon. But how could I ever explain Elijah and the curse? He would never believe me.

In the hallway, the few early students greet me with ugly looks. Insults are spoken just loud enough for me to hear. I clench my jaw to keep from crying.

As I turn the corner, a nondescript door opens. I can just make out Elijah's angled face in the shadow. I head straight for it and slip inside. The door clicks shut. It's pitch black, and my shoe hits something hard. I grab on to Elijah. He flicks on the light switch.

It's a custodial closet with barely enough room for both of us. Our chests are only inches apart.

For a moment, we're both silent. Shadows fall on his cheekbones, and his lips part slightly. I have the sudden desire to be closer to them. I lean forward before I realize what I'm doing.

"How's my dad?" I ask, bringing my heels back down to the ground.

"Well cared for."

Good. "Did you find anything, or do you just like broom closets?"

A small smile forms on his lips. "I found the story of Cotton at George Burroughs's hanging. You see, Cotton wrote another book about witchcraft called *Wonders of the Invisible World* after the Trials."

I can barely understand *Memorable Providences*.

"After which, a man named Robert Calef wrote a book called *More Wonders of the Invisible World*. This contained the story of which you had the vision."

"Why was Calef's book title like Cotton's?" I ask, realizing I'm still holding on to Elijah's arm. I make no effort to let go. He feels so solid and alive.

"Robert Calef was making a commentary on the Witch Trials. He had a lot of unpleasant things to say about Cotton."

"Wait, so Calef was Cotton's enemy? And he boosted his own fame by destroying Cotton's reputation?" I hear people bustling in the hallway, but I don't care. "Then it's possible that story about Cotton and Burroughs isn't true? Why would Cotton show me a story some dude told to make him look bad?"

"It is hard to say. Cotton wrote in his journal that he did not believe Calef's book would ever make it to print. And if it did, that none would take the book seriously. Tell me again what Cotton said about Burroughs after he recited the prayer."

"Something about how wicked people can pretend to be good. So don't let them deceive you." I readjust my feet in the small space between the buckets, and my body brushes against Elijah's for a moment. He puts his hand on my waist to steady me, and my stomach drops like I came over a hill too quickly.

He lets go. "Potentially, it is a metaphor. He may be pointing someone out, someone who seems good and is not."

"Actually, if we take the whole Calef thing into consideration, it would be someone who spun a story about me *and* appears to be good but really sucks. Lizzie? I mean, she's been awful to me, but everyone else in school thinks she's awesome."

"Or one of the other Descendants," Elijah says.

The thought that Mary or Alice or Susannah could be my secret enemy makes my chest ache. *Not Susannah. Anyone but her.* "Did you get a chance to look for the cause of the rash?"

"No, but now is the perfect time—empty houses."

The first bell rings, and I grab on to his shirt. I don't want to go out there. I want to stay in this lemon-scented closet with Elijah. He knows all the weird things that are happening to me, and he doesn't think I'm crazy; he thinks I'm special. Heat spreads through my body like flame with dry wood.

He lifts his hands up and holds my face. His fingers are gentle, and he brushes my hair back. "I'm right here with you. And I will be for as long as you need me. You are not alone."

The comfort in his words wraps around me like a hug. He pulls my face toward him and kisses my forehead. Before I say a word, he blinks out. I'm left gripping the air where Elijah's shirt used to be and feeling the weight of his absence. I flick off the light and exit into the sea of people.

I rush to my homeroom, and when I open the door the hostility is palpable. The Descendants' seats are empty. I sit down in my usual place. Behind me, hushed voices discuss John's death. The bell rings.

Mrs. Hoxley doesn't need to quiet everyone. The room goes silent by itself. "There will be a special assembly this afternoon, an opportunity to discuss the tragedy that occurred yesterday. If anyone feels they need to discuss the event individually, please ask for a pass to the counselor's office."

I put my forehead in my hands. My tiredness and anxiety mix as my unbrushed hair falls around my face. I'm sure by now Alice and Mary know about my blunder at Susannah's house. I had no idea they didn't see the vision of John when I did. My telling it to them after what happened to John does look suspicious. Alice already suspects me as the cause of all this. If only I can explain. There's no guarantee how much time we have before Susannah . . . I can't even think about that. I won't let the same thing happen to her.

The bell rings. I open my eyes, and my head feels heavy. On my way out, a guy bumps into me. I stumble, but he doesn't turn around. *Great, a day of this type of thing.* I wouldn't be surprised if they lynch me in that assembly.

Wait, what if they do? My stomach rumbles with nerves and lack of food.

I make my way into history class and catch Jaxon watching me. I feel terrible, but I don't know what to say. Lizzie's not in her seat, either. Are all the Descendants together? Would Susannah have told Lizzie about my visit to her house? If so, this is all going to get a lot worse.

The bell rings.

"I'm not sure there's a good way to begin today," says Mr. Wardwell, and he proceeds with his lesson. I stare out the window, not listening.

What Elijah told me this morning about an enemy gnaws at me. It was definitely a warning. Cotton was furious when he said I was focusing on the wrong things.

Elijah blinks in, and I jump. Jaxon notices.

"I found something you will want to see," Elijah says.

I raise my hand, but Mr. Wardwell doesn't call on me. I can see the bathroom pass is already gone from his desk. He continues for a few more seconds while my hand is in the air.

"Yes, Sam." Mr. Wardwell sounds annoyed.

Am I imagining it, or is he being a real jerk? Does he think I had something to do with John's death, too? Maybe Jaxon was wrong; maybe Wardwell is a descendant. "May I have a pass for the counselor's office?" I really don't want to see Mrs. Lippy, but he can't say no.

"Just go." He waves his hand toward the door.

I grab my bag. As I pass one of the girls in the front row, she says, "Don't come back."

I rub my face as I enter the hallway. "What did you find?"

Elijah hands me a tiny piece of paper. I carefully unroll it. There are symbols written in black ink, smeared in places from some kind of liquid. "What is this?"

"That is parchment paper, and those symbols are a spell."

I open my mouth to argue the legitimacy of this and remember the promise I made to my dad last night that I wasn't gonna resist believing in this stuff. "Where was it?"

"Artfully concealed in a ruffle of the dress Susannah wore to the party."

"So this was most likely the cause of the rash since she got it the worst, right?" I always assumed the rash somehow manifested by itself, like a sign of the apocalypse or something. "This doesn't explain why I didn't get the rash when everyone else did, though."

"You see spirits, and have visions. You are many things, but typical is not one of them."

Maybe this is what Cotton meant by his warning. "If Lizzie was trying to set me up, my not getting the rash would be the perfect way to do that." *Or Alice.* Oh man, I so hope it's not her.

One of the classroom doors near me opens and we start walking toward Mrs. Lippy's office.

I should show this to the Descendants. Susannah would get that someone planted it and trace it back to Lizzie. Who else knows witchcraft besides these girls? "Oh no! Susannah came to my house before the party. That makes me a prime suspect."

"I considered that."

"Is there any way to prove who wrote this?"

"Not to my knowledge."

I stare at the little paper that possibly caused all this trouble. "Can I keep this?"

"Certainly," Elijah says as we arrive in front of the counselor's office.

My bad luck rears its head, and Mrs. Lippy steps out of

the door. "I thought I heard a voice in the hallway. You're in luck, Sam. I'm currently free."

I take one last look at Elijah before he blinks out, and step inside her office. I tuck the spell into my wallet and notice the business card Captain Bradbury gave me when he questioned me.

"I'm glad you came down here. It was the right choice."

I was hoping this place would be packed and I would spend the rest of the period in the waiting room. I sit down at her desk.

"I imagine you're here about the tragic event."

I nod. "I'm not sure what to think."

"Were you close to John?"

"He was in my class."

"How did you feel when you saw him? You found him, correct?" If she knows this, everyone in the school knows I was the only one with him when he died.

I sigh. "Honestly? Numb. I couldn't move."

"And when the numbness left?"

I pause. "Guilt."

She releases her breath as though she's relieved we're getting somewhere.

"I felt like I should have been able to stop it." I hated John, but I didn't want him to die.

"Hindsight is twenty-twenty, Sam. It might help if we talk about the events leading up to this incident. See if we can find the source of the problem." She pulls out a paper full of notes. "Have you been in any physical altercations recently?"

"As in physical fights? No."

"Have you touched anyone and then realized they were sick shortly after?"

So much for my moment of honesty. "No."

"Have you purposefully sabotaged anyone's grade during a quiz?"

"I'm not sure I understand." So this is the list of complaints Mrs. Lippy was trying to go over with me yesterday.

"Have you ever wished anyone ill will with your eyes?"

That has to be the most ridiculous thing I've ever heard. "So people are coming in here making these crazy complaints about me? Or, their parents are?" Elijah was right. The whole school wants to vilify me. They might not openly attack me, but the result is the same.

"It may be that some of these are more of a stretch than others," Mrs. Lippy concedes. "But this many people can't all be wrong. I believe if we break this pattern you seem to have with the other students, we'll get somewhere."

Break this pattern? But it's not my . . . Wait a second. Maybe I *can* break the pattern I have with them. Everything about this curse seems to be a pattern. If I can break one link in the chain, it might help. Elijah did compare my social situation here to the Witch Trials.

"Sam?"

"Sorry, Mrs. Lippy. I actually think you helped me figure something out."

Mrs. Lippy beams. "All part of my job."

I need some time to think this through. "Is there a place where I could sit quietly for a little while? An empty classroom or something?"

"It's not exactly school policy."

"You gave me a lot to think about. I'm afraid if I go back to class I'll lose all this progress we've made."

Mrs. Lippy wavers. "Are you sure we can't talk this out?"

"Believe me, I have to think about things privately first. Then I can share."

She nods and begins filling out a slip of paper. "This is for room one twenty-seven. It's usually empty at this time." She hands me the pass. "This will give you a half hour."

"Thank you so much!" I smile at her, and she looks pleased. I pick up my bag and bolt out of her office.

As soon as I'm in the hallway, I start whispering Elijah's name. By the time I open the door to the empty classroom, he is standing right in front of me. "You whispered?"

"Sorry," I reply. "I don't really know how else to get in touch with you."

His face softens. "I do not mind if you call me."

"Elijah, how do you know that I'm calling you if you aren't watching me?"

"I have not quite figured it out myself. I believe it is correlated to the amount of time I focus on you. I must be tuned in to you. I can hear when you say my name. Names have power."

I like that he's tuned in to me. "I think I stumbled across something while talking to Mrs. Lippy. Did you know people were complaining that I messed up their grades and got them sick with my eyes and all kinds of nonsense?"

"Not exactly those things. But I did have an idea."

"Remember how you said my situation is like the accused witches' in the sixteen hundreds? And that silence is a death sentence." He nods. "I was thinking my situation is more like that than I initially thought. That it might all be part of a larger pattern."

"Elaborate."

"So, the deaths occur in a pattern. That we know. And we figured out that they were occurring only when descendants of all the main Witch Trials families were in Salem at the same time. What if the pattern is more complex than we thought? What if the original Trials are re-created? As in, the same basic thing happens, just in a different form. In this case, it would be my being accused as a witch and everyone else falling in line to kill me off, at least metaphorically."

He tilts his head. "It is a better rationale than anything we have come up with thus far."

"Right?" I'm so excited that my sleepiness fades. "Let's review the major causes of the Trials. Maybe if we stop some of those things from happening we can break the curse . . . or at least slow it down." I pull out a piece of paper and pen to make notes. "To start with, there was Cotton's book."

"To *start,* we must look farther back. Witchcraft was a common crime in those times. In only a few hundred years there were upward of eighty thousand witchcraft executions in Europe. And before the Salem Trials, approximately fifteen people had been executed in New England."

I wince. "So witchcraft was something that people accepted as real."

"Indeed. And, as I have told you, Massachusetts Bay Colony was a Puritan community. The political leaders were all members of Puritan churches and consulted their ministers frequently. Puritans were Calvinist—all rituals besides the approved ones were associated with paganism."

I write quickly in my notebook. "Basically, anything outside of the norm was jumped on as evil or something."

Elijah nods. "Also, Salem Village was a quarrelsome place. Villagers fought over land and church-related matters. Almost every villager could come up with a list of complaints about his or her neighbors."

That's high school in a nutshell. "I bet once the accusations started flying, they spread like wildfire."

"Certainly. Now, what you said about Cotton's book was correct. It provided people with the information they needed to make their accusations plausible." Elijah sounds regretful.

"So it was the perfect setting for things to get out of hand." I pause for a moment. "Which is like my situation here. High schoolers immediately go for the throat of the different person. And once the war starts, it just rages on until someone is broken."

Elijah frowns. "I guess witchcraft accusations have not disappeared. They have just transformed."

I was hoping for a more straightforward task. "How am I going to change a whole system? Something that's been happening forever?"

Elijah smiles at the word *change*. "I wanted you to understand the context of witchcraft accusations in Salem. We can look at it more specifically, examining which things are necessary to convict a witch."

"Okay." I'm more comfortable with that idea. "You tell me what happened during the Trials, and I'll find the equivalent for my situation."

I write in my notebook:

How to Hang a Witch

Witch Trials   Now

"To start with, you need a fearful community," Elijah says. "In addition to what I have already said about the towns-people, the French and Indian battles made New Englanders particularly skittish. There were people in Salem who had been attacked, lost ones they loved, or were refugees. They feared the wilderness and were always ready for something bad to happen. They wanted something to explain their losses and fears."

"Like all the mysterious deaths and weirdness in Salem. Alice said they were looking for an explanation."

Elijah nods. "And most of the accusations were formed by a select group of people."

"The Descendants."

"Once that group decided to turn against a witch, no one in the town would stand up for that individual. They feared that they would also be accused if they said anything."

"My whole school's scared to stand up to the Descendants, especially to Lizzie. Maybe the town is, too." Connecting these dots is too easy. I don't like it.

"Oftentimes, the complaints about the witch would increase in frequency. More townspeople would join in and reinforce the idea that there was something wrong with that person."

"The complaints Mrs. Lippy read . . ."

Elijah nods. "Then proof was provided in the form of physical harm and visions, going so far as to blame past murders on the witch."

"The rash and John's death." It's pretty morbid.

"The evidence was reviewed by the magistrates and the community in the court. When everyone agreed that the evidence was sufficient, the witch took a hanging sentence."

My heart pounds. There's no way they could hang me, right? Even if it's a metaphor, the idea is sick and disturbing. My mind goes to the drawing in the dirt at Gallows Hill Park and the noose on my coffee cup. "On this one, I got nothin'."

How to Hang a Witch

Witch Trials	Now
1) fearful community (French/Indian battles)	descendant deaths in Salem
2) convictions by select group (who no one would stand up to)	the Descendants
3) increasing frequency of complaints about accused witch to reinforce that there is something wrong with that person	what parents and students are telling Mrs. Lippy and Brennan
4) proof of witchcraft (visions, murder, etc.)	the rash, John's death
5) evidence reviewed in court	???
6) hanging sentence	

"I'm not sure what could be the equivalent of going to trial," I say. "Also, most of those things have already happened. I can't stop them. Was it ever possible to escape a death sentence?"

"Occasionally, yes. But that individual needed a good deal of support and a way to make her voice heard. You will need an audience and you will have to be convincing."

My stomach drops so low, I feel it in my toes. "Like a speech?"

"Yes, I suppose so." He pauses, and I know what he's going to say next. "Also, our courts were not formal the way you might imagine them. They were more of a community event. Will the school gather to discuss John's death?"

I stare at my hands, which have stopped taking notes. "Yes. There's an assembly today."

"Providence."

"You mean worst thing ever."

CHAPTER THIRTY-EIGHT

Reasons for Disliking Me

I grip the paper written in my crappy handwriting and take the last seat in the last row of the auditorium. People speak in hushed voices, but the energy is high.

Principal Brennan clears his throat at the podium. "As you all know, one of our own students died tragically yesterday."

I tune him out and look over my speech. My hands shake and the paper rustles. *Just don't let me faint*—which I have done twice since I came to Salem for some crazy reason. *And don't let anyone throw anything.*

"Samantha, if you are not careful, it will tear," Elijah warns. I ease my grip.

I look at the backs of the students' heads and involuntarily begin to count them. When I get to five hundred, I start to dry-heave.

Elijah appears calm, but I can tell by the slight wrinkle in his brow that he's worrying. "If you must regurgitate your food, I suggest doing so before the speech."

"I didn't eat anything today," I say.

He lifts his brow. "I suppose that is good fortune."

I can't help but agree.

"Now I would like to hand over the microphone to some of John's closest friends," Brennan says, concluding his brief introduction.

The Descendants take the stage wearing floor-length black dresses and appearing almost to float. Lizzie carries a bundle of roses such a deep shade of purple, they look black from a distance. She places them near a picture of John on the stage.

Those roses! They're the same kind I saw by the lamppost in town. My mind races. Could they have been from her as well? Susannah did say that Lizzie's been affected more than most and that she blames me. Did something happen to someone else she loves?

Lizzie takes the podium with the three girls behind her. "I cannot give you a carefully constructed speech about how special John was, or what a good life he had until yesterday. You all knew him. You all know." Her demeanor's cold and commanding. "I'm not going to make you laugh or cry or even tell you how I feel without him. My feelings are obvious. I can sum them up in one word—anger."

The Descendants, behind Lizzie, glance at each other. I guess she's not giving whatever speech they were expecting.

"He shouldn't have died. It was not an accident. And the responsible party must pay. We all know who that is: Samantha Mather."

Sweat breaks out on my forehead, and I slink down in my chair as far as I can. Nausea throbs through my body, and the edge of my vision flickers like camera flashes.

"Susannah was there when Samantha tried to attack him in the hallway. I was there when she threatened him in class.

And Jaxon was there to discover her bite mark on his lifeless palm."

My heart nearly stops when I hear Jaxon's name. He talked to the Descendants about me? He was the only one there when I told Bradbury about biting John's hand. Has he been lying to me all along? The betrayal stabs at me, and all I want to do is run. Surprised reactions ripple through the crowd in gasps and whispers. Many turn around and search for me. Elijah fumes. This is my conviction. Brennan stands, looking like he is going to interject.

"That's all we have to say." Lizzie turns away from the podium. Susannah hesitates near the microphone, but Lizzie grabs her arm. They follow her off the stage. Lizzie convinced them I had something to do with John's death. And Jaxon . . . I want to cry.

A flustered Brennan takes the microphone. "Uh . . . I would just like to say that the police report indicated that John's death was most likely an accident, as I said earlier. Now I would like to introduce Dr. Myers, a grief therapist, to the stage." Dr. Myers takes the microphone.

"Maybe this isn't such a good idea," I say.

"Samantha, there is no retreating. You either go up there or your trial is concluded. Lizzie is victorious."

"How can I change people's minds after that?"

"You simply have to introduce doubt. Make them question their dislike of you. That should be enough to buy us time. This is your chance. Do not miss it."

I take a breath. I have to focus on why I'm trying to break the curse. My dad . . . and now Susannah. I saw her hesitate on stage. She doesn't agree with Lizzie—at least not completely. I need every shred of support I can get.

My whole body shakes as I stand. Thankfully, everyone's

watching Dr. Myers. I hug the wall and make my way toward the front of the auditorium. I don't look at anyone because I can't bear knowing what I'll see. I walk up the stairs to the stage.

"Steady, Samantha," Elijah says.

Dr. Myers looks confused as I approach the podium.

"I have to say something." My voice is quiet.

Brennan attempts to get on the stage, but Myers stops him with a hand gesture. To my surprise, Myers puts the microphone back on the podium and steps away from it. I'm not sure whether I'm grateful or wish that he stopped me.

I place my crinkled speech on the podium. The room's unnaturally silent. No one moves. I don't look at the crowd. I can't. I just focus on my paper and try to keep my voice steady.

"I . . . well . . . I know that . . . I haven't made a good impression on most of you. Some of you . . . well, you have legitimate reasons for disliking me."

People begin to whisper, and the counselor hushes the room.

"Get off the stage!" someone yells, and a few people boo me.

I'm making this worse for myself. "There are many . . ." The boos increase.

Lizzie yells, "Murderer!" and others echo her.

I lift my head and take in the audience for the first time. Angry faces stare at me. I clear my throat, and Brennan and Dr. Myers attempt to quiet the hostile students. I straighten my speech, hoping people will stop booing long enough for me to get the words out.

In one jerky movement I knock the piece of paper off the podium and over the edge of the stage. Elijah grabs it mid-fall. It takes me a second before I realize the auditorium has gone silent. Slowly, Elijah lifts the paper. Everyone stares at it, floating in the air. I take it, but finding my place in my speech now seems silly. How can I go on like nothing strange just happened?

I scan the auditorium the way I peek at a bad cut. I have the Descendants' attention. Good. I spot Jaxon in my peripheral vision, but don't look directly at him. I fold my speech and tuck it into my back pocket. "I'm not perfect. I'm far from it. I'm weird. The strangest things happen around me all the time. I don't know why, and maybe I never will.

"I can explain that paper, though. It was a spirit. I can't make friends at school, but I can with the dead. So at least I've got that." There are a few nervous laughs that end as abruptly as they start.

"And I'm pretty sure I know why John died, even though I don't know how." The tension in the room is palpable. "But to explain that, I have to back up a bit. You see, there were three times in the years since the Trials when a whole bunch of descendants died. My spirit friend helped me figure out that these deaths happen in a pattern. All the major Witch Trials families have to be in Salem at once. A few weeks ago, the Mathers were the only major family missing. And as you may have noticed, when I moved here, people started dying quickly."

To my surprise, the crowd's not acting like I've said the most ridiculous thing they've ever heard. With a quick glance, I catch Jaxon putting his head in his hands. My lip trembles.

"You said that I'm cursed. I am. And so are the Descendants, their families, and possibly this town." Actually owning these words feels oddly light. I've been running from them for a long time. "I am trying to figure it out. But I don't think I can do it by myself. I'm not asking you to like me. I'm asking you to stop hating me long enough for me to work this thing out." The whispers start. "That's all, I guess. Thanks for listening."

As I walk away from the podium, a girl yells, "Prove that you can see a ghost!"

Not this again. The room waits for my reply. "No." But as the word leaves my mouth, Elijah lifts me by my waist. The audience bursts into shocked conversation. No one tries to get control of the situation. I make eye contact with Susannah, and Elijah sets me back on my feet. She nods calmly while Alice and Lizzie battle it out on either side of Mary, who looks ill.

I don't sit back down in the auditorium. I steal a glance toward Jaxon, but he's not in his seat. I walk through the heavy double doors and then out of the school entirely.

CHAPTER THIRTY-NINE

A Crow and a Noose

Books and old transcripts of the Trials cover the table where Elijah and I sit. The reference room of the public library is as stuffy as ever, but at least it's private.

I gesture at the book I'm reading. "This says Cotton was prejudiced against Burroughs for his unorthodox beliefs. As far as I can tell, Burroughs's hanging was the only one Cotton attended. I haven't read the trial transcript yet, though."

Elijah nods. "I remember Burroughs. He had an unfortunate history with my fiancée's family. He owed them money. Although he eventually repaid it, my fiancée was well acquainted with gossip concerning him. When she twisted the gossip properly, she formed it into an allegation of witchcraft. He became pinned as the ringleader of the witches because he was a minister."

It must be strange for him to research all these people his fiancée accused. "I'm not sure how these things tie together. It's so tangled. But there has to be some sort of common thread we're missing."

"Indeed."

I play with the cap of my pen. "I'm just thinking out loud. But what have we learned from the things I've seen? My first dream had a crow and a noose. The second was Cotton's sermon about witchcraft, and it had another noose. And my visions consisted of John being crushed and the girl hanging from a rope. The one time I actually called on Cotton, I saw Burroughs hanging. Before he turned into Susannah, that is."

Elijah and I are both silent, considering for the hundredth time how these events connect. "Riddles, metaphors, double meanings," I say. "Did you find anything on the crow woman Mrs. Meriwether said my grandmother used to dream about?"

"Nothing near the time of the Trials. But people were more superstitious then and would refrain from committing to paper anything that could attract a curse or black magic. It is possible I am not looking closely enough. I will search for more-recent diaries, from the eighteen hundreds. It may even be that the bird is wrong. Or that I am not considering the right metaphors for a bird."

Metaphors for a bird . . . flight, flying, feathers. Feathers carved into a windowsill. House in the woods. Woman-with-dead-birds story. "I missed something," I say, putting my pen down. "I think I blocked it out, honestly. It happened before I believed most of this stuff could be real. Remember that day I spent with Jaxon, when you were waiting at my door? Did you see where I went that day?" Saying Jaxon's name out loud creates a sharp pain in my chest.

"No. I was engaged in my own research."

The one time it would have been helpful to have him watching me, he wasn't. "We were in the woods. We went to find a house that's hands-down the creepiest place I've ever been. It has a bedroom with walls covered in scribbled rantings from some lunatic. And the windowsill has feathers carved into it. Jaxon told me a story at the time about an old woman who lived there and ate birds. It sounded so crazy that I disregarded it completely."

Elijah sits unnaturally still.

"And my name and my dad's name were written on the wall. Our first names, anyway. I never thought those feathers could be related to the crow woman." I'm really frustrated with myself for not considering it.

He snaps the pencil he's holding and puts it on the table. How could I be such an idiot? I should have told him about those names from the beginning.

"Where is this house, Samantha?"

"I can draw you a map."

"Quickly."

I draw the streets and what I remember of the woods. "Jaxon could see an old trail that led to the house, but I'm not positive of its angle. I'm pretty sure the place is haunted."

"Did you see someone?" Elijah asks. He's almost frantic.

"No, but I heard a woman crying."

He blinks out. I still think Jaxon's story is bull, but there might be some piece of truth in it. Like the birds piece. Birds, feathers, crows. It doesn't take a genius to put these things together. Thinking about Jaxon hurts more than I thought it would. I can't believe he would talk to the Descendants about me. I bet they had a good laugh about how he fooled me into thinking he liked me.

I flip through the pages of a book without reading it. My eyes well up, and I push my feelings away, hiding them with all the others that I can't deal with right now. Jaxon's not the first friend who's turned on me, and I'm sure he won't be the last. This is exactly why I don't let people near me.

This dimly lit room that seemed sort of old-world romantic when Elijah was in it suddenly feels isolated and devoid of oxygen. I prop open the wooden door to get some air, and there's a freshman from my school in the book aisle. He eyes me curiously. I return to the round table to pack up my things.

"Mather?" he says.

"Huh?" My heart beats a little faster.

"I saw your speech today." He leans against the doorway. He isn't particularly tall, but he's stocky and takes up most of the entrance.

"Okay." I eye the space between him and the doorway, trying to decide whether or not I could squeeze past him if he turns out to be a creep.

"I know all about your family."

"Great." I'm not sure if he's making fun of me or trying to talk to me.

"Can I take a picture of you?" he asks, pulling out his cell phone.

"Seriously, no. Go be weird somewhere else." I want people to stop hating me, not treat me like a sideshow.

"Cheese," he says. Only before I can say "What?" that little punk flashes his cell phone light in my face and takes the worst picture ever. Then he runs down the aisle, laughing.

"I will break that phone!" I yell after him as the white-haired librarian comes around the corner. I'm developing a phobia about this library.

"Keep your voice down," she says. "Five minutes until closing." Then she peers at me in a you-know-what-you-did way and walks off.

I grab my shoulder bag and head toward the stairs. Why did that boy take a picture of me? Is that a sign that people might not hate me, or does that just mean they're finding new ways to torment me?

As I exit the library, I fold my arms against the cold night air.

"More spells," says Elijah, blinking in.

"What?"

"The house . . ." He looks more agitated than when he left. "There are stones by the windows and doors bound with string and sealed with black wax. I do not know the exact meaning, and I do not dare cross the barrier."

I try to remember if I saw that, but in all likelihood I wouldn't have noticed. "But you're already dead. What's the worst that can happen?"

His look tells me I don't know the half of it. "I need to talk to you. Important conversations are not intended for the street."

I smile at his formality. "There's a garden right over there." I point toward the Ropes Mansion, where I met the Descendants.

"Yes, that will do." He walks at such a fast pace that I almost have to run to keep up. I've never seen him like this.

I follow him under the trellis and into the labyrinth of flowers. Even in the dark, this place feels alive. The Gothic tower looms over us in the moonlight. He winds along the dirt paths to a bench under a canopy of vines. I sit before he asks me to. He sits next to me.

Elijah collects his thoughts. "Reading through old diaries, I found accounts regarding my fiancée that were disturbing. I did not tell you because I believed them my personal business, and irrelevant. You see, my fiancée formed an obsession with my death. She buried my body at the edge of her property."

That's right. If you commit suicide you can't be buried on hallowed ground, or whatever. I vacillate between curiosity and dread.

"Her family found her wailing over my grave night after night. She spoke to me freely around her house, refusing to accept I was gone." I'm reminded of what Jaxon told me about his mom when his dad died. "Out of spite, her witch accusations became more frequent and demanding. When the Trials concluded, she snapped. She became vicious and incoherent. She had luck on her side, though. Because the shame of the Trials was so great and her family so influential, they refrained from arresting her."

"You could be arrested for being crazy?"

"If your fits cause others physical harm, then yes. And her fits were . . . terrifying, from what I have read. Even though they spared her arrest, she was banished from the town. She refused to leave on the grounds that she would not be parted from me."

"So you think she lived in that house? The one in the woods?" I interrupt, feeling anxious.

"I know it. Her parents bought it for her because it was just outside the town limits. That house was remote even then, well surrounded by trees. For a while, her mother visited her. My fiancée was losing her mind, and her violent outbursts increased. After a while, her mother stopped going altogether. I found a letter saying she saw my fiancée from a distance years later, feral and dirty."

"Okay." My voice is measured. "What does this have to do with the feathers I found on the windowsill and the story about the birds Jaxon told me?"

Elijah looks regretful. "Like everyone else at the time, I kept a diary. It was leather-bound, with a feather on the front.

It was part of a set, and she had the matching one. She inspired the purchase, in fact. She used to say my hair was as black as a raven's, and her nickname for me was Bird. She would tell me that when we died we would fly away together." He looks away.

Suddenly the writing on the walls seems way worse. And the crying I heard when I touched the carved feather. My brain is on overload. *Why was my name there, and what is that place used for now?*

"Elijah, maybe the stories about the evil old woman that lived there with birds were about your fiancée, not the crow woman . . ." My voice trails off as I try to figure out how the crow woman and Elijah's fiancée could be different people. I can't.

"I did not associate the word 'crow' with my fiancée. I am frustrated that I did not make this connection sooner. There was something about your grandmother's drawing that struck me as familiar. The way the woman's hair fell. The way she held her body. I just could not put my finger on what it was until now."

My heart races. "Why would my grandmother draw your fiancée?"

"And why would Cotton show you a crow in a dream?" He sounds as anxious as I feel.

Elijah's fiancée is the crow woman. There's only one thing that explains this. "She's wrapped up in the curse. She must be."

"I just never imagined . . ." He doesn't finish.

He told me several times she was one of the main accusers of witches. It makes sense she would be involved in the curse. "She helped start the hysteria."

"Yes. And if she is involved, I do not believe myself exempt from this situation, as I once did," Elijah says.

"Are you suggesting you're part of the curse, too?"

"Indeed. It is possible. I was the one who disapproved of her actions at the time. Then I killed myself because of the Trials, and left her alone. And here I am again, helping you attempt to stop the curse. She has every reason to seek revenge."

"If you're tied to this and we figure it out, what will happen to you?" I always thought he was stuck here because of his suicide, not the curse.

"Are you inquiring whether I will remain a spirit?"

I nod at him.

"I cannot say."

A tightness forms in my chest. For the first time since I learned about the curse, the idea of solving it doesn't feel like a relief. "Do you want to stop being a spirit?"

His face is unreadable, but he maintains eye contact. "I have often wished it."

The tightness spreads. "Of course."

"In truth, I have not enjoyed these years. I have loathed many of them. And returning to Salem only increased my suffering. Then . . ."

As he talks, it becomes increasingly hard to breathe. "Then what?" I whisper.

"I recalled the reason I was in pain. Loss of beauty, of connection. Abigail's singing while I painted. How we laughed so when no one was watching. And how finding a black-eyed Susan tucked into my business contracts reminded me of why I was doing that business in the first place. To really care for another is a reason to live. When that beauty was blotted out of my world, I no longer wanted to be in it."

I understand him completely. Without my dad, I don't know who I am.

"You reminded me of that beauty again. Not in one

minute of my death have I wished for my life back, until I met you."

Under the vines, on that little bench, I stare into his gray eyes. Before I can consider what I'm doing, I lean forward until I'm only inches from his face. He gently brushes my hair behind my ear. "Samantha, I—"

"I don't care," I whisper.

He doesn't argue with me. Instead, he leans forward and presses his lips to mine. Softly at first, then with pressure. The coolness of his mouth warms against my own. Everything about him feels alive and hungry. His hand moves under my hair to my neck and pulls me toward him.

His tongue slips into my mouth, and my body tingles from my lips to my thighs. *I want this, you, all of it. I don't care if it doesn't make sense.* I reach out, entwining my fingers in his clothes and pulling him closer. He holds me tightly, the tips of his fingers pressing into my back. Then, like flipping a switch, he stops kissing me.

I look at him, confused. There's a pause before I release my hands from his body. "What?"

He shakes his head and stands. "This cannot be, Samantha. You are living."

CHAPTER FORTY

Midnight Mission

The clock on my bedside table reads 2:27 a.m. I snuggle farther into my down comforter. With the crap sleep I've gotten recently, I should have passed out hours ago. But all the details of the curse won't leave my head, and it's driving me crazy that I can't connect them. How much time do I have left?

There is a soft tapping on my window, and I launch myself from my bed in a tangle of blankets. I squint at the crouched silhouette on my roof and can just make out the shape of a bun. "Susannah?"

"Sorry," she says, but her voice is muffled by the glass.

I kneel on the window seat and open the window.

"How did you get on my roof?" I peer behind her just to make sure she's alone.

She slides into my room and closes the window. "I climbed the latticework and jumped up."

She scaled my house?

I flip my bedside lamp on. She's wearing green plaid pajamas and a fluffy white winter coat. Okay, so she's not wearing black, she's a mini ninja, and she's on a midnight mission. What else don't I know about this girl?

"Everything's a mess, Samantha," she says, and sits down on my window seat.

"Yeah, I know," I say. I'm not sure how to process this visit. I'm partly relieved and partly suspicious, especially after Lizzie's hateful speech.

"No, I mean it's gotten worse. I need to know—have you had any more visions?" she says, and I can hear the fear in her voice.

"You mean other than the one of you?" I wish I had phrased that better.

"Yeah. Anyone else? Even someone you don't know?"

I recognize the look on her face. I've worn it myself. "Your sister . . ."

Her eyes widen.

"No, I mean, I didn't see your sister. But did something happen to her?"

Her panic deflates. She nods. "She was admitted to the hospital not long after I came home from school. She collapsed." Her voice shakes.

I sit down next to her. "I'm so very sorry. I don't know what to say."

"And she's not the only one. Lizzie's brother and cousin got in a car accident. Her cousin's dead and her brother's in the ICU. And Alice's uncle, the one who owns The Brew, had a heart attack."

Lizzie's brother and cousin? *That's what those purple roses in town were about.* It takes all my self-control not to jump up and start pacing. "It's escalating."

"I think you might be the key to figuring all this out."

I'm so nervous, I almost laugh. "You guys have been keeping me in the dark. Why would you do that if you think I can solve the curse?"

"That's why I'm here. Anything I know that can help you, I'll tell you."

I definitely didn't expect that answer. "What changed?"

She takes a breath. "We did the clarity spell with Lizzie and it didn't work."

"Do you mean you didn't see the blurred faces?"

"Let me back up. Alice, Mary, Lizzie, and I have been friends since we were little. Our mothers were friends, and their mothers. And from the time we were ten or so we were casting. It took us a long time before we could make anything work, and it wasn't until recently that any of us besides Lizzie could do spells individually. We always needed the circle. We still do, for most things."

"The circle?"

"Four of us."

"What about John?"

Susannah hesitates at the mention of his name, and I regret bringing him up. "He wasn't as interested as we were. When he was there, it was mainly for Lizzie."

"So everyone knows you do witchcraft—they're not just spreading rumors?"

"Not exactly. People make guesses, but we never discuss it with anyone outside of ourselves. That's why I didn't answer when you were asking me questions the day I came to your house."

I was right. They're like a secret society. "But you did a spell with me. Isn't that a violation of your secrecy?"

"Yes and no. The thing is, I get feelings about people. Not

everyone, but certain people I just know things about. And as much as Lizzie and Alice kept saying you were the bad thing coming to Salem, I knew the moment I met you that wasn't true. Alice argued with me, but Lizzie wouldn't hear it. Eventually, Alice agreed that if I could prove it, she would help me convince Lizzie. That's when we met you in the garden, and that's why Alice agreed to do that spell."

Alice reads bones and Susannah reads people? I'm really not sure which end is up anymore. "You were testing me?"

"Yes. The clarity spell should have told us something about you, brought to light the truth. But those blurred faces were something no one planned on. Nothing like that had ever happened before. When we saw Cotton, Alice and I started arguing all over again. We decided to go back one more time to sort it out before discussing it with Lizzie."

"But why were you arguing with your friends about me?" *What does she see when she reads me?*

She places her hand on mine. "Samantha, Alice's bones kept directing us to you. You are obviously connected to us for better or for worse."

"And so what happened with Lizzie?"

"We tried the clarity spell in the same spot in the woods, and we didn't even get a normal reading. We got nothing. It didn't work at all."

"Could it be a fluke?" I don't know how this stuff works, but it sounds like I need to. I look at my dad's picture.

Susannah shakes her head. "Things like that don't happen randomly. You made that spell work; I'm sure of it."

I open my mouth to protest, and shut it again. "Did you ever tell Lizzie?"

Susannah fidgets with the zipper on her coat. "Alice brought you up in the auditorium, right before . . . everything happened."

Oh no. That has to be the worst timing ever.

"Lizzie's not thinking clearly. She's coming after you. She's convinced that these deaths and accidents are your fault, and she's doing everything she can to convince the town of the same thing. And because she's angry with us, she's not telling us what she's planning. But it's not just gossip. Her family is well connected here."

"What do I do?"

"Meet us tomorrow in the woods behind Walgreens at midnight. We'll bring Lizzie, and we'll sort this thing out. If we can't work together, then we're all gonna lose. These divisions are costing us time."

A chill runs through me. "Okay."

Susannah pulls out her phone. "I have to run. My parents are expecting me back at the hospital." She lifts my window and slips through it.

"Susannah, be careful. That vision I had . . ."

"Just meet us tomorrow," she says, and closes my window behind her.

CHAPTER FORTY-ONE

Becoming a Witch

I rub my eyes against the early morning light as I walk into the kitchen. Coffee's brewed and everything's quiet. Vivian's car isn't in the driveway. Looks like she's avoiding me now. Somehow this hurts worse than the anger. She's the one who sold the apartment and lied to me; she's the one who slapped me. How is it fair that she's now mad at me, on top of everything else?

I pull down a mug and fill it with coffee, half-and-half, and a bit of cinnamon. There are new empty wine bottles in the recycling can. Maybe Vivian's just waiting for my dad to die to get rid of me. I have no family and nowhere to go. Why doesn't she care about me anymore? I shake my head. I need to stop thinking about this.

"Elijah," I say as I sit down at the round wooden table in the kitchen.

He blinks in, with an old leather-bound book in his hand. He takes a seat at the table and smiles. "Good. You are awake."

I immediately blush and look at my coffee. Seeing his dimples just makes me remember the way his lips felt. I shift the conversation to our usual morning topic. "How's my dad today?"

"Very much the same."

It's Saturday, a week since I was at the hospital, and the separation's panicking me. "I really wish I could go see him."

Elijah looks sympathetic. "You are helping him more by staying here."

I'm grateful for the reinforcement. "What's the book?"

"It is an old spell book. I am using it to figure out what kind of spell is around the house in the woods. It took me all night to locate one that I did not suspect was protected by some enchantment or another."

"It surprises me that anything can hurt you." Not that anything makes sense anymore.

"Understand that my existence as a spirit has no guaranteed end date. I would surely hate to spend the next few hundred years suffering over a spell because I was not cautious."

The idea that objects can hold that kind of power is unsettling. "Could that really happen?"

"Samantha, death reveals that the world is more fantastical than you thought, not less. The veil between possible and impossible is often lifted."

"I think I need to get on board with this spell stuff, too. I feel like I've been on the sidelines."

"How so?"

"Well, I have that parchment you gave me. Maybe there's some sort of identity-revealing spell that I can use to figure out who wrote the thing." On the off chance it does work, it will save me a bunch of time.

Elijah smiles. "Becoming a witch, are we?"

I feign annoyance. "Not funny. So, did you find out what those stones and things at the old house meant?"

"I believe they are some form of binding spell to keep things in or shut things out. I am not positive. They could also be a way of hiding the house from general view. I have not gotten far enough in my research."

I wonder why Elijah's using an old spell book to decipher a new spell. I freeze, and my coffee cup only makes it halfway to my mouth. "Elijah, do you think there's any way your fiancée could still be around?"

His lips tighten. "Yes. I do. It is one of my greatest fears. One of the reasons I did not come back to Salem."

"But you haven't seen her? Right? You'd see her if she was here." All I need is a crazy spirit obsessed with Elijah to make this situation worse.

"My first few days after I returned to Salem, I was on guard for her. When she did not appear, I began to relax a little. Eventually, I assumed she had passed on. It was not until yesterday that my fears about her resurfaced."

I'm sure that if she knew where his spirit was, these past three hundred years would have been unbearable. "What's her name? It's weird to keep calling her your fiancée."

"As I told you yesterday, names have power. I have been careful not to say it all these years, and I ask that you do not say it, either. But you know her name. She accused Burroughs and Giles Corey. . . . She testified against Susannah Martin. . . ."

I would be lying if I said I hadn't already been considering this. And these details definitely confirm my suspicion. I bet anything his fiancée was Ann. She was the leader of the girls who claimed to be afflicted by the accused. I nod. "I won't say her name. Can I see the spell book?"

He hands it to me, and the weight is surprising. The leather cover is old and cracked and has silver accents. I gently open it, and the pages are thick and soft like cloth. The spells are handwritten in the same type of calligraphy Elijah uses. The book has a homey feel to it—the way old houses have a personality.

I skim the titles of the spells. They are about love, protection, growth, and harmony. It must have belonged to a good witch. I almost laugh at the thought.

After some page-flipping, I come across a spell entitled "The Origin of a Spell." I skim the text. "This says it reveals a witch's signature, so you know who's casting against you."

Elijah's eyebrows push together. "I do not know, Samantha. If this does work, you risk drawing the witch's attention. She may sense you searching for her. Someone powerful enough to cast the spell that caused that rash is not someone you want to attract."

He could be right. But this is our best option. "Maybe. But I think we have to take the risk. Besides, if it's Lizzie, she already hates me."

"And if it is not Lizzie?" he asks.

The vision Cotton showed me of Burroughs suggested I have a secret enemy. But it's only a secret to me, not to my enemy. This is something concrete that might level the playing field. "Then we deal with that as it comes. I'm already in the middle of this. . . . You aren't thinking it could be your fiancée, though, right?"

"No. The dead cannot conjure." His voice has finality in it, so much so that I wonder if he has tried magic himself.

At least I can rule her out. I study the required list of ingredients. I don't recognize all of them, but then again, I've never been good with plants. Oh, crap. It specifies that everything must be freshly cut by the spell caster.

Elijah stands behind my shoulder. "How do you plan on getting those ingredients?"

My options are limited without a car and without asking Vivian. I look out the kitchen window. "I can ask Mrs. Meriwether. I'm guessing her huge garden has some, if not all, of these things." I don't want to go anywhere near Jaxon right now, but this isn't about me and my wants. Plus, Mrs. Meriwether loves cooking. I'm sure she could tell me where to get something if she doesn't have it.

I grab a pen and paper from the kitchen drawer and make a list of ingredients. Elijah frowns. "I do not like this at all."

"Me neither, but we need to take anything we can get at this point. Susannah stopped by last night and told me about more injuries in Salem. The problem is getting bigger, faster." Judging by his look, I know he agrees with me.

I finish my list, and he blinks out and takes the book with him. That's okay. It's probably easier to talk to Mrs. Meriwether without him there.

I take one final sip of my coffee and put my mug in the sink. I walk out the back door and onto the grass toward Mrs. Meriwether's. There's always the chance Jaxon's asleep.

I knock on the back door. It only takes a moment for her rosy cheeks and warm smile to greet me. "Top 'o the mornin' to ya," she says in a playful Irish accent.

I smile, and step through the doorway. "And the rest of the day to yourself."

Mrs. Meriwether lights up. "How'd you know that was the right response?"

"I went to Ireland with my dad when I was a kid." I listen

for Jaxon as I follow Mrs. Meriwether down the hall, but everything's quiet.

"Come in and sit awhile." She walks through the arched doorway and into the kitchen.

I take a seat at the island, which is once again covered with beautiful desserts. She offers me my pick, and I gladly accept.

"I was wondering if I could have a few things from your garden?" I ask between bites.

"Of course you may! What is it you're looking for?"

Her enthusiasm makes this all a little easier. I pull the list out of my hoodie pocket.

"Wild leek. Checkerberry. Fiddlehead." She reads to herself and then looks at me curiously. "What are you using these for?"

"Uh . . . a recipe I found."

"Did you know that these are all native New England plants?"

That makes perfect sense if the spell book was from Elijah's time. The witch it belonged to would need to use local ingredients. "No. How funny." My voice is higher-pitched than usual.

"Checkerberries are found in the forest."

That's not good. "So you don't have them?"

She smiles. "Actually, I do. I use them for a Native American medicinal tea. The thing is, that besides tea, I've seen only one other recipe that calls for them—a seasonal muffin."

Crap. She knows this is a weird ingredient. I should've taken a few minutes to research before marching over here. This is where impulsiveness gets you. "Oh."

Mrs. Meriwether walks to the island. "Samantha, leek and checkerberry do not belong in the same recipe."

I look at the desserts, hoping they'll provide me with some advice. "I'm afraid you'll think I'm crazy."

"You would be surprised at the things I can accept, especially if they're the truth." She's so calm and nonjudgmental that I feel awful.

What made me think I would sneak this one past a woman who bakes for a living? "They're for a spell."

To my great surprise, she laughs. "You sound so much like your father. We used to spend hours raiding our parents' gardens trying to mix together any magical concoction. I half thought that was why he grew up to be a spice importer and I, a baker."

I almost choke on my pastry. My dad, mixing spells? That seems like the last thing in the world he'd do. He wouldn't even let me get one of those fortunes out of a vending machine at a carnival. I suddenly see his spice business in a whole new light. How many things did he change about himself after my mother died? "Did the potions ever work?"

"Oh no, not exactly. But it didn't stop us from trying." She laughs again. "You cannot imagine how angry Charlotte was the day we used up all the mint she liked in her lemonade."

I smile now, too. "So you don't think I'm nuts?"

"I live in Salem. There are ten stores within walking distance that have tonics and potions for true love and any other thing you desire. Everyone swears by my happy cakes. Nothing like the magic of triple chocolate to perk a body right up." She winks.

I never considered that spells could be part of the culture here. "I'm sorry for not telling you. I really am."

"Not to worry. Trust is grown over time. You're still just planting your first seeds." She brushes her hands on her apron. "Shall we get what you need?"

I shove the last bite of a cinnamon and sugar challah knot into my mouth. She leads me out the door and down a small stone pathway toward her enormous garden. Part is enclosed in a greenhouse, and a short stone wall surrounds the rest.

Mrs. Meriwether points to the stones. "My mother always told me stones like these were New England's winter crop. Because every year when the snow left there would be loads of them sticking out of the ground. Only made sense to build walls."

She brings me to the checkerberries first and hands me a wooden bowl to collect them. She urges me to try one, and they taste just like wintergreen. As we move through the list, she explains the plant flavors and shows me which plants can be used to treat anxiety, illnesses, or even be used for beauty products.

My bowl fills quickly, and I'm strangely satisfied with the experience. As we walk back to the house, I find myself smiling. I can see why she was my dad's best friend. She's one of the most good-natured people I've ever met.

"Now, Samantha," Mrs. Meriwether says as we return to the kitchen. "Would you like to bring over that spell so I can help you with it?"

If I do the spell here, there's no risk of Vivian coming home and finding out. Also, the instructions looked complex, and it would be nice to have help. But I'll have to explain what the spell is for.

"Oh, come on. It'll be fun. And when Charlie wakes up, we can tell him all about it. I'm sure we'll all have a good laugh." She looks so happy about the idea.

The bit about my dad tips the scales. I'm not sure he'll find it funny, but I do like the idea of him waking up and us all laughing together. "Okay. I'll be right back."

I put down the bowl and run next door through the grass. When I open my back door, Elijah's standing there. "I heard," he says.

I'm not sure if he means that as a good or a bad thing. He hands me the book. I open the door again, but he doesn't follow me. I stop. "You coming?"

"I will be along in a while. I am searching for something."

By his vagueness, I'm sure it has to do with his fiancée.

"Okay. See you soon. Good luck with your search," I say, and head back out the door.

I return to Mrs. Meriwether's kitchen and place the old book on her counter.

"Isn't this something? This must be two or three hundred years old." She examines the leather. "I would've loved to have this when I was a girl."

She flips through the pages, oohing and aahing at the spell names. "Which one are we doing?"

"'Origin of a Spell,'" I say, and she waits for an explanation. Might as well just dive in. "I don't know if Jaxon told you, but I got blamed for the rash at the party. I'm trying to figure out who did it 'cause I think that person set me up."

I remove the tiny piece of parchment from my wallet and hand it to Mrs. Meriwether. "This was found at the party."

She unrolls the paper as I flip the pages of the spell book. "And here I thought we might be doing a true love spell," she says, looking more serious than she did a moment ago. She examines the spell I've chosen. "Well, it's certainly worth a try."

"Mom . . . Sam?" Jaxon enters the kitchen in his pajamas, his blond hair messy and falling in his eyes.

My heart gallops, and I instinctively block his view of the

spell book. I yank back the wave of emotion that threatens to crash. He looks from one of us to the other suspiciously.

"Breakfast, Jaxon? There's some lovely warm broccoli-and-cheddar quiche, and your orange juice is in the fridge."

Jaxon stares at me. "What are you guys doing?"

"A spell," Mrs. Meriwether says matter-of-factly.

Watching the shock register on Jaxon's face is uncomfortable. "You're definitely not doing a spell in my kitchen, Sam."

I set my jaw and stare at him.

"You may help if you like, dear," his mother continues. "But otherwise, will you please take your quiche into the dining room? I suspect we'll have to concentrate."

"Mom! I'm not kidding!"

Mrs. Meriwether pauses. "Okay, sweetheart. What's bothering you?"

"You know what. For years everyone thought you were crazy because of her . . ." He looks frustrated.

"My grandmother," I guess, and I know I'm right. He told me his mother was shunned because people thought she was crazy. He said there were "other reasons" besides depression. I just never put it together till now.

"It's finally blown over, and now you're doing spells? And you—" He looks at me but doesn't finish his sentence. His eyes are accusatory.

Mrs. Meriwether watches her son wrestle with his emotions. "I'm in my own kitchen. You shouldn't worry so much about what other people think. Besides, you know Charlotte was as much my mother as my own. I don't regret one moment I spent with her, no matter what the small-minded townspeople thought. I raised you better than that."

Jaxon looks straight at me. "You were right. You do hurt the people around you."

"And what about you?" I mean this to sound confident, but my voice falters. "Helping the Descendants crucify me."

He looks down and shakes his head. "I knew you'd think that was true. I don't know why I bother." Jaxon's look makes me wish I could take it all back. He turns and walks away.

"Jaxon," I say, but he keeps walking.

Mrs. Meriwether stops me before I chase after him. "Give him time. Jaxon's one that needs to process. If you push him now, it will only get worse."

"I'm so sorry, Mrs. Meriwether."

"No need for apologies. You've done nothing wrong."

Yes I have. I've thought the worst about someone who was nothing but nice to me. I turn around and look at everything she helped me pick and just feel rotten. "I'll leave."

Her expression softens. "You'll do no such thing. We have a spell to do. No sense in everyone being unhappy."

"What about Jaxon?"

She smooths her apron. "I know you're worried about him. It's sweet of you. My Jaxon is a very practical soul, bless his heart. Just like his father. But sometimes people need to be believed in more than they need to be told what is so. In time, he'll learn this. Just be patient with him, Samantha."

Does she mean he needs to believe in me or I need to believe in him? "Thanks for being so nice."

She reties her apron. "Alrighty now. What do we do first?"

I turn to the book and try to ignore my sadness. "We have to boil the berries."

Mrs. Meriwether gets a small but heavy-looking pot. "This is called a chowder. It's where they got the name for the soup."

She fills it halfway with water and puts it on to boil. Then we drop the checkerberries in, which makes the whole room smell like minty gum. We read the directions together. Thankfully, she understands, because I have no clue how to "finely shred" leafy greens.

Mrs. Meriwether gives me a cutting board and a knife. "First, cut the root off the leek. Like this. Then slice it lengthwise. Now brace it with your fingers and chop it in nice even pieces."

I'm amazed at how fast her hands move. I take the knife and try to replicate it. Unfortunately, I'm at twenty percent her speed and zero percent of her finesse. Together, we cut all the greens into their proper forms and place them into the chowder pot.

"Whoo. That is one strong smell," Mrs. Meriwether says as we watch our ingredients boil together in a thick soup.

I double-check the instructions, and Mrs. Meriwether pulls a small baster from a drawer. We clear a portion of the counter near the pot, and I carefully unroll the tiny piece of parchment paper. There's something exciting about doing this with her. It's how I always imagined some kids baked cookies with their moms.

I take a deep breath and concentrate on the words. "What is hidden, come to view. Make plain the hand with which you drew. Your magic mark I wish to see. With these three drops reveal to me."

I pull the hot liquid from the pot into the baster and squeeze three red drops onto the parchment. We both stare at it, afraid to blink. The red liquid coats the tiny piece of paper, causing the remaining black ink symbols to bleed. Then, all at once, the red potion moves to the center of the parchment in a concentrated dot. It slowly curves and winds itself, like there's a pen instructing it where to go. After a moment of this, it makes an elegant red feather.

I stare at it, trying to will it to turn into something else. Anything but a feather. My stomach twists in on itself, and I almost drop the baster on the floor.

"The crow woman," Mrs. Meriwether says in a hushed voice.

I grab the edge of the paper, trying to touch it as little as possible. "I'm really sorry, but I have to run." I pick up the book. *I need Elijah. Now.*

"What does this mean, exactly?" Mrs. Meriwether looks serious, with none of the bubbly sweetness of her usual demeanor. "Your grandmother said—"

I cut her off. If I don't go now, I'll have a panic attack. "I'm not sure. If I can explain, I promise I will. I'm sorry again for taking off like this." I run out of the kitchen before Mrs. Meriwether has time to respond.

"Elijah," I say as I sprint across the grass.

When I open the back door of my house, he's in the hallway. I hand him the parchment. His face shows more than surprise. He's angry.

"Not possible," he says to himself. "Turn around, Samantha. We are leaving."

The front door slams shut. "Sam?" yells Vivian.

If I run now, she'll see. I stand still, unsure what to do. "Yeah?"

Elijah grabs the book and the parchment from me as Vivian appears in the hallway.

"Where have you been? I called the house and your cell three times. I think we—" She sees my face and stops. "Did something happen?"

"Um, yeah." I know she'll never believe that nothing's wrong.

"Quickly, Samantha," Elijah urges. "I will carry you out of here if you do not find another way."

His insistence makes it harder to think. "I forgot that I have a paper due on Monday."

The worry leaves her face. "I thought we could go visit your father. And on the way, we can talk about all the fighting we've been doing lately. I know this hasn't been easy for you, and I know I've been on edge recently."

This surprises me. She never tries to resolve things like this. But then again, we've never fought this badly, either. Part of me really wants to say yes, wants to forgive her and believe there is an explanation for that medical bill. But I need to go with Elijah and figure out what this feather means. "I have to meet my group at the library." I turn toward the back door. I hate to leave, but I can't stay.

"Here I am trying to do something nice when really I should be the one mad at you for the way you acted. And I didn't say you could leave this house," she says, the hurt in her tone turning to anger.

I reach for the door handle and grab it. I take one look at her. She's fuming mad. I run.

"Don't you dare run from me!" she yells so loudly I hear her from the driveway.

I don't look back. It's too late to change my mind. But part of me worries that shrugging off Vivian's offer might have broken our relationship for good. My dad always softened me and Vivian, like a disk between vertebrae. Now we're just rubbing together in the worst and most painful way. Maybe we don't work without him.

"This way," says Elijah, keeping pace with my sprint.

CHAPTER FORTY-TWO

There's No Way Out

I wipe sweat from my forehead as I enter a small cobblestone street just outside town. I stopped running five blocks back, but my body didn't get the message.

"I'm in so much trouble."

"I could not risk you staying there," Elijah says.

"Okay, but *why*?" I stop, not wanting to leave this sleepy street, where I can talk to him.

"You called attention to yourself with that spell today. My fiancée's attention."

I feel exposed. "So she knows where I live now?"

"I imagine she already knew where you lived. After all, you live in the house that used to belong to me. What she would not have known is that you could do spells."

"You're saying I just announced myself as a threat?"

"I would think so."

If I wasn't a threat before and she was already casting spells, I might as well paint a target on my forehead now. "But you told me spirits can't do spells."

"They cannot."

"Am I missing something?"

He nods, looking uncomfortable.

"Sam?"

I whip around as Jaxon turns the corner. I'm partly relieved and partly terrified that he's seeking me out. Did he see me talking to Elijah? "You followed me?"

"I know you like this boy, but there is no time for this. I must tell you something," Elijah says, and I get the feeling I'm not going to like whatever it is.

Jaxon walks up to me. "Yeah, well, you saw someone die, then you levitated onstage. I find you doing spells with my mother, and then I see you running full sprint down the street. I think it makes sense that I followed you."

"You never told Lizzie about me biting John's hand, did you?"

"What do you think?"

"Jaxon, I . . . I'm sorry. I don't know what to say."

"Why don't you start by explaining."

"Samantha," Elijah says. I don't need to look at him to know this isn't a good idea.

"I don't have time." It's the most truthful thing I can say.

"Why?"

"You wouldn't understand." I twist my fingers together.

Jaxon waits for me to continue. When I don't, he asks, "Why don't you trust me?"

My heart aches. "It's not that."

Elijah throws his hands in the air.

"Then why don't you tell me anything?" Jaxon asks. "I found out with the rest of the school these things happened to you. Even the Descendants knew more than me." I open my mouth, but he stops me. "Don't try to tell me they didn't. I saw their faces. Then, you believe Lizzie's lies about me.

They aren't even nice to you. Meanwhile, I do everything I can for you, and you shut me out."

I bite my lip. I completely misunderstood why Jaxon was angry with me. I can't help but agree with him. "I never meant to shut you out," I whisper.

"Then stop," says Jaxon.

Elijah paces. "The longer you delay, the more danger you are in."

Which means Jaxon is in danger being near me. "It's not safe for you to be here," I say.

Jaxon looks at the historic houses and quaint benches. "We are on a quiet street in an expensive neighborhood. *And* it's still light out. I don't really think it gets much safer."

I blush, embarrassed by how paranoid I sound. "I *know* that. I'm not suggesting the trees are gonna eat us. I'm saying that it's not safe for *you* to be with *me*."

"And again, I ask why." I've never seen Jaxon act like this. He's dead serious.

How do I tell him anything that will make sense to him? "I want to tell you; I just don't know how."

"Do you have feelings for me, Sam?" He takes a step toward me and my heart picks up speed. "I have to know. Because if you do, I will stand here fighting you all day until you let me in. But if you don't . . ."

I glance at Elijah, who grumbles unhappily and walks off a few feet to give me space. My instinct is to bolt. I'm impossibly nervous, and I'm not going to have this conversation in front of Elijah. But I can't ignore Jaxon's question. There's no way out.

"Sam? What are you looking at?"

My eyes meet Jaxon's with fear.

"Wait . . . it's here?" Jaxon asks.

"He," I correct him.

"Great. *He* is here?" Jaxon scans the street again and Elijah walks toward us.

"Yes, I am here. Trying to keep her safe. Not attempting to discuss my feelings for her while she is quite obviously distressed," Elijah snaps at Jaxon.

"It's not his fault; he doesn't understand," I say to Elijah before I catch myself.

"What did he say to me?" Jaxon asks.

"Go home, Jaxon, before you cause her harm," Elijah says.

"Sam?" Jaxon takes a step forward, not shying away from this uncomfortable situation.

I want to cry. It's not like I can lie; Elijah's standing next to me. "He said for you to go home before you cause me harm." I cringe at every word. And by the way Jaxon's face falls, I know I shouldn't have said them.

"Is that how you feel?" Jaxon asks quietly.

It's more complicated than that. But if I say that, he'll stay. It takes all my will to say, "Yes."

Jaxon nods, and his eyes glisten. "I guess that's my answer." He waits for me to say something else, anything else. After a few moments of silence, he walks away.

"Jaxon! I'm sorry." Pushing Jaxon and Vivian away within the same hour is killing me. Maybe I *am* the problem. Maybe Lizzie's right. All I do is hurt people.

He stops and starts to turn toward me, but changes his mind. He shakes his head and continues down the street. With every step he takes, the ache in my heart grows bigger.

I look at Elijah. "I know," he says, and wraps his arms around me. I bury my face in his chest and cling to his shirt. He smells like old books. "I just could not put you at further risk. It is safer for everyone, including him, if he goes home."

I nod against his body. "What did you want to tell me?"

Elijah holds me for a second longer before releasing me. "While you were with Mrs. Meriwether, I searched again for diary entries."

"You found something, didn't you?"

He nods. "One in the late seventeen hundreds that referenced a woman living with crows in the woods. The writer claimed that no one would walk past her house for fear of being cursed."

"Wouldn't she have been over a hundred by the late seventeen hundreds?"

"That is precisely what worried me. So I looked in the eighteen hundreds. I found two more mentions of her. Then one in the early nineteen hundreds."

How could people write about the same person over hundreds of years? "Maybe they were just repeating stories they heard from other people and never actually saw her."

Elijah pushes his dark wavy hair back. "What gives me pause is that the descriptions were extremely similar."

"What are you saying, exactly? That you think she's lived for hundreds of years? That's impossible." My words don't hold the conviction I'd like. I just did a spell with my next-door neighbor, and my best friend's a spirit—who I've kissed. The word "impossible" holds a much looser definition than it did in NYC.

"Is it impossible?" Elijah asks. I can only imagine how freaked out he must be.

I fidget. "If she's casting spells, she has to be alive in some way, right?"

"I think we can assume definitively that she is the unknown enemy Cotton was referencing in your Burroughs vision."

The blood drains from my face. "Cotton said I was paying attention to the wrong things. But why wouldn't Cotton just tell me your fiancée was my secret enemy instead of all these coded messages?"

"Names have power. He was trying to protect you or himself, I imagine."

If Cotton's frightened of her, what does that mean for me? I glance around the street, feeling like a sitting target. "Do you think she's out to get me because of Cotton?"

"Potentially."

"But my dad's name was written alongside mine." If she gave people that rash, I bet she's responsible for other things. The pastries that got everyone sick? John's death? "So now there are two things that can hurt my dad . . . the curse *and* your fiancée."

"I think they are one and the same. I am just not sure where the connection lies." A car door slams shut, and I jump.

I step closer to Elijah, lowering my voice to a whisper. "How do we find her?"

"We go to a café or some public place where you are at less risk, while I try to make sense of it all."

"No way. I'm not hiding out drinking a latte while you go looking for her."

"If I can speak with her, I may be able to persuade her to stop." He looks every bit as determined as me.

"No. Cotton and your fiancée were at the top of the food chain." I picture my "How to Hang a Witch" chart. "Cotton couldn't have started the witch hysteria without her, or she without him. Oh man, and my coming to Salem inadvertently started the chain of deaths. I would bet money that she's involved in these deaths and accidents, too. Probably *not* inadvertently. And if we were the ones to start it, she and I are the only ones who can stop it." The moment I say it, I know I'm right. Susannah said I was the key to solving this. Alice thinks I'm the problem. They might both be right. The thought makes me dizzy.

"I dislike that idea greatly." Elijah's upset only confirms my suspicions.

"I'm not wild about it, either." That's an understatement. "But Cotton could've stopped the accusations all those years ago if he'd tried, which would've saved the lives of innocent people. If everything's as parallel as we think, I'm the one who needs to try." As I speak, my theory makes more sense to me.

He frowns. "Do not forget you are the witch in this version of the pattern."

"Your fiancée lost everything. If she wanted to blame anyone for the Trials, Cotton would be a likely choice. What would be a better revenge than to brand a Mather as a witch and make that Mather look responsible for all the deaths?"

"How could Cotton have stopped my fiancée?"

"Expose her as a fraud. Uncover her lies," I say. In which case, that spell I did was a step in the right direction. I look at the spell book on the bench a few feet from where we stand. "But in order to do that, I need to know where she is."

Elijah follows my eye line. "A spell is not a good idea, Samantha."

"What choice do we have? If I need to stop her, I can't stand here waiting for her to take me by surprise."

"It is not safe," Elijah says definitively. "We do not know enough yet."

More than anything, I want to agree. But if I don't track her down, I will continue to be behind the horse, like Cotton said. "Elijah, we need to come up with a plan. And then I need to try one of those spells."

"What plan? We do not know what we are planning for." His voice deviates from its evenness. "I do not want you to get hurt."

My heart thuds. "If I die, then I guess we'll be spending lots of time together."

He grabs my arms and holds on to me as though he will shake the idea out of me. "Do not ever say that, Samantha. You have your whole wonderful life ahead of you. You cannot imagine all the experiences you will have. I would never wish this upon you so young."

"But how can I have those things if I don't stop your fiancée?" I match his passionate tone, and my voice rises. "And how many other people won't get to live their lives if I don't break this curse?"

"You will break it. You just need to be reasonable." He pulls me forward a couple of inches.

Our faces are close together. "John's already dead. Susannah's next. Not to mention all those others. I can't know that I had the answer and didn't take action. I would never be able to live with myself. I'm not going to be like Cotton, sit back and watch it unfold." I'm getting more determined by the minute. I have no desire to meet Elijah's fiancée. But I'll be damned if I'm going to miss my chance because I'm too cautious.

"You do not know what she is capable of." He pulls me closer again, like he's trying to shield me with his body.

Suddenly his role in this curse makes sense. "You know the enemy this time, Elijah."

He looks at me questioningly.

I steady my voice. "You couldn't protect Abigail because you didn't know who the enemy was. Now you're trying to protect me. Difference is, we know who we're fighting."

His eyes go wide, and he releases me. He sits down on the bench. "I killed myself last time I failed."

I sit down next to him, my voice gentle. "I can't do this without you."

He turns toward me. For a few seconds we're quiet. His gray eyes are big and sad. "I cannot live the rest of eternity knowing I failed you, too."

My breath catches in my throat. "You could never fail me. . . ."

He sighs. "Okay, Samantha. I will bend to your will."

I exhale. But my victory's short-lived. Police sirens blare in the distance. Elijah blinks out. I stand, examining my surroundings, and realize Ms. Edelson is peering through a curtain from a second-story window. When we make eye contact, she shuts the drapes. How could I be so stupid as to stay in one place for so long? It must look like I'm arguing with myself.

Elijah blinks back in. "Run!"

I take off down the cobblestones.

"Turn right," he says, and I duck into an alley. The police sirens get louder. "The park."

I sprint onto the sidewalk, almost knocking down a pedestrian. I quickly check the traffic and run across the street into a patch of trees. I stop by the trunk of a big maple. The police car passes us and heads in the direction we came from.

"You need to get off the street," Elijah says. "That officer had a notepad full of comments about you."

"Wait, why?"

"I did not stay to find out. We need to get you to Mrs. Meriwether's."

"What!" I stare at him in horror. "No."

"Can you think of a better location to do a spell?"

CHAPTER FORTY-THREE

What the . . . ?

"I will unlock the door," Elijah says as I crouch behind a bush in Mrs. Meriwether's front yard. I grip the spell book to my chest and scan my house. Vivian's car is in the driveway and the lights are on. Elijah opens Mrs. Meriwether's front door.

I bolt across the lawn in the fading light, my heart pushing against my rib cage. I take the two entrance steps in one jump, clumsily barreling through the doorway. I close it behind me with a bang.

"Hello?" says Jaxon from the living room. I want to run at the thought of facing his hurt look. Within a few seconds he's standing in front of me.

"Hey," I say, looking at my feet.

"Did you just break into my house?"

"I didn't want anyone to see me. But I didn't mean to break in." It's the truth.

"Why do you care if someone sees you come into my house?"

Elijah frowns. "Time is passing quickly."

I'm silent for a few seconds, unsure how to answer either of them. "Well, I . . . ." I run through the various explanations, but they all suck.

There is only one thing I can say. "I should never have believed Lizzie's lie. I know I made you uncomfortable with all the spell stuff and the auditorium. And then again in the street today. I'm really sorry. I so want to tell you something that will explain it all . . . and convince you that I never meant to hurt you, that I care. I just haven't sorted it out myself yet."

"You care?" I've never seen Jaxon vulnerable before. It makes me feel so much worse.

"Samantha," Elijah warns. I give Elijah a please-give-me-a-minute look. I know he's afraid that I'll get lost in this conversation, but I don't want to hurt Jaxon any more than I already have.

I nod. "Yes."

Jaxon's face relaxes slightly. "As long as I know that, I can deal with the rest of it. Even the ghost." He says the last part unhappily.

Elijah scowls. Guilt overwhelms me as I look from one to the other. *How did I get myself into this mess?*

"Samantha?" Mrs. Meriwether enters the front hall. "I was worried."

I tense. "I'm sorry I ran off."

"When I saw that feather, I . . . Well, to be perfectly up-front, the idea that your grandmother was correct about the crow woman has been haunting me all day."

I take a deep breath. "I need to track her down . . . the crow woman." Mrs. Meriwether nods as though she expected this. "And I could really use your help."

Jaxon's upset expression returns. "So you came here to apologize, huh?"

I've really botched this up. At this point, all I can do is hope he doesn't hate me.

"Jaxon, I'm gonna tell you the truth. No lies, no omissions. But I can't explain everything. There just isn't time. You're gonna have to believe me for now. Can you do that?"

His eyebrows push together, and he looks at his mother before answering. Maybe she talked to him? "Only if you promise not to shut me out like that again. I felt ridiculous."

I release my breath. "I promise." He's way more forgiving than I might be. "So . . . the reason I've been acting so crazy lately is 'cause I'm positive John's death was part of a larger pattern. Susannah is next. And I'm betting my dad and I are close behind."

Mrs. Meriwether and Jaxon exchange looks again. What did they talk about today?

"If you really think this, you need to go to the police," Jaxon says.

The mention of the police tenses me even more. Could Lizzie somehow be behind them coming after me? Susannah did say her family was well connected.

"This is one of those things you just need to trust me on," I say, and I can tell that Jaxon wants to argue.

"Dear, let's go to the kitchen and discuss what you need," Mrs. Meriwether says.

"Clever woman," says Elijah.

I nod, grateful for Mrs. Meriwether's support, and follow her down the hallway toward the kitchen. To my surprise, Jaxon comes as well.

"I swear I'm not on something," I say under my breath to Jaxon as we walk.

The beginning of a smile tugs at his lips. "Debatable."

"Are you sure you want to know all of this? It'll sound wacky."

"I saw you float in midair. If I can handle that, I don't think a spell is gonna make me faint." His voice is moving back toward its usual playfulness.

"Fine, but this is difficult enough for me to accept. If you laugh, I will knock you out."

Jaxon smiles. "I'm counting on it."

We walk into the kitchen, and Mrs. Meriwether clears some counter space. "Tell us your plan, Samantha."

Elijah paces, deep in thought.

I sit down at the island, and Jaxon sits next to me. "The only way I think I can stop the deaths is to find this crow woman and expose what she's doing. I'm pretty sure she's setting me up to take the fall for all the weird things that happened recently, and if I'm not careful, the deaths will get pinned on me, too." Lizzie's no help, either.

I put down the spell book and can tell Jaxon's impressed by it. It *is* kinda beautiful. I flip through the pages, looking for a location spell. When I land on one, Elijah reads over my shoulder. He grabs a basket from the counter and blinks out.

"So what's the reason this crow woman's out to get you?" At least Jaxon isn't making fun of me, even if his tone is doubtful.

"There's a lot of bad blood between her and the Mathers. I think she's enjoying branding me as a witch, and will try to hang me for it. Metaphorically, or whatever."

"Sam, you're in my kitchen with a *spell book* doing *spells* with my mother. Is there a different definition of a witch I don't know about?"

I open my mouth and close it again.

Mrs. Meriwether looks at the location spell. Her face is serious. "Your grandmother was searching for information about the curse before she died. She talked to me about it constantly. I even helped her do research."

I knew Mrs. Meriwether helped her. I figured it was one of the reasons she wasn't pressing me for details.

"One of the things she was most interested in was the location of the hangings, which Jaxon tells me you've already sorted out," Mrs. Meriwether continues.

So this is what they were discussing today. In my grandmother's last journal entry it said she found the address to the house in the woods and planned to go visit it. But since she didn't write any more, I figured she never did. "We actually got the idea from her journal."

"Yes, well. One evening, Charlotte came to my house ranting. She always had some odd ideas, but I never saw her this worked up. She kept calling your father, insisting she saw the crow woman, and that your family was in danger. She was so frantic that I could barely understand her. I thought she was unwell. I desperately tried to calm her."

"She went to the house in the woods, didn't she?" The hairs on my neck stand up.

"She died that night, Samantha." Mrs. Meriwether pauses. "I was fearful when you started asking me about the curse. You sounded so much like Charlotte. I had no idea you and Jaxon had found her research and went to that house. Even I couldn't find it. I wish . . ." She's too full of emotion to continue.

Of course Mrs. Meriwether couldn't find my grandmother's notes. They were in the secret study. What happened to my grandmother when she went to that house?

"I remember that night. My dad left me with Vivian while

he came here to make arrangements. He never told me what happened." I remember my dad's face when he came home, distant and sad.

"I blame myself," Mrs. Meriwether says, shaking her head. "I helped her, but I didn't always believe Charlotte. I thought because your grandmother dreamed of the crow woman so often, she was confusing dreams with reality. And when I saw that feather today, all I could think was that I was dreadfully wrong all these years. If I could go back, I—"

"It's not your fault," Jaxon says. "You can't even be sure what happened."

"I cannot change the past, I suppose." She pats her eyes. "But I can help you, Samantha. I won't doubt this story a second time. If there's a way to find her, it must be done."

Mrs. Meriwether's comments about believing in people all make sense now. "Jaxon's right. It's better that you didn't go to that house."

She stops patting her eyes. "Which ingredients will you need?"

Elijah blinks in with a full basket of plants and places it on the counter. Jaxon jumps when he sees it appear. Mrs. Meriwether's face brightens with the novelty of it.

"Well, there is the location spell, which Elijah already got ingredients for." I blush a little, not sure how to explain him. "But I think I need to do another one, too."

Jaxon can't hide his annoyance. "The ghost I told you about, Mom."

"How very curious!" Mrs. Meriwether says, examining her newly full basket and clasping her hands together. "He's here now?"

"Yeah," I say, making eye contact with him. *He's always here when I need him.*

"What other spell were you thinking of?" Mrs. Meriwether asks, looking around her kitchen for signs of Elijah. I can't help but enjoy her interest in him.

"Well . . ." If I were Cotton, I would have to expose the crow woman as a fraud. "I don't know much about her plans. Maybe something about clarity or truth?"

Elijah nods and comes to my side. I flip through the pages with all three of them leaning in. I move past all the good-fortune and beauty spells without reading the titles.

"Maybe something to fight her with?" Jaxon says as I flip past the healing section.

Elijah shoots Jaxon an icy glare. "I chose this book specifically because I did not want Samantha using spells that were intended to harm."

He picked this book for *me*? "She's three hundred years ahead of me in learning magic," I say to Jaxon. "If I try to battle her, I'll lose for sure."

Jaxon flinches at "three hundred years" but refrains from commenting. I keep flipping.

"A justice spell?" Mrs. Meriwether suggests.

"Hmmm." I flip the next couple of pages with excitement. " 'Inside Out'—it says it brings a person's inward self to the surface. Like a truth serum?"

"That sounds like a strong contender," says Mrs. Meriwether.

"She relies on manipulation," Elijah agrees. "Take that away, and you would succeed in disorienting her."

Both Jaxon and Mrs. Meriwether read the description. "Just pulling out what she knows and what she's planning would be great," I say.

"I should have some of that to use on you when this is all over," Jaxon jokes.

Elijah frowns.

"Samantha, don't you think you should do something for protection?" Mrs. Meriwether now flips through the pages herself.

"Yes," Elijah chimes in.

"I thought about that. I just don't know how much time I have." I don't bother to say that at any moment the crow woman could hunt me down. Ugh. Now that I've thought it, I feel guilty not warning Jaxon and Mrs. Meriwether. "There is . . . I need to be honest with you. I'm worried she might be looking for me, now that I revealed her spell." I glance at Elijah. He seems to know my intentions.

To my surprise, it's Jaxon who answers. "Didn't you just say she's trying to frame you?"

"Yeah. So?"

"So why would she storm my house to get you? Wouldn't that blow her whole plan?"

Holy crap. Jaxon's making some serious sense.

Mrs. Meriwether nods. "You're like family. There's no way we'd leave you to do this alone."

"Not too much like family," Jaxon says, which earns him another hard look from Elijah. Mrs. Meriwether points to a protection spell she found.

It's called "Shield and Protect." There's a drawing of a familiar knot next to the title. *I've seen it before. Where? Oh, right. It's the same as the pendant on Vivian's necklace. She lent it to me for the party. What the . . . ?*

My hands are suddenly cold, and my mouth is dry. Is that what kept me from getting that rash? Elijah takes a protective step toward me.

"Samantha? Are you okay?" Mrs. Meriwether asks.

"Do you know what this is?" I say, pointing to the drawing of the knot.

"Yes, dear. It's a witch's knot. It protects people and

objects. Charlotte always wore one," Mrs. Meriwether answers easily. "Why?"

"I just . . . I was wearing one the night everyone got the rash except me. It looked like an antique. Could it have been my grandmother's?" I stare at the book, trying to make sense of it.

"Your grandmother lost hers the night she died. But with the state she was in, it doesn't surprise me that it's in the house. Did you find it in her bedroom?" Mrs. Meriwether asks.

"Vivian lent it to me. She has my grandmother's old room. Do you think that's what stopped me from getting the rash?" Vivian could have said something about finding it. I was mostly in my own head at the time.

Elijah stiffens. "It may also be that my fiancée was at that party without my knowing it."

I shudder at the idea that I may have already met her.

"Can you get it? We could use it in this spell," asks Mrs. Meriwether.

I hesitate. Going into Vivian's bedroom does not sound awesome. I glance at Elijah.

"Happy to oblige," he replies to my unspoken request.

"Elijah will," I say to Mrs. Meriwether.

She nods, and picks up a large wooden bowl. "Now I'm going to get those additional things from the garden. Jaxon, offer Samantha some food." Mrs. Meriwether turns and heads for the back door. Elijah blinks out.

"I'm not hungry," I say to Jaxon.

He looks down for a moment. When he looks back up, his expression is kind. "Sam, I . . . I honestly had no idea what you were going through. I mean, your father, people dying in front of you, and even though I'm having trouble believing it, this crow-woman thing. I shouldn't have come down on you for not including me. I seriously don't know how you're dealing with all of this."

"Thanks, Jaxon. But you were right. I do need to learn how to trust people more. I was so suspicious of you when we met, and you were sincerely trying to be nice."

Jaxon's cheeks turn slightly pink. "Actually . . . my mother kinda made me promise to go over and see you in the beginning. And to talk to you at school, too. Charlotte meant a lot to her. I told her you were gonna think I was some crazy stalker, but she wouldn't hear it."

My heart sinks.

Jaxon's pink deepens to a full blush. "Then I talked to you the day you moved in. You flat out refused my help and wiped your lip gloss all over me. Then I got to know you a little better and realized that you were smart and stubborn and fearless enough to stand up to anyone. At that point, she couldn't have convinced me to stay away from you."

I look down. "So you're attracted to girls who are difficult?"

"If that's what you are, then, yes." There's not the usual humor in his tone.

Conflicted feelings creep through me. The back door opens, and I'm grateful for the distraction. I stand and grab the chowder pot.

"Okay, which one first?" Mrs. Meriwether sets a full basket down on her counter.

"We should do the location one last. Just in case that somehow tells her I'm coming. So I guess the inside-out spell and then the protection one," I reply.

She removes greens from the basket while I read the

directions. She places the needed items in a small pile near the cutting boards.

Mrs. Meriwether joins me at the spell book. "It says to use one inch of water in the pot."

I put the pot under the faucet as Mrs. Meriwether reads on. "Jaxon, I need you to mince the sage as small as it will go." She hands him a knife and a bundle of dark green leaves.

He's not as fast as Mrs. Meriwether, but he's certainly skilled. I pause to watch him.

"I'll take the dill and coriander, if you want to start on the bachelor's buttons," she says.

"No problem." I grab the brilliant blue flowers and drop the petals into the water.

Elijah blinks in with the necklace. I push it into my pocket, and mouth "thank you."

I return to the spell book as Jaxon and Mrs. Meriwether dump ingredients into the pot. "Only the pansy petals left," I say, grabbing the deep purple flower from the counter.

Then all I have to do is pour five drops into the person's food or onto their skin for it to work. I'm sure that's gonna go over smoothly. *Hey, Elijah's fiancée, I know you hate me, but will you just hold still while I pour this liquid all over you?* Yup, should be a real breeze.

I look down at the bubbling leaves and carefully pull the petals off. As I drop them in, I clear my mind and repeat the words "Truth be known," three times. When the last petal lands, the mixture takes on an iridescent sheen. I really hope that means it worked.

I pull the necklace out of my pocket.

Mrs. Meriwether approaches me. "Charlotte's necklace . . ." She holds it gently.

Before I can ask her anything, sirens blare outside the

window. A car bounces up my uneven brick driveway. Elijah blinks out, and Jaxon and Mrs. Meriwether go to the back door. I follow them.

Car doors slam. I can make out faint voices but can't understand their words. Jaxon steps back inside. "Two officers headed for your door." He searches my face for an answer.

My stomach churns. I put my hands on my forehead. Is it Lizzie's doing or Elijah's fiancée's?

Worry lines wrinkle Jaxon's brow. "I'll check it out."

"Come," says Mrs. Meriwether, putting her arm around my shoulders. "Let's go bottle that spell and start on the next one. No sense in biting our nails off waiting."

CHAPTER FORTY-FOUR

Plan or No Plan

The few minutes Jaxon's gone feel like ten years. I clench my hands and stare at my feet. The back door slams, and my body flies forward toward the sound. Jaxon's footsteps are quick in the hallway as he heads back to the kitchen.

The bad news is clear by the tension in his jaw. "It's the Descendants. They're missing."

"What?" I yell. I knew something was going to happen to Susannah, but I wasn't expecting this. What if I'm too late? "Which Descendants?"

"All four of them."

"I have to talk to those cops." I move toward the door.

"Sam." Jaxon grabs my arm. "You can't. They're looking for you. They think you're involved in their disappearance. Something about a threat you made in front of Susannah's mother. And then ranting on the street, talking to thin air." He gives me a knowing look.

Mrs. Meriwether speaks calmly as she separates the

ingredients into piles. "Breathe. You need to focus. We must do the location spell."

She's right. I have to focus. I dart back to the spell book. "Jaxon, was there anything the police knew?"

He shakes his head. "They didn't say much." There's an edge in his voice. He's looking at me more seriously than he did before.

Mrs. Meriwether hands Jaxon a few greens to chop.

Elijah blinks back in. "Susannah, Mary, Alice, and Lizzie went missing this afternoon according to the policeman's notepad. They told their parents that they were going to Walgreens and would be back home in an hour."

"Wait, I wasn't supposed to meet them there until tonight. Why would they be there this afternoon?" Were they setting me up? Susannah wouldn't do that, would she?

Elijah raises a knowing eyebrow at me. "I cannot say."

"Maybe they got caught up in what they were doing and didn't go home? Or they were too far in the woods and the cops couldn't see them?" I would love to believe they aren't gone.

Mrs. Meriwether and Jaxon watch me talk to Elijah.

"I searched," Elijah tells me. "There is no sign of them other than Mary's Jeep in the parking lot."

"They've been missing for hours, then. Someone could already . . ." I don't finish that thought, because I don't want it to be true.

"The story of their disappearance has already begun to spread throughout the town. It is known that you are a main suspect. It is only a matter of time before the townspeople send out a search party for you."

I picture them lining up outside my house, screaming and waving torches.

Elijah looks uncomfortable. "Samantha, it is most likely a trap."

I pause. His fiancée has been messing with me all this time and I couldn't predict a single move. In fact, the things I've done to try to solve the curse only gave her ammo to use against me. "You think she knows I'll look for them?"

"I think she is counting on it. You were the only one there when John died. Then Lizzie accused you of murder at the assembly, and Susannah's mother claims you threatened her daughter. If she makes it appear that you were the responsible party for the Descendants' disappearance, the consequences will be great. You will be formally accused."

"If I don't track her down, I run the risk of someone dying."

I can't even send the police. She'd probably punish me by killing them slowly.

Jaxon stops chopping. "I'm coming with you, Sam. To find her."

I shake my head. "No. It's not safe."

"So you think I should just let you go do this dangerous thing by yourself? I'm coming."

I clench my hands so tightly that my knuckles turn white. There's no way I'm bringing Jaxon with me. And now there's also no way I'm getting out of here without a fight.

Mrs. Meriwether interjects. "Dear, we can't hear Elijah. Does he have information?"

"He said they went missing hours ago. I tried to warn Susannah the other day about the curse and the danger she might be in and her mother heard. That's why the cops came looking for me. If the crow woman was planning to set me up, this would be one way to do it." I grab a bunch of chives.

I chop as fast as my untrained hands will go. What if Jaxon follows me out of here? He'd just be one more target for her. I dump the cut chives in the pot and return to the book, but I don't continue with the directions. Instead, I flip back a few pages to a sleep spell. This spell might be the last straw. He might never forgive me. But putting him in danger is worse.

I skim the directions. For potent long-lasting spells, a potion is required. But to temporarily disarm someone, a series of symbols can be written. Elijah hands me a piece of paper and I copy the elaborate symbols. *Just in case,* I tell myself. I hand the paper to Elijah. Mrs. Meriwether walks toward me, and I flip back to the location spell as fast as I can.

"Only the rosemary left, and you'll have to put that in," says Mrs. Meriwether.

She grabs a handful from the basket. I move to the pot and close my eyes. I attempt to form the image of Susannah in my mind, but the vision that comes is of her hanging. I shake my head and try again.

Just her face. I just need to focus on her eyes and her hair. When I'm sure I can hold the image of her, I drop the rosemary into the pot. The green liquid sizzles, and I open my eyes. We all wait anxiously as black steam begins to form. No one breathes.

The steam rises slowly at first, then forms large puffs like exhaust from a coal-fueled train. It doesn't disperse like normal steam. Instead, it makes a cloud over the pot. We all lean forward.

Like the red drops did on the parchment, it twists and turns. The first shapes it makes are trees. I need something more specific. And why is it always those damn woods, anyway?

The trees part and branch out to form a path. At the end of the path, the black steam creates another shape—a house with broken windows. Any hope I had of the Descendants' disappearance being a mistake is extinguished like burning wood doused with water.

Jaxon is so much calmer than I am. "At least we know where that is."

Mrs. Meriwether grips her hands together.

That's the worst possible location—it's so isolated. "My fingerprints are in that house already." I grab the counter, hoping the solidness of the stone will steady me.

"We need to call the police," Jaxon says.

"No! You can't call the police. It'll put the Descendants at risk." I don't want them to suffer because I'm scared.

Mrs. Meriwether paces. "It's not a good idea, Samantha, to go to that house. We all need to think about this. I'm not sure that Jaxon's wrong."

They want to protect me, but I don't think they can. It's just a matter of time before Elijah's fiancée lures me in. I can't have more deaths on my head.

The doorbell rings and we all jump.

"Stay here, both of you," says Mrs. Meriwether.

Jaxon's eyes follow his mother with concern. I wish I could make this whole situation go away.

Elijah blinks in. "It is done. You should check on her."

My heart thuds. I run toward the front door. Jaxon follows, close by my heels. When we get to the hallway, Mrs. Meriwether is braced against the wall, holding the piece of paper with the sleep spell in her hand.

"This was left on the stoop." Mrs. Meriwether's volume trails off at the end of her sentence, like it's a real struggle for her to speak.

"Mom!" Jaxon takes one of her arms and I take the other.

"I'm okay. It's just . . ." Mrs. Meriwether yawns as we bring her into the living room. "I'm just so . . . tired."

We set her down on the couch. Jaxon shakes her, but her eyelids are heavy. He removes the spell from her hand and looks at it. I don't stop him. He, too, falls back on the couch.

"Sam?" he says in confusion, his voice heavy with drowsiness.

Elijah stands by the fireplace.

I look from Jaxon to Mrs. Meriwether and feel horrible. "Jaxon, I'm so sorry." I fight to steady my voice. "This is all my fault. I shouldn't have involved you guys. I never wanted . . ."

They both blink without responding. The recognition of what I've done appears in Jaxon's eyes. "You . . ." He starts the accusation but yawns instead of finishing it.

I breathe deeply and fight through my guilt. "Lay thee down and slumber take. A peaceful rest before thou wake."

Their eyes close, and I'm not sure if I'm relieved or horrified. I grab the spell from Jaxon's hand, tear it up, and throw it in the fireplace. The flames consume it.

"How long will they sleep?" I ask.

"Could be a few hours or a few days."

Am I a bad person? "Come on. Let's go. I don't want this to be for nothing."

I take one final look at Jaxon sleeping on the couch and run to the kitchen. I snatch up the small bottle of the inside-out spell and pull the knot pendant off my grandmother's necklace. No need to advertise my defense system. I drop the chain on the counter with a clang, and put the silver knot in my pocket.

I turn to Elijah. "Now we need a strategy. What can you tell me about her?"

Elijah's face is full of worry. "In the many years I have spent thinking about what happened, I have come to realize that control was the most important thing to her."

I focus all my attention on his words. I *need* this information.

"The one thing she could not control was my affection for my sister. I believe that was the reason she set out to ruin her. What she did not count on was that I did not care if the whole world turned against Abigail. Even if Abigail were the witch ringleader, I would have loved her the same. In fact, it only made me protect her more. It was the job I had dedicated my life to."

"She must've been furious when she saw that she couldn't come between you."

He nods. "When I stayed by Abigail's side, she doubled her efforts. And when Abigail did pass, my fiancée momentarily got what she wanted. I went to her for comfort. She became the only person of consequence in my world."

So that's what she was after. She didn't want to share him with anyone, even his sister.

"She almost succeeded in convincing me that it was a foolish accident that got out of control. Her lies were well spoken and calculating. But I could see in her eyes that she was secretly delighted Abigail was gone. I knew in that moment I could never be near her again." Elijah's eyes brim with pain.

I can't imagine the weight of that betrayal. And to know that he was the one who told her about Abigail's singing and her secret love in the first place. What a heavy guilt to carry around. And all these hundreds of years, he hasn't been able to escape it.

"Understand, Samantha, that if you take away her sense of control, you may be able to stop her. I believe it is the only way."

Elijah's strategy seems useful but super difficult to carry out. I'll have to do something big, something to take her by surprise. And more than that, it needs to be clever. "Is it enough to expose her as a fraud and get her to admit to her lies? One person knowing that the witch accusers were lying wouldn't have made a difference."

"The public has to know in order for the perception to shift."

"That house is in the middle of the woods. There's no way to make it public. Plus, I just knocked out the people who would believe me."

"Indeed."

Great, so I have to expose her publicly, but I also have to go to that house alone. "I hope there's a way I can convince her all by myself to stop what she's doing."

To my surprise, he reaches out for me, pulling me into his body. "I will be there with you," he says gently, his face bent down toward mine. I press into him, wanting to soak in the feeling of his arms holding me for even this brief moment. "I will do everything and anything to keep you safe." He flickers slightly.

"What was that?"

"Samantha?" Elijah's voice is strangely faint. He flickers again. The counter behind him becomes visible through his body.

My hold on him weakens. I grab at the air, but it doesn't

make a difference. He only fades faster. Elijah opens his mouth, but no sound comes out. He's barely visible anymore. Then all at once, he's gone.

"No!" I scream.

I scan the room for an answer, but no one's there, and everything's still. It was *her*—I just know it. I run for the front door. Plan or no plan, I'm going to get Elijah back.

CHAPTER FORTY-FIVE

Stunning and Vicious

I stop to slow my heart rate and examine the imposing trees before taking my first step into the pitch-dark woods. I never thought I'd come here alone.

I pull my cell phone from my hoodie and scroll through the icons until I land on the flashlight. I shine my phone at the forest floor. With each step into the darkness, the damp scent of fallen leaves gets stronger. I keep my eyes trained on the ground to avoid the full view of my surroundings.

A branch smacks me in the face. I touch my stinging cheek. The skin's raised, and I feel a few droplets of blood. My dream comes rushing back like a slap to the head. *In the dream where I scratched my cheek, I saw . . . a noose and a crow.* Sweat forms on my palms. Cotton knew this was going to happen.

I point the light in front of me again and force myself through the trees. What does it mean that he knew? That it's fated to happen? If it's fated, how can I stop it? I could just be playing into the pattern, contributing to another century of deaths.

Ahead of me a light flickers. *The house.* I crouch down and cover my phone with my hand. I'm about to shut it off when I notice the camera icon. I press the video option, and my shoes, surrounded by dark leaves, appear on the screen. I pull out Bradbury's business card from when he questioned me and snap off my phone case. I tuck the card against the back of my phone before putting the case back on. My conversation with Elijah about public opinion plays in my thoughts.

"Even if I don't make it through this, I hope that someone finds this video and knows that I tried to stop her. And that I tried to save them," I whisper at my phone.

I creep toward the light and stop twenty feet from the house. The shadows on the black, decrepit walls look alive in the moonlight. I study a jagged window for clues of what awaits, but it's covered with vines.

I step forward and crunch a twig. Panic stabs me, and for a brief second, I hold my breath and listen to the rustling wind. If I don't do this quickly, I'll lose my nerve.

I run to the front door and fling it open with a bang. As my feet hit the old wooden floorboards, I take in the large room. It's not empty anymore. There's a single stool in the center and a large wooden table covered with jars, candles, and bowls to the right. The fireplace blazes. Near the left wall are four more stools—standing on them are Mary, Alice, Susannah, and Lizzie, nooses around their necks.

Their eyes are closed as though they're asleep. Is this a trick? There's no sign of Elijah's fiancée. *Don't you dare fall before I can get you down.* High heels click in the nearby hallway.

I stop so abruptly, it's as though I slammed into an invisible wall. A familiar wavy-haired shadow appears on the floor. "Vivian?"

She steps gracefully into the room, wearing a dark blue dress and a cloak, as though nothing's awry. I shake my head at her, trying to will her to disappear. Her body language suggests that she's in perfect control, the way it always does. In control . . . I gag. *No, I don't accept this. I don't want to know this.*

I stand frozen, feeling like someone sucker-punched me in the gut. *I know you; I live with you. You're supposed to be some awful stranger.*

"We were never people to indulge in our emotions. Why start now?" She moves toward the table strewn with spell ingredients, and her dress swooshes behind her.

I stare at the Descendants and bite my lip hard in an effort to stop the overwhelming sadness that threatens to come. There's no good way to get all four down at once.

Vivian turns to face me. "If you try to help them, you'll regret it." The door slams.

I don't look at her. Maybe I can drag that other stool over and slip the ropes off their necks. I take a step toward them. The stools start rattling and the girls' feet vibrate on top of them.

"No!" I yell, looking straight at her now. Vivian was never one to make idle threats. I back away, and the stools stop shaking. *Vivian is Elijah's fiancée. Vivian knows witchcraft. Vivian isn't Vivian.* The idea could choke me. Why did Elijah never recognize her? And where is he? Did she do something to him?

Vivian sorts spell ingredients with the self-assurance that comes through practice.

As I watch her here, in what is clearly her element, my

mind struggles to make sense of this. What does it mean for my entire childhood? What does it mean for the time we've been in Salem? "Did you cause that rash?"

She nods.

"And you killed John?"

She stops breaking apart dried leaves. "Obviously."

"Now what? You'll kill these girls and make it my fault, too?" I can't hide the hurt in my voice.

"'Hang' would be more accurate. And that's up to you."

I dig my nails into my hand to keep myself from having a breakdown. "I thought Elijah would be here."

She pauses.

I want to hurt her. I want her to feel just a fraction of what I'm feeling. "Oh, wait. He killed himself to get away from you."

Anger flashes in her eyes. She moves away from her herbs and grabs my chin with her hand. Her nails dig into my face so hard, I'm sure she'll break the skin. "I warned you once— you don't want me for an enemy."

I set my jaw and stare back at her. She releases me with a push, and I land on the floor.

"This is a business arrangement, Sam. Don't cry. Don't beg. Don't instigate. If need be, I'll mute you."

I stand, and rub my jaw where her hand was.

Vivian examines the sleeping Descendants. "I'm going to give you a choice." Vivian wiggles her fingers, and the stools begin to dance, one after the other.

The girls open their eyes. Confusion, then panic, washes over them as they realize they have nooses around their necks. They desperately try to steady themselves. Mary screams.

Vivian looks at me pointedly. "Which one should we hang?"

The word "we" makes me sick. I look at Lizzie and immediately feel guilty about it. Alice locks eyes with me, her fear quickly turning to accusation. When we did the clarity spell, their ancestors were telling me about their hangings. Cotton didn't stand up for them. If I have any hope of breaking this chain of accusation and hanging, I have to change that. "Me," I whisper, and the word sticks. "I choose me."

Susannah shakes her head. "Samantha, don't."

Vivian's expression goes dark. "You would hang for someone who threw a rock through your window with DIE written on it?"

This catches me off guard. So it *was* Lizzie. And Vivian knew?

"Of course, she's been punished," Vivian says, and by the way she flaunts those words I know I'm not the only one meant to hear them.

Lizzie's eyes widen. "Punished? Throwing a rock does not equal killing my cousin and paralyzing my brother!" There's a hysterical edge to her voice. What did Vivian say or do to these girls before I got here?

Vivian flicks her wrist, and Lizzie bends forward in pain. Her footing becomes wobbly as she strains against the rope. In a few seconds, she will slip from the stool. My stomach turns.

"Stop! I choose me! Please stop!"

The stools settle abruptly. "Fine, Sam. If you want to hang, then that is exactly what you'll get." Her voice is angry. *I don't understand this at all. What is she after?*

I face Vivian. "That rock wasn't even directed at you."

"Indirectly, it was."

Mary sobs, and Vivian wrinkles her nose. "Continue to

make that sound, and I'll tear your vocal cords out." Mary's cheeks pale and her mouth closes.

I make eye contact with a fuming Alice, and Vivian returns to her spell ingredients. I can't bear to look at Susannah. Vivian knows I've been spending time with these girls, and now she's manipulating me with them.

Vivian lifts a cloth-wrapped book off the table. She unwraps it like it has great value. It's an old leather-bound journal. When she puts it down, I can just make out the feather on the cover.

"When you bring someone back to life, Sam, you need a personal item of theirs."

My eyes fix on the journal. Elijah told me they had a matching set. *I thought this was about revenge. This is about bringing him back to life? Did she lure me here to be part of her spell?* The moment I think it, the horrifying truth sets in. She didn't drag me by my hair because she must need a willing participant. It's the only way baiting me with the Descendants makes sense.

"This is why we moved to Salem," I say quietly. Everything I knew about my world is crashing down around me.

She opens a jar of black powder and pinches some with her fingers. "Don't convince yourself this is personal. This spell took lifetimes to perfect, and you just happen to be the one here for it."

No one spends years spinning a false relationship if any schmo off the street would do. This *is* about me specifically. But why? Because I'm a Mather? If I'm the key to bringing Elijah back to life, I could also be the key to unraveling her plan. "How did you figure out the spell?"

For a split second she looks up at me with curiosity, like I've said something right. She places a few dried herbs into a worn wooden bowl. "I first succeeded by reversing the death of a crow back in the seventeen hundreds. I didn't know then that breaking the barrier of death would give me such a great reward—my eternal life."

It's as though she were explaining the latest fashion. The familiarity of her voice stabs at my thinning composure. "Why didn't you bring him back to life, then?"

"I tried." She stops her mixing.

I move closer to the table to inspect the journal.

She sighs. "It took me centuries to figure out that the reason I could bring that bird back to life was because I was the cause of its death."

But she was the cause of Elijah's death, too, at least indirectly. There's something I'm missing. She watches me, waiting for me to figure it out. The Descendants watch me, too.

She lifts a small knife. "Give me your right hand."

I stick my hands in my hoodie pockets and shake my head.

She raises an eyebrow. "Do you imagine for a moment that I won't make you?"

I reluctantly take my right hand out. My left grips the pendant.

Vivian places my hand over a small bowl. "Repeat these words: 'I give my blood. I welcome the knife. The soul I took, I call to life.'"

I know I shouldn't. My gut screams at me not to. But if I refuse, she will kill the Descendants. I don't doubt that. I repeat the spell. Vivian pulls the knife easily over my palm. The blade slices into my skin, and I choke back a whimper. My blood flows in a steady stream into her bowl.

"Do you know what the cause of Elijah's death was?" she asks.

I force myself to think through the pain. If Vivian wasn't the direct cause, then it was the town, it was . . . "The Trials?" I ask through clenched teeth.

She smiles.

She and Cotton couldn't have started the Trials without each other. That's why she needs a descendant from Cotton Mather to bring him back. And I just said the words that confirmed my part in her spell. The room spins, and I look away from my hand.

Why me instead of some other Mather?

All the blood drains from my face. I bet she tried other Mathers but it didn't work. Maybe even my grandmother. The past clicks into place at a sickening speed. She dated my dad to build trust. When she figured out he wouldn't willingly return to Salem, she put him in a coma. Then I came here willingly. To Salem, to this house in the woods. I offered myself in the place of the Descendants.

She drops my hand, and I pull it to my body, trying to stop the bleeding and trying to shield myself from the intensity of the betrayal. My bottom lip trembles and I bite it. I can't get lost in my feelings right now or I won't be able to think clearly. I need to do something she won't expect. I steal a glance at the journal.

Vivian picks up a jar of red powder and walks toward the center of the room. I pull out the protection knot, hiding it in my fist. She opens the jar and starts slowly pouring the powder out to form a large circle on the floor around the stool. A noose hangs above it.

I wait until her back is turned and slip my hand behind me to find the edge of the book on the table. I attempt to push the pendant under the leather cover of Elijah's journal, but it's difficult to do with one hand. Any second, I'll be in her line of vision again.

"You put the nooses in my uncle's store, didn't you?" Alice asks.

Vivian glances toward the girls just as I get the pendant securely in place. *Thank you, Alice.* I yank my hand away from the journal. With a look, Mary sends a silent, terrified plea for Alice not to antagonize Vivian.

Vivian puts down the powder and takes a step toward the girls. "I thought I made it clear—"

I know that tone. I can't let her hurt them. "What if I tell you I changed my mind about being part of your spell?" I reach for the bowl she put my blood in.

She turns back in my direction. Her eyes are dangerous. I don't break eye contact.

She approaches me so fast, it's as though she flies across the floor. She grabs my cut, outstretched hand and squeezes it. "Then I'd tell you that I can always torture your father until you agree again."

Her nails dig deeper into my open wound, sending shooting pains up my arm. My knees get weak. "Okay. I agree." She doesn't let go. "I agree!"

She releases my cut hand. "I had a suspicion you might feel that way."

She's too angry. What am I missing here? I nurse my bleeding palm. She eyes me for a second before she returns to forming her circle. I hope like hell the protection knot buys me a little time.

Vivian mutters in a language I don't recognize. The air shifts around her, and her clothes move as though she's caught in a strong wind. Her hair darkens and grows. Her face becomes younger, eighteen maybe. Her blue eyes turn light brown, and they tilt at the corners. She shrinks until she's shorter than I am, and her curves soften, giving her a much slighter frame. She almost appears dainty. *Ann.*

She shakes her arms and looks at me. I believe she interprets my shock as approval, because she wears a smug expression. She runs her hands through her waist-length waves. She's stunning and vicious. No wonder Elijah fell in love with her.

CHAPTER FORTY-SIX

The Witch of Salem

The transformed Vivian kicks off her high heels, and her cloak slips to the floor. She stretches like a cat. "Much more comfortable." Even her voice is different.

The Descendants are having the same stunned reaction that I am. Mary's mouth is agape.

Vivian walks around the stool and circle, chanting the words of a spell with new confidence. The air flickers in the circle. *Elijah!* I move toward him as he materializes.

He looks from her to me. His eyes fill with dread. "Samantha, you are bleeding."

"Elijah . . ." I take another step toward him.

She lets out a sigh of relief when I say his name. "See, that's one thing I could never do. I can't see spirits . . . but you can."

Elijah tries to step out of the circle, but he can't cross the line. He struggles against it. *He's trapped.*

"And if you can't see them, you can't do spells on them.

You must know where a spirit is in order for it to work." She says this part slowly and deliberately.

So I'm the Mather she chose because I can see spirits? My tiny happiness from knowing that Elijah's okay disappears. She heard me talking to him in the foyer. She even invited me out for a celebratory dinner. *It's my fault.*

Vivian faces the circle. She fidgets in a way I've never seen before, like a nervous girl. "I *am* sorry I kept you in limbo for so long, my little bird. I hope you'll forgive me."

Elijah's face stiffens. She glides back to the table.

I walk toward him. "I'm so sorry," I whisper.

"It should be me apologizing to you," he replies, and his eyes contain a deep sadness.

I reach my hand out, and it passes easily through the circle's invisible boundary. *It must only trap spirits.* My fingers touch his.

"Give me your hands," Vivian commands from behind me.

I glance over my shoulder; she holds a slender rope. *Not good.*

"Run, Samantha. Get out of here," Elijah pleads.

He doesn't understand. I mouth the words "I can't."

Vivian touches my back and pain slides down my legs. I scream and pull away from her.

"Hands!" she repeats.

This time, I listen. She yanks at the rope as she wraps it around my wrists, tying my hands behind my back. The rope's pressure makes my palm bleed less, and the warm liquid stops running down my fingers.

"Get on the stool." Her eyes linger on the circle before she walks back to the table.

My heart pounds so hard that I fear it'll break free of my chest. I step into the circle and onto the first rung of the stool, trying to balance without my hands. Vivian bends down behind the table and grabs the edge of an old gray wool blanket. Elijah helps me steady myself.

"Left pocket," I whisper to him as Vivian drags the blanket toward the circle.

He pulls the small potion bottle out of my hoodie. I lift my right foot onto the top of the stool, and he supports me as I take the final step.

Vivian turns to face us. She mumbles something, and the noose slips itself over my head. The rope is rough against my neck. My hair sticks to my sweaty face and I spit it out of my mouth. I look at the lumpy blanket, and my stomach churns.

"Turn fully toward her," Elijah says. "Do not let her see your hands."

I adjust myself so that my arms are hidden. Only Elijah and the Descendants can see them.

"I will catch you," Elijah says.

I swallow. Hanging is one of the worst things I can imagine.

She stirs her large bowl as Elijah loosens the rope around my wrists. Not so much that it comes off, but enough so I can slip it off. He places the inside-out potion bottle in my uncut hand.

She takes one final look at me, challenging me to change my mind. I no longer have to imagine how those people in the Witch Trials felt looking down at their friends who had accused them. People they had known their entire lives. "How could you?" I ask, and my voice wavers.

She flicks her fingers, and the stool flies backward and out of the circle. My body drops downward at a dizzying speed, and the rope scrapes against my neck, burning my skin. Elijah's arms wrap around my thighs before my full weight hangs from the noose. I cough and sputter.

"Relax, Samantha, or you will not be able to breathe! If I lift you any higher, she will know I am supporting you and she will hurt you. Please, stop fighting. Please!"

I gasp for breath, but it comes out as more of a wheeze.

"Samantha!" Susannah's voice yells from behind me.

Vivian stares at the blanket and begins to chant. "Life and death a circle make. What's alive must wither, and what's dead shall wake." Elijah flickers. His grip loosens ever so slightly, and the rope tightens around my neck.

She repeats her words. The third time, I actually understand them. *Reverse life and death? Wait.* Does that mean the spell might work on her, too? If I can get my hands on it, I can use it against her.

She cuts her own finger and lets her blood mix with mine. Then she pours our blood into the larger bowl with the rest of the potion. Elijah flickers more dramatically.

"I fear that I cannot hold you much longer," he says, straining.

The wool blanket starts vibrating next to us, and then its corners fly open. From inside it, a skeleton sits straight up. I want to close my eyes, but they refuse to do anything other than watch the whole horrible thing play out. I gag and the rope cuts into my skin. There are gasps of surprise from the Descendants, behind me.

"How dare you!" Elijah says.

The skeleton moves toward Elijah as though Vivian's controlling it with strings. It fits itself into his body and wraps around me where his arms are supporting my weight. Vivian's smile vanishes when she realizes where Elijah actually is. Her nails gouge the table.

There's no time left. I slip the rope off my wrists, and the fibers prick my open cut. I pop the top off the tiny bottle containing the inside-out spell.

Vivian lifts the bowl of potion she's been mixing over Elijah's journal. She allows three drops to fall on the leather. Nothing happens.

"Now," I whisper, and drop the rope. Elijah and his skeleton lift my head out of the noose.

She puts down the bowl and stares at the journal like it betrayed her. I'm on the floor in one swift movement and running toward her with the bottle of potion. She lifts the journal cover, and the protection knot falls out. Her mouth opens.

"You!" she shrieks, throwing her hand in the air and making a fist.

Whatever spell she's using makes my heart tighten and burn like it's being ripped out of my chest. I scream and force myself to keep moving through the intense pain.

"You'll suffer before you die!" she yells.

It takes every molecule of my will to lunge forward and fling the open bottle at her. My movements are jerky, and the bottle spins in the air, spraying us both. She gasps as the potion hits her skin, and she drops her hand. The pain in my chest subsides. I suck air into my aching lungs.

She mutters spells at a dizzying rate as her hair turns white and her skin wrinkles. In a matter of seconds, the inside-out spell strips the youth from her entirely. She becomes a seventy-year-old version of herself. I focus on her spell bowl. I'm at the table in two strides. I reach for it, but she's faster and pulls it away.

"No!" I yell, searching for something to use against her. I grab the protection knot and Elijah's journal in one hand.

And in my other, I take a lit candle. I hold it near the journal so that the flames almost touch the old pages. It all happens so fast that for a couple of seconds there's complete silence while we assess each other.

One of her hands makes circular movements over her face. Streaks of brown return to her hair, and her skin is younger in places. But the transformation's only partial, like our spells are fighting each other.

"I had no idea you could make a spell like this," she says. "I guess I have those nitwits to thank." She looks confused. One of her partially wrinkled hands flies to cover her mouth. "Why did I say that? What is this? What did you do to me?" Her voice is muffled through her fingers.

"What did *I* do to *you*? You're my goddamn stepmother and you want to hang me!" It feels worse saying it out loud, as though it makes it more real somehow. I try to focus on the fact that she doesn't look like my Vivian. Some part of me wants to believe she isn't.

We face each other from opposite sides of the table, her with the potion, and me with the journal and the candle. We both have something the other wants.

Her eyes are piercing and defiant. For the first time since the physical transformation, she reminds me of my Vivian. "And you want to kill me with my own spell."

The truth of her words stuns me. "Yes, I do. Oh, holy hell. Why did I say that out loud? No! The truth serum's messing with me, too."

"You will give me that journal one way or the other." She points a finger at me, and my arm holding the journal moves toward her.

I clench the protection knot and focus. "Not if I can use this protection knot." I pull backward and bring my hand to a stop. "This spell blows. It's supposed to tell me your plans, not have me tell you mine."

The room's silent. Not even the Descendants make a noise. I glance at them. "Lined up in a row, you remind me of the group hangings at the Trials. Wait." I shift my focus back to Vivian. "You brought four of them. Why not one or two?" I bite my tongue to stop from talking. I realize I've overlooked something. "You've been the one killing them for centuries, haven't you? Just like you did in the sixteen hundreds."

"Yes."

"Why?" I blurt out. "They were the victims."

"They all need to go. The Trials killed my Elijah. I'm erasing them." She stamps her bare foot and mumbles under her breath.

My thoughts tumble over each other and out my mouth. "The pattern of deaths. You try to kill us all every time you think you've perfected the spell to bring him back, don't you? Maybe it's even part of the spell. No wonder all my relatives are dead. But how did you know Elijah would be in Salem?" I ask, half angry with her and half with myself for not being able to shut up.

"The moment you found Abigail's letters I knew he would come back to chase you off."

My eyes widen. "You were using me as bait."

She grinds her teeth together in frustration. "I knew that if I threw those clothes out of your armoire, you would eventually find the letters. I also knew he would hate you for being a Mather. A dark shadow staying in his sister's old room."

"It worked. He did hate me." I narrow my eyes, an expression I learned from her. "But he also hates you."

She screams low in her throat. "Enough!" She points a

finger at me. "Burn!" The flame from the candle redirects itself toward my body.

It singes my cut hand and I lose my grip on the candle. It falls to the floor, putting itself out. I pull the journal toward my chest.

"The knife!" yells Alice. I scan the table, looking for it.

I glance at Vivian, but she doesn't advance. Instead, she reaches her hand out and Alice's body starts twitching. Alice screams in agony. Her knees buckle under her.

"She's going to fall! Stop!" I yell at Vivian. I abandon the idea of the knife and run to Alice, whose back arches unnaturally. I slip the protection knot into her boot. Slowly her body relaxes and she regains her balance, but the look of horror remains in her eyes.

"You continue to choose them over me!" Vivian says behind me.

What does she mean? Before I can turn around, my neck tilts backward. My body flies to the ground and slams down so hard that all the wind whooshes out of my lungs. I gasp for air as my body slides across the wooden boards. A spell pulls me by my hair toward her. I brace the journal with one hand and my other hand clenches my hair.

I come to a stop and my head smacks into the ground. My waist is exactly on the circle line, pain radiating down my neck and along my spine. I attempt to stand but can't. It's as though I'm stapled to the floor.

Elijah bends down and brushes the hair back from my sticky face. His eyes are demanding. "You cannot stay in this circle or she will kill you. I told you once you are powerful. You need to focus."

Tears blur my vision. I don't know what he thinks I can do—I just barely learned how to cast a spell a few hours ago. I try to lift my head, but it's no use. I'm not changing things or bringing peace, like he thinks I am. *And I'm not more powerful than she is.* "I gave Alice my protection knot." My voice is raspy from hanging. He flickers.

Vivian carries the bowl of potion. Her bottom lip quivers as she watches him sitting next to me. "You think she's innocent? Well, she's not! We're alike, she and I. We both kill to get what we want!" Her eyes are wild.

We're alike. Her words ring in my ears—*We both kill to get what we want.* How am I better than Cotton? I tried to kill her.

"I vowed never to speak to you again," Elijah says to her, struggling to talk while under her spell. "Do you know why?"

She leans close to him, as though she can only barely make out his words.

"Everything beautiful in you died centuries ago," he continues. "Now you live to crush and abuse. How many people have you killed? All the spells in the world cannot make you beautiful again."

She stiffens. "I'm doing this all for you."

He shakes his head. "No, you are doing this to control me. I will give you a chance now to do the right thing. The only one I will ever give you. If you stop hurting these girls, I will stay here with you and do as you want. But if you continue, and you harm Samantha further, I will do more than despise you. I will forget you entirely."

She pauses. "That's the problem, Elijah. You can't do what I want." Her voice wavers. "You look at her the way you once looked at me. You love this girl."

Heat seeps into my battered cheeks. She grips the bowl of potion until her knuckles turn white, waiting for Elijah to deny it. A tear runs down her cheek. She steps toward me. More of her hair turns brown, and her skin gets younger. My spell's wearing off. She holds the bowl above the journal on my chest and spills a few drops onto it.

Some of my life force is yanked out of my chest. My mouth opens, and I wheeze. Elijah flickers violently. The blood she poured on the journal lifts into the air and swirls around him, attaching itself to his skeleton. He falls to the floor, his head near mine. He grabs on to his arm where the blood is forming veins and grits his teeth.

"I will make you remember how you once felt about me," Vivian says through her tears. "I will erase her from your memory."

"You cannot cover truth with lies," he says, his voice pained. He tries to stand, but his new body won't support him.

She makes sure she has my attention and points at Alice. The pendant I put in her boot flies out and onto the floor, rendering it useless. "I'm sick of your protection spells. How will you protect your father when you're dead?"

Protection spell on my dad? I never put a spell on my dad. Did I? Elijah tries to say something, but his voice is too strained.

"I always wondered if it was my fault. If the spell I killed your mother with somehow gave you these abilities." She pours a couple more drops of the potion on the journal.

My mother. My heartbeat slows. I barely have the energy to resist. My life is slipping away.

"But when you're gone, I'll make sure Charles suffers."

"No!" I scream.

An awful expression takes over her face. "When the police find you here, all evidence will point to you. I'll explain to your father how you lost your mind, how you killed these girls and took your own life. Before he dies, he'll think you're a monster."

She's going to take everything from me. Vivian curls her hand into a claw, and the Descendants squirm with pain.

"Please stop," Mary pleads.

Susannah whimpers. Above my head the noose dangles like in my visions. All my visions are coming true. I cut my cheek, Susannah will hang, and Vivian is the crow. Standing up for the Descendants wasn't enough. And if I give up now, I'm no better than any of the Salem townspeople back in the sixteen hundreds. *No. I refuse to die like this.*

Determination pulses through me and I push against her spell to lift myself off the floor. My veins bulge. I concentrate on my neck and head, pulling them with all my might. They lift an inch. Then another inch. Elijah's journal falls off my chest and onto the floor.

She watches me, genuinely confused. "Why is your face doing that? Who's helping you?" Her words are fast and jumbled.

I push again, harder. It's like the strings that make up her spell and secure me to the ground are snapping. I sit up. She drops her hand and lifts the bowl. I fling the journal out of the circle before another drop hits it. It slides near the fireplace.

Her eyes widen. "Cotton!"

She sees Cotton when she looks at me? I force myself out of the circle and immediately feel stronger. I run for the journal. She mutters a few words and my knees give out, hitting the floor with a bang.

"No," I say definitively, and use my hands to force myself back into a standing position.

The journal lifts into the air. I grab it as it whizzes past my head. It tugs against my hands, but I maintain my grip. She shrieks behind me, and her feet pound against the wood floor. I run for the fireplace.

I take only two strides before her nails scrape down my neck and pull at my shirt, choking my already sore throat. I throw the journal toward the fire, and it lands on one of the burning logs. We fall to the ground, her weight on my back. As my chin smacks onto the floorboards, the edges of the old pages catch fire. The taste of blood fills my mouth.

She pushes herself up, using my body as leverage to propel herself forward. I grab her dress and she comes toppling down again. She tries to stand, but I jump on her. I get one knee on either side of her waist and use her neck to smack her head into the floor.

She spits out a spell. Hot pain runs up my arms like they are being dipped in boiling water, and I lose my grip. Her hands shove me backward and I hit the floor. She moves toward the journal again, pulls it out of the logs, and tries to pat out the flames with her hands. But it's already fully alight, and burn marks appear on her palms.

I jump to my feet as the pain in my arms subsides. She frantically chants spells at the journal. I grab a heavy iron forked poker from an old set of fireplace tools and swing it. It connects with her head and she falls backward with a loud thud. A trickle of blood runs down her forehead.

I step over her, and her eyes meet mine. She brings her palm to her head and looks at the blood on her fingers. I lift the forked tool to hit her again.

"Cotton," she says once more, only with less force this time.

I freeze. The poker hangs above her in midair, ready to strike. *What did she say before?* We're alike, both killing to get what we want. My big plan turned out to be hunting and killing a witch. Beating her with a pitchfork. I thought I was breaking the pattern of the Trials, and here I am repeating it. And like Cotton three hundred years ago, I believe I'm eliminating evil.

A small smile forms on Vivian's lips.

"Hit her!" demands Lizzie.

I'm not Lizzie. I can't kill her. And if I do, I'll be continuing the curse. The poker lifts in the air, but it's not me doing it. Cotton stirs inside of me. *Maybe that inside-out spell had more consequences than I realized.*

"No," I say to myself as Cotton makes my arm take aim.

Vivian looks like she's won something. Susannah's stool flies out from under her. She drops. The rope makes a horrible snapping sound as it straightens and the beam creaks under her weight.

"Put this down!" I yell at Cotton as Susannah chokes. "I need to help her!" My legs won't move—Cotton and I are fighting for control over them.

"She has been killing our family for centuries—we must put an end to this," I say in a voice I don't recognize. It's a hybrid of Cotton and me, like we're both speaking at the same time.

"Sam, help her, please." Mary's voice is so thick with sobs it's hard to understand her. Mary's stool drops. *Snap, creak.*

Fear and helplessness swirl around me like a black fog as I watch Susannah and Mary hang. I fight my own body, but it won't budge. "They're going to die!" I plead with Cotton.

"Then stop this woman," he answers with my mouth.

Vivian's eyes sparkle with interest.

"You're not letting me," I say with such heaviness that I almost give way to my grief. "Don't you get it? She wants me to repeat the Trials. Prove that I'm like you."

"They can't breathe, Sam." Alice's voice is surprisingly

even. She's inching her stool toward Susannah so that Susannah can get her leg onto it. She's actually *doing* something. That is, until her stool flies out from under her. *Snap, scream.*

Vivian gloats and lifts her head off the ground. Blood drips into her brown waves.

"Kill her, Sam!" Lizzie shrieks. "She hurt my brother and your father. My *brother,* the one person I could rely on!" Her voice wavers as her deep sadness falls out of her like water from a broken vase.

Vivian shrugs, and Lizzie's stool drops, too. *Snap.*

Four girls hanging, the deaths of countless others, and my dad's safety all hovering before me like a rainstorm in the distance.

"I *will* save them," I say to Vivian, searching myself for every ounce of courage to follow through on my words.

Susannah rotates toward me on her rope, her hair falling into her face. Tears stream down her bright red cheeks. *You believed in me, Susannah. Elijah believed in me.* I close my eyes and tears seep through my eyelashes.

When I open my eyes again, I concentrate on the wood beam that holds the ropes. *I need to break it.* It's the only way to get them all down at once. I stand a little straighter, fighting my urge to give in to the blinding panic and the gasps of suffocation that fill the room. I picture breaking the beam in the center, splintering the wood. I throw all my terror and frustration at it, punching it with my mind. I gather every ounce of strength I have left and direct it at that old piece of wood. There's a small creak. My heart makes one deafening thud. *Is it working?*

Vivian turns toward the Descendants, then looks at me like a cat looks at a mouse. I push harder, faster. I hit the beam with my thoughts. There's a cracking sound, like the beam is holding too much weight. It buckles downward a bit. A force flings me backward a few feet.

Vivian stands. "I guess you *are* my daughter in some ways."

Her words tear at my most inner self. I use my grief to direct my energy more aggressively. There's a loud splintering sound, and the girls tumble to the ground gasping and coughing.

Vivian frowns.

I stare at her with more confidence. "It was Cotton's fault he didn't stop you three centuries ago. And I won't make that mistake again. But I won't do it by killing you," I say with our hybrid voice, and I can feel Cotton considering my words.

She twists her fingers, and it's as though a thousand needles are pricking me over and over. I want to tear my own skin off.

"Kill me? I was just a girl. He went off and had a life, wrote books about it. I had no life. Everything I had was taken from me." Her words feel raw and new, like she never wanted to admit them.

I fight to keep my thoughts clear with Cotton in my head. "That power and importance you thought you had by hanging witches was a delusion. You weren't rooting out evil. You and Cotton were misguided bullies, crushing the dreams and the lives of the people around you." As I speak, Cotton stops fighting me. He loosens his grip on my body and the stiffness slips away.

"After everything I've done for you . . . You have no loyalty!"

Everything she's done for me? That's how she sees it? To my surprise, it's Cotton who answers her. "I'm truly sorry for all

of your pain. But I'm not the cause of it anymore. You are."
Now it's me considering his words.

A high-pitched noise comes from her throat, and the forked poker lifts into the air above my head. I reach my hand toward it. It stops mid-swing. We stare at each other, both struggling to control the tool, both determined.

"Look at us. We're all trapped together, making the same mistakes over and over. You were right; we're not that different. I'm not good the way I once imagined. And you're not purely evil." For the first time, Cotton and I answer together.

The poker falls with a clang. She throws an arm in the direction of the Descendants, still bound and struggling to catch their breath on the ground. "They took your hair, and I sent them a warning with those pastries. They wrote *PSYCHO* on your locker, threw a rock through your window, and turned the damn town against you. So I gave them a rash. I showed them there were consequences."

What is she saying? Is she trying to tell me she did these awful things because of me? "You killed people."

"I was the *only* one defending you! I gave you the choice not to die, to help me. To kill them instead. And after everything I've done for you, you still turn on me. No one ever chooses me. Not you, not Charles, not Elijah!"

This is about her being chosen? My heart thumps. It's just like when she killed Abigail. She couldn't handle not having the top spot in Elijah's life. Everything spins. She lunges for me, knocking me backward. We hit the floor hard, her weight on my chest. My back screams in pain from the impact. I grab her wrists before her nails make it to my face. She struggles to get out of my grasp but doesn't seem to have the energy. Her face contorts and her body heaves in exhaustion.

She turns her head toward Elijah. "I have nothing anymore. I have no one." Tears mix with the blood on her face.

I've never seen weakness from Vivian, or any sign of vulnerability. I don't know how to process it.

"You took the last person who cared about me," she says with the weight of three-hundred-year-old longing. She elbows me in the ribs, her wrists still in my hands.

I grunt from the blow, and my aching body begs for the struggle to finish.

"Ann . . . nothing is going to change unless you make different choices," Elijah says, using her real name.

She whimpers and her face collapses on my chest. Her breathing is heavy and her shoulders shake lightly. I lie still, unsure what to do. I let go of her wrists. Her fingers curl into my hoodie next to her cheeks. She makes no effort to lift her face as she cries into my bloody shirt.

My skin tingles, and the air around me stirs. Cotton's arms lift out of my own and he pulls himself from my body until he stands, looking down at us. His clothes are antiquated, like in my visions of him, and his posture is straight. There's pride showing in the lines of his face that reminds me of my dad.

Vivian doesn't seem to notice but instead pushes brown waves back from her damp cheeks. Something deeply hidden in me stirs, like a small candle at the end of a long hallway, and I bite my lip. I wrap my arms around her. *She's so small.* All this time, I thought she was the big one with all the power. I had no idea how breakable she was.

My own chest lifts a little. "All my life, bad things have happened to the people around me." I don't know how to ask what I want to ask, and I hope she understands.

"They deserved it," she says. *That's just like Vivian. No apology.*

My bottom lip quivers. She killed John when he attacked me, and planned on killing the rest of them. Who knows what she was up to during my childhood, all those birthdays that ended with someone getting hurt? I'm even seeing the girl that tripped on the stairs at my fifth-grade graduation in a different light. It's so sick and misguided. And she was doing it for me, in a way. Or doing it to isolate me so that I would need her more. We're no good together. Maybe we never were. But some part of me is still heartbroken.

I rest my cheek on her head, and a tear runs into her blood-streaked hair.

She chokes a little. "My bird," she says in barely a whisper.

Her fingers uncurl from my hoodie and air pushes out of her lips. Her body becomes dead weight in my arms. I sit slowly, holding on to her. Her arms fall limply, and I support her head in the crook of my arm.

"It is finished," Cotton says gently. "You broke the curse."

I shake my head. "I don't know how."

He bends down beside me, slipping his arms under Vivian's back and knees. "A curse is just a cycle, which may only exist because people want it to. We all played our roles. For centuries we have been making the same choices we did during the Trials, hurting and blaming each other. There is no real power gained by harming others."

Cotton lifts Vivian off me, and I feel so odd letting her go. I push myself up onto wobbly legs. From the Descendants' bodies, four women rise. The original accused witches of Salem. They look at the young Descendants and help the girls untie their hands from behind their backs. The older women glow faintly.

Cotton looks from them to me. "All these many years, I thought I knew witches better than anyone. You can imagine my surprise to find one in my own family. Not the wretched being I once studied in my books, but a lovely young woman.

You see, 'witch' is merely a title. It is not the title that is inherently bad but the people who decide what that title means."

"How do you mean?" I ask.

"If a man fears dogs, he may beat one with a stick when he sees it. As is the nature of all creatures, that dog will bite him. And then he may tell everyone that he was right about dogs, that they are evil. But I ask you, who is at fault in this scenario, the man or the dog?"

"The man," I say.

"Now picture this story again, only with two men."

"Funny thing is," I say, "dogs are friendlier and more loyal than men."

He smiles. "You will grow to be a powerful woman, Samantha. There is much to come that you will struggle against. And many scenarios where it may seem easy and tempting to dominate. Do not use your power the way that I did, labeling and damning others."

"I won't," I say, nodding at him. "I promise."

The body in Cotton's arms hums. Out of it comes Vivian's spirit as a girl in her late teens. She jumps from Cotton's arms and lands on the ground with all the grace and pep of a dancer. She briefly examines Cotton holding the lifeless body before walking straight to Elijah.

She sweeps her foot from side to side, pushing away the red powder on the floor and breaking her own circle. There's a loud crackling in the air and the bones and blood fall out of Elijah, tumbling to the ground. He now stands easily and approaches her.

"Yes," he says, nodding. He doesn't look angry. She must have said something, but I didn't hear it.

She returns to me and Cotton. She kisses her former self on the cheek and smiles, making her eyes tilt even more.

The anger has left her, and her young face begins to glow. Cotton's and the accused witches' faces do, too. The Descendants and I squint against the light that now consumes the room. Then all at once it's gone, and they fade into nothingness.

"Elijah!" My voice catches in my burning throat. I turn fully around, but he's not there. I fix my gaze on the circle where we were trapped, too afraid to move, to even think he might have gone with them. My breath is shallow.

He blinks back in right next to me. I suck in air, and it trembles on the edge of a sob. Elijah reveals a cloth in his hand. His eyes roam my many injuries by the light of the fireplace.

"We need to stop the bleeding," he says, gently lifting my cut hand.

He applies pressure to the fabric he places over my wound. For a few seconds we're both silent. He ties the cloth tightly and makes a neat knot.

"She said your name. Right before she died." My voice is barely louder than a whisper.

He nods.

"Was what she said true?"

He cradles my bandaged hand in his own, and I wonder if my heart will explode. "That I love you . . . Yes. Easily. You are strong and stubborn. You risk everything for the people you love. And more important, you are kind to the ones you do not." He nods toward Lizzie, who is trying to steady her breathing.

I can't find the right words, so I reach out with my uncut hand. I touch his lips with the tips of my fingers, and he kisses them. He places my palm on his chest and leans forward. His face is close to mine, and he ever so gently tilts my chin up.

His lips move toward mine inch by inch, and the world is

filled only with the solidness of him under my fingers. Our lips tease each other and our mouths move together. He runs his hand along my cheek and down my neck. Our tongues touch, and I push harder. He pulls me by my lower back into him, his arms enfolding me.

His mouth releases mine, but his eyes are hungry and longing dances on his lips. "If only I were alive."

"I don't care that you're a spirit."

"You must live your life, Samantha," he says, but holds me, still.

Dread slithers into the warm space of our touching bodies. My words fight me on their way out. "You can't leave."

"I think it would be better for you if I did."

My heart ping-pongs in my chest like a caged bird. I shake my head, unsure how to keep myself from drowning us both in my emotions. "I don't want to do this without you."

"You have already done it."

"But I'm in love with you." My voice teeters like a kitten before her eyes are open.

The front door to the house flies open, and I jump backward, breaking our embrace. Jaxon stands in the doorway, panting from running through the woods. *He came to help me after everything I did to him?*

His eyes land on me like a gavel on wood. "Sam?" Jaxon runs toward me, stopping short when he sees the blood that streaks my clothes and skin. He wraps his arms around me. His heart beats forcefully against my shoulder.

Elijah looks at us and smiles. *No!* I want to yell at him. I can tell what he's thinking. That I'm safe, that this is how it should be.

"I'm okay." My voice is raspy.

Jaxon pulls back. "You look anything but okay." He scans my beat-up body.

"Jaxon, will you give me a minute?" I ask, my eyes fixed on Elijah. "And will you call for help?"

He nods, but steps away reluctantly. He moves toward the Descendants as they rub their wrists and check their wounds.

I grab on to Elijah with all my might. "Please, don't go," I whisper. "I barely had any time with you. We only had one floor picnic."

He holds my face in his hand and tickles my ear with his breath. "And I enjoyed it immensely."

I press my cheek into his. *This can't be goodbye.* How could I ever tell him what he means to me? I wouldn't know where to start.

The air next to us shimmers. A faint breeze billows the ashes from the fire and flickers the flames. A beautiful girl with long dark hair appears.

She wears the same content smile she did in her painting. "Abigail . . . ," I whisper. My arms slip from Elijah's body.

He turns toward her, tension vanishing from places on his face I never noticed it was hiding. Immediately, he seems lighter, freer. *I can't take this moment away from him.* I can't plead with him to stay. I would have to be the most self-ish person in the world. I pull both my arms into my chest, trying to shield myself from the heartache that has started there.

"My sweet brother," she says, her voice ethereal and sur-prisingly playful.

He takes her small hand in his. "How long I have waited to see you."

"In three hundred years, not one haircut," she teases.

He smiles, dimples and all. "I was not born with your natural beauty. I will make a better effort."

"Beauty, my eye. You were prettier than half the girls in town," she replies, and I'm now sure that they're repeating familiar banter.

Their shared look is intoxicating. They're bonded in a way that I've never experienced.

Abigail shifts her gaze to me. She has the same intense gray eyes Elijah does. Without warning, she reaches her delicate arms toward me. Warmth fills me as she holds on to my shoulders. "The witch of Salem." There's silence for a long moment. She leans close to my ear and whispers, "Your father just woke up, Samantha."

My cracked heart tries to leap out of my chest, breaking the tenuous hold I had on it. I immediately start sobbing. All the tension and heartache I've felt for the past four months pours out of me. I have wanted this more than I ever wanted anything in the world. And now that it's real, I can't breathe. Elijah gently touches my face, intercepting my stream of tears.

He mouths "I will always love you," and disappears with Abigail. I sob harder. I don't know whether to collapse or jump for joy. My body probably couldn't stand either.

"Sam?" Jaxon asks in a worried tone, slipping his phone back into his pocket.

"My dad's awake," I say through my staggered breaths.

Jaxon walks toward me. My upset about Elijah and my happiness about my dad mix together in a confusing way.

I wipe tears away from my cheeks. "I'm sorry I put you to sleep with that spell. I really am."

Jaxon shakes his head. "You always threatened to knock me out. I guess I should have expected it."

"How did you wake up from it?" I ask as Susannah comes to my side.

He pulls my grandmother's pendant out of his pocket. "I woke up and this was on my chest."

Elijah! He knew Jaxon would come here to help. I almost can't take this.

"You should be happy you slept through this," Mary says as she stands.

Alice nods, free from her usual ice. "You get to show up at the end, Jaxon, and look cool for having discovered us."

"I wish I could've been here to help," Jaxon says.

"Nah, better to let the girls handle it," says Susannah in her raspy voice, and the girls laugh. She slips her delicate hand into mine.

Jaxon examines the room and spots the bones, the blood splattered on the floor, and the noose. "Was someone hanged?"

It's Lizzie who answers. "All of us. If it wasn't for Sam, we'd be dead."

"The crow woman?" Jaxon asks me. "Where is she?"

"Gone. Very much gone." *She died in my arms,* I think, but I don't say it.

CHAPTER FORTY-SEVEN

Black-Eyed Susan

I take the last couple of stairs slowly, one foot at a time. With each movement, my bandaged body protests. The smell of French toast and eggs motivates me to attempt a faster pace. Pans clink and clatter.

I step through the arched doorway of the kitchen, and Jaxon and his mother turn, with matching Meriwether smiles on their faces.

Jaxon puts down a plate of biscuits and approaches me. "Sam, you're not supposed to get out of bed."

"And how do you propose I pee, then?" I ask, breathing in the scent of delicious freshly brewed coffee.

Jaxon smirks. "I could carry you."

"Yeah, fat chance that's gonna happen."

Mrs. Meriwether comes to inspect me. "I'll run you a hot bath after breakfast and make another poultice. We'll get you feeling shipshape in no time."

I smile at the fitting expression. "Thanks, Mrs. Meriwether."

"Why don't we all head into the dining room," Mrs.

Meriwether proposes as she scoops fresh whipped cream into a bowl.

"Need help, Sam?" Jaxon asks.

"If you keep treating me like I'm helpless, I will bop you," I reply with a smile that hurts my face.

"Now that you can do spells, I guess I better be careful." Mrs. Meriwether grins at us. I follow them down the hall to the dining room and stop dead in my tracks. I've never seen so much food, and it is a thing of beauty.

"There are four place settings," I say to Mrs. Meriwether as she puts down her bowls of strawberries and whipped cream.

"Yes, dear. Your father will be joining us." She winks.

I grab a nearby chair for support. "He's coming here already?" They wouldn't even let me speak to my dad these past couple of days. They kept saying they didn't understand how he could recover so quickly, and they wanted to run more tests. *I guess broken spells don't act the same way real illnesses do.*

"He cannot wait to see you." Her smile is kind. Jaxon beams.

Tears form droplets on my eyelashes, and I put my hand over my mouth. I turn around and head for the back door.

"You okay, Sam?" Jaxon runs after me.

"Yeah! I just need to get something."

I run through the grass, stray leaves crunching under my feet. I forget my aches as I enter my house and head for the kitchen. I open the cabinet and push the front cups aside. I pull down the #1 DAD mug. He won't have his coffee without it.

I swing the back door open again, anticipation fueling my steps, and stop. A single freshly cut black-eyed Susan rests on the doormat. I search the porch, but no one's there. I smile. *Elijah.*

Cotton Mather was the third generation of Mathers in America, and I'm the twelfth. I've known this since I was a kid, not because we have the same last name and he's in history textbooks, but because my grandmother Claire Mather told me so. Gram walked me through her house, telling me stories of presidents, forbidden love, and inventions. I recognized my own eyes in my ancestors' paintings and appreciated their humor from their letters. History isn't some distant remembrance in my family; it has a pulse.

My relatives have done everything from fighting in the Revolutionary War to surviving the *Titanic*. They're a colorful and diverse group who definitely made their mark on American history. But Cotton was always a point of controversy. Even when my father was a kid and studied the Salem Witch Trials in school, the other kids gave him a hard time for his last name.

I was always so curious about this infamous man and the reactions he got out of people, even three hundred years later. So I started doing some research. And what I found was surprising—Cotton was *way* more complex than I had ever imagined. He fought for implementing smallpox inoculations, he wrote America's first true-crime book, he conducted one of the first experiments in plant hybridization, and he was instrumental in founding Yale. Many writers after him looked to his books as a record of early American Puritan culture.

Nothing about Cotton was straightforward. Historians argue about his role in the Witch Trials. But that's not just because of Cotton's complexity. It's because the Witch Trials were a perfect storm. And the further I dug into the mysterious circumstances surrounding them, the more I wanted to know. So I went to Salem and began poking around.

One of the first things I did there was go to a bookstore and order an out-of-print book about my relatives. When I arrived at the address, it wasn't a shop like I was expecting, but an old house filled with books. I wrote my name on the order form, and the woman raised her eyebrows and said, "Mather . . . that isn't a popular name around here." I wasn't offended; I was completely intrigued. No one had ever reacted that way to my last name before. Was I a historical villain of sorts in Salem, if nowhere else?

I knew then that visiting wasn't enough. I wanted to actually spend a few nights and get a real feel for the place. I walked along cobblestone streets with black houses, took tours, and got goose bumps hearing all the (sometimes creepy) historical stories. But what I wasn't prepared for was the bed-and-breakfast I chose to stay in. It was a converted old mansion with winding hallways and staircases that stopped and started at random. Beautiful, no doubt. But when I found my room, I couldn't help but feel like something was off.

I kept looking over my shoulder (and under my bed). I went all the way back down to the reception desk and asked if there was any chance the place was haunted. The woman at the desk nodded and said, "Definitely." Then she told me how scared she was to lock the place up at night by herself.

She said to look in the guest books if I wanted to know about the ghosts. Everything in me told me not to. But of course, I just couldn't help myself. It was page after page of people waking up to screams, rocking chairs rocking by themselves, and messages written on the steamed mirrors after showers. People traveled from all over the world to stay in this haunted inn, and I had accidentally and unknowingly booked a room there.

I flipped. I'm a huge scaredy-cat. I slept—if you could call it that—the entire night with one eye open and the light on. But what I learned the more time I spent in Salem was that almost everywhere you went there was a haunted house, a curse, or a graveyard. People didn't ask you *if* you believed in ghosts, but instead *when* was the last time you saw one. After a few days, I was utterly charmed by the mysterious history of the town and the secrets that were hidden there. So I wrote a book.

With this story I really wanted to highlight some of the fascinating historical personalities I found in Salem and give them another chance to have a voice. A lot (but not all) of the history in this book is accurate. If there's a better explanation for the hanging location than Sidney Perley's essay "Where the Salem 'Witches' Were Hanged," I haven't found it. However, the causes of the Salem Witch Trials are more complicated than I can tackle in this fictional narrative. But that's okay, because this story wasn't only written to revisit history. It was written to be learned from and to specifically show the parallel between hanging a witch in Salem and modern-day bullying.

To understand more about what led up to the Salem Witch Trials, it's important to consider what we know and how we know it. Then we should examine the lens through which we view the events. Otherwise, it becomes super easy to shake a finger at history while shouting, "You're all nuts, and your clothes look uncomfortable!"

While addressing the causes of the Salem Witch Trials in my book, I definitely took some artistic liberties. My character Ann, for instance, is only loosely based on Ann Putnam, Jr., who was twelve years old when the accusations started and not the teenager I made her in this story. The black house in the woods is imaginary, but there *was* an actual house that belonged to John Symonds's relatives (which is quoted in Perley's essay and Sam's grandmother's journal) from which it was possible to see the hanging location. Unfortunately, this house no longer exists. Also, Cotton's writings and his role in the Trials themselves are way more involved than what I could capture here. However, there are many real landmarks from old and modern Salem in this story that are worth visiting and exploring.

Even though not all of the historical sites still stand and some information was lost over time, the lessons of the Trials remain relevant. On a basic level, social uncertainty and fear created an unstable emotional environment that allowed things to spiral out of control in Puritan Salem. Some citizens were singled out and made an example of by powerful groups that the community both admired and feared. And once the community supported an accusation of witchcraft, it became nearly impossible for the accused to escape conviction—and punishment.

Where once witchcraft accusations were the norm, bullying has taken its place. And just as during the Trials, it's not always the usual suspects who get bullied; it can happen to anyone for any reason. But the only way it happens is if the community supports it. Group agreement and group silence are equally as deadly. The moment someone speaks up, it's possible to stop that cycle. It's not the easiest thing to do, but greatness is never without risk. And there is nothing greater in the whole world than kindness—kindness to someone being bullied, kindness to a stranger, kindness to an injured animal. Every act counts.

ACKNOWLEDGMENTS

Sometimes you just get lucky, as in "win the lotto and a lifetime supply of donuts on the same day" lucky. For me, this was Halloween 2014, when the genius coordinating my cosmic matchmaking directed me to Rosemary Stimola and Nancy Hinkel. They are kind, humorous, and fiercely clever women whom I am honored to call friends. That Ro is my agent, Nan is my editor, and I get to work with them only adds donuts to my lotto. My love and respect for them is big.

On top of that, Knopf/Random House is a magical place, where everyone adores books and there are illustrations of familiar book-friends on the walls. I'm especially grateful to Julia Maguire for all her hard work and amazing dedication; without her this journey would not have been the same. And the entire team continues to impress me. Barbara Marcus, Stephen Brown, Melanie Cecka, Dawn Ryan, Artie Bennett, Janet Wygal, Lisa Leventer, Marianne Cohen, Trish Parcell, Alison Impey, Kim Lauber, Mary McCue, Judith Haut, John Adamo, Dominique Cimina, Adrienne Waintraub— thank you all for being wonderfully creative people and my story's supportive village.

Also, a special thank-you to Marilynne K. Roach, an insightful Salem historian. Her own wonderful books made a real contribution to my understanding of Salem history.

Now, before Ro saw this manuscript, when I was still wondering "what in the heck is a plot?" there were friends and family who read and gave me invaluable feedback. My Right Club—Cristen Barnes, Leah Briesé, Kristin Minter, and Raj Velu—were there from the beginning. So were Frank and Claire Mather, Marcia Wood, Peter Ciccariello, Ron Wood, Linda Levy, Candis Wood, Saul Levy, Mollie Warren, Allie Merriam, Meghan Best, Maggie Conlon, Nan Shipley, Patrick Maloney, Matt Daddona, Michael McDonagh, Kara Barbieri, Geoffrey Gordon, Samantha Joyce, Jeff Zentner, and Kali Wallace. A big thanks to Dani Bernfeld for her generosity from day one; it will forever be appreciated. And thanks to Anya Remizova for always being supportive, to my cats for their superior snuggling skills, and to all my friends and family for their love.

But truly, I wouldn't have written this book if it weren't for my mama (Sandra Mather) and my pirate (James Bird). The way they love and encourage me is astounding. Their support may also be unwise. I believe in every way that anything is possible, which I'm sure will get me into trouble one of these days. And then these two will be cheering on my starry-eyed optimism. So I would like to preemptively blame them for any future folly. And thank them with everything I have for giving me a bit of space in the world to fill with dreams. In the words of ee cummings, "I carry your heart; I carry it in my heart."

le tour du monde
équitable

Design graphique : Josée Amyotte
Traitement des images : Mélanie Sabourin
Révision et correction : Brigitte Lépine

Pages de garde : Étoile de Noël en feuille de palmier
habilement fabriquée par Anita Joychar, artisane
chez Keya Palm, au Bangladesh.
P. 1 : Itanish Wolde et ses collègues de la coopérative de
café équitable de Negele Gorbitu, en Éthiopie, chantent
pour s'encourager durant la longue et fastidieuse sélection
manuelle.
P. 2 : Récolte au jardin de thé Dunsandle, dans les collines
du Nilgiri, en Inde.
P. 6 : Anita, artisane chez Hajiganj, près de Saidpur,
au Bangladesh.

Catalogage avant publication de Bibliothèque et Archives
nationales du Québec et Bibliothèque et Archives Canada

St-Pierre, Éric, 1971-

Le tour du monde équitable : des femmes et
des hommes qui sèment l'espoir

ISBN 978-2-7619-2749-9

1. Commerce équitable. 2. Commerce équitable - Afrique.
3. Commerce équitable - Amérique latine. 4. Commerce
équitable - Ouvrages illustrés. I. Titre.

HF5416.5.S24 2010   338.5'22   C2010-940803-9

DISTRIBUTEURS EXCLUSIFS :
Pour le Canada et les États-Unis :
MESSAGERIES ADP*
2315, rue de la Province
Longueuil, Québec J4G 1G4
Téléphone : 450 640-1237
Télécopieur : 450 674-6237
Internet : www.messageries-adp.com
* filiale du Groupe Sogides inc.,
  filiale du Groupe Livre Quebecor Media inc.

Pour la France et les autres pays :
INTERFORUM editis
Immeuble Paryseine, 3, Allée de la Seine
94854 Ivry CEDEX
Téléphone : 33 (0) 1 49 59 11 56/91
Télécopieur : 33 (0) 1 49 59 11 33
Service commandes France Métropolitaine
Téléphone : 33 (0) 2 38 32 71 00
Télécopieur : 33 (0) 2 38 32 71 28
Internet : www.interforum.fr
Service commandes Export – DOM-TOM
Télécopieur : 33 (0) 2 38 32 78 86
Internet : www.interforum.fr
Courriel : cdes-export@interforum.fr

Pour la Suisse :
INTERFORUM editis SUISSE
Case postale 69 – CH 1701 Fribourg – Suisse
Téléphone : 41 (0) 26 460 80 60
Télécopieur : 41 (0) 26 460 80 68
Internet : www.interforumsuisse.ch
Courriel : office@interforumsuisse.ch
Distributeur : OLF S.A.
ZI. 3, Corminboeuf
Case postale 1061 – CH 1701 Fribourg – Suisse
Commandes :
Téléphone : 41 (0) 26 467 53 33
Télécopieur : 41 (0) 26 467 54 66
Internet : www.olf.ch
Courriel : information@olf.ch

Pour la Belgique et le Luxembourg :
INTERFORUM BENELUX S.A.
Fond Jean-Pâques, 6
B-1348 Louvain-La-Neuve
Téléphone : 32 (0) 10 42 03 20
Télécopieur : 32 (0) 10 41 20 24
Internet : www.interforum.be
Courriel : info@interforum.be

04-10

Dépôt légal : 2010
Bibliothèque et Archives nationales du Québec

ISBN 978-2-7619-2749-9

Gouvernement du Québec – Programme de crédit d'impôt pour
l'édition de livres – Gestion SODEC – www.sodec.gouv.qc.ca

L'Éditeur bénéficie du soutien de la Société de développement des
entreprises culturelles du Québec pour son programme d'édition.

Conseil des Arts   Canada Council
du Canada   for the Arts

Nous remercions le Conseil des Arts du Canada de l'aide accordée
à notre programme de publication.

Nous reconnaissons l'aide financière du gouvernement du
Canada par l'entremise du Programme d'aide au développement
de l'industrie de l'édition (PADIÉ) pour nos activités d'édition.

éric st-pierre le tour du monde
équitable

des femmes et des hommes qui sèment l'espoir

Collaboration à la rédaction :

Emerson da Silva et Mathieu Lamarre

LES ÉDITIONS DE
L'HOMME

Une compagnie de Quebecor Media

sommaire

L'expérience de petits producteurs de café autochtones du sud de l'état d'Oaxaca, au Mexique, a été à l'origine du projet d'un *label* de certification équitable. Envoyé par un évêque catholique mexicain – qui était préoccupé par la pauvreté et la famine sévissant chez les indigènes Zapotec et Mixe – pour les aider, j'ai découvert et adopté leur réalité quotidienne en effectuant la cueillette du café en leur compagnie.

En 1981, 150 d'entre eux se réunirent dans une vieille église au cœur des montagnes pour faire un «état des lieux» de leurs communautés – des routes à peu près inexistantes, des maisons sans eau courante – et constatèrent leur dépendance face aux petits « barons » locaux qui les exploitaient, les maintenant sous un joug qui empêchait toute forme de progrès. Pour changer les choses, ils décidèrent de mettre sur pied une organisation paysanne, l'Unión de Comunidades Indígenas de la Región del Istmo (UCIRI). Malgré leurs moyens limités et à force d'apprentissage, ils s'organisèrent. Petit à petit, ils apprirent à communiquer et à transiger sans intermédiaires avec les torréfacteurs. Parallèlement, en 1985, 17 communautés indigènes faisaient le saut vers l'agriculture biologique.

Trois ans plus tard, je me rendis aux Pays-Bas avec un groupe de petits producteurs qui voulaient faire part à différentes organisations de leur désir de faire du commerce autrement plutôt que de recevoir de l'aide charitable. Ces cultivateurs, situés au bas de l'échelle, savaient trop bien que leur sort ne se réglerait pas par le biais d'une approche économique « à la sauce occidentale ». Pour eux, il ne pouvait y avoir de véritable évolution

Le commerce équitable, un apprentissage constant

sans un réel changement de culture, sinon de paradigme ; ils devaient proposer une nouvelle façon de faire du commerce. En 1988, la certification équitable, identifiable par un *label,* voyait le jour et profitait des acquis des réseaux de « magasins du monde » déjà établis dans plusieurs pays.

De toute évidence, c'était là un défi lancé au modèle économique prédominant, qui lui ne se base pas sur des notions sociales ou scientifiques mais plutôt sur une foi presque aveugle dans les sacro-saintes « lois » du marché, et qui semble parfois relever de la pensée magique.

Aujourd'hui, le néolibéralisme et sa sainte trinité – déréglementation, innovation et mondialisation – font face à une crise, et l'on découvre que l'idée en vogue du « développement durable » est, à toutes fins pratiques, un oxymore. L'occasion est peut-être propice pour repenser nos façons de faire et contrer la contagion de l'individualisme et du *consumérisme,* même s'il n'est jamais facile d'aller à contre-courant.

Le commerce équitable propose une alternative basée sur des notions de justice sociale, de qualité de produit et de respect de l'environnement. Il se nourrit d'une mise en relation plus directe des producteurs et des consommateurs, ces derniers pouvant enfin exercer leur pouvoir décisionnel en sachant clairement quels sont les vrais coûts de production et les vrais dangers de l'exploitation sociale et environnementale ; son dessein en est un d'implication solidaire.

Dans les montagnes de l'isthme mexicain, nous avons beaucoup appris de nos démarches. Bénéficiaires, sinon tributaires de leur expérience, les paysans soumettent le concept d'une « pauvreté décente » comme espoir modeste mais réalisable. Déjà, la pauvreté a sa propre sagesse, une créativité lui permettant de repousser la mort grâce à l'amour et la vie – et cela n'a rien d'une perspective romantique. En même temps, elle procure une persévérance riche en enseignements. Une éducation qui, avec l'avènement du commerce équitable, a mené progressivement vers l'autodétermination sociale, culturelle et politique et à laquelle souhaite s'ajouter l'autodétermination économique. Pour ce faire, les producteurs autochtones de café savent qu'ils doivent se préparer à une longue et âpre lutte. En ne se satisfaisant pas d'une simple niche dans le marché, ils doivent logiquement anticiper une confrontation avec le système établi.

Les images qui réussissent à traduire le rude vécu, voire l'âme des petits cultivateurs, leur résilience ou encore leur souci de produire des aliments de qualité pour eux-mêmes et les autres, sont tout aussi importantes que les longues dissertations sur les manières de changer le monde pour le mieux. Tel un remède contre l'impuissance, le découragement et la médiocrité, elles soulignent l'espoir invincible qui rejaillit des paysages et, bien sûr, des visages de ceux – hommes ou femmes, enfants ou vieillards – qui aspirent à une vie digne. Ce livre est un signe qu'un autre monde est possible.

Dr Francisco Van der Hoff,
membre de l'UCIRI, Oaxaca, Mexique
et cofondateur du *label* Max Havelaar aux Pays-Bas

Devant moi, suspendue dans un cadre, Rosanalia a beau cacher sa bouche avec sa main, ses yeux rigolent. De son sourire émane la dignité des paysans de l'isthme mexicain, qui luttent courageusement contre l'oppression d'un système économique asservissant.

Cette magnifique photographie, Éric St-Pierre l'a prise lors de notre premier séjour dans les communautés de l'Unión de Comunidades Indígenas de la Región del Istmo (UCIRI), en 1996. Chaque fois que je la regarde, elle me rappelle les raisons d'être du commerce équitable. J'y vois l'importance de passer de la parole à l'action. J'entends Luc De Larochellière chanter : «J'suis né du bon bord, du bord de l'Amérique, de l'Amérique du Nord ». J'aurais pu être la belle Rosanalia. Et alors, qu'aurais-je attendu de tous ces gens en Occident qui vivent dans l'opulence? De la charité ? Non, de la justice.

Après une décennie d'expansion rapide, voilà que ce mouvement est à la croisée des chemins. Deux solutions s'offrent à lui : faire croître le marché équitable en volume avec les critères actuels, voire des critères plus ouverts (notamment en acceptant des plantations dans des filières réservées aux coopératives) ou le faire croître en qualités sociales et environnementales, afin qu'il serve de locomotive au développement d'un système d'échanges véritablement équitable, et ce, à l'échelle globale.

Comme le démontrent les images et les témoignages présentés dans ce livre, la réponse n'est pas simple. Le débat est animé, au Nord comme au Sud. Le défi est de taille, soit de préserver les valeurs fondamentales qui ont donné naissance au commerce équitable tout en faisant en sorte qu'un nombre croissant de petits producteurs, d'artisans et de travailleurs en bénéficient. Chaque stratégie a ses avantages et ses risques. Le mot « équitable » ne résonne d'ailleurs pas de la même manière pour tout le monde. Au sein de ce mouvement pluriel, comme sur une grande mosaïque, chacun apporte sa couleur et sa forme en fonction de sa réalité. C'est aussi la beauté de ce livre, qui nous fait découvrir des hommes et des

Unidos pour un commerce plus juste

femmes de tous les continents qui, sans se connaître, font partie du même mouvement.

Leur histoire nous rappelle que, malgré la croissance fulgurante du commerce équitable, nous ne sommes en fait qu'aux premiers battements d'ailes d'un papillon encore bien fragile. Le commerce équitable n'occupe qu'une infime fraction des échanges internationaux. L'équité dans le commerce fait encore exception. Il y a pourtant plusieurs décennies que l'on observe les écosystèmes se dégrader et le fossé entre riches et pauvres se creuser avec le bulldozer de l'exploitation globalisée. Il est temps non seulement de souhaiter un commerce plus juste, mais surtout de passer à l'action individuellement et collectivement.

S'il est vrai que l'achat de produits équitables contribue à faire une différence dans la vie de milliers de gens, il ne doit pas nous faire oublier l'importance de transformer, pour la majorité des habitants de la Terre et les générations futures, les règles d'un commerce mondial actuellement inéquitable. Cette transformation ne peut s'opérer sans nous, citoyens et citoyennes, quelle que soit la place que nous occupons dans la société. Nous devons convaincre les décideurs de tous lieux que l'équitable n'est pas qu'un choix entre deux produits; il doit être un critère incontournable pour tous les échanges. Nous en serons tous gagnants.

À mon ami Éric, je dis merci d'avoir fait ce tour du monde pour nous permettre de mieux comprendre la réalité de ces femmes et de ces hommes du commerce équitable. Merci de nous prêter ton œil de grand photographe – un œil qui nous fait voir que là-bas c'est ici, et que ces gens, c'est nous aussi.

Laure Waridel,
sociologue, auteur et pionnière du commerce équitable
et de la consommation responsable au Québec

☑ Rosanalia Teran Guzmán, de Guadalupe,
dans l'État d'Oaxaca, au Mexique.

« L'équitable, tout en étant supérieur à une certaine justice, est lui-même juste... (Il) n'est pas le juste selon la loi, mais un correctif de la justice légale. » Le fait qu'Aristote pensait déjà, au troisième siècle avant Jésus-Christ, « à l'équité et à l'équitable » ne fait que témoigner de l'intemporelle légitimité de ces concepts pour celles et ceux dont ne s'apaise la soif de justice. Il y a plus de 60 ans, des courants chrétiens états-uniens, néerlandais, anglais et français posèrent les premières pierres de ce qui deviendra l'actuel réseau mondial du « commerce équitable ». En passant par les « magasins du monde » jusqu'à la certification des produits à la fin des années 1980, le marché équitable a fait des pas de géant, pour atteindre aujourd'hui près de cinq milliards de dollars de ventes. En 2001, quatre grandes institutions de l'équitable définissaient le mouvement ainsi :

> Le commerce équitable est un partenariat commercial fondé sur le dialogue, la transparence et le respect, dont l'objectif est de parvenir à une plus grande équité dans le commerce mondial. Il contribue au développement durable en offrant de meilleures conditions commerciales et en garantissant les droits des producteurs et des travailleurs marginalisés, tout particulièrement au sud de la planète. Les organisations du commerce équitable (soutenues par les consommateurs) s'engagent activement à soutenir les producteurs, à sensibiliser l'opinion et à mener campagne en faveur de changements dans les règles et pratiques du commerce international conventionnel.

Cette définition ne fait pas toujours l'unanimité et ne cesse d'être réécrite par ce mouvement non seulement en forte croissance sur le plan économique mais qui rejoint de nouveaux adeptes jour après jour, qu'ils soient producteurs au Sud, consommateurs au Nord, industriels, commerçants, étudiants, universitaires ou autres décideurs nationaux et internationaux.

introduction

Depuis près de 15 ans, à titre de photojournaliste, mon commerce équitable à moi s'est principalement défini sur le terrain, auprès des familles qui sont à la base du système. Un tour du monde équitable qui a débuté en 1996, avec Laure Waridel, auprès des membres de l'Unión de Comunidades Indígenas de la Región del Istmo (UCIRI) au Mexique. Avec Felix, Adela, et l'ineffable Francisco Van der Hoff, nous avons travaillé, discuté, observé et appris. Je suis retourné, à quatre reprises sur dix ans, visiter les membres de l'UCIRI. Les enfants sont devenus adultes, et plusieurs ont quitté leur village vers les centres urbains, la capitale ou même – illégalement – vers les États-Unis. En 25 ans d'histoire, l'UCIRI a mené à bien de nombreuses réalisations : services de santé, magasins de denrées de base, coopératives d'autobus, etc., mais le prix équitable du café n'a guère changé depuis les débuts de la certification, alors que le coût de la vie au Mexique a progressé sans cesse. Le commerce équitable, malgré toutes ses vertus, n'est pas une panacée qui, à elle seule, peut régler toutes les inégalités régionales ou mondiales.

Après le commerce du café, que j'ai documenté dans huit pays, j'ai fait la découverte des autres denrées équitables : cacao, sucre, artisanat, banane et autres, pour un total de 14 produits différents et autant de pays d'Amérique du Sud, d'Asie et d'Afrique qui sont présentés dans ce livre. Mis bout à bout, ces séjours représentent plus de 600 jours à vivre auprès de paysans, d'artisans et d'autres travailleurs. J'ai partagé le quotidien de ces gens, dormant sous leur toit, partageant leur repas. Avec eux, j'ai appris à battre le riz, à reconnaître la bonne fermentation d'une fève de cacao ou à déguster le thé, qu'il soit vert, noir ou blanc. J'ai tenu à ce que nos différences culturelles et économiques ne soient pas des barrières au partage et aux rencontres. Les êtres humains pris dans leur essence ne sont pas si différents, qu'ils proviennent de la campagne burkinabé ou des hauts plateaux boliviens. Tous aspirent à vivre dignement et à assurer un avenir prometteur à leurs enfants.

J'ai voulu transmettre, à travers ces images, le respect que je porte à ces hommes et ces femmes. Sans être complaisantes, elles ont été saisies telles qu'elles se sont présentées à moi, laissant la magie des lumières et des moments s'exprimer sur la pellicule ou le capteur numérique. Images de semis, de récoltes et de transformations, c'est souvent toute la chaîne de production que vous pourrez découvrir pour chacun des produits présentés. Au fil des chapitres, les principaux produits équitables sont traités – et même certains moins connus, tels le quinoa et le karité, et d'autres en attente de certification (comme le guarana) sont présentés. Les textes débutent avec un regard historique, mythique – parfois même lyrique – sur ces denrées, suivi d'un récit ponctué de rencontres et d'expériences sur le terrain. Dans chaque chapitre, on retrouve un texte repère, qui traite de l'aspect botanique du produit en question et qui compare son commerce conventionnel et équitable (quelques statistiques viennent s'ajouter à ces informations de base), et un texte thématique qui aide à illustrer un enjeu important du commerce équitable.

Sans vouloir redéfinir l'équitable, je crois que ce mouvement doit être pour et par les producteurs du Sud. Ce livre est donc une multiplicité de rencontres avec ceux et celles qui sont à la base du mouvement : les artisans, les paysans et les travailleurs de plantations qui luttent, dans l'adversité aveugle d'un marché mondialisé, en empruntant un chemin pavé d'espoir et de solidarité. Le commerce équitable n'est pas un geste de charité, mais bien un pacte de justice avec certains des plus marginalisés de notre planète. Au Nord, nous détenons le pouvoir sur une part importante des aspirations du mouvement. Comme l'a si bien illustré Laure Waridel dans son livre *Acheter, c'est voter*, notre rôle de consommateur mérite d'être valorisé. La dignité des producteurs, elle, mérite d'être respectée.

© Rabeya Begum, artisane chez Biborton à Agailjara, au sud du Bangladesh, déplace des feuilles de papier de soie qui sèchent au soleil.

l'artisanat

« ...Et le sixième jour, Dieu prit de l'*adamah* et fit Adam. » Ainsi, l'union de destins entre la terre et l'homme commença par l'art, avant même que ne fût l'agriculture. Chez les Babyloniens, la glaise est fécondée par le sang d'un dieu-démon. La main du grand artisan façonnant la glaise à son image n'est certes pas le seul mythe partagé par les anciennes cultures à l'aube de l'Histoire, car pour plusieurs d'entre elles, les créatures firent à leur tour des œuvres qui n'ont pas toujours été jugées dignes aux yeux de l'artisan premier. Les bruyants descendants d'Adam perturbèrent le divin sommeil et Dieu décida de les exterminer par le

Déluge. Mais si nous pouvons aujourd'hui rappeler ces récits à notre imagination, c'est bien parce qu'il y a eu une deuxième chance. Dans la mythologie grecque, lorsque Zeus envoya le Déluge pour anéantir les hommes violents de la race de fer, c'est à Deucalion, le fils de Prométhée, et à Mirrha, sa femme, que revint la tâche de recréer les hommes. Avec des pierres – de l'*adamah*, tout de même – cette fois-ci. Dans une pièce perdue d'Euripide, Prométhée lui-même s'en charge en modelant les nouveaux hommes avec l'abondante argile de l'Après-Déluge, encore toute fraîche.

Que ce soit lors de la Création ou de la seconde chance, dans toutes les cultures, Dieu est toujours cet artisan producteur de la plus-value originale. Le souffle de la parole instaurera l'Histoire, c'est-à-dire le débat universel autour de la création et de l'usufruit des richesses qui ne peuvent être créées que par la fécondante force de travail. Il n'est ainsi point surprenant de retrouver, aux origines du commerce équitable, la mise en valeur des objets créés par des artistes et des artisans partenaires d'un projet mondial de solidarité. « Commerce solidaire », tel était le terme utilisé pour désigner les premières initiatives de ce que l'on appelle aujourd'hui le « commerce équitable ». La vente de produits artisanaux du Bangladesh est un jalon important dans l'histoire de cette mouvance. En effet, le soleil du commerce équitable s'est levé lui aussi à l'Orient.

|||||||||||||||||||||||||||||||||||||||||||||||||||||||||||||||||||||||||||||||||||||

L e jour se lève le long de la rivière Bagdha, dans la région d'Agailjara, au sud du Bangladesh et déjà, la campagne est envahie par les paysans, les pêcheurs, les écoliers et nombre de rickshaws. De partout, la vie transpire. Je suis dans le pays le plus densément peuplé de la planète, avec plus de mille personnes au kilomètre carré. Au petit atelier de la Charity Foundation, des femmes arrivent une à une vêtues de saris colorés. L'endroit est modeste : un toit, des nattes tressées sur le plancher de terre battue, des ventilateurs au plafond et de petits bancs de bois entourés de fibres multicolores. Elles s'assoient en cercle et chacune travaille à son rythme en tressant des paniers. Elles seront rémunérées, selon la nature des items et le nombre d'items produits, entre 2000 et 2500 takas par mois (30 et 40 $). C'est la valeur d'une heure de travail d'un cadre moyen dans les pays riches industrialisés, mais pour ces femmes c'est suffisant pour mettre la nourriture sur la table, vêtir et éduquer les enfants.

« Maintenant je peux offrir trois repas par jour à mes enfants, et même faire venir un professeur à la maison pour aider aux leçons », m'explique Hanufa Begum, qui travaille à la Charity Foundation depuis huit ans et qui a récemment été promue superviseuse. « Lorsque mon mari est décédé, j'étais enceinte de trois mois de mon deuxième. Après mon accouchement, j'ai commencé à travailler ici. »

L'histoire d'Hanufa, c'est aussi celle de Salina, Shefali, Gita, ou encore Sanjita. Des mères monoparentales, parfois âgées d'à peine 25 ans, mais

⌃ Hanufa Begum, superviseuse à la Charity Foundation.

dont un second mariage reste fort improbable dans leur contexte culturel. «Au début, nous ne visions pas directement les femmes, mais plutôt les plus démunis et vulnérables de la société bangladaise», m'explique Doug Dirks du Mennonite Central Committee (MCC), une organisation nord-américaine qui, au début des années 1970, développait de nombreux programmes de coopération internationale au Bangladesh. Ce pays venait tout juste de sortir de sa guerre d'indépendance avec le Pakistan. «Chaque fois, on nous suggérait d'aller vers les femmes des communautés minoritaires du pays – les Hindous au Sud et les Biharis au Nord – et de penser surtout aux femmes monoparentales, qui avaient encore moins d'opportunités de travail et davantage de besoins.» Au fil des ans, le travail du MCC au Bangladesh a permis la création de dizaines d'organisations d'artisans dans l'ensemble du pays, qui ont pu profiter, entre autres, des réseaux de boutiques Dix Mille Villages du MCC au Canada et aux États-Unis.

L**A FILIÈRE DE L'ARTISANAT A UNE PLACE** toute spéciale au sein de la petite histoire du commerce équitable, à titre de tout premier germe d'une idée, sinon d'une philosophie, égalitariste planté, selon la légende, dans le fond d'un coffre de voiture !

L'aventure débute en 1946, avec l'initiative d'une humble bénévole du Mennonite Central Committee (MCC) états-unien en séjour à Porto Rico. Charmée par le travail des couturières artisanes de l'endroit, mais également préoccupée par leur niveau de pauvreté, Edna Ruth Byler entreprend de rapporter chez elle, en Pennsylvanie, des échantillons qu'elle vendra directement de sa voiture aux dames de sa communauté. Le proverbial effet boule de neige fait son œuvre et aboutit, une vingtaine d'années plus tard, à l'établissement d'un réseau de boutiques baptisées SelfHelp, dont la croissance mènera, en 1996, au renouvellement de son appellation ; aujourd'hui, on compte plus de 130 magasins Dix Mille Villages (Ten Thousand Villages) en Amérique du Nord.

Mais puisqu'une bonne idée ne reste jamais orpheline très longtemps, on évoque également l'avènement européen d'une démarche similaire de la part de l'organisme anglais Oxfam à la fin des années 1950, cette fois en faisant la promotion d'artisanat issu des réfugiés chinois à Hong-Kong. Au cours de la décennie suivante, différentes organisations néerlandaises emboîtent le pas et créent le concept des « magasins du monde », avec une première boutique européenne en 1969. L'évidence qu'un commerce alternatif n'est pas une utopie ni une série de cas isolés sera d'ailleurs soulignée lors de la deuxième édition de la toute jeune Conférence des Nations Unies sur le Commerce et le Développement (CNUCED), en 1968. On y lança le slogan « *Trade, not Aid* », message de la part des pays démunis que le commerce (idéalement équitable) vaut mieux que la charité.

Comme l'araignée qui tisse sa toile, le commerce de l'artisanat équitable tendit ses fils aux quatre coins de l'Europe et de l'Amérique du Nord. Le réseautage de ses intervenants ne tarda pas à accoucher,

1946 Edna Ruth Byler vend des broderies d'artisanes de Porto Rico.

1968 Conférence des Nations Unies sur le Commerce et le Développement (CNUCED) à Delhi.

1969 Premier « magasin du monde » en Europe (Pays-Bas).

dans les années 1970 et 1980, de multiples organisations associatives nationales, qui elles-mêmes se regrouperont une autre décennie plus tard dans des structures internationales, dont la World Fair Trade Organization (WFTO), anciennement l'International Fair Trade Association (IFAT), qui regroupe 350 organisations de commerce équitable, au Nord comme au Sud.

La voie ainsi tracée par la filière de l'artisanat sera logiquement la porte d'entrée initiale du commerce des denrées alimentaires, démarré aux Pays-Bas avec le sucre à la fin des années 1960, puis le café en 1973. Avec le temps, ce tout autre domaine démontre un potentiel de croissance qui change la perception (et les intérêts) autour de l'équitable. L'apparition, en 1988, du *label* Max Havelaar de certification des produits – puis son émulation – ouvrira effectivement les vannes et décuplera la visibilité de l'équitable auprès du grand public.

« Au Nord, nos membres ont parfois développé le marché alimentaire au détriment de l'artisanat », soumet Paul Myers, président de la WFTO ; mais l'homme a bien l'intention de faire profiter cette filière fondatrice du même décloisonnement qui a si bien servi le café, le thé et les autres : « Au Sud, nos groupes d'artisans nous demandent de développer plus de marchés. Nous allons donc créer pour eux un *label* similaire à ce qui se fait pour les produits alimentaires », et qui replacera peut-être l'artisanat à l'avant-scène du commerce équitable.

5 milliards $

⊡ Action Bag, du Bangladesh, produit des sacs, ainsi que d'autres articles en jute et en coton.

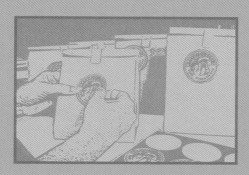

1988 Max Havelaar Pays-Bas, le premier *label* de certification équitable, est lancé.

1997 La Fairtrade Labelling Organizations International (FLO), regroupant 19 initiatives nationales de certification équitable, est fondée.

2008 Les ventes de produits équitables à travers le monde atteignent près de cinq milliards de dollars.

2008

Madhabi Adhikary, lors de l'assemblée annuelle de Keya Palm qui propose des objets décoratifs faits de feuilles de palmier. Shahana Begum et ses compatriotes de l'entreprise Bagdha filent la fibre de chanvre. Après avoir été filée, la fibre de chanvre est tricotée par les mains habiles d'artisanes comme Shova Roy. Mère de trois enfants, elle travaille chez Bagdha depuis neuf ans.

IIIIIIIIIIIIIIIIIIIIIIIIIIIIIIIIIIIIIIIIIIIIIIIIIIIIIIIIIIIIIIIIIIIIIIIIIIIIIIIIIIIIIIIIII

Sept organisations d'artisanes du MCC sont aujourd'hui réunies au sein de Prokritee, dont le nom signifie « nature » en bengali. Prokritee coordonne le design, la mise en marché et le soutien administratif de ces entreprises. En ce mois de mai, elles tiennent leur assemblée annuelle. C'est le moment des bilans et des festivités. Chants, pièces de théâtre éducatives et danses traditionnelles sont au programme. Quelques enfants arborent des tuniques élaborées et de flamboyants maquillages à la hauteur de leur prestation. Les artisanes y attendent également l'annonce des profits, qui seront répartis sous forme de primes annuelles. Pour les quelque 125 femmes de l'entreprise Bagdha qui tricotent la fibre de chanvre, l'année fut particulièrement faste, grâce à une commande supplémentaire de leur principal client. C'est une grande satisfaction pour Suraiya, la dynamique designer en chef de Prokritee. « Il y a quelques années, nous avons pratiquement dû fermer les portes de Bagdha, alors que les ventes étaient anémiques », raconte celle qui soutient les artisanes comme une mère ses enfants. « Nous sollicitions depuis longtemps une grande entreprise spécialisée dans les soins corporels, mais nous n'arrivions pas à satisfaire ses standards de qualité. Après une première commande refusée de 3000 gants de bain, j'ai dû travailler extrêmement fort avec les artisanes et auprès du client pour sauver le contrat. » Le deuxième envoi fut le bon et les commandes ont progressé d'année en année, pour atteindre 90 000 gants en 2008. Le bonus conséquent fut de 22 000 takas (300 $) par artisane, doublant pratiquement leurs revenus annuels.

⌃ Nazma, en compagnie de son fils Noshad.

|||||||||||||||||||||||||||||||||||||||||||||||||||||||||

Dissimulée sous sa burka noire, Nazma marche d'un pas rapide dans les passages étroits d'un des camps biharis de Saidpur, dans le nord du Bangladesh. De confession musulmane, les Biharis ont quitté l'Inde et sa majorité hindoue lors de sa partition en 1947. Plus de 20 ans plus tard, lors de la guerre civile entre le Pakistan Est et Ouest, ce peuple a été pris entre deux feux et ni son pays de résidence, le Bangladesh, ni le Pakistan ne voulurent le reconnaître. Ils sont aujourd'hui environ 240 000 Biharis à vivre en apatrides, marginalisés, souvent dans des camps de fortune. Nazma rentre enfin chez elle. En retirant sa burka, elle révèle un sourire chaleureux. Sa maison, toute en ciment, contraste avec celles de ses voisines. « Avec le bonus de fin d'année de l'an passé et un petit prêt de mon employeur, j'ai pu construire ma propre maison », raconte-t-elle fièrement. Dans la pièce principale d'à peine quelques mètres carrés, ses deux filles s'affairent à terminer une broderie. « Avant, je pouvais gagner 300 à 400 takas (5 $) par mois avec mon travail de broderie, mais depuis que je suis chez Action Bag, je gagne dix fois plus et mes filles ont pu retourner à l'école. »

Débutant ses activités au milieu des années 1970, l'entreprise Action Bag fut fondée pour la fabrication des sacs en jute, au moment où une campagne contre les sacs en plastique battait son plein en Europe. « En 1976, avec les commandes d'organismes comme Gepa, en Allemagne, nous exportions 25 000 sacs en jute par mois », raconte monsieur Ghayasuddin, directeur général d'Action Bag. « À cette époque, les femmes recevaient deux takas par sac en salaire et deux takas en épargne. Lorsqu'elles accumulaient 5000 takas, elles pouvaient retirer le montant et lancer leur propre entreprise. » Au fil des ans, c'est plus de 1500 femmes qui ont pu ainsi travailler chez Action Bag, mais désormais, on préfère y fidéliser la main-d'œuvre ; aujourd'hui, 75 artisanes comme Nazma sont employées permanentes et 30 sont temporaires, au sein de l'entreprise.

▷ La mosquée de Saidpur, fondée en 1863.

⊙ Dans le petit atelier de Hajiganj, situé près de Saidpur, Rashida prend quelques secondes pour s'occuper de Shumy, son fils de huit mois, tout en tenant avec ses pieds le couvercle d'un panier tressé avec de l'herbe *kaisa* et des feuilles de palmier. Ce travail lui permet, depuis près de dix ans, de subvenir à ses besoins et à ceux de ses enfants.

À 100 kilomètres au nord de Dhaka, la ville de Mymensingh est reconnue pour la rareté des véhicules motorisés dans ses rues... mais aussi pour ses embouteillages de rickshaws ! Dans un local au centre-ville, une dizaine de jeunes bangladaises sont rassemblées. Les programmes du MCC dans cette agglomération de plus de 300 000 habitants visent cette fois des défavorisés d'un tout autre ordre. Ces femmes ne sont ici ni réfugiées, ni veuves, ni victimes de catastrophes naturelles. « Nous les présentons souvent comme des survivantes », me précise avec pudeur Bita Narua, intervenante du MCC Bangladesh. Il y a à peine deux mois, celles-ci arpentaient les rues du *redlight* de Mymensingh à la recherche de clients. « Grâce à l'aide de partenaires locaux, nous avons recruté un certain nombre de filles, qui devaient être disposées à laisser complètement leur ancien travail pour joindre le programme. »

Réunies autour de l'animatrice de la rencontre, elles relatent leur douloureux passé, parfois avec des rires mais surtout avec des larmes. Avec ses cicatrices à l'œil gauche et une maturité qui détonne par rapport à ses 22 ans d'âge, Shilpi donne l'impression d'avoir beaucoup vécu. « Plus jeune, je travaillais comme bonne dans une famille aisée, où je me suis fait violer. Nous avons voulu poursuivre le coupable en Cour mais parce que ma famille était pauvre et la sienne riche, nous n'avons pas réussi », raconte-t-elle en essuyant une larme. « On nous persécutait de toute part, mon père a même perdu son emploi parce que sa fille était "une petite garce" », lance-t-elle sèchement.

Plus tard, dans la modeste maison qu'elle occupe avec sa mère et ses trois enfants, Shilpi me raconte sa descente aux enfers : « Je me souviens que mon père devait faire du porte-à-porte pour quémander un peu de riz. J'avais 15 ans quand il est décédé d'une crise cardiaque. C'est là que j'ai commencé à travailler dans la rue. Je prenais les robes de ma mère, car je n'avais même pas de quoi m'habiller. » Elle essuie à nouveau ses yeux rougis. « La rue, ce n'est pas une vie. Tu t'entends avec un client mais tu te retrouves entourée de cinq hommes. Souvent, je n'étais même pas payée ou on me battait. » Tout à coup, des cris de l'extérieur viennent couper son récit. Elle me dit : « Tu entends ? Tu entends ? Ce sont d'anciens clients. Ils disent : "Tu ne te fais plus de Bangladais, tu te fais des étrangers maintenant ?" » Elle se lève pour inspecter autour de la maison, séparée de la rue uniquement par quelques sacs accrochés à une clôture de fortune. « J'ai peur pour ma fille dans ce quartier. J'ai voulu entrer dans le programme [du MCC] pour changer de métier, pour offrir à mes enfants une meilleure éducation pour qu'ils puissent avoir un bon travail. Raconte mon histoire ; utilise mon nom. Je ne veux pas que d'autres jeunes filles vulnérables tombent dans le même piège. Être une travailleuse du sexe n'est pas une solution, personne ne nous respecte, on nous refuse toute dignité. »

☑ Shilpi et ses enfants. ☑ Fatima visite le quartier de son enfance, où vit toujours sa mère, dans un abri de fortune sur le bord du chemin de fer. ☑ Les savons Sacred Mark sont distribués à travers le monde.

⌃ Shilpi se remémore un passé douloureux.

À quelques minutes de marche de la demeure de Shilpi, dans un petit atelier, je retrouve un autre groupe de jeunes femmes toutes de bleu vêtues. « Ce sont les premières à avoir joint le programme et terminé leur formation. Le premier semestre est consacré à la formation personnelle et le deuxième à la formation technique », m'indique Bita, l'intervenante. Les artisanes sont à l'œuvre. Elles mélangent des huiles de palmier et de noix de coco en plus d'autres ingrédients. Sur les tablettes de séchage s'empilent des savons, étiquetés selon leur parfum – *neem,* gingembre ou lavande. Fatima, à peine 18 ans, a un visage d'ange. Elle raconte : « J'avais 15 ans lorsque j'ai été violée par mon cousin. Ma mère m'a jetée de la maison. Je suis partie pour Dhaka, où j'ai été agressée de nouveau. Quand je suis revenue à Mymensingh, j'ai commencé le travail du sexe parce que j'étais furieuse contre moi-même. J'avais tout perdu. » Bita souligne que Fatima a passé un an dans le *redlight* de Mymensingh avant de joindre le programme du MCC et qu'elle est aujourd'hui une de leurs expertes dans la fabrication des savons.

Assistée de deux collègues, Fatima s'empare d'une estampe et d'un cube de cire. La substance fondue par des charbons ardents est déposée sur un savon, pour ensuite y apposer le sceau représentant une empreinte digitale. « L'empreinte est une marque que Dieu donne à chaque personne ; nous l'utilisons pour souligner l'identité unique de celles qui sont à la source de nos produits », m'explique Austin, le designer états-unien responsable de la mise en marché. « Ce symbole est également en lien avec la marque de commerce de nos savons – Sacred Mark –, qui évoque les mots d'un poème célèbre de Tagore : "Laisse-moi porter en secret (...) cette marque sacrée imprimée de Ta main". »

Les écrits de Rabindranath Tagore (1861-1941), écrivain nobélisé de l'ancienne Inde unifiée, ont su non seulement cristalliser les traits des sociétés indienne et bangladaise (notamment dans leurs hymnes nationaux) mais aussi interpeller les destins des artisanes de Mymensingh. Puisque la nouvelle vie qu'elles construisent de leurs mains est une résurrection ayant exigé une mort préalable, leur attachement à ces autres paroles fatidiques est immédiatement compréhensible : « Laisse-moi naufrager, laisse-moi mourir ! » Cette mort n'est pas à craindre car : « (...) le lac de cette résurrection (...) ignore les profondeurs. »

« Je n'oublierai jamais le jour de la célébration de notre nouvelle vie. C'était un mardi, le 9 juin. Nous avons coupé un grand gâteau et reçu un superbe sari bleu », se rappelle Fatima, les yeux brillants. « Ma colère est disparue. J'ai pu la changer pour quelque chose d'heureux », conclut-elle.

Au moment où j'écris ces mots, j'ai appris qu'à l'été, Fatima s'est mariée et travaille toujours chez Sacred Mark. De son côté, Shilpi poursuit sa formation d'artisane. Toutes deux vivent pleinement cette deuxième chance et marchent à présent sur un chemin pavé de dignité.

▷ Un sceau pour marquer dans la cire une empreinte digitale, l'emblème des savons Sacred Mark.

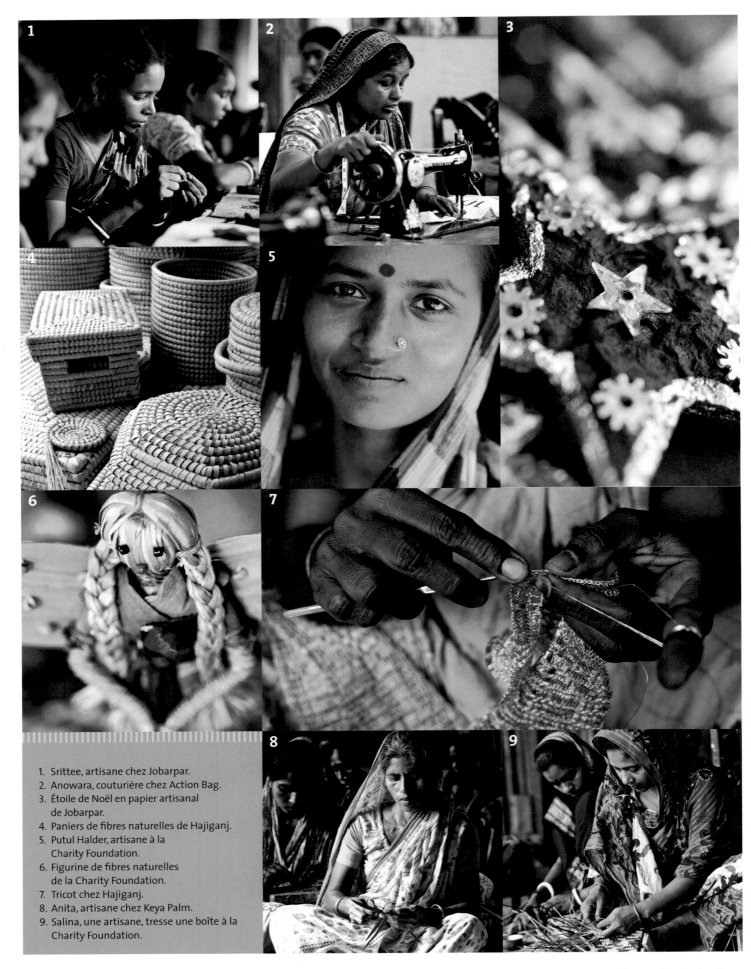

1. Srittee, artisane chez Jobarpar.
2. Anowara, couturière chez Action Bag.
3. Étoile de Noël en papier artisanal de Jobarpar.
4. Paniers de fibres naturelles de Hajiganj.
5. Putul Halder, artisane à la Charity Foundation.
6. Figurine de fibres naturelles de la Charity Foundation.
7. Tricot chez Hajiganj.
8. Anita, artisane chez Keya Palm.
9. Salina, une artisane, tresse une boîte à la Charity Foundation.

▷ En haut : Rita Sarkar, artisane chez Biborton, façonne un livre de papier à partir de jacinthes d'eau.
▷ En bas : Nurjahan et Renu Begum récoltent des jacinthes d'eau dans un canal de la région d'Agailjara, au sud du Bangladesh.

▣ Nadra, artisane chez Hajiganj à Saidpur, a appris le crochet avec sa mère et sa grand-mère. Confectionner un foulard lui demande quatre à cinq jours de travail.

le café

K aldi trouva ses chèvres bien stimulées après qu'elles eurent mangé les baies rouges d'un arbuste. Ce berger abyssinien du premier millénaire fit alors part de sa découverte aux moines, qui trouvèrent ces baies fort salutaires car elles leur permettaient de rester éveillés pour s'adonner davantage à la prière. Consommé en Arabie dès le XIIe siècle, le café s'y répandit, profitant de la prohibition de l'alcool par l'islam. C'est également là que débutent la culture et l'exportation des grains de café vers le nord de l'Afrique, la Turquie et ensuite l'Europe.

Au XVIIe siècle, le café partit dans les bateaux coloniaux pour conquérir l'Asie, les Caraïbes et les Amériques. Aujourd'hui, cultivés dans plus de 60 pays situés sous les tropiques, les caféiers produisent plus de sept millions de tonnes de grains, dont 80 % sont destinés à l'exportation. Cultivé au Sud et consommé surtout au Nord, le café est objet d'une spéculation boursière continue, où les sacs changent de mains sans quitter leur entrepôt. Ainsi exacerbé, le commerce du café est souvent considéré comme le deuxième marché de matières premières au niveau mondial, après le pétrole.

En Éthiopie, 15 millions de personnes sont concernées par sa production, qui constitue 50 % des recettes d'exportation du pays. Les hauts plateaux de ce vaste territoire de la corne de l'Afrique ont vu naître les premiers caféiers et comptent aujourd'hui près de 5000 espèces endémiques. Par contre, cette paternité ne s'est pas reflétée dans le nom botanique *(coffea arabica)* que les scientifiques donnèrent au caféier en 1753, vu sa dissémination à partir du Yémen. Près de Jimma, dans la province de Kaffa, l'arboretum du Centre de la biodiversité du café est une mosaïque d'*arabica* des quatre coins du pays. « À chacun sa morphologie, selon la région d'origine », explique Jara Nagash, un employé du centre. « La ville de Jimma a été désignée comme lieu de naissance du café, car on y trouve des forêts où poussent des caféiers sauvages, dont certains vieux de 200 ans. À moins d'un kilomètre, des symboles inscrits sur une grande roche témoignent d'un ancien lieu de commerce ; Kaldi, le berger, est sûrement passé par là ! »

Pour Tadesse Meskala, fondateur et directeur de L'Union des coopératives de caféiculteurs d'Oromia, « Le café vient précisément de la région d'Oromia. Le mot *buna*, qui signifie "café", est le nom d'une communauté près de Jimma. » Essentiellement rurale, Oromia produit 60 % du café national. L'Union des coopératives de caféiculteurs d'Oromia a vu le jour en 1999, avec 34 membres. Aujourd'hui, elle compte 129 coopératives qui fédèrent 230 000 familles. « Avant, les producteurs obtenaient 30 à 40 % du prix d'exportation. Aujourd'hui, c'est au minimum 70 % », déclare Meskala, que l'on peut voir dans le documentaire britannique *Black Gold* sur les caféiculteurs éthiopiens et le marché mondial du café. La région d'Oromia compte certains des plus célèbres terroirs du pays comme Limu, Sidamo et surtout Yirgacheffe, dont les collines, qui s'élèvent à 2000 mètres, offrent des conditions idéales pour la culture caféière.

||||||||||||||||||||||||||||||||||||||||||||||||||||||||||||||||||||||||||||||||||||||||

Dans sa petite plantation de Yirgacheffe, Beyene Udesa récolte avec des voisins les fruits rouges de petits arbustes ; « Ma famille a toujours cultivé les caféiers », annonce-t-il. Au-dessus de nous, plusieurs arbres indigènes font ombrage. De grands singes colobes beiges et noirs viennent nous saluer, sans oublier, en guise d'accueil pour le nouveau venu, de marquer leur territoire ; « Non, ce n'est pas de la pluie », m'indique l'un des paysans. Tout le monde rit chaleureusement – même les primates haut perchés poussent des cris qui ressemblent à s'y méprendre à des ricanements.

Le caféier donne ses fruits après quatre ans d'entretien et restera productif pour au moins 20 ans. Les baies vertes sont laissées sur l'arbre pour le prochain passage des cueilleurs. À l'écart du labeur de ces derniers, un mouvement dans un arbre attire mon attention. En me rapprochant, je peux observer le va-et-vient d'un petit oiseau apportant à sa couvée d'oisillons affamés de petits insectes de toutes sortes. Ce spectacle témoigne de la grande biodiversité – animale

☑ Tadesse Meskala (au centre à droite), directeur de l'Union des coopératives de caféiculteurs d'Oromia. ▷ Beyene Udesa, producteur de café, est membre de la coopérative de Negele Gorbitu, dans la célèbre région de Yirgacheffe.

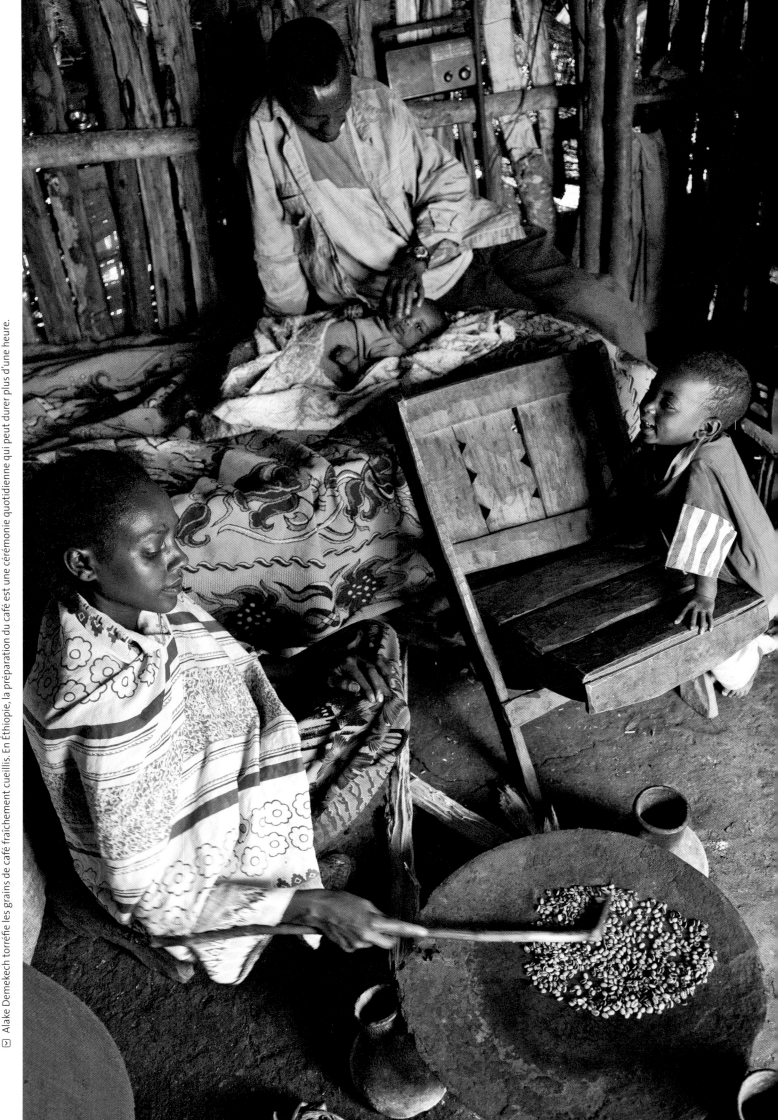

Alake Demekech torréfie les grains de café fraîchement cueillis. En Éthiopie, la préparation du café est une cérémonie quotidienne qui peut durer plus d'une heure.

comme végétale – qui prévaut dans les plantations de café sous couvert forestier. Les essences de bois régionales côtoient les avocatiers, les papayers et les manguiers. De loin, ces écosystèmes ne laissent pas entrevoir qu'ils abritent une plantation, et l'œil du profane n'y voit qu'une forêt naturelle. En Éthiopie, 400 000 hectares sont consacrés au café. Dans l'ensemble des 60 pays producteurs de café, on évalue que 10 millions d'hectares sont consacrés à la culture du café, soit l'équivalent du territoire du Portugal. Une large proportion de ces terres est aujourd'hui transformée en monoculture, au détriment de riches habitats et parfois même de refuges pour une multitude d'oiseaux migrateurs, entre autres espèces.

À 11 heures, Beyene place un lourd panier de baies rouges sur sa tête et dit : « J'apporte ces baies à la maison. Ma femme va préparer le café pour la pause du midi. » De tous les pays producteurs de café que j'ai visités au fil des ans, l'Éthiopie est, sans contredit, celui où la tradition de consommation du café est la plus riche. Sa préparation est un cérémonial quotidien qui s'étire sur plus d'une heure, et qui est aussi courant dans les huttes paysannes que dans les restaurants huppés d'Addis-Abeba.

À la maison, Alake, la femme de Beyene, prend une grande poignée de fruits qu'elle dépulpe habilement, en serrant les cerises entre son pouce et son index. De chaque fruit, elle récupère deux grains, les semences du caféier. Lorsque son bol est plein, elle dépose une première fois les grains sur une grande assiette métallique, replace quelques bouts de bois et ventile les braises. Après quelques minutes, elle retire les grains, les dégage de leur parche et les remet à nouveau sur le feu pour la torréfaction. Avec un petit bâton, elle brasse les grains verts pour qu'ils grillent de manière uniforme. Rapidement, l'arôme du café remplit la pièce, pendant que Beyene joue sur le lit avec son quatrième enfant d'à peine trois mois.

Après avoir été bien torréfiés, les grains sont déposés dans un mortier et Beyene empoigne le pilon, tandis qu'Alake met la cafetière de terre cuite sur le feu. Elle ajoute la poudre de café résultante, en petites quantités à plusieurs reprises, jusqu'à l'ébullition du mélange, puis délicatement, elle verse le riche élixir dans les tasses. L'huile remonte doucement à la surface et je peux alors déguster le café le plus frais de la planète. « Chaque jour, un voisin différent prépare le café et tous viennent discuter, prendre des nouvelles », me dit Beyene.

⊡ Un nid d'oiseau dans un caféier, un signe de la biodiversité des plantations traditionnelles sous couvert forestier.

AU SENS PROPRE, ON NE PEUT QUALIFIER LE CAFÉ de « drogue » – aucune loi ni règlement n'encadrent ou ne prohibent sa consommation. Mais si l'on s'arrête pour contempler les chiffres reliés à sa diffusion et son adoption planétaire, le mot « stupéfiant » est tout indiqué pour le définir au sens figuré : sept millions de tonnes produites par 125 millions de paysans et travailleurs, pour remplir, en bout de ligne, 400 milliards de tasses par an.

On dénombre 60 espèces différentes du genre *coffea* appartenant à la famille des rubiacées arbustives ; de ce lot, deux genres se partagent la plus grande part du commerce – l'*arabica* et le *robusta* (ou *canephora*), complétés par d'autres variétés plus marginales, comme le *liberica* et l'*excelsa*. L'*arabica*, aux arômes plus fins, se cantonne généralement aux régions montagneuses plus fraîches et tend à être moins productif et plus sensible aux infections – mais il demeure tout de même le plus largement cultivé, avec 70 % de la production mondiale. Le *robusta*, prisé des amateurs d'expressos, est moins capricieux quant au terrain de culture et donne un rendement supérieur, avec des grains au mûrissement plus long et au taux de caféine plus élevé.

En général, la demande et les prix de l'*arabica* sont plus élevés que ceux du *robusta*. Blue mountain de Jamaïque et kona d'Hawaii sont, certes, des appellations célèbres d'*arabica*, mais c'est une variété très particulière de *robusta* qui rafle les honneurs du café le plus onéreux ; à 350 $ le kilo, les grains du kopi luwak indonésien doivent, en effet, être altérés par l'appareil digestif d'une civette – un petit mammifère indigène – avant de mériter leur gloire auprès des puristes.

Près des trois quarts des productions caféières mondiales sont de petite superficie, mais tous ces petits joueurs pèsent individuellement peu dans la balance d'un marché contrôlé à près de 70 % par cinq multinationales et régi par les lois spéculatives des grandes bourses. Que ce soit à New York (pour les cours de l'*arabica*) ou à Londres (pour ceux du *robusta*), les prix du café sont notoirement volatils. La forte croissance de la production brésilienne et l'arrivée tonitruante du *robusta* vietnamien sont pointées du doigt dans l'explication du contexte récent de surproduction et de déflation tarifaire.

Fort heureusement, l'avènement du commerce équitable dans l'univers du café a permis de limiter les dégâts pour les petits producteurs regroupés en coopératives qui ont choisi cette voie alternative. En assurant des conditions avantageuses aux paysans, la filière a pu fidéliser ses fournisseurs au Sud pendant que son travail de conscientisation auprès des consommateurs, au Nord, récoltait des dividendes croissants. En se jetant dans l'arène commerciale de la deuxième matière première la plus transigée au monde (après le pétrole), le mouvement équitable allait faire du café sa tête d'affiche et le produit phare de la certification.

⊡ Fleur de caféier *arabica*.

le café en chiffres

COMMERCE CONVENTIONNEL

Production mondiale : 7 792 960 tonnes
Commerce mondial : 11 075 000 000 $

PRINCIPAUX PAYS PRODUCTEURS

Brésil	27 %
Viêtnam	14 %
Colombie	9 %
Indonésie	9 %
Éthiopie	4 %

COMMERCE ÉQUITABLE

Année de certification : 1988
Importations mondiales : 65 808 tonnes
Ventes au détail : 1 784 230 000 $
Croissance de 2007 à 2008 : 14 %

ORGANISATIONS CERTIFIÉES

291 organisations de petits producteurs, dans 25 pays.

ORIGINE DES ORGANISATIONS CERTIFIÉES

Mexique	16 %
Pérou	14 %
Colombie	12 %

PRINCIPAUX PAYS IMPORTATEURS

	Importations (t)	Croissance (2007 à 2008)
États-Unis	24 141	7 %
Grande-Bretagne	9642	16 %
France	7116	8 %
Canada	5029	49 %
Allemagne	4787	10 %

PRIX ET PRIMES

Prix équitable : *arabica* lavé : 2,75 $/kg ; *robusta* lavé : 3,31 $/kg
Prime équitable : 0,22 $/kg
Prime biologique : 0,44 $/kg
Proportion de café biologique : 48 %

La récolte du jour. Chaque baie contient deux grains, les semences du caféier.

À la fin de la journée, Beyene apporte les baies récoltées à la petite coopérative de Negele Gorbitu. À l'usine de lavage du café, hommes et femmes s'activent. Les uns sont au moulin pour le dépulpage des cerises, les autres brassent le contenu des grands bassins de fermentation, et d'autres encore transportent les grains fraîchement lavés vers l'étape du séchage. Sur des dizaines de longues tables couvertes de jute, les grains dorés reposent. Itanish Wolde et ses collègues chantent pour s'encourager durant la longue et fastidieuse sélection manuelle. Ces grains seront acheminés à l'Union, pour son propre marché extérieur ou pour l'encan d'Addis-Abeba. L'an dernier, l'Union a exporté 3250 tonnes de café certifié équitable, soit moins de 5 % du café produit par ses membres. Mais comme le spécifie le directeur Tadesse Meskala, «Tous nos nouveaux clients viennent du marché équitable.»

Le petit hôtel de Yirgacheffe est un carrefour où se croisent acheteurs et exportateurs du grain d'or. À chaque année, Jean-Pierre Blanc, le directeur des Cafés Malongo, rend visite aux organisations avec lesquelles il travaille. Son implication dans le commerce équitable a été inspirée par sa rencontre, au début des années 1990, avec Francisco Van der Hoff, missionnaire néerlandais, membre fondateur de la coopérative de café UCIRI au Mexique et cofondateur de Max Havelaar, le premier *label* de certification équitable. «J'ai compris que c'était la voie de l'avenir, qu'il ne pouvait y avoir de saines entreprises de café sans le respect des producteurs, explique Jean-Pierre Blanc. Aujourd'hui, près de 50 % de nos importations sont des cafés certifiés équitables.» L'entreprise, dont le chiffre d'affaires avoisine les 80 millions d'euros, est le leader du café équitable en France.

Deux autres représentants d'une grande entreprise caféière sont venus rencontrer Tadesse Meskala. Ils travaillent pour Nestlé, qui contrôle, entre autres, 55 % du marché mondial du café soluble – un géant parmi les géants. En 2005, Nestlé a obtenu une certification équitable pour l'une de ses lignes de café en Grande-Bretagne. «Ce fut un grand choc pour certains, mais nous les avions approchés depuis plusieurs années», raconte Ian Bretman, vice-président du conseil d'administration de la Fairtrade Labelling Organizations International (FLO) et directeur de la Fairtrade Foundation en Grande-Bretagne de 1997 à 2008. «Nestlé importe de nombreux conteneurs annuellement et nous n'avons jamais eu de difficulté à nous entendre sur les prix», me dit Tadesse. J'ai bien pu serrer leur main, mais une entrevue m'a été catégoriquement refusée.

☑ Les grains de café sont raclés régulièrement pour qu'ils sèchent uniformément.

⌃ Itanish Wolde et ses compatriotes de la coopérative de Negele Gorbitu
sélectionnent manuellement les grains de café.

Francisco Van der Hoff rappelle : « J'aurais souhaité qu'un minimum de 10 % soit demandé avant qu'une entreprise puisse utiliser le *label* équitable, car des compagnies pourraient faire un peu d'équitable juste pour l'image, tout en poursuivant des pratiques abusives sur 99,9 % de leur café. » Pour Ian Bretman, « L'engagement initial n'est pas aussi important que le résultat final. Aujourd'hui, 100 % des cafés expresso de Starbucks en Grande-Bretagne sont certifiés équitables, mais nous y sommes arrivés progressivement. » Dans le monde du café, Starbucks frappe l'imaginaire. Ses 10 milliards de dollars de chiffre d'affaires n'équivalent qu'à 10 % des revenus annuels de Nestlé, mais la compagnie est le leader des cafés de spécialités, qui sont en forte croissance. Après avoir obtenu sa certification équitable en 2000, Starbucks torréfia 9000 tonnes de café équitable en 2008 – soit 5 % de ses importations – mais cette quantité lui confère tout de

même le titre de plus importante distributrice de café équitable au monde, avec 15 % du marché. En 2009, l'entreprise s'est engagée à accroître ses importations équitables à 20 000 tonnes.

L'adhésion de Starbucks à l'équitable est le résultat de nombreuses batailles. L'Éthiopie fut au cœur de l'une d'elles. En 2004, Starbucks déposait une demande aux États-Unis pour enregistrer l'appellation « Sidamo », nom de l'une des plus célèbres régions caféières de l'Éthiopie. Les autorités éthiopiennes ont vite réagi en déposant leurs propres demandes de marques de commerce pour les noms « Sidamo », « Yirgacheffe » et « Harar ». Après d'âpres négociations, une entente entre les deux parties reconnaissait à l'Éthiopie la propriété intellectuelle des noms. L'initiative éthiopienne n'inclut aucune redevance financière directe, mais mise sur une meilleure reconnaissance de ses cafés pour augmenter les prix et ainsi mieux valoriser le travail des caféiculteurs.

⌂ Au point d'achat du café de la coopérative, les birrs changent de mains.

||||||||||||||||||||||||||||||||||||||||||||||||||||||||||||||||||||||||||||||||||||||

À quelques kilomètres de Negele Gorbitu, la coopérative d'Hoomma compte près de 1000 membres dans six villages. En fin d'après-midi, Amara Elema quitte la coopérative avec une liasse de birrs éthiopiens et sa calculatrice, en direction du village de Buchessa, l'un des trois points d'achat de baies. Des centaines de personnes arrivent avec de lourds sacs sur le dos. Trois acheteurs ont leur espace dans la place centrale du village. Les fruits seront payés sur le champ – près de 6 birrs le kilo (0,50 $), soit le double du prix de l'an passé. « L'année a été exceptionnelle, affirme Tadesse. Avec la signature de l'accord avec Starbucks, des acheteurs locaux ont rapidement affiché des prix très élevés en début de saison, et nous avons suivi la tendance. Nos clients équitables sont au courant de la situation et sont disposés à payer plus pour nos cafés. »

Avec l'accroissement des revenus, les kiosques de viande se multiplient dans ce pays où la viande crue est une importante tradition culinaire. « Pendant la récolte, on abat des bœufs à tous les jours, mais dans six mois, il n'y aura plus que du *ko'cho* (galette de faux bananier) à se mettre sous la dent », commente Tadesse. Nous visitons la région avec Takile, le jeune gérant de la coopérative d'Hoomma, qui poursuit : « Ici, plusieurs cultivent des terres louées et doivent partager les revenus. Certains s'en sortent bien, mais plus des trois quarts des familles de la région sont pauvres. Leurs problèmes surviennent surtout en juillet et août, quand l'argent du café est disparu et que les réserves de nourriture sont basses. Obtenir un prêt ici coûte 100 % d'intérêts. »

« Même si le prix des baies atteignait 20 birrs, il ne permettrait pas de faire vivre dignement toutes ces familles et leurs enfants. Il faut davantage d'éducation et de nouvelles opportunités de travail pour réduire le nombre de gens dépendant de la caféiculture », précise Tadesse. Dans l'ensemble des six villages desservis par Hoomma, trois écoles primaires ont pu profiter d'améliorations et une clinique médicale a été construite grâce aux primes équitables. « L'an prochain, les membres souhaitent construire deux petits magasins de denrées de base et, si possible, une école secondaire ; sinon, l'école la plus proche est à 45 km ! », m'instruit Takile. De retour à la coopérative de Negele Gorbitu, les professeurs de l'école primaire du village sont fiers de montrer les quatre nouvelles salles de classe. Au total, les coopératives certifiées de l'Union (28 sur les 129) ont construit plus de 20 écoles primaires, 4 dispensaires et 36 puits d'eau potable avec leurs primes équitables.

Reconnaître la provenance de nos biens de consommation et surtout valoriser le travail qui se fait par ceux et celles qui sont à la base de ces marchés sont certains des principes fondateurs du commerce équitable. La certification équitable appuie directement plus d'un million de familles productrices. Les ventes de produits équitables atteignent aujourd'hui les cinq milliards de dollars annuellement. Ce marché équitable ne crée peut-être pas d'immenses richesses au Sud, mais fait souvent la différence entre misère et dignité, entre désillusion et espoir. « Il n'y a pas de problème à vivre pauvrement, c'est l'exploitation qui est inacceptable », dit Francisco Van der Hoff, en réaffirmant des valeurs évangéliques qui ne sauraient en aucun cas être confondues avec le maintien d'un *statu quo* fondé sur l'injustice. « Le commerce équitable n'est pas une question de charité, mais bien de justice », conclut « *el padre* ».

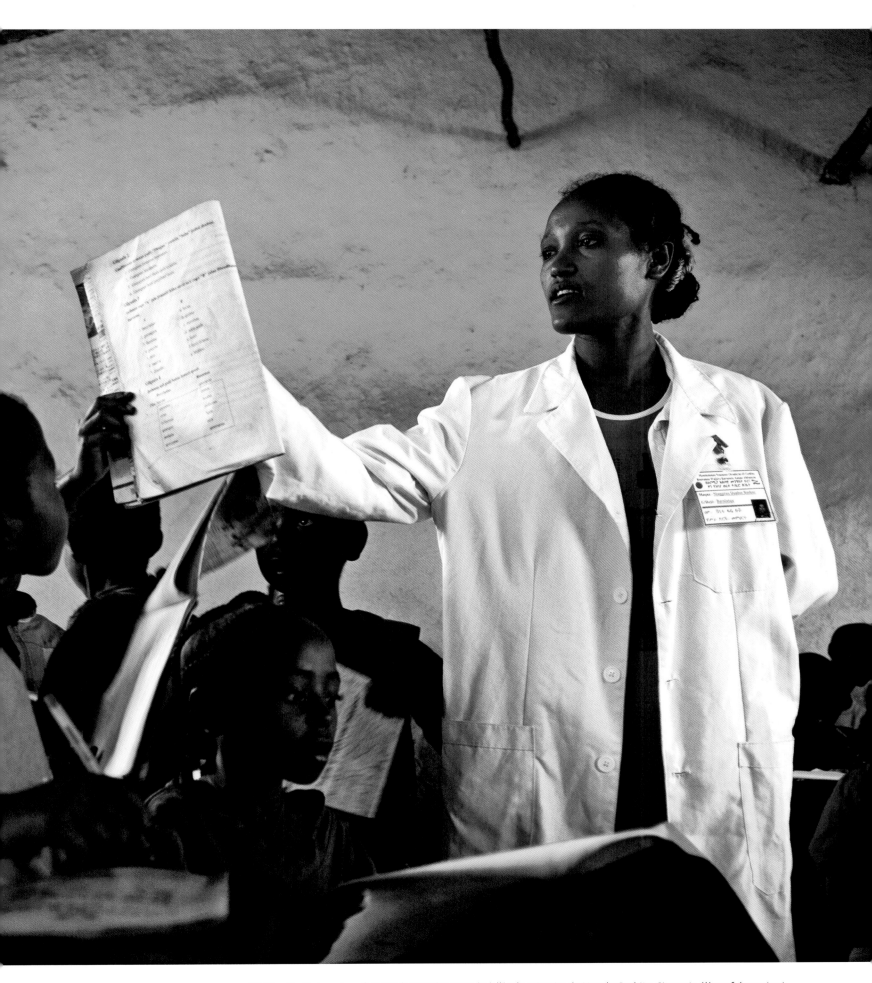

⌃ Shegitu Dube est professeur de troisième année à l'école primaire de Negele Gorbitu. Six cents élèves fréquentent
cette école, où quatre nouvelles salles de classe ont été construites grâce aux primes équitables de la coopérative.

la certification équitable

En 1985, le prêtre-ouvrier Francisco Van der Hoff rencontre son compatriote Nico Rozen, un économiste œuvrant auprès de l'organisation d'aide internationale Solidaridad. Assis à une table dans la gare d'Utrecht, aux Pays-Bas, les deux hommes jettent les bases de la certification équitable; le moment est charnière dans l'histoire du mouvement. Pour les petits producteurs et leurs coopératives, cela se traduit par des prix minimums garantis couvrant les frais de production, des primes au développement, le préfinancement sur demande et une saine gestion environnementale. Pour le consommateur, elle légitime le produit et sa réelle valeur sociocommerciale. « Ces critères ont été inscrits sur une serviette de table... qui existe toujours ! », se rappelle Van der Hoff. Trois ans plus tard, l'organisme Max Havelaar – qui évoque le héros justicier d'un roman de la littérature néerlandaise – voyait le jour aux Pays-Bas. Aujourd'hui, on compte 19 initiatives nationales de certification équitable sous l'égide de la Fairtrade Labelling Organizations (FLO), fondée en 1997.

⌃ Les *labels* pour les produits certifiés équitables au Canada (en haut) et à l'international (en bas).

« La certification a été développée pour décloisonner le commerce équitable des limites des réseaux alternatifs, pour mieux l'offrir à un plus vaste bassin de consommateurs », explique le « père » de la certification. En certifiant des produits – et non des organisations –, ceux-ci peuvent être importés par de grandes entreprises et distribués plus aisément dans les grandes surfaces avec, sur leur emballage, un *label* garantissant les principes d'équité de cet échange commercial.

La croissance du mouvement est spectaculaire (1300 % entre 2000 et 2008), mais les critiques sont aussi au rendez-vous; l'hégémonie de la certification de la FLO, mais aussi la participation croissante des multinationales en inquiètent plusieurs. « Nos règles sont strictes et les mêmes pour tous; nous haussons continuellement nos exigences auprès des distributeurs de produits équitables », assure Ian Bretman, de la FLO. « Nous ne sommes pas un organisme de certification comme les autres, nous sommes une organisation de développement qui utilise la certification comme outil. »

Après 20 ans de certification, le commerce équitable peut compter à son actif des succès probants. « Le café équitable couvre 22 % du marché en Grande-Bretagne; en Finlande, 20 % des ananas sont certifiés et en Suisse, 53 % des bananes vendues sont équitables », rappelle Bretman. Actuellement, la FLO certifie plus de 6000 produits, issus de 746 organisations de producteurs et distribués par 2700 entreprises, pour des ventes au détail évaluées à près de cinq milliards de dollars. « Notre défi est de poursuivre la croissance au profit des producteurs du Sud, sans compromettre l'intégrité de nos principes », conclut-il.

« La certification a été développée pour décloisonner le commerce équitable des limites des réseaux alternatifs, pour mieux l'offrir à un plus vaste bassin de consommateurs. »

⌃ C'est l'heure de la pesée dans le petit entrepôt de la coopérative de Negele Gorbitu.

1. Baies du caféier.
2. Récolte des baies.
3. Tadesse Dechasso et sa récolte de café.
4. Tables de séchage à la coopérative Kenteri.
5. Tsegaye Abela fait sécher ses baies au soleil.
6. Tri manuel à la coopérative de Negele Gorbitu.
7. Sacs de café à la coopérative de Negele Gorbitu.

▷ En haut : Galgale Shorbo, membre de la coopérative d'Hoomma.
▷ En bas : Maison traditionnelle dans la région de Yirgacheffe.

Ⓒ Un majestueux *hornbill* survole les collines de Yirgacheffe. Sous la canopée se cachent des caféiers *arabica*, d'où proviennent certains des meilleurs cafés au monde.

le Cacao

Pas même les rivières de miel qui irriguent les vallées dans nos plus généreux mythes de l'abondance ne pourraient faire oublier l'âcre saveur du fielleux commerce mondial de cacao. Du sang versé par une princesse toltèque naquit le cacaoyer, plante aux fruits imprégnés de cette amère souffrance originelle. Toltèques, Mayas et Aztèques firent du cacao un élément central de leur culture. Largement utilisées comme monnaie d'échange, les fèves de cacao étaient aussi grillées et broyées sur des pierres brûlantes et mélangées avec de l'eau pour en faire une pâte à laquelle on ajoutait de la vanille, du poivre, de la cannelle, de l'anis ou d'autres épices. Cette préparation était la base d'une boisson sacrée appelée *xocolatl*, mot composé à partir des termes *xocolli* et *atl*, qui signifient respectivement « amer » et « eau » en langue nahuatl. La « nourriture des dieux » était donc passablement amère, mais la saveur dominante du chocolat n'était pas repoussante pour ces peuples, dont la notion d'équilibre faisait autant de place à l'amertume qu'à la douceur.

Il en allait tout autrement pour l'élite européenne, qui mélangea le chocolat à un autre produit colonial alors également rare et dispendieux : le sucre de canne. Envoûtée par son goût transformé et par ses effets, la naissante bourgeoisie s'appropriera le fruit du cacaoyer jusqu'à en faire un élément essentiel de son nouveau confort. Pour répondre à une demande croissante de chocolat, de grandes plantations cacaoyères seront développées dans le continent Abya Yala, alors rebaptisé Amérique. Les nouveaux maîtres du monde violèrent un autre continent, l'Afrique, où ils se procurèrent la force de travail nécessaire aux nouvelles cultures coloniales. Bien plus tard, ce sera au tour du cacao lui-même de se faire expatrier vers l'Afrique. Aujourd'hui, le tiers de la production mondiale de cacao vient de la Côte-d'Ivoire. Avec le Ghana et le Nigeria, l'ouest de l'Afrique produit près des deux tiers de cette denrée.

||||||||||||||||||||||||||||||||||||||||||||||||||||||||||||||||||||||||||||||||||||

La cabosse rouge vif est proéminente sur le tronc du cacaoyer. Fauto Aureo, producteur de cacao dominicain, muni d'une longue perche à l'extrémité tranchante, taille quelques branches à la cime de l'arbre. « Il faut bien entretenir sa plantation si l'on veut obtenir une bonne récolte », dit-il. Avec ses quelque 40 000 producteurs, la République dominicaine produit 50 000 tonnes de fèves annuellement, ce qui équivaut à près de 1 % de la production mondiale. Au-dessus des cacaoyers se déploie la forêt naturelle dominicaine. Du haut des airs, rien ne laisse présager qu'une plantation s'y cache. L'exploitation des cacaoyers occupe 25 % des forêts du pays ; dissimulée dans son environnement sylvestre, elle fait contraste avec celle d'autres régions cacaoyères – nommément en Afrique, où les monocultures ont déjà souillé 10 millions d'hectares de la forêt équatoriale, dont 13 % de la surface totale de la Côte-d'Ivoire.

La déforestation n'est malheureusement pas le plus grave des drames de l'industrie cacaoyère. Des études menées par l'Institut international d'agriculture tropicale ont révélé l'emploi massif d'une main-d'œuvre infantile – voire un esclavage pur et simple – dans les champs de cacao de l'ouest de l'Afrique, où 284 000 enfants sont ainsi contraints à effectuer des tâches dangereuses, dont la manipulation de produits chimiques toxiques, tel le lidane, un insecticide proche du DDT.

Exploités par des producteurs eux-mêmes sous-payés, ces enfants sont les victimes caricaturales de cet échange inégal. Si les pays exportateurs de cacao retirent annuellement deux milliards de dollars de cette activité, l'industrie chocolatière occidentale s'en sort bien mieux, avec plus de 60 milliards de dollars. L'amer cacao, produit par de petites mains blessées, est transformé par une industrie qui, ironiquement, destine une grande partie de ses produits aux enfants du Nord.

||||||||||||||||||||||||||||||||||||||||||||||||||||||||||||||||||||||||||||||||||||

Dans sa plantation, en République dominicaine, Francisco Alcantara fait le tour de ses cacaoyers pour vérifier la maturation des cabosses. « La couleur n'est pas un indicateur garanti ; vaut mieux cogner sur la cabosse pour savoir si elle est bien mûre », dit-il. Avec une machette, il détache délicatement une cabosse du tronc de l'arbre, sans endommager les fleurs et les jeunes fruits. « En décembre, ce n'est que la petite récolte ; toutes ces jeunes cabosses vont mûrir en avril et là, on aura beaucoup de cacao. » Le sac rempli, les cabosses sont déchargées à un point de congrégation, au centre de la plantation. Francisco s'assoit et, d'un geste précis, fait une entaille dans la cabosse pour la séparer en deux ; les graines blanches apparaissent en grappe. L'écabossage dure tout l'après-midi et un monticule blanc s'accumule dans un tronc de bananier. « Il est temps d'acheminer le tout à la coopérative », m'indique-t-il.

Francisco est membre du « Bloc 2 » de la Confederación Nacional de Cacaocultores Dominicanos (CONACADO). La CONACADO est une fédération nationale de huit coopératives régionales (baptisées « Bloc ») regroupant 150 associations et 10 000 producteurs. « Nous représentons 25 % des producteurs de cacao du pays ! », souligne Isodoro de la Rosa, directeur exécutif de la CONACADO. Pourtant, dix ans après sa fondation (en 1988), et malgré son nombre important de membres, la fédération n'exportait que 7 % du cacao dominicain. « Tout a changé avec l'ouragan Georges ». En fait, Georges n'a pas été tendre lorsqu'il a traversé la République dominicaine, le 22 septembre 1998 ; la tempête a fait des centaines de morts et 185 000 réfugiés. Pour l'industrie cacaoyère, l'ouragan a ravagé de grandes régions, coupant des deux tiers la récolte annuelle. « Nous avons reculé cinq ans en arrière », précise-t-il.

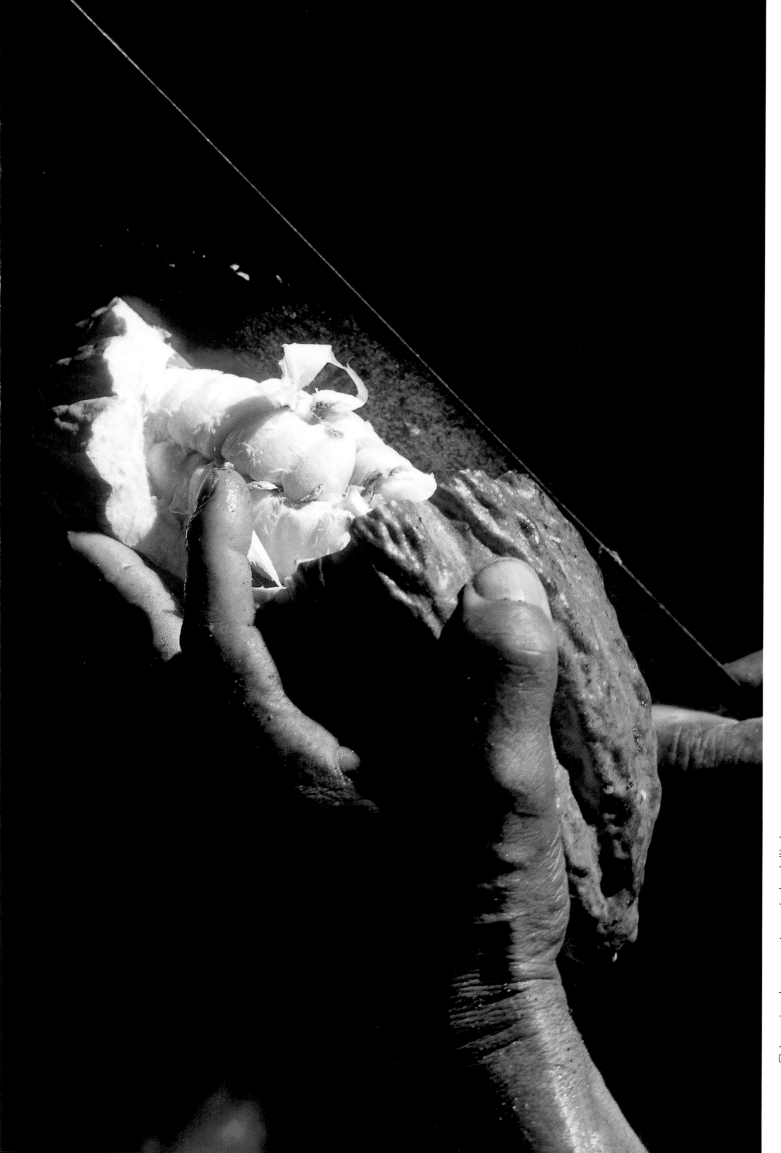

Les graines de cacao sont exposées lors de l'écabossage.

le cacao

LE CACAOYER EST UN ARBRE de la famille des sterculiacées, genre *theobroma*. Ce terme signifie littéralement « nourriture des dieux ». C'est une plante cauliflore, c'est-à-dire dont les fruits poussent directement sur le tronc ou les rameaux. La graine de cacao contient de la caféine et de la théobromine. Bien qu'originaire du Mexique, le cacaoyer a été introduit dans les Caraïbes, en Amérique du Sud et en Afrique – cette dernière produisant près des deux tiers du cacao mondial.

L'économie du cacao est caractérisée par une forte concentration. Quatre-vingts pour cent du marché du chocolat sont contrôlés par six transnationales, dont trois Européennes : la Britannique Cadbury-Schweppes, l'Italienne Ferrero et le géant suisse Nestlé.

Seuls le Brésil et la Malaisie font du cacao selon le modèle des grandes plantations. À la base, ce sont surtout de petits producteurs et leur famille qui assurent 90 % de la production mondiale de cacao. Dans des pays africains tels la Côte-d'Ivoire (plus grand producteur mondial) et le Ghana, la culture et la commercialisation du cacao constituent la principale activité économique de millions de familles, ce qui rend ces pays extrêmement dépendants des cours de cette denrée.

Le cacao équitable provient de 30 organisations de producteurs de l'ouest de l'Afrique, des Amériques et des Caraïbes. Plus de 10 000 tonnes de cacao équitable furent exportées en 2008. Au Canada, 22 millions de tablettes de chocolat ont été vendues avec le *label* équitable. Ce chiffre risque de doubler avec le lancement de la Dairy Milk équitable de Cadbury, qui soutiendra 40 000 cacaoculteurs ghanéens et 6000 petits producteurs de sucre.

le cacao en chiffres

COMMERCE CONVENTIONNEL

Production mondiale : 4 161 631 tonnes
Commerce mondial : 8 380 000 000 $

PRINCIPAUX PAYS PRODUCTEURS

Côte-d'Ivoire	33 %
Ghana	18 %
Indonésie	15 %
Nigeria	12 %
Brésil	6 %
République dominicaine (14ᵉ)	0,8 %

COMMERCE ÉQUITABLE

Année de certification : 1997 (FLO)
Importations mondiales : 10 299 tonnes
Ventes au détail : 275 300 000 $

ORGANISATIONS CERTIFIÉES

30 organisations de petits producteurs, dans 15 pays.

ORIGINE DES ORGANISATIONS CERTIFIÉES

Pérou	27 %
République dominicaine	13 %
Côte-d'Ivoire	10 %
Nicaragua	10 %

PRINCIPAUX PAYS IMPORTATEURS

	Importations (t)
Grande-Bretagne	3612
États-Unis	1745
France	1349
Allemagne	694
Pays-Bas	518

PRIX ET PRIMES

Prix équitable : 1600 $/t
Prime équitable : 150 $/t
Prime biologique : 200 $/t
Proportion de cacao biologique : 48 %

⌄ Au Bloc 2 de la CONACADO, Pepin Gregoria racle les fèves de cacao pour qu'elles sèchent uniformément.

⌃ Contrôle de qualité des fèves suite à la fermentation et au séchage. ⌐ Roque Pérez Cruz choisit ses plants de cacao à la pépinière de la CONACADO, financée par les primes équitables.

Avant le passage de Georges, les paysans, qui ne bénéficient de revenus que quelques mois par année, avaient recours au crédit dans les magasins généraux pour acheter des denrées de base, des matériaux de construction ou des outils agricoles. « L'intérêt était de 3 à 5 % par mois ! Et tout était garanti par le cacao à venir », s'indigne Fauto Aureo – un cercle vicieux d'endettement qui forçait les paysans à vendre toute ou en partie leur récolte à ces magasins liés aux grandes compagnies d'exportation du pays. À la suite du passage de Georges, les petits producteurs étaient incapables de rembourser leurs dettes. Le gouvernement dominicain a donc mis sur pied un programme pour régler les emprunts. Si les créanciers en ont été les premiers bénéficiaires, il n'en reste pas moins que les petits producteurs dominicains ont été libérés de leurs dettes et de l'obligation de vendre aux acheteurs privés. Plusieurs producteurs ont alors joint la CONACADO. « Nous avons plus de membres, et nos producteurs vendent maintenant tout leur cacao aux coopératives de la confédération », précise Isodoro. Lors de la récolte de 2002, alors que la production de cacao dominicain avait atteint les trois quarts de son niveau d'avant Georges, la CONACADO exportait 30 % de la production nationale, se classant pour la première fois au sommet des exportateurs de cacao du pays ! « C'était un moment exaltant, mais on a fait des jaloux sur l'île », chuchote Isodoro. Pour Fauto, la situation actuelle est complètement différente de celle du passé : « Si j'ai besoin d'un prêt pour des travaux agricoles, je vais à ma coopérative et je peux l'obtenir à un bon taux d'intérêt. »

En fin d'après-midi, aux entrepôts du Bloc 2 de la CONACADO, les paysans arrivent les uns après les autres pour apporter la récolte du jour. Les graines blanches sont alors transvidées dans des bacs de plastique pour en vérifier la qualité. « Quelques graines de mauvaise qualité et c'est tout un lot de cacao qui écope », lance José, le directeur de la coopérative. « Par le passé, le cacao dominicain était pénalisé à cause de sa mauvaise qualité ; c'est maintenant une priorité d'améliorer nos standards. » Les graines sont aussitôt transférées dans de grandes boîtes en bois pour la fermentation. Étape très importante, la fermentation permet d'éliminer la pulpe, mais transforme surtout la graine en fève, en tuant l'embryon et en donnant naissance aux précurseurs chimiques qui donnent tout son arôme au cacao. Dionisio, l'un des travailleurs, place quelques feuilles de bananier au-dessus des graines, sous le regard de Michel, un expert européen venu évaluer et conseiller la CONACADO pour améliorer la qualité de son produit. « Traditionnellement, le cacao dominicain était seulement séché (cacao sanchez), mais l'hispanola, qui est fermenté, est plus recherché et se paiera 10 à 15 % de plus sur le marché mondial », précise Michel. Avec des primes biologiques et équitables, le cacao de la CONACADO est l'un des plus valorisés au monde.

Après six jours de fermentation, le mucilage blanc a complètement disparu et les fèves chaudes et visqueuses sont étendues sur des plates-formes de bois, où elles sécheront naturellement au soleil. La cour arrière du Bloc 2 est un labyrinthe de ces plates-formes sur roues, avec leur toit de tôle qui sert à recouvrir le cacao en cas d'orage. Pepin Gregoria, un employé, déambule de plate-forme en plate-forme avec son râteau pour retourner les fèves, afin qu'elles sèchent de manière uniforme.

Durant une période d'une à deux semaines, ces fèves passeront d'un taux d'humidité de 60 % à 8 %.

À l'entrepôt, Dionisio et les autres travailleurs se relaient pour transporter sur leur tête les sacs de 60 kilos. L'un des employés coupe en deux les fèves d'un échantillon qu'il étale sur une petite planche quadrillée. « Une fève brune, pleinement fermentée, est de première qualité, alors qu'une fève brune-pourpre ou pourpre est de seconde ou troisième qualité », me précise-t-il. Notre seuil de tolérance aux défauts est de 5 %, pas plus. »

À deux pas des entrepôts, Roque Pérez Cruz arrive à la pépinière de la coopérative pour y récupérer 200 semis. « Des cacaoyers, mais aussi des arbres indigènes », m'indique-t-il en remplissant son camion de petits arbustes. Il souhaite reboiser une partie de sa plantation vieillissante qui a été touchée par le dernier ouragan. Cette pépinière a été construite grâce aux primes équitables.

⊡ Dionisio Arcangel dépose une feuille de bananier sur les graines de cacao, qui fermenteront ensuite pendant six jours.

« UN PRIX JUSTE DANS UN CONTEXTE LOCAL ou régional est convenu après dialogue et concertation. Cela couvre non seulement les coûts de production, mais permet également une production socialement juste et respectueuse de l'environnement. » Cette citation est tirée des dix principes du commerce équitable de la WFTO. Pour la FLO, « Le prix équitable garantit que les producteurs couvriront leur coût moyen pour une production durable. Il agit comme filet de protection pour les paysans lorsque les cours mondiaux baissent. Sans lui, les paysans seraient complètement à la merci du marché. »

Le marché du cacao, coté à Londres et à New York comme celui du café, est hautement volatil et souffre de la spéculation boursière. Les quantités de cacao et de café négociées sur les marchés financiers sont largement supérieures à celles effectivement produites. Les désastres naturels ou encore les crises politiques qui affectent les principaux pays producteurs influencent grandement les cours. Si une gelée au Brésil fait gonfler soudainement les prix du café, les récentes tensions politiques en Côte-d'Ivoire, de la même façon, ont fait grimper les cours du cacao. En novembre 2009, ils étaient de 3300 $ la tonne, soit plus du double du prix minimum équitable (1600 $), alors qu'en novembre 2000, ils étaient de 700 $, moins de la moitié du prix équitable.

Il faut comprendre que le prix équitable n'est pas fixe mais représente un prix minimum garanti. Lorsque les cours dépassent le prix minimum équitable, les acheteurs doivent payer le prix supérieur du marché. Producteurs et clients peuvent négocier des prix supérieurs selon la qualité, la spécificité ou d'autres attributs du produit exporté. Une production biologique, quant à elle, assure une prime de 200 $ la tonne dans le cas du cacao.

Une prime équitable au développement s'ajoute aussi au prix de base (150 $ la tonne pour le cacao), un aspect fondamental pour le mouvement. « Ces montants vont dans un fonds commun, au bénéfice des travailleurs et des paysans, pour l'amélioration de leurs conditions sociales, économiques et environnementales. Leur utilisation est décidée de manière démocratique par les producteurs », spécifie la FLO. Plus de 60 millions de dollars en primes équitables ont été versés en 2008.

En plus du prix minimum et de la prime, les compagnies qui commercialisent des produits équitables doivent payer une avance de 60 %, six semaines avant la livraison lorsque les organisations de producteurs le demandent. Ce paiement constitue un préfinancement à la production absolument nécessaire dans bien des communautés de producteurs où les crédits sont onéreux et souvent inaccessibles. Ces préfinancements ont dépassé les 150 millions de dollars en 2008. Les entreprises du Nord doivent aussi signer des contrats qui permettent aux organisations du Sud de planifier à long terme et de maintenir des pratiques de production durables.

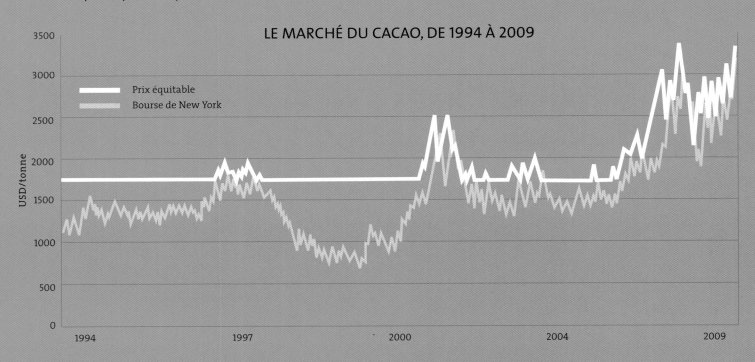

LE MARCHÉ DU CACAO, DE 1994 À 2009

Prix équitable
Bourse de New York

USD/tonne

Francisco Antonio racle ses fèves de cacao sur une plate-forme de séchage qu'il a pu construire à côté de sa maison grâce à un prêt de sa coopérative.

Voisine de Fauto Aureo, Carida m'invite à déguster un vrai chocolat chaud maison. « Nous devons nous rendre à ma petite maison dans la forêt », me dit-elle. Le pas assuré malgré ses 71 ans, Carida évite les racines et enjambe les rigoles, un parapluie à la main. Elle ajoute : « Je ne viens plus très souvent ici depuis que je vis seule. » De manière rudimentaire, elle grille les fèves de cacao dans un grand bol d'acier au-dessus d'un feu de bois. Broyées à la main dans un mortier, les fèves de cacao se transforment en pâte qui, une fois séchée, forme un bâton dur qui se préservera de longs mois. « Celui-là n'est pas pour aujourd'hui, mais j'en ai d'autres en réserve », avance-t-elle. Elle râpe alors un bâton qu'elle agrémente d'une pincée de sucre et de quelques épices, selon la recette locale. À la surface du breuvage brunâtre, les huiles naturelles de la fève de cacao suintent lentement ; l'arôme est délicieux et le goût incomparable. Carida sort une pipe à tabac et prend une pause bien méritée.

À des milliers de kilomètres de là, une autre recette de chocolat chaud suscite un enthousiasme certain. À Ottawa, la coopérative La Siembra fabrique les produits Cocoa Camino avec le cacao équitable de la CONACADO depuis sa fondation, en 1999. En 2006, lorsque la CONACADO a fait l'acquisition d'une usine de transformation des fèves, les dirigeants de La Siembra ont choisi d'intégrer le cacao en poudre produit par les producteurs dominicains dans leur chocolat chaud. « Dès que l'occasion s'est présentée, nous avons essayé le cacao provenant de Cafiesa (le nom de l'usine en question) et avons constaté avec bonheur la qualité du produit », explique Henk Van der Molen, directeur des opérations. Au-delà des prix et primes équitables sur le cacao, cette mesure assure aux producteurs une plus grande part de la valeur ajoutée. Comme l'ancienne boisson sacrée des ancêtres, nourriture des dieux concoctée par les mortels, ce cacao équitable sert à célébrer un nouveau pacte de justice entre les hommes et la terre.

▷ Carida.

1. Fleurs sur le tronc d'un cacaoyer.
2. Sélection des graines de cacao.
3. Manutention des graines de cacao, au Bloc 2 de la CONACADO.
4. Fèves de cacao fermentées.
5. Séchage des fèves de cacao.
6. Fèves de cacao broyées dans un mortier.

▷ En haut : Carlos Bonilla, producteur de cacao, est membre du Bloc 8 de la CONACADO.
▷ En bas : Dionisio Arcangel transporte des sacs de cacao de 60 kilos dans l'entrepôt du Bloc 2 de la CONACADO.

© Anthony Rodriguez transporte de la canne à sucre sur la plantation La Pressa de CoopeAgri, au Costa Rica.

le sucre

L'arc de Kâma, divinité hindoue de l'amour charnel, est une tige de canne à sucre. Séduire est la mission de Kâma, être d'une irrésistible beauté et d'une infinie douceur.

Sarkara en sanscrit, *sukkar* en arabe, *seker* en turc, *saccharum* en latin, *zucchero* en italien, *sucker* en allemand, *sugar* en anglais, *azucar* en espagnol, ζάχαρη en grec, le sucre est dans toutes les langues, toutes les bouches, mais l'histoire de cette omniprésente denrée n'a pas grand-chose à voir avec l'équité et la justice. On ne rappellera jamais assez les liens siamois entre le sucre et la traite négrière. Des millions d'hommes et de femmes furent sacrifiés dans la production de cette poudre qui, dès sa commercialisation, a contribué à accélérer le processus d'accumulation du système économique naissant.

Pourra-t-on préciser un jour l'ensemble des dégâts écologiques provoqués par l'introduction des cultures sucrières chez les peuples soumis par le mercantilisme planétaire? L'ingénieur agronome Narciso Aguilera Marin, professeur à

⌃ Wilson Conejo Guzman, producteur de canne à sucre.

l'École d'Agriculture de Granma à Cuba, rappelle qu'à l'arrivée des Espagnols, 94,5 % du territoire cubain était recouvert de forêts : «La monoculture de la canne à sucre est en grande partie responsable de la réduction de cette couverture à seulement 14 % en 1959 ! Nous avons mis 40 ans pour revenir à 24,5 %.» Comprendre l'histoire du sucre et ses effets ravageurs sur les civilisations peut nous amener à nous poser bien d'autres questions dérangeantes. Pourquoi les sociétés acceptent-elles de payer si passivement les coûts astronomiques – en termes de santé publique – engendrés par la consommation abusive de ce produit ? Et comment se fait-il que, même aujourd'hui, le monde tolère que l'économie du sucre pérennise des relations de production, comme celles dont sont victimes les travailleurs haïtiens dans les *bateyes** de République dominicaine, qui ressemblent à s'y méprendre aux vieux rapports esclavagistes des siècles passés ?

Quoi qu'il en soit, le sucre est là pour rester, étant devenu un produit incontournable pour l'ensemble de l'économie. Bâtir des relations de justice autour d'une telle production est un défi majeur pour les producteurs et les consommateurs unis par les liens du commerce équitable.

||||||||||||||||||||||||||||||||||||||||||||||||||||||||||||||||||||||||||||||||||||||||

F ier de ses 74 ans, Wilson Conejo Guzman roule sur sa bicyclette entre deux champs de canne à sucre, au Costa Rica. «Depuis 45 ans, je me promène à vélo, c'est comme ça que je garde la forme », explique le septuagénaire. «Je ne passe pas une journée sans prendre mon vélo. Mes terres ne

||||||||||||||||||||||||||||||||||

* Campements où vivent les coupeurs de canne, en République dominicaine et à Cuba.

▷ Plantation de canne à sucre dans le comté de Pérez Zeledón, au Costa Rica.

sont qu'à un peu plus de deux kilomètres de la maison. » Wilson est membre de CoopeAgri, une large coopérative qui façonne depuis plus de 45 ans le paysage du comté de Pérez Zeledón, au Costa Rica. Fondée en 1962, avec 391 membres, CoopeAgri compte aujourd'hui plus de 10 000 membres dans une région de 125 000 habitants. Quinze pour cent des membres de Coope-Agri produisent de la canne à sucre, alors que la grande majorité produisent du café. « J'ai eu du café, du tabac, mais depuis 11 ans, je me dédie à la canne », raconte Wilson, qui cultive trois hectares de canne à sucre sur ses cinq hectares. « Je cultive aussi des piments et d'autres légumes que je vends à la foire agricole les jeudis et vendredis. » Ce père de six enfants et grand-père de plusieurs petits-enfants circule dans sa plantation pour vérifier le niveau de maturation de ses plants. Haute de plus de deux mètres, la canne prend 12 mois avant d'arriver à maturité. Sa petite-fille Pamela, le regard rieur, nous rejoint dans la parcelle. Son grand-père coupe alors un bout de canne, qu'il épluche, et lui remet un morceau qu'elle déguste avec avidité.

||||||||||||||||||||||||||||||||||||||||||||||||||||||||||||||||||||||||||||||||||

À quelques kilomètres des terres de Wilson, c'est jour de récolte sur la plantation La Pressa, propriété de CoopeAgri. « Ici, la récolte est sans brûlis », m'annonce Miguel Navaro, l'un des cueilleurs. Les brûlis sont souvent utilisés pour réduire la charge de travail des cueilleurs, mais ils affaiblissent les sols, réduisent la qualité du sucre et causent leur lot de gaz à effet de serre. « Mais il faut faire attention aux serpents », précise Miguel, une machette à la main. Les grands roseaux sont coupés, défoliés et déposés méthodiquement. Les cueilleurs coupent la canne à quelques décimètres du sol pour permettre la repousse. La canne à sucre peut se régénérer ainsi quatre ou cinq ans avant que ne soient labourées les terres et que la canne soit replantée, cette fois par boutures.

De mètre en mètre, la plantation s'effrite, mais il reste encore beaucoup de canne sur les 11 hectares. « Nous en avons pour quelques jours avant de terminer », dit Miguel. On y récoltera 50 à 60 tonnes de canne à l'hectare, un rendement comparable à la moyenne mondiale de 58 tonnes. La canne à sucre est cultivée dans 150 pays. Sa production mondiale atteint la somme astronomique de 1,56 milliard de tonnes annuellement, un poids qui dépasse largement celui de l'ensemble de la population mondiale. En fin d'après-midi, Miguel et les autres cueilleurs commencent à ramasser les tiges coupées, qu'ils chargent en hauteur sur des remorques. Un lourd ballot sur l'épaule, ils montent tour à tour sur une précaire petite échelle pour aller au sommet de la meule.

⊡ Les travailleurs chargent la canne à sucre pour l'emmener à l'usine. ⊡ Coupe des tiges de canne à sucre.
⊡ Miguel Navaro sur la plantation La Pressa.

⌃ C'est le temps de la récolte sur la plantation de Carlos Salasar, membre de CoopeAgri.

L E MOT « SUCRE », PRIS DANS SON SENS LARGE, évoque initialement une saveur, mais également un composé alimentaire à la valeur énergétique appréciable, idolâtré des uns et honni des autres, mais qui ne laisse personne indifférent.

Si la famille des saccharides inclut le sucre naturel des fruits et du miel (fructose) ou celui de l'amidon (glucose), c'est le saccharose, une combinaison des deux, extractible en grande quantité de la canne à sucre et de la betterave sucrière, qui est transformé depuis des siècles en sucre commercial. De ces degrés de raffinage ou de mélasse résiduelle seront obtenues les différentes variétés de sucre – complet, roux, blond, blanc –, avec leurs avantages et inconvénients alimentaires respectifs. De façon générale, le raffinage se fait au profit du goût, mais aussi au détriment des qualités nutritives, avec une perte notoire de sels minéraux, de potassium, magnésium, calcium, phosphore et fer, tous nécessaires à une bonne métabolisation, et qui seront sinon puisés à même les ressources corporelles.

⌃ Doña Maria, la marque maison de CoopeAgri.

La production mondiale se scinde en deux pôles : au Nord, avec environ 20 % de part du gâteau, l'exploitation de la betterave, avec la France comme plus gros producteur ; au Sud, la canne à sucre demeure historiquement la principale source d'approvisionnement, à des coûts environnementaux et humains hélas répréhensibles. Le Brésil et l'Inde produisent à eux seuls 56 % de tout le sucre de canne.

Entre ces deux végétaux géographiquement opposés se dessine une compétition inégale, où protectionnisme et subventions (surtout du côté européen) ont créé, dans les années 1990, une situation de surproduction et de *dumping* au détriment des prix consentis aux producteurs moins bien nantis du Sud. Depuis 2004, l'Organisation mondiale du Commerce (OMC) arbitre la partie en vue d'un rééquilibrage des forces.

De son côté, le sucre équitable passe souvent « sous le radar » lorsque comparé au café, à la banane et autres denrées vedettes de la filière – bien qu'il représente, en termes de poids, le troisième produit en importance du commerce équitable, avec une production de 57 000 tonnes. L'ingrédient industriel – grâce notamment au chocolat – pèse évidemment plus dans la balance que la denrée achetée séparément au supermarché.

Le problème est que le sucre – équitable ou non – est *persona non grata* pour bien des consommateurs soucieux de leur alimentation ; si la nicotine équitable existait, elle aurait le même problème de marketing ! À défaut de pouvoir inscrire « sans sucre », les entreprises alimentaires évitent de mentionner outre mesure sa présence, passant ainsi sous silence les efforts d'équité dans cette filière.

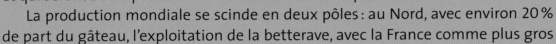

le sucre en chiffres

COMMERCE CONVENTIONNEL

Production mondiale (canne à sucre) :
    1 557 664 978 tonnes
Commerce mondial : 20 092 000 000 $

PRINCIPAUX PAYS PRODUCTEURS

Brésil	33 %
Inde	23 %
Chine	7 %
Thaïlande	4 %
Pakistan	4 %
Costa Rica (34ᵉ)	0,3 %

COMMERCE ÉQUITABLE

Année de certification : 1997 (FLO)
Importations mondiales (sucre) : 56 990 tonnes
Ventes au détail : 257 440 000 $

ORGANISATIONS CERTIFIÉES

15 organisations de petits producteurs, dans sept pays.

ORIGINE DES ORGANISATIONS CERTIFIÉES

Paraguay	40 %
Costa Rica	20 %
Philippines	13 %

PRINCIPAUX PAYS IMPORTATEURS

	Importations (t)
Grande-Bretagne	43 832
États-Unis	3364
Allemagne	1701
France	1588
Belgique	1038

PRIX ET PRIMES (sucre blanc)

Prix équitable : 520 $/t
Prime équitable : 60 à 80 $/t
Prime biologique : 120 $/t
Proportion de sucre biologique : 13 %

▷ Récolte de canne à sucre sur la plantation de Carlos Salasar.

Le jour même, la canne est apportée à l'usine pour y être traitée. Plus la transformation est rapide, plus la teneur en sucre est élevée. Tout près de la rivière Peñas Blancas, l'usine de CoopeAgri règne en maître au centre de vastes plantations. Une fumée blanche s'élève des installations. Des remorques remplies sont alignées près de la grue qui viendra les alléger de leur fardeau. Les tiges sont englouties dans le système de digestion mécanique : elles sont coupées et entrent dans le défibreur, où elles seront broyées. L'extraction du jus (qui compose les trois quarts du poids) laissera de côté la bagasse, utilisée sur les lieux comme combustible dans le processus d'épuration du jus. Ce jus est premièrement blanchi à la chaux, ce qui cause la précipitation des impuretés, qui sont ensuite filtrées. Suit l'évaporation par ébullition. Le sirop résultant est alors déversé dans une cuve sous vide et alimenté de sucre en poudre pour en accélérer la cristallisation. Les cristaux de sucre seront lavés, séchés, avant d'être tamisés, classés, pesés et stockés. Ils contiennent 99,5 % de saccharose. Pour chaque tonne de canne, l'usine tire 120 à 130 kilos de sucre, une production totale de plus de 35 000 tonnes disponibles pour l'exportation.

En 1974, il était rarissime qu'une organisation de petits producteurs possède une usine de transformation du sucre, telle celle de Coope-Agri. Même aujourd'hui, obtenir leur propre usine est un défi pour les petits producteurs de plusieurs pays, comme au Paraguay, où l'on retrouve six des 15 coopératives de sucre certifiées équitables et une longue tradition de travail collectif. « Le coopérativisme est ici le prolongement d'une tradition culturelle, celle des *mingas*, les travaux collectifs fondés sur l'entraide. Ce mouvement a été interrompu pendant la dictature militaire, lorsque toute organisation populaire était "maudite". Aujourd'hui, il y a plus de 800 coopératives. Entre 1,5 million et 2 millions de Paraguayens sont membres d'une coopérative », témoigne Andres González Aguilera, directeur de la coopérative Manduvirá, au Paraguay, fondée en 1975 et aujourd'hui composée de plus de 1000 membres.

Manduvirá a dû attendre trois décennies avant de transformer elle-même sa canne à sucre. « En louant notre propre usine, en 2005, nous avons brisé un schéma. Nous avons défié des castes qui se réservaient le privilège de la propriété des usines », explique Andres. Au Canada, Martin Van den Borre, de la coopérative de travailleurs La Siembra, se souvient de cette époque : « Lorsqu'on a commencé à importer du sucre équitable pour nos barres de chocolat, il était difficile d'avoir une relation directe avec les producteurs, à cause des moulins privés qui contrôlaient la mise en marché. C'était l'oligarchie blanche face aux paysans indigènes guaranis, explique-t-il. Lorsque certaines coops ont repris des moulins, plusieurs acheteurs équitables n'ont pas cru que les producteurs réussiraient à faire du sucre de qualité. Nous avons importé le premier conteneur de sucre que les gens de la coopérative Manduvirá avaient eux-mêmes transformé et ils ont toujours été très reconnaissants de cette marque de confiance. Même si plusieurs acheteurs nous disent avoir des problèmes à trouver du sucre biologique, Manduvirá a toujours du sucre pour nous. Nous avons pu bâtir une relation de fidélité avec eux. » Pour Andres, au Paraguay, l'aventure ne fait que commencer : « Grâce au commerce équitable, nous avons pu faire un premier pas en exportant notre sucre. En 2011, nous aurons notre propre usine. Ce sera briser encore un autre tabou. »

Au Costa Rica, l'usine de sucre de CoopeAgri n'est qu'une des vastes installations de l'organisation. En plus de son usine pour le traitement du café, elle compte une unité pour la production de compost avec une production annuelle de plus de 100 000 sacs d'engrais biologique. Dès sa fondation, CoopeAgri a su assumer pleinement son rôle dans le développement du comté de Pérez Zeledón. En 1969, alors qu'un premier « magasin du monde » ouvrait ses portes aux Pays-Bas, CoopeAgri

◁ ▽ L'usine de sucre de CoopeAgri, près de la rivière Peñas Blancas.

inaugurait le premier supermarché de la région. Aujourd'hui, l'organisation opère quatre supermarchés, un centre de produits agricoles, une quincaillerie, un café et même une station d'essence avec son atelier de mécanique. Ces activités commerciales représentent 55 % du chiffre d'affaires de la coopérative, qui a atteint plus de 80 millions de dollars en 2008.

« Les programmes sociaux sont le cœur de la coopérative, c'est pour cela qu'elle a été fondée », indique le directeur général Victor Hugo Carraza. « Nous offrons un travail aussi professionnel que les autres compagnies. Ce qui nous différencie, c'est notre bilan social. » Avec ses bourses d'étude, son fonds d'urgence, son assistance technique et sa clinique médicale, CoopeAgri investit plus de 750 000 $ annuellement dans ses programmes sociaux. De ce montant, 1 66 000 $ sont issus des primes équitables, mais la balance, plus des trois quarts, provient de ses propres fonds. « Nous avons un médecin dont les consultations sont gratuites pour tous nos membres et leur famille », ajoute Victor Hugo. En 2008, plus de 15 000 personnes ont visité le médecin de la coopérative. « Nos différents services touchent directement 50 000 personnes, c'est près de la moitié de la population du comté », conclut-il.

||||||||||||||||||||||||||||||||||||||||||||||||||||||||||||||||||||||||||||

À quelques pas des bureaux de CoopeAgri, la succursale de Credecoop grouille de gens. Fondée par CoopeAgri en 1994, Credecoop est une organisation indépendante ouverte à l'ensemble de la population du comté. Ici, les prêts agricoles ; là, le paiement pour les ventes de café ou de canne, les placements à court ou à long terme, les devises étrangères, les cartes de crédit, on se croirait dans une succursale du mouvement coopératif Desjardins, en plein centre-ville de Montréal. Au 31 décembre 2008, l'actif de Credecoop était de plus de 20 millions de dollars et comptait 22 000 membres.

||||||||||||||||||||||||||||||||||||||||||||||||||||||||||||||||||||||||||||

Le secteur forestier est très certainement un autre domaine où CoopeAgri fait sa marque. Le promoteur forestier Raphael Solones gravit la montagne en direction de la petite ferme de Silencio Cortez, dans la communauté de Santa Fé. La forêt est douce et humide, riche et verdoyante, représentative des forêts tropicales du pays. « Nous avons un bon réseau de parcs nationaux, mais il y a aussi une bonne proportion de terres privées où dominent des forêts qui n'ont subi pratiquement aucune perturbation, grâce à leur emplacement », m'explique Raphael. Ici, de grandes fougères ; là, un toucan vient nous saluer ; plus loin, une source jaillit du sol et ruisselle de rigoles en cours d'eau. « Grâce à un programme financé par des échanges de carbone, nous avons pu protéger des milliers d'hectares de terres privées », m'annonce-t-il. En 2008, le programme forestier atteignait 15 000 hectares de forêts, plus de 20 fois la superficie du parc Manuel-Antonio, l'une des plus célèbres zones protégées du pays. Raphael continue : « Les propriétaires reçoivent une compensation financière, mais doivent, en retour, maintenir les forêts telles qu'elles sont. Nous créons de cette façon des corridors migratoires entre les parcs nationaux. »

Bien que la culture sucrière ait eu son lot de tragédies et d'abus – même encore aujourd'hui – il existe des organisations où la démocratie et le travail collectif permettent de mettre à l'avant-plan les besoins des membres producteurs, et ce, avant l'hégémonie des « profits à tout prix ». Le bilan de CoopeAgri est plus que reluisant – programmes sociaux, développement régional, protection de l'environnement –, la coopérative est une force incontournable du comté de Pérez Zeledón. Et tout ce travail fut lancé bien avant l'arrivée du commerce équitable et va bien au-delà des primes. En s'associant à des organisations démocratiques de petits producteurs, le commerce équitable ajoute son soutien à des institutions qui sont ancrées dans leur communauté et qui offrent une réelle alternative de développement, bel et bien issue de la base.

⊳ Le promoteur forestier Raphael Solones (à droite) admire la forêt vierge sur la terre de Silencio Cortez.

« **D**EPUIS 46 ANS, NOUS OBTENONS DES RÉSULTATS POSITIFS grâce aux efforts continus d'un groupe d'hommes et de femmes qui croient en un modèle d'organisation d'économie sociale qui se développe sous une vision entrepreneuriale », a écrit Amado Castro Fernandez, président du conseil d'administration de la coopérative CoopeAgri.

Selon l'Alliance Coopérative internationale (ACI), une coopérative est « une association autonome de personnes volontairement réunies pour satisfaire leurs aspirations et besoins économiques, sociaux et culturels communs, au moyen d'une entreprise dont la propriété est collective et où le pouvoir est exercé démocratiquement ». Les sept principes coopératifs de l'ACI :

1. une adhésion volontaire ouverte à tous ;
2. un pouvoir démocratique exercé par les membres ;
3. la participation économique des membres ;
4. l'autonomie et l'indépendance des membres ;
5. l'éducation, la formation et l'information des membres ;
6. la coopération entre les coopératives ;
7. l'engagement des coopératives envers la communauté.

Au Nord comme au Sud, le mouvement coopératif jouit d'une longue et riche tradition. En Tanzanie, la Kilimanjaro Native Cooperative Union (KNCU) a été fondée, il y a plus de 75 ans, sur les flancs du plus haut sommet d'Afrique. Au Québec, la coopérative d'épargne et de crédit fondée par Alphonse Desjardins, en 1900, compte 5,8 millions de membres.

Coopératives, unions, fédérations, les organisations démocratiques de petits producteurs ont toujours été au cœur du commerce équitable. Selon la FLO, pour qu'une entreprise soit considérée comme une coopérative, « une majorité des membres de l'organisation doit être composée de petits producteurs qui ne dépendent pas de travailleurs salariés à temps complet, mais qui administrent leur ferme principalement avec leur propre labeur et celui de leur famille. Les profits doivent être distribués de manière égale entre les producteurs, et tous les membres doivent avoir une voix et un vote dans le processus décisionnel de l'organisation. »

Le premier rôle des coopératives est souvent de fédérer les ressources pour permettre une activité commerciale sans dépendre d'intermédiaires locaux, et ainsi assurer une plus grande part des revenus d'exportation aux producteurs. Les infrastructures – entrepôts, camions et équipements collectifs de transformation –, permettent d'améliorer la qualité du produit et sont une grande source de fierté pour les producteurs. Sur le plan social, les coopératives elles-mêmes sont des moteurs de développement régional dont les bénéfices s'étendent finalement aux communautés dans leur ensemble. Leurs initiatives sont hautement participatives et diverses – transport collectif, microcrédit, centres de santé, alphabétisation et formations de toutes sortes, orphelinats, eau potable, jardins communautaires, reboisement – et hautement participatives.

> Une coopérative est « une association autonome de personnes volontairement réunies pour satisfaire leurs aspirations et besoins économiques, sociaux et culturels communs, au moyen d'une entreprise dont la propriété est collective et où le pouvoir est exercé démocratiquement ».

⌂ Un travailleur transporte la canne à sucre sur la plantation de Carlos Salasar.

1. Jeune pousse de canne à sucre.
2. Canne à sucre mature.
3. Préparation des champs de canne à sucre pour leur régénération naturelle.
4. Transport de la canne à sucre sur la plantation La Pressa.
5. Broyage de la canne à sucre à l'usine de CoopeAgri.
6. Sucre raffiné d'exportation de CoopeAgri.

▷ En haut : Pamela, la petite-fille de Wilson Conejo Guzman, déguste un bout de canne à sucre.
▷ En bas : Elisio Alisondo mène ses bœufs, qui transportent la canne à sucre vers l'usine.

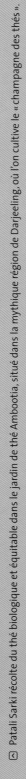

le thé

Certains disent que des feuilles de théier sont tombées dans l'eau bouillante d'un empereur quasi divin. D'autres encore affirment que les feuilles ont trouvé repos dans le bol de Gautama Bouddha pendant sa méditation... Son origine demeure mystérieuse mais sa popularisation ne fait nul doute. En effet, un sacré coup de vent balaya les feuilles du théier à travers la Chine et ailleurs quand l'Empire britannique en répandit des jardins à travers ses colonies. Peu de temps s'est écoulé entre les premières graines plantées, en 1840, dans le jardin du docteur Campbell à Beechwood, Darjeeling, en Inde, et la fin du monopole de la production chinoise. Des plantations pullulèrent dans le paysage indien pour répondre à une demande mondiale croissante. À Assam, des jungles entières cédèrent la place à ces nouvelles productions.

Le thé s'installa dans l'économie mondiale et dans les cultures. L'Inde millénaire l'intégra comme un nouveau dieu dans le panthéon hindou. Le thé y devint une icône culturelle, une boisson nationale façonnant divers aspects de la vie. La conversion au thé ignora d'ailleurs toutes les frontières : après l'eau, le thé est aujourd'hui la boisson la plus bue au monde.

En route vers les hauts sommets de l'Himalaya, le train venu d'une autre époque monte de mètre en mètre, à la «lenteur» d'une cérémonie de thé japonaise. Loin des rues bondées et de la chaleur torride de Calcutta, le Darjeeling est doux et plutôt serein. Les temples bouddhistes bordent les petites routes et lorsque le temps se sent généreux, quelques sommets majestueux, dont le Kangchenjunga (troisième sommet mondial, à 8598 mètres), viennent repeindre l'horizon. En bordure des routes, les théiers s'étendent à perte de vue dans le relief escarpé. C'est une région mythique où, selon les experts, on cultive «le champagne des thés».

Au milieu de ce paysage grandiose, on retrouve le jardin de thé Ambootia, avec au centre la grande maison du directeur, le *director's bungalow*, qui est en fait bien plus une maison de visiteurs, le propriétaire vivant à Calcutta. Botu, l'affable intendant, m'y accueille avec son plateau d'argent garni de deux tasses de porcelaine fine qui fument un arôme délicat. À quelques centaines de mètres, les cueilleuses s'affairent à la récolte du thé. Avec leurs vêtements colorés, leur panier sur le dos avec une courroie posée sur le front ou sur les épaules, leurs mains gantées ou leurs bandages autour des doigts, elles butinent rapidement d'arbuste en arbuste pour en prélever les jeunes pousses. «La récolte est faible, car c'est le début de la saison, mais ces premières feuilles, les *first flush*, sont les plus recherchées et valent le plus cher», précise le directeur de la plantation qui, avec ses shorts et son polo, fait

contraste avec les travailleurs. Pour la première fois, je visite une grande plantation privée certifiée équitable.

À la pause, une employée circule dans le champ avec une théière remplie d'eau fraîche qu'elle offre à chaque cueilleuse. Les conditions de travail sont régies par le *Plantation Act*, promulgué en 1951, qui octroie, entre autres, le droit à l'organisation syndicale, fixe un salaire minimum et détermine les conditions de travail (vêtements, outils, pauses, jours fériés) et de vie (habitations, routes, écoles, garderies, cliniques médicales, etc.) des employés. À l'instar des villes ouvrières du passé industriel d'un capitalisme paternaliste, les jardins de thé sont de réelles petites cités où vivent et travaillent parfois plus d'un millier de personnes.

«Je suis venu au monde dans le *director's bungalow*», raconte quelques semaines plus tard le propriétaire Sanjay Bansal dans son bureau climatisé de Calcutta. «Mon père a été gérant du jardin et il en est devenu le propriétaire au milieu des années 1980. En Inde, il n'y a pas plus d'une demi-douzaine de gérants qui soient un jour devenus propriétaires!»

Ambootia a reçu de nombreux prix pour la valeur de ses thés aux encans de Calcutta. Son secret: des thés de qualité. «On trouve toujours un marché pour un bon thé, lance Sanjay. Devenue propriété de ma famille, Ambootia a fait sa conversion au biologique et aujourd'hui même,

⊡ Les cueilleuses d'Ambootia en route pour la récolte matinale. ⊡ Récolte des jeunes pousses de théiers.

⌃ Une pause bien méritée pour les cueilleuses d'Ambootia.

les jardins des travailleurs sont certifiés.» Biologique, biodynamique et équitable, la recette d'Ambootia est très simple, selon son propriétaire : «Nous sommes directement impliqués dans toutes les étapes, des théiers jusqu'à la vente du thé. Trois pour cent de nos thés sont vendus dans les réseaux équitables. Pour nous, le commerce équitable est un marché de niche comme un autre.» Au cours des trois derniers mois, Ambootia a fait l'acquisition de cinq nouveaux jardins «en difficulté», dans la région de Darjeeling. Sanjay explique : «Notre production est passée de 150 000 à 600 000 kilos de thé annuellement. Ça ne s'est jamais vu dans la région. Voyons comment nous allons réussir !» Aujourd'hui, quelques années plus tard, Ambootia Tea Group Exports compte 11 jardins.

Après nombre de visites, au fil des années, dans différentes coopératives de petits producteurs, la visite de grands jardins de thé certifiés équitables est pour moi quelque peu déroutante. Legs du colonialisme britannique, il s'y reproduit une hiérarchie traditionnelle, avec un propriétaire roi et maître à la tête de ses travailleurs. «Nous sommes responsables d'une grande population», précise Sanjay. Cela signifie beaucoup de responsabilités, certes, mais beaucoup de pouvoir également. De l'aveu même du propriétaire d'Ambootia, le mariage commerce équitable et jardins privés n'est pas des plus naturels. Dans les jardins certifiés, il n'est pas rare de croiser des travailleurs qui parlent de leur propriétaire comme de leur «roi» ou de leur «dieu»... Nous sommes loin des associations de petits producteurs, emblèmes du commerce équitable, où la démocratie et l'autosuffisance des familles membres sont d'importants principes.

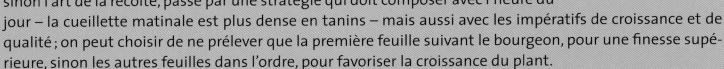

VINGT-CINQ MILLE TASSES À LA SECONDE – le temps de lire ces mots, c'est la consommation mondiale de thé qui vient de s'écouler dans d'innombrables gosiers. Qu'importe la diversité des hypothèses mythologiques entourant leur avènement ou encore la multiplicité de leur taxinomie colorée – blanc, noir, vert, bleu, rouge et même jaune – tous les thés viennent d'un seul type d'arbre, le *camellia sinensis*, comportant deux variétés, *sinensis* et *assamica*, disséminées naturellement aux quatre coins de l'Orient, mais historiquement concentrées en Chine.

À l'état sauvage, le *camellia sinensis* peut atteindre 20 mètres de hauteur – ce qui est peu pratique pour la récolte! La domestication du théier le bride plutôt à une taille de 1,20 mètre pour optimiser le rendement et la cueillette. La science, sinon l'art de la récolte, passe par une stratégie qui doit composer avec l'heure du jour – la cueillette matinale est plus dense en tanins – mais aussi avec les impératifs de croissance et de qualité; on peut choisir de ne prélever que la première feuille suivant le bourgeon, pour une finesse supérieure, sinon les autres feuilles dans l'ordre, pour favoriser la croissance du plant.

Par la suite, ce seront les décisions concernant la fermentation des feuilles – légère, modérée, pleine ou simplement inexistante – qui créeront les différents types ou «couleurs» de thé. Les Japonais ont fait du thé vert (non fermenté mais torréfié) leur unique passion, alors que les thés semi-fermentés (oolong) sont d'inspiration chinoise. Le thé noir, résultat supposément inopiné d'une fermentation étirée au cours d'une livraison en retard au XVIIe siècle, a tant séduit les sujets de la Couronne britannique qu'ils ont exigé cette méthode pour la suite du commerce, et lors de l'implantation de sa culture en Inde et en Afrique, au XIXe siècle.

De nos jours, le marché conventionnel du thé est contrôlé par un nombre restreint de multinationales qui influencent grandement les prix aux enchères régionales. La surproduction des dernières années pousse les cours à la baisse et l'on tente conséquemment de stimuler une plus grande consommation dans les pays producteurs (Inde et Chine), qui sont pourtant déjà quantitativement les plus gros buveurs. Par contre, *per capita*, l'Indien se contente de 650 grammes par année, comparativement à 2200 grammes pour le Britannique.

Du côté de l'équitable (qui incorpore dans son équation les autres infusions à base d'herbes comme la camomille, la menthe ou le rooibos sud-africain), on assiste à une explosion de la demande – une croissance de 112% entre 2007 et 2008 –, principalement due à la fidélisation d'une des plus grandes chaînes alimentaires en Grande-Bretagne à la fin de 2007. Ce dénouement triplait l'offre d'un seul coup, en accaparant 10% des parts de marché pour les thés équitables chez les consommateurs clés que sont les Anglo-Saxons.

le thé en chiffres

COMMERCE CONVENTIONNEL

Production mondiale : 3 871 339 tonnes
Commerce mondial : 3 750 000 000 $

PRINCIPAUX PAYS PRODUCTEURS

Chine	31%
Inde	25%
Kenya	8%
Sri Lanka	8%
Indonésie	5%

COMMERCE ÉQUITABLE

Année de certification : 1996
Importations mondiales : 11 467 tonnes
Ventes au détail : 294 640 000 $
Croissance de 2007 à 2008 : 112 %

ORGANISATIONS CERTIFIÉES

31 organisations de petits producteurs et 43 organisations avec travailleurs salariés, pour un total de 74 organisations, dans 12 pays.

ORIGINE DES ORGANISATIONS CERTIFIÉES

Inde	25%
Kenya	23%
Sri Lanka	16%

PRINCIPAUX PAYS IMPORTATEURS

	Importations (t)	Croissance (2007 à 2008)
Grande-Bretagne	9330	149%
États-Unis	600	33%
France	432	33%
Canada	271	215%
Allemagne	202	2%

PRIX ET PRIMES

Prix équitable : entre 1,20 et 2,00 $/kg
Prime équitable : 0,50 $/kg
Proportion de thé biologique : 17 %

⌄ Pour un thé de qualité, on récolte une ou deux feuilles et le bourgeon, alors qu'une récolte royale se compose strictement de bourgeons.

Dans le jardin de thé Makaibari, à première vue, tout transpire la tradition. Le propriétaire, Rajah Banerjee, est de la quatrième génération de « planteurs » de sa famille. « Mon trisaïeul fut le premier Indien propriétaire de jardins de thé », dit-il. Aujourd'hui, sur les 87 jardins de thé de Darjeeling, Rajah est le seul propriétaire à demeurer sur sa plantation. « C'est l'heure du thé », lance-t-il avec un sourire espiègle, comme pour suggérer que toute heure du jour est bonne pour un thé. Les tasses sont toutes alignées et, devant elles, les différentes feuilles : thé vert, thé noir, et le légendaire *silver tips* de Makaibari. « En 1996, ce thé a raflé le record des prix de vente à l'encan de Calcutta », s'enorgueillit Rajah, pointant le certificat accroché au mur. Il sent d'abord le thé, pour ensuite le goûter. Regardant fixement son directeur de plantation, son verdict est sans équivoque : « C'est bien, mais on peut faire mieux ! »

À quelques pas des bureaux, les planchers de bois sculptés par le temps des vieux bâtiments de la *factory* ont vu passer bien des tonnes de thé. À midi, cueilleuses et cueilleurs arrivent avec leurs paniers pour peser les feuilles de la récolte matinale. Dès lors, les feuilles sont étendues sur de longs grillages pour qu'elles flétrissent, une étape durant laquelle elles perdront 50 % de leur contenu en eau.

Après les salutations d'usage à Ganesh, le dieu indien de la sagesse et de l'intelligence, Rajah m'emmène chez une famille de travailleurs. « Il faut absolument que tu voies la production de biogaz. Plusieurs familles ont reçu des vaches et le système pour produire du carburant à partir du fumier. Elles peuvent maintenant cuisiner sans couper d'arbres et les résidus sont compostés pour fertiliser les théiers », précise l'enthousiaste propriétaire avant d'ajouter : « Les théiers ne couvrent que 30 % de nos terres, le reste est une forêt vierge qui regorge de diversité animale, on y retrouve même des léopards ! »

Chez lui sont d'ailleurs empaillés tigres et autres chats sauvages, trésors de chasse familiaux de la période coloniale britannique. « C'était une autre époque », convient-il. Pour Rajah, le modèle de plantation du passé colonial doit également être revu : « Le système de jardins de thé était un modèle fort rusé qui forçait la dépendance des travailleurs et, en fait, s'approchait de l'esclavage. » L'objectif de ce propriétaire hors normes : permettre à ses travailleurs d'obtenir des parts de son jardin. « Je ne vais pas leur donner. Il faut

⊡ Sujata, superviseuse de cueillette chez Makaibari. ⊡ Rajah Banerjee, propriétaire de Makaibari, le premier jardin de thé de Darjeeling certifié équitable.

qu'ils les gagnent. Mais d'ici quelques années, je crois que ce sera possible. Et je pense surtout aux femmes », ajoute-t-il.

Chez Makaibari, déjà sept femmes ont été promues aux fonctions de supervision, un fait rare dans les plantations indiennes de thé. Sujata, 23 ans, a obtenu son emploi lorsque sa mère a pris sa retraite. Elle raconte : « En 2003, j'ai suivi une formation pour être infirmière, mais nous étions six candidates pour seulement un poste au dispensaire de la plantation. Je n'ai pas eu l'emploi, mais quelques mois plus tard j'étais promue superviseuse, mon salaire est passé de 1000 à 1500 roupies par mois (38 $), et je dirige un groupe de 20 cueilleurs. Oui, oui, tous des hommes de 19 à 49 ans ! »

Sujata est également membre du comité mixte responsable des fonds liés au commerce équitable, où Makaibari vend 15 % de sa production annuelle. Ce comité administre les primes équitables (0,50 $ par kilo de thé) destinées à la mise en place de projets sociaux, dont la formation de sages-femmes, des cours d'informatique, des microcrédits pour les travailleurs et un ambitieux projet d'écotourisme. Rajah m'explique : « Le projet d'écotourisme est totalement géré par les travailleurs et contribue à leur autonomie. » Le comité est composé de 12 membres, dont une majorité de femmes. Rajah en est tout de même le président. « Les travailleurs ont insisté pour que ce soit moi, dit-il, tout ne change pas du jour au lendemain. Le comité se réunit toutes les semaines. Je souhaite que son rôle aille bien au-delà de la gestion des primes équitables. »

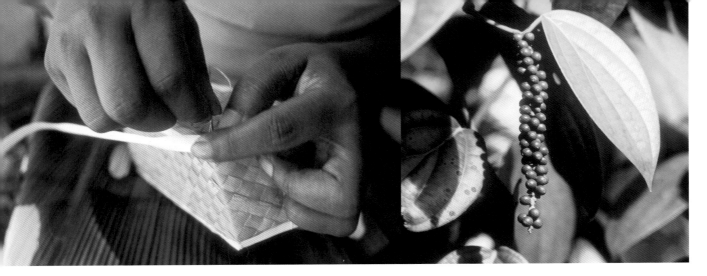

⌐ Boîte de roseau artisanale pour l'exportation du thé et des épices de la SOFA. ⌐ Grappe de grains de poivre.
⌐ Sripali, membre de la SOFA, récolte des feuilles de thé biologique.

Bien qu'une majorité du thé équitable soit issue de grandes plantations, il existe aussi des associations de petits producteurs, dont la première vit le jour au Sri Lanka. Fondée au milieu des années 1990 avec 193 membres, la Small Organic Farmers Association (SOFA) regroupe aujourd'hui près de 2500 petits producteurs de thé et d'épices biologiques et équitables. Les producteurs travaillent en partenariat avec Biofoods, une entreprise familiale responsable de la transformation et de l'exportation, qui est au cœur du développement de la SOFA.

Près de Kandy, au centre de l'île de Ceylan, l'usine de Biofoods se fond dans la riche forêt tropicale. Le docteur Sarath Ranaweera, fondateur de Biofoods, approche une à une les tasses de thé de son visage pour humer leur fragrance. « Notre thé vert biologique est particulièrement aromatique, mais il est difficile à vendre à cause des prix offerts par la Chine pour son thé vert biologique. Biofoods fut fondée en 1993 et quelques années plus tard, nous avons créé des organisations de producteurs. Au début des années 2000, la SOFA était autonome, mais avec une très forte collaboration », explique-t-il.

Dans le village de Nillembe, Chamdi et Sripali, membres de la SOFA, se déplacent de théier en théier pour recueillir les feuilles fraîches. Autour d'elles, il y a des poivriers, des girofliers, des canneliers et des vanilliers, orchidées grimpantes dont on extrait la vanille. Tous les producteurs de la SOFA ont une agriculture diversifiée, ils cultivent le thé, les épices et différentes denrées de subsistance. « Nous récoltons le thé les lundis et jeudis car ce sont les jours d'achat », me précise Chamdi. En fin d'après-midi, le camion arrive, on accroche une balance sur un arbre, et on pose une calculatrice et un livre comptable sur un tabouret. Les sacs de feuilles sont pesés un à un. Les producteurs sont payés sur le champ. « Ma petite terre me donne un tiers de mes revenus, mais la majorité d'entre nous ont un autre travail en plus de leur ferme », me raconte Chamdi, qui a aussi travaillé quelques années comme aide familiale au Moyen-Orient avant de se marier.

Dans le village voisin, dix femmes sont réunies, leurs mains agiles pliant et repliant de frêles roseaux en de magnifiques petites boîtes. Elles serviront à l'exportation du thé et des épices de la SOFA. « C'est un revenu d'appoint qui est important pour nous », me précise l'une des théicultrices. Quinze roupies (0,13 $) pour chaque boîte vont à l'artisane, huit roupies pour l'achat des matériaux et une roupie pour le fonds social. Avec ses ventes de thé dans les réseaux équitables, la SOFA touche des primes sociales de l'ordre de cinq millions de roupies (45 000 $) annuellement, qui permettent le développement agricole avec des semis de théiers offerts gratuitement, et même des animaux pour diversifier les revenus des membres et fournir du fumier pour leur agriculture biologique. Le fonds social de l'association est aussi utilisé pour des fournitures scolaires et des projets d'abduction d'eau potable, un service pour l'ensemble de la communauté, membres et non membres de la coopérative.

En plus de la SOFA, 31 organisations de petits producteurs, dont seulement deux en Inde, exportent 29 % du thé équitable. Après la révolution biologique du thé indien dans les années 1980, souhaitons que le commerce équitable puisse semer cette graine du changement et inspirer une révolution démocratique dans le Darjeeling et dans l'ensemble des traditionnels *tea estates* du pays aux mille divinités. Un vent de changement pour poursuivre le travail du Mahatma Gandhi, de Nehru et autres pères de la plus grande démocratie sur Terre.

▷ La famille de la petite Sirome est membre de la SOFA, l'une des 31 organisations de petits producteurs qui exportent du thé équitable.

LA CERTIFICATION DES PLANTATIONS DE THÉ, EN 1997, créa une onde de choc dans le mouvement équitable, avec son lot de résistance. Pour la première fois, des normes équitables étaient développées pour des producteurs privés dépendant de travailleurs salariés – une différence marquée avec les organisations démocratiques de petits producteurs qui étaient jusqu'alors l'emblème du mouvement équitable.

La réponse fut particulièrement forte dans la filière café, où les organisations certifiées représentent 400 000 petits producteurs, soit la moitié de tous les petits producteurs certifiés par la FLO. Comme ces organisations n'exportent que 50 % de leur café dans le marché équitable, l'entrée des plantations dans l'équation n'est pas justifiée. Aujourd'hui, 16 filières certifiées par la FLO (dont le sucre, le café, le cacao, le riz et les épices) demeurent réservées aux organisations de petits producteurs, alors que cinq comptent également de grandes plantations (les jus de fruits, les fruits frais, la banane, le thé et le vin), et que deux ne proviennent que d'entreprises privées dépendant de main-d'œuvre salariée (les fleurs et les ballons de sport).

« Les travailleurs sans terre font partie des producteurs les plus défavorisés au monde », évoque la FLO, qui base sa certification des plantations sur les normes de l'Organisation internationale du Travail (OIT) de l'ONU et quelques principes généraux :

- Un comité mixte, composé de travailleurs et de membres de la direction, doit gérer la prime équitable ;
- La prime doit être utilisée pour améliorer les conditions de vie et de travail ;
- Le travail forcé et le travail d'enfants de 15 ans et moins sont prohibés ;
- Les travailleurs ont le droit de mettre en place ou de joindre un syndicat indépendant ;
- Les salaires doivent être égaux ou plus élevés que la moyenne régionale ;
- Des mesures de sécurité doivent être mises en place pour éviter les accidents de travail.

« Dans les débuts de la certification des plantations, on demandait qu'elles aient un comité mixte et une forme de négociation collective, mais souvent sans plus », explique Markus Staub, de Max Havelaar Suisse, qui fut à la genèse de la certification équitable dans l'industrie des fleurs, au début des années 2000. « Avec l'expérience acquise grâce aux fleurs, nous avons pu faire évoluer les standards de certification. En plus des primes et des comités mixtes, la certification équitable aborde aujourd'hui l'organisation des travailleurs pour que ceux-ci puissent concrètement améliorer leurs conditions de travail. Ces travailleurs doivent avoir un système, tel un syndicat, qui leur permette de s'organiser. Leur employeur doit leur accorder du temps pour se réunir et rencontrer la direction régulièrement », conclut-il. La FLO certifie 206 entreprises au Sud, qui emploient 150 000 personnes.

« Les travailleurs sans terre font partie des producteurs les plus défavorisés au monde. »

▷ C'est l'heure de la récolte chez Makaibari.

1. Radhika Tamang récolte les feuilles de thé chez Ambootia.
2. Récolte dans le jardin de thé Samabeong.
3. Un cervidé visite le jardin de thé Korakundah.
4. Davika Chitri boit du thé froid, chez Ambootia.
5. Flétrissage des feuilles de thé de la SOFA.
6. Ouvrières au travail dans l'usine de thé de Biofoods, au Sri Lanka.
7. Thé vert biologique et équitable de Biofoods.

▷ Josmaya Sorma, neuf mois, à la garderie de Makaibari.

les fleurs

Les os brisés de nos cousins de la grotte de Shanidar en disent long sur leur capacité de solidarité. Ces brisures, survenues à la jeunesse de ces individus trépassés en pleine vieillesse néanderthalienne, témoignent d'une race de nobles sentiments, dont les plus forts prenaient soin des plus faibles jusqu'à la mort. Une mort au-delà de laquelle il y avait un horizon pour ceux qui n'étaient pas encore des hommes, mais qui fabriquaient des outils, s'habillaient et enterraient leurs morts sur de complexes tapis de fleurs, signes d'une foi naissante dans l'existence d'un ou de divers dieux.

Les fleurs ont toujours été intimement liées aux divinités. Botticelli nous rappelle que Vénus est née avec les roses devant le couple Zéphyr et Flore, dont les célébrations, les Floralies, ont donné lieu à de douces réjouissances ainsi qu'au déchaînement de passions et de conflits.

⌃ Boutons de roses dans les serres d'Agrogana, en Équateur.

Car si les fleurs fascinent tant les hommes, ce n'est pas seulement par la promesse de résurrection qu'elles annoncent. À chaque saison, elles nous reviennent d'une mort récente dont elles ne cherchent pas à effacer le souvenir, mais leur merveilleux éclat cède vite place au dépérissement et à la pourriture grâce auxquels le cycle se pérennise. D'un extrême à l'autre, l'humain peut associer les fleurs à tout : à la naissance et à la mort, à la paix et à la guerre. Dans la mythologie romaine, c'est à Flore que Junon, en colère contre Jupiter, demande une fleur qui lui permettra de concevoir un enfant toute seule. Ce troublant désir serait à l'origine de Mars, qui pousse les hommes à la guerre depuis la naissance des jumeaux fondateurs.

À travers les siècles, les femmes recevront des fleurs, messagères de l'amour des hommes, bien que celles-ci ne cessent jamais d'évoquer d'autres amours aussi mystérieux que leurs secrets inaudibles. Inaudibles à la plupart des mortels, mais pas aux poètes. « Le matin j'écoutais les sons du jardin, le langage des parfums des fleurs », annonce le philosophe chanteur sicilien Manlio Sgalambro, revisitant *Les fleurs du mal* de Baudelaire à travers l'émouvante voix d'un autre sicilien, chanteur philosophe celui-ci, tout autant envoûté par d'étranges senteurs, *il maestro* Franco

Battiato. Son triptyque musical commencé par *Fleurs 1*, suivi de *Fleurs 3* et conclu avec *Fleurs 2* (sa façon d'éviter les séries infinies), est un véritable jardin dont les fleurs témoignent d'impossibles amours médiévales et de subtiles caresses.

Fleurs des plus belles espérances des hommes, mêmes vaines, qu'importe! La Rose au poing aura inspiré des générations de « ceux qui refusaient de ramper jusqu'à la vieillesse », dont se souvient Jacques Brel dans *Jaurès*, et c'est avec des œillets à la pointe de leurs fusils que des capitaines portugais ont rendu la liberté à leur peuple le matin d'un 25 avril. De l'autre côté de la langue, le poète brésilien Vinicius de Moraes nous enjoignit de ne pas oublier la « Rose de Hiroshima, la rose héréditaire, rose radioactive, stupide, estropiée, la rose à la cirrhose, l'anti-rose atomique, sans couleur sans parfum, sans rose, sans rien. »

Rassuré d'un mythe à l'autre à travers les ères, l'humain s'incline toujours pour cueillir des fleurs, mû par d'ineffables forces d'une Nature dont il s'est cru définitivement séparé. Une Nature d'abord désacralisée et ensuite réduite à l'avilissante condition de « ressource ».

Les oracles de notre temps ont dit que la culture intensive de fleurs pour l'exportation était un bien pour les nations ayant le « privilège » des « avantages » comparatifs : bas salaires, lois environnementales minimales, précarisation de la force de travail... ce que le langage des mythes modernes définit comme une « large flexibilisation des conditions de production ».

Ainsi, le Kenya, l'Équateur, le Zimbabwe, la Zambie et la Colombie, entre autres, sont devenus les pays floriculteurs de la « mondialisation heureuse ». Dans leurs serres, où l'on produit nos symboles d'amour, 65 à 70 % des travailleurs sont des femmes exclues du romantisme de cette chaîne mondiale qui commence pourtant dans leur ligne de production. Travaillant plus de 60 heures par semaine, elles sont exposées en permanence à la pollution chimique. Leur « globalisation » passe par le harcèlement sexuel, les maladies épidermiques et respiratoires, et des genoux estropiés à force d'adopter trop souvent la position des humiliés de ce monde.

C'est dans ce contexte que le commerce équitable a été appelé, une fois de plus, à faire pencher la balance du côté de la justice. « Au début des années 1990, il y a eu des campagnes pour sensibiliser les consommateurs suisses et allemands aux mauvaises conditions de travail et à l'utilisation massive de produits chimiques dans l'industrie des fleurs », explique Markus Staub, de Max Havelaar Suisse, qui fut à la genèse de la certification équitable dans l'industrie des fleurs. L'idée a fait son chemin, mais il y a eu des réticences pour sa certification équitable. « Le produit n'était pas alimentaire, les fournisseurs avaient des travailleurs salariés et non de petits producteurs regroupés en coopératives. De plus, les fleurs sont exportées par avion, ajoute Markus. Aujourd'hui, nous savons que la production de roses aux Pays-Bas cause cinq à six fois plus d'émissions de CO_2, dues au chauffage, que leur production au Kenya et ce, malgré le transport aérien. » Il fallait vaincre les préjugés pour apporter des changements pragmatiques dans une industrie qui en avait grand besoin. « Nous avons été la seule initiative nationale de certification à soutenir et structurer ce nouveau produit équitable, précise Markus. En 2001, 21 millions de tiges de fleurs certifiées équitables du Zimbabwe et du Kenya ont fait leur entrée en Suisse. En 2004, nous étions déjà à 89 millions. Nous avons réussi à combler 50 % d'un marché national, un fait très rare dans le commerce équitable. Nous n'aurions pu le faire sans la participation des producteurs du Sud. »

|||||||||||||||||||||||||||||||||||||||||||||||||||||||||||||||||||||||||||||||||||||||||

À mi-chemin des 140 kilomètres qui séparent Quito, la capitale de l'Équateur, et les serres de Nevado Ecuador, le blanc sommet du volcan Cotopaxi caresse les nuages, à 6000 mètres d'altitude. Le soleil brille de tous ses rayons, mais juin est frais sur l'Altiplano équatorien. « Ici, à 2750 mètres, les conditions sont optimales pour la culture des roses », dit Roberto Nevado, le propriétaire de Nevado Ecuador. « C'est le parfait équilibre pour un maximum d'ensoleillement, sans risque de gel. » Depuis plus de 40 ans, ce ressortissant espagnol travaille dans le marché des fleurs. Il continue : « J'ai été courtier pendant 30 ans, avant d'être producteur. » Fondée en 1998, Nevado Ecuador compte 45 hectares de serres où s'activent 550 employés. C'est l'une des 46 plantations de fleurs certifiées par la FLO.

Dans une allée bordée de magnifiques inflorescences, Miriam Chusing avance d'un pas rapide tout en sélectionnant les boutons matures. Elle coupe une tige, vérifie la corolle, enlève parfois un pétale et dépose la rose dans un bac qu'elle glisse sur le sol. Lorsqu'elle a suffisamment de fleurs, elle les regroupe, les aligne et les enveloppe délicatement dans un grand filet de plastique.

Celui-ci est ensuite déposé sur un système de rails pour aller à l'usine de postproduction, où les roses sont rassemblées par variétés. Nevado Ecuador cultive 50 variétés, dont quelques-unes lui sont exclusives et certaines ont été créées sur place. « Nous récoltons 60 000 tiges par jour, dit Roberto, et ça peut monter à 180 000 pour la Saint-Valentin ! » Dans l'usine, quelques hommes, mais surtout une cinquantaine de femmes travaillent. Leur salaire est d'un peu plus de 200 $ par mois. Elles portent un chandail chaud et une tuque à l'effigie de la compagnie, des gants et un tablier jaune imperméable. Celles qui doivent rester sur place sont sur une plate-forme en bois qui les protège contre la fraîcheur du plancher de ciment.

Patricia Coronel prend une rose d'un blanc immaculé, dont elle vérifie la longueur et le bouton, pour la déposer derrière elle avec d'autres de même taille. Plusieurs fleurs mesurent un mètre ou plus. « Certaines de nos roses atteignent deux mètres ! », m'annonce Roberto avec fierté.

Il manque un élément à cette expérience sensorielle. Aucun arôme, nul parfum délicat ni douce fragrance ne viennent éveiller mon odorat. « La majorité des roses commerciales n'ont aucune senteur », m'apprend Roberto. Parmi les 50 variétés conventionnelles de Nevado, une seule dégage un arôme. Nevado développe aussi depuis quelques années des roses biologiques. Pour Markus Staub de Max Havelaar

Suisse, ces roses biologiques sont la preuve de l'évolution des techniques agricoles alternatives : « Il y a à peine 10 ans, on nous avait dit que les roses biologiques étaient une aventure impossible. Aujourd'hui, on en trouve de plus en plus. » Quatre des huit roses biologiques de Nevado dégagent de douces fragrances.

Dans une autre section de l'usine, Juliana Ataballo rassemble les roses en bouquets de 10, 12, 20 ou 25. Ces roses sont délicatement enveloppées dans un carton protecteur. Juliana jette un court regard dans un miroir pour s'assurer du bon alignement. Elle dépose son dernier emballage sur le tapis roulant. Il est 13 heures, elle doit assister à la réunion du comité mixte responsable de la gestion des primes équitables, dont elle est la vice-présidente. « La compagnie nous octroie quatre heures par mois pour les réunions et autres activités du comité », explique-t-elle. Ces comités sont une exigence de la FLO pour l'obtention de la certification équitable. « La prime équitable et sa gestion par un comité mixte furent le premier pas pour valoriser les travailleurs », précise Markus Staub. Pour chaque fleur exportée avec une certification FLO, une prime de 10 % est versée dans un compte séparé dont le comité mixte a la responsabilité, et qui doit être utilisé pour des projets sociaux bénéficiant à l'ensemble des travailleurs.

Les 16 membres du comité mixte de Nevado Ecuador, à parité entre hommes et femmes, sont

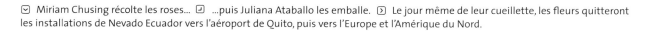

⊡ Miriam Chusing récolte les roses... ⊡ ...puis Juliana Ataballo les emballe. ▷ Le jour même de leur cueillette, les fleurs quitteront les installations de Nevado Ecuador vers l'aéroport de Quito, puis vers l'Europe et l'Amérique du Nord.

MALGRÉ LA DIVERSITÉ DES ESPÈCES COMMERCIALISÉES sur les étals colorés de nos marchés, une fleur s'adjuge le titre de « best-seller » à travers le monde occidental et récolte conséquemment une bonne partie de l'attention des producteurs. Cultivé depuis les temps immémoriaux, de la Chine antique à l'Égypte, en passant par la Perse et la Grèce, le genre *rosa* aura fasciné et suscité les passions jusqu'à nos jours. Des excès souverains de Cléopâtre et Marc Antoine – dont on raconte que les nuits se déroulaient sur une couche de pétales de roses de près d'un demi-mètre d'épaisseur – aux 189 millions de tiges vendues à la Saint-Valentin seulement aux États-Unis, les roses provoquent tous les superlatifs chez leurs consommateurs, mais également leur lot de désarroi chez ceux qui les font pousser.

Si les Pays-Bas sont une plaque tournante du commerce de la fleur, les producteurs s'établissent de plus en plus dans les zones équatoriales du globe, où la stabilité climatique et la main-d'œuvre bon marché jouent en leur faveur. La Colombie et l'Équateur alimentent ainsi une partie de la demande nord-américaine, tandis que le Kenya, l'Éthiopie et l'Inde fournissent principalement l'Europe.

En comparaison avec les filières alimentaires, la floriculture n'est pas légalement régie par quelque quota que ce soit quant à la quantité de pesticides utilisée pour éradiquer les menaces d'insectes – elle peut être jusqu'à 75 fois plus élevée que dans l'agriculture conventionnelle au Nord. Les conséquences désastreuses sur la santé humaine et écologique ne se font pas attendre et affectent les travailleurs (surtout des femmes), auxquels les propriétaires n'offrent souvent aucune protection.

Voilà bien une filière où les préceptes du commerce équitable permettent d'effectuer de véritables changements. L'initiative pionnière des Suisses dans le développement des fleurs équitables est éloquente : en quelques années, les roses équitables se sont accaparé les 50 % du marché national. C'est la preuve qu'à son extrémité de la chaîne, le client du Nord ne s'objecte pas à payer un peu plus pour un achat qui n'est pas de première nécessité, mais qui se fait dans le respect des travailleurs. Les primes équitables, gérées de manière consensuelle, soutiennent le développement de projets sociaux qui améliorent les conditions de vie des communautés de floriculteurs. Qui plus est, l'initiative équitable permet de réduire l'empreinte environnementale de ces fleurs cultivées loin des marchés occidentaux (on élimine jusqu'à 90 % des pesticides), qui polluent moins que celles produites localement au Nord dans des serres énergivores.

les fleurs en chiffres

COMMERCE CONVENTIONNEL

Commerce mondial : 3 716 800 000 $

PRINCIPAUX PAYS PRODUCTEURS

Pays-Bas	56,5 %
Colombie	14,1 %
Israël	4,2 %
Kenya	2,7 %
Équateur	2,7 %

COMMERCE ÉQUITABLE

Année de certification : 2004 (FLO)
Importations mondiales : 311 000 000 de tiges
Ventes au détail : 255 950 000 $
Croissance de 2007 à 2008 : 31%

ORGANISATIONS CERTIFIÉES

46 organisations avec des travailleurs salariés, dans huit pays.

ORIGINE DES ORGANISATIONS CERTIFIÉES

Kenya	43 %
Équateur	28 %
Zimbabwe	15 %
Colombie	4 %
Tanzanie	4 %

PRINCIPAUX PAYS IMPORTATEURS

	Importations (tiges)	Croissance (2007 à 2008)
Grande-Bretagne	105 400 000	26 %
Suisse	88 000 000	0 %
Allemagne	46 800 000	138 %
Finlande	14 000 000	40 %
Suède	13 500 000	35 %

PRIX ET PRIMES

Prix équitable : n.d.
Prime équitable : 10 % du prix d'exportation
Proportion de fleurs biologiques : 0 %

⌃ Nevado Ecuador cultive 50 variétés de roses, dont certaines lui sont exclusives.

représentatifs de tous les quarts de métier de la plantation, incluant la direction. Ruben, le président, qui travaille dans les serres, m'accueille avec diligence avant de commencer sa présentation : « En 2008, nous avons reçu 123 690 $ en primes équitables, qui ont été répartis en cinq projets : 42 000 $ pour des jardins biologiques collectifs et l'achat d'outils pour les jardins personnels des employés ; 15 000 $ pour la clinique dentaire, à même la plantation, avec des consultations gratuites pour les travailleurs et leurs enfants (la plantation compte déjà les services d'un médecin et d'une infirmière ainsi qu'une garderie) ; 25 000 $ sont allés dans un programme de microcrédit pour améliorer les maisons ou pour certaines urgences ; 29 000 $ ont été destinés aux bourses d'étude pour les travailleurs et surtout pour leurs enfants ; finalement, un centre d'informatique et diverses formations en économie familiale, en nutrition, etc., ont été mises sur pied. » Les projets sont variés, dynamiques et participatifs. En 2008, plus de 200 travailleurs ont obtenu des prêts de 150 à 250 $. « Avant, lorsqu'on empruntait, on devait rembourser le double », précise Ruben. Aussi, 250 jeunes ont reçu des bourses d'étude, deux fois plus qu'en 2007, et tous les employés ont bénéficié d'une première consultation chez le dentiste.

Juliana a par contre une inquiétude. « Pourrais-tu nous dire pourquoi la prime fut baissée de 12 à 10 % ? » Markus explique : « Suite à l'expérience positive de la Suisse, les fleurs sont devenues un produit certifié par la FLO en 2005. Certaines initiatives nationales de certification ont alors fait beaucoup de pressions pour diminuer la prime équitable. Elles voulaient offrir 5 % de prime seulement, alors qu'il n'y a même pas de prix minimum garanti. Nous avons trouvé un compromis à 10 %. »

Les fleurs sont l'un des seuls produits certifiés par la FLO qui n'ont pas de prix minimum garanti. « J'ai toujours voulu établir des prix garantis, mais avec tant de variétés de fleurs, ce n'est pas commode. J'ai même demandé à l'industrie de nous faire des propositions. Aujourd'hui, il y a beaucoup de pressions sur les prix ; le moment serait opportun pour développer une bonne méthode de prix équitables », précise Markus.

⌂ Maria Tipantuna appose les *labels* de certification équitable qui garantissent aux consommateurs que ces fleurs sont produites et commercialisées selon les critères de la FLO.

E N PLUS DE LEURS LOGOS DOÑA NATALIA et Nevado Ecuador, les emballages et même les fleurs des deux floriculteurs arborent de nombreux *labels* : Flower Label Program (FLP), FlorEcuador, Veriflora, Ecocert, USDA Organic, Rainforest Alliance, Max Havelaar-FLO ou autres. Nevado Ecuador est certifiée par dix organismes internationaux ! Je n'en avais jamais vu autant pour une seule entreprise.

◩ *Label* international de la FLO.

Tous ces *labels* représentent des frais pour les producteurs qui se chiffrent en milliers de dollars. « Nous payons 4000 $ en moyenne par *label,* mais ces frais ne représentent que la certification elle-même ; nous devons également faire d'autres investissements, payer de meilleurs salaires et autres bénéfices, explique Roberto Nevado. Nous avons estimé qu'au sein des fermes certifiées par la FLO, nos coûts de production par tige étaient supérieurs de 17 % à ceux des producteurs conventionnels. » La FLO perçoit également, auprès des importateurs, des frais de licence sur les volumes importés qui, en moyenne, représentent 1,4 % du prix de vente des produits équitables. Ces recettes de certification représentent globalement des dizaines de millions de dollars pour la FLO et ses initiatives nationales de certification.

Ces organismes de certification n'importent ni ne vendent aucun produit. La FLO est une tierce partie indépendante d'une transaction entre producteurs et importateurs certifiés, qui assure le respect des critères du commerce équitable et l'intégrité de son *label*. La FLO établit les standards équitables de concert avec les producteurs, alors que FLO-CERT, une compagnie de certification indépendante affiliée, est responsable des inspections et de la certification des producteurs et des importateurs selon ces standards. Contrairement à l'agriculture biologique, le commerce équitable ne jouit d'aucun cadre juridique national ou international. Plusieurs peuvent donc se vanter d'être « équitables », et un consommateur averti en vaut deux.

UTZ Café, qui certifie également des plantations, a un système de traçabilité des plus sophistiqués, mais ses critères n'incluent aucun prix minimum garanti pour les producteurs. Ecocert, qui a une longue expérience de la certification biologique, a ajouté une série de normes sociales sous l'appellation Ecocert ESR (équitable, solidaire, responsable) à ses critères environnementaux. Le fait qu'Ecocert ESR ne perçoive aucun frais de licence basé sur les volumes importés rend sa certification beaucoup moins onéreuse pour les distributeurs de produits équitables. Pour la WFTO, « Tous les membres doivent faire l'objet d'un processus de suivi fondé sur une autoévaluation en regard des dix principes du commerce équitable. » Une certification formelle est en chantier pour les membres de la WFTO.

Les grandes entreprises ont également développé de nombreux programmes parfois en lien avec des initiatives caritatives, comme Coffee Kids, ou en élaborant des codes d'éthique internes. Malheureusement, sans tierce partie pour garantir ces engagements, les compagnies sont souvent les seules à vérifier les résultats et la véracité de leur engagement.

Contrairement à l'agriculture biologique, le commerce équitable ne jouit d'aucun cadre juridique national ou international. Plusieurs peuvent donc se vanter d'être « équitables », et un consommateur averti en vaut deux.

⊡ Cette rose sera bientôt coupée... ⊡ ...puis emballée, à l'usine d'Agrogana.

‖‖

Non loin de Nevado, les serres d'Agrogana regorgent également de roses équitables. « Toute notre production est cultivée selon les règles de l'équitable, mais nous n'en exportons que 15 à 20 % dans ce marché », explique Anita Orozco, responsable de la production chez Agrogana. Fondée il y a dix ans par les frères Espinosa, Agrogana emploie 150 personnes pour 14 hectares de serres et exporte 30 000 roses par jour. « Faire des fleurs équitables est plus coûteux. Il faut des pesticides et des herbicides admissibles, payer trois semaines de congé, améliorer la protection des employés et payer les heures supplémentaires. Autrement dit, nous devons pleinement respecter la loi, ce que les plantations ne font que rarement par ici. »

Sur tous les emballages de roses d'Agrogana, un petit chapeau coiffe la marque Doña Natalia, nommée en souvenir de l'arrière-grand-mère des fondateurs. « Son héritage est notre dévotion envers l'agriculture, notre engagement envers la qualité et l'humanité », peut-on lire sur les murs de l'usine de postproduction. Le commerce international des fleurs reste majoritairement marqué par de déconcertantes contradictions capables de faire faner l'enthousiasme des amoureux, mais l'expérience équitable est déjà là comme une alternative concrète. Pour la Suisse, avec 50 % du marché, c'est encore plus qu'une alternative mais bien une nouvelle norme. Les symboles multicolores de tendresse s'offrent bien mieux sachant qu'ils furent récoltés par des ouvrières travaillant dans des conditions respectueuses des lois. L'accès à la dignité du travail sera toujours une étape à partir de laquelle les mains productrices de richesses se feront créatrices d'avenir.

Rosa San-Pedro bénéficie de trois semaines de congés payés annuellement grâce aux normes de certification équitable pour les organisations avec des travailleurs salariés.

le riz

Avec lui commença la culture de la terre. Plante du début des temps, don de la nouvelle alliance de l'homme dorénavant sédentaire avec la terre où il développera des racines, le riz, céréale proche des graminées les plus primitives, est toujours l'aliment de base de près de trois milliards d'humains, soit la moitié de la population mondiale. Symbole de l'abondance et de l'immortalité, graine d'un divin cultivateur ou fruit de l'étreinte amoureuse entre le ciel et la Terre, le riz se multipliera à travers les continents. Lorsque les Veda nous parlent de 500 000 variétés de riz, il faut plutôt accueillir le chiffre comme l'expression d'une extraordinaire diversité. En effet, on estime qu'il y a plus de 130 000 sortes de riz, cultivé ou à l'état sauvage. Plus de 650 millions de tonnes de riz sont récoltées annuellement, dans 113 pays.

La Thaïlande assure pour moins de 5% de cette production, mais reste néanmoins la plus grande exportatrice de la noble céréale. Il y a une réelle autosuffisance alimentaire des producteurs de riz en Thaïlande, où la moitié des terres agricoles sont consacrées à la riziculture. Dans ce royaume, où l'on dit que « la souffrance du riziculteur est la souffrance du pays », le riz n'est pas qu'une base de l'économie, mais un réel pilier de la culture nationale.

Les subtiles tonalités du tendre vert des rizières thaïlandaises s'étendent gracieusement sur les campagnes. Les abris de repos en bambou qui bordent ces immensités vertes viennent compléter cette bucolique et caractéristique image thaïe. Le regard apaisé du visiteur pourrait prendre un tel effet chromatique pour un fait de la nature ou pour un caprice artistique de Mae Phosop, l'omniprésente déesse, la mère de la Terre.

En bordure de son lopin de terre, Kampun a placé un petit récipient en feuilles de bananier garni d'offrandes à la déesse. C'est le geste essentiel dans ce pays où le riz est divinisé par nombre de rituels qui font partie de la vie quotidienne. Il met la main dans son panier pour attraper une grande poignée de riz à peine germé qu'il lance sur les petits monticules de terre. « C'est mon propre riz, que j'ai laissé quelques jours dans la rivière pour qu'il germe » explique-t-il. Son voisin Pirun arrive au champ, où il est accueilli par un « *gin khao* » – terme couramment utilisé pour demander « Comment ça va ? », mais qui veut dire précisément « As-tu mangé du riz ? ».

Pirun nous invite à visiter ses champs, où de jeunes brindilles ont déjà fait leur apparition et scintillent sous des gouttes de rosée. Au côté des semis, des plants matures arborent déjà leurs premiers grains de riz. « C'est du riz collant que j'ai semé il y a 12 semaines. Celui-là, c'est pour la maison, dit Pirun. Je fais un tiers de riz collant pour deux tiers de riz jasmin sur mes deux hectares. » À deux pas, une vingtaine de vaches broutent dans un petit enclos. « Grâce à elles, je peux tout cultiver de manière biologique », m'informe Pirun avec fierté. Kampun continue : « Avant, j'utilisais des fertilisants chimiques, mais leur prix augmentait année après année alors que ma production baissait. Plus je produisais, plus je m'endettais. Il me restait moins de 10 % du prix de vente pour mon travail ! Depuis que je cultive de manière biologique, mon travail représente 50 % du prix de vente et j'ai pu rembourser toutes mes dettes. »

En Thaïlande comme ailleurs, la révolution verte a signifié une augmentation de la production fondée sur l'utilisation de semences à haut rendement, et l'emploi massif de pesticides et d'engrais chimiques. Outre les problèmes de santé, de contamination des sols et des nappes phréatiques, ces pratiques, qui exigent beaucoup de capital, ont aggravé l'endettement de la petite paysannerie et favorisé la concentration foncière. Avec l'agriculture chimique, seules les exploitations intensives sur de grandes étendues peuvent espérer, par des économies d'échelle, une rentabilisation des investissements. J'ai retrouvé ce même cercle vicieux de l'endettement chez les

☑ Offrande à Mae Phosop, déesse de la Terre. ☑ Kampun ensemence sa terre. ☑ Kam Pa laboure un lopin de terre inondé qui se transformera sous peu en rizière.

Abris de repos en bordure des rizières, au nord de la Thaïlande.

producteurs de café, de cacao, de coton et de bien d'autres denrées. Dans ce contexte, le choix du biologique par Kampun relève d'une bonne dose de bon sens paysan et de sa volonté de continuer de vivre de l'agriculture.

Tous deux membres d'une petite coopérative regroupant 36 familles dans la province de Chiang Maï, au nord de la Thaïlande, Kampun et Pirun exportent leur riz jasmin biologique à travers Green Net, le premier exportateur de produits biologiques de la Thaïlande. Le but de cette organisation pionnière dans le développement du commerce équitable en Thaïlande est de garantir des prix justes aux paysans pour leur permettre de se libérer du cercle vicieux de l'endettement, freinant ainsi l'exode rural. Green Net, qui regroupe 1000 paysans dans cinq associations régionales, se donne aussi pour mission de fournir aux consommateurs thaïlandais et internationaux des produits biologiques de haute qualité.

le riz

« LE RIZ, C'EST LA VIE »; le slogan de la récente Année internationale du riz, décrétée par l'Organisation des Nations Unies en 2004 (la deuxième, après celle de 1966), résumait la place légitime qu'occupe cette céréale dans l'équation humaine sur la planète. C'est la seule céréale majeure à pouvoir subsister et même prospérer dans un milieu submergé – le genre *oryza sativa*, d'origine asiatique, et son cousin de l'ouest de l'Afrique, *oryza glaberrima,* prennent soin de nourrir la moitié des habitants de la Terre.

Le prodigue grain de riz, initialement recouvert de sa « balle » non comestible, est composé d'une couche brune, le son, et d'un intérieur d'amidon blanc, l'albumen. Lorsqu'il quitte son plant, le paddy (riz à l'état brut) devient riz brun (ou « complet ») au moulin et passe ensuite au raffinage, qui lui fait perdre sa peau ambrée – mais hélas aussi une portion non négligeable de ses substances nutritives – au profit d'un temps de cuisson réduit et d'un meilleur potentiel de conservation. Le riz blanc compte pour la grande majorité de la consommation mondiale.

La plus importante des cultures vivrières mondiales est principalement pratiquée par de petits agriculteurs pour alimenter leurs compatriotes – seulement 7 % de la production de riz traverse une frontière internationale. Si la Chine et l'Inde en sont de loin les plus gros producteurs, la Thaïlande et le Viêtnam en sont les principaux exportateurs.

La démarche équitable en matière de riz débuta en 2000. Avec ses 4685 tonnes importées en 2008, le riz équitable fait figure de grain, si l'on peut dire, dans le grand carré de sable de plus de 650 millions de tonnes de la production mondiale. Au Canada, il représente à peine 0,0006 % de l'offre commerciale. La Suisse est le principal pays importateur de riz équitable, avec près de 1300 tonnes.

le riz en chiffres

COMMERCE CONVENTIONNEL

Production mondiale : 651 742 616 tonnes
Commerce mondial : 10 527 000 000 $

PRINCIPAUX PAYS PRODUCTEURS

Chine	29 %
Inde	22 %
Indonésie	9 %
Bangladesh	7 %
Viêtnam	5 %
Thaïlande (7e)	4,3 %

COMMERCE ÉQUITABLE

Année de certification : 2001
Importations mondiales : 4685 tonnes
Ventes au détail : 28 270 000 $
Croissance de 2007 à 2008 : 11 %

ORGANISATIONS CERTIFIÉES

15 organisations de petits producteurs, dans quatre pays.

ORIGINE DES ORGANISATIONS CERTIFIÉES

Thaïlande	59 %
Inde	27 %
Laos	7 %
Égypte	7 %

PRINCIPAUX PAYS IMPORTATEURS

	Importations (t)	Croissance (2007 à 2008)
Suisse	1298	-2 %
France	953	-1 %
Grande-Bretagne	833	33 %
Allemagne	451	48 %
Italie	289	17 %

PRIX ET PRIMES (Thaïlande)

Prix équitable :	231 à 354 $/t
Prime équitable :	24 $/t
Prime biologique :	20 à 32 $/t
Proportion de riz biologique :	44 %

⌃ Après avoir reçu du riz en guise d'offrande des paysans de la région de Yasothon, ces moines bouddhistes prennent leur déjeuner, leur seul repas de la journée.

⌃ Une libellule dans une rizière biologique est un signe de bonne santé environnementale. ⌐ Samon Skiradee repique, à intervalles réguliers, des bouquets de trois à cinq brins de riz. ⌐ En Thaïlande, 90% des rizières sont irriguées pour permettre le repiquage, augmenter les rendements et réduire le travail de désherbage.

IIIIIIIIIIIIIIIIIIIIIIIIIIIIIIIIIIIIIIIIIIIIIIIIIIIIIIIIIIIIIIIIIIIIIIIIIIIIIIIIIIIII

Dans la région de Yasothon, au nord-est de la Thaïlande, le repiquage bat son plein. Les rizières sont toutes inondées (90 % des rizières de Thaïlande sont irriguées) et chacun s'affaire à sa tâche respective. Dans un champ, les jeunes pousses dépassent déjà 30 cm et sont prêtes à être arrachées. Les paysans frappent délicatement les racines sur leurs talons pour en retirer la terre. D'autres prennent de grandes perches pour transporter les gerbes, balancées de part et d'autre de longs bambous. Ces gerbes sont transportées un peu plus loin, dans une nouvelle rizière submergée, pour le repiquage. Ici et là, le dos courbé et les pieds plantés dans la terre visqueuse, les paysans replantent les tiges de riz en grappes de trois à cinq brins. Leurs mains, qui saisissent les semis, et leurs pieds, qui marchent dans la boue semblent adopter les mouvements d'une danse rituelle offerte en célébration de la vie.

⌐ Les gerbes de riz sont transportées de rizière en rizière pour le repiquage.

⌃ Chutima et son fils Haleem.

|||||||||||||||||||||||||||||||||||||||||||||||||||||||||||||||||||||||||||||||||||||||

En compagnie de Chutima, la jeune technicienne de la coopérative de Yasothon (Nature Preservation Club), fondée au début des années 1970, je visite Ta Wee et Son Mai, de typiques petits producteurs de la région. Leurs trois hectares sont un jardin d'Éden. On y trouve des arbres fruitiers, des légumes, des étangs à poissons et même un élevage de grenouilles – preuves d'une riche diversité écologique et alimentaire. En Thaïlande, l'agriculture biologique du riz revêt une approche toute particulière qui encourage la diversification. Il n'est pas rare que les organisations de promotion de l'agriculture biologique demandent aux petits paysans de produire des dizaines de variétés de produits agricoles sur leurs terres – une production diversifiée qui favorise l'auto-suffisance alimentaire.

« Mon père est devenu un ardent défenseur de l'agriculture biologique après être passé bien près de mourir des suites d'un cancer », raconte Chutima. Man Samsee, membre fondateur de la coopérative de Yasothon, avait remarqué que bien des paysans souffraient d'étourdissements et de maux de tête ou d'estomac les jours d'épandage. Lorsqu'il a reçu le diagnostic de cancer, il a rapidement fait le lien. La maladie de son corps était celle de son corpus social. En faisant le choix de l'agriculture biologique, Man Samsee s'est engagé dans la lutte pour recouvrer sa santé et celle de son environnement. La leçon a été bien comprise par Chutima : « Le choix du biologique, c'est pour ma santé, celle de mon enfant et aussi celle de ceux qui vont manger le riz que je cultive. »

INTERVIEWÉ PAR UN JOURNALISTE qui lui demandait depuis quand il « faisait du bio », un vieux paysan français répondit sans hésitation : « Depuis toujours. Lorsque j'ai commencé à cultiver, il n'y avait pas de production empoisonnante. » Si « faire du bio » signifie produire des aliments sans utiliser aucun pesticide chimique, engrais de synthèse ou organisme génétiquement modifié, force est de constater que l'agriculture biologique a été très longtemps la règle depuis que l'homme sème.

L'enrichissement des sols par des additifs artificiels a commencé au milieu du XIXe siècle, lorsque le chimiste allemand Justus von Liebig, père de « l'agriculture chimique », dénia toute fonction nourrissante de l'humus et annonça le salut agricole par l'utilisation de la triade azote (N), phosphore (P) et potasse ou carbonate de potasse (K). Les prophéties de von Liebig firent le bonheur des patrons des mines allemandes de potasse et des industries chimiques. L'agriculture chimique s'est imposée et quelques décennies ont suffi pour que s'ensuive une nette dégradation des sols et des aliments.

En 1924, le penseur Rudolf Steiner lança les bases de ce qu'il appela l'agriculture biodynamique : « Une agriculture assurant la santé du sol et des plantes pour procurer une alimentation saine aux animaux et aux hommes. » L'agriculture prônée par Steiner prend en compte le cycle des saisons, le cycle lunaire, celui des planètes, et utilise des préparations pulvérisées sur le compost et les plantes pour améliorer le rendement des cultures. L'International Federation of Organic Agriculture Movements (IFOAM), fondée en 1972, base, quant à elle, sa définition de l'agriculture biologique sur quatre grands principes : la santé, l'écologie, l'équité et la précaution. Pour l'IFOAM, « L'agriculture biologique est un système de production qui maintient et améliore la santé des sols, des écosystèmes et des personnes. Elle s'appuie sur des processus écologiques, la biodiversité et des cycles adaptés aux conditions locales, plutôt que sur l'utilisation d'intrants ayant des effets adverses. »

Dans son rapport présenté en 2007, même l'Organisation des Nations Unies pour l'alimentation et l'agriculture (FAO) reconnaît que l'agriculture biologique peut satisfaire la demande alimentaire mondiale sans nuire à l'environnement, comme le fait l'agriculture moderne. Rappelant qu'en 2006 « l'agriculture biologique était pratiquée dans 120 pays pour une surface cultivée de 31 millions d'hectares, et représentait un marché de 40 milliards de dollars », la FAO a exhorté les pays membres de l'ONU à œuvrer en faveur de ce type de production.

Aujourd'hui, la vente de produits arborant l'épithète « biologique » et son abréviation « bio » implique une certification (AB, Ecocert, USDA, etc.). Aussi, dans plusieurs pays, cette certification est encadrée par des lois, ce qui n'est pas le cas pour le terme « équitable ». Globalement, près de 50 % du café, du cacao et du riz certifiés équitables sont également certifiés biologiques. Au Canada, 59 % des ventes équitables concernent des produits également biologiques. Le reste de la production équitable doit suivre des pratiques agricoles respectueuses de l'environnement et limiter l'utilisation de pesticides.

L'agriculture biologique encourage la culture de variétés locales de riz. Pour Kankamkla Pilandi c'est une vraie passion, et sa terre est un laboratoire à ciel ouvert où sont cultivées plus de 75 variétés de riz, dont une qu'il a créée lui-même.

Phakphum Inpaen cultive, de manière biologique, six variétés de fèves, 12 sortes de fruits, 15 sortes de légumes, plus de 20 sortes d'herbes comestibles et du riz à profusion sur quelques hectares de terre.

ⓐ Sumanta Matkhao récolte son riz.

IIIIIIIIIIIIIIIIIIIIIIIIIIIIIIIIIIIIIIIIIIIIIIIIIIIIIIIIIIIIIIIIIIIIIII

Les mois ont passé et octobre a redessiné de reflets dorés les rizières desséchées. Chez Kampun, la récolte bat son plein. « Nous travaillons souvent collectivement pour nous encourager les uns les autres », dit-il. Après un dur labeur vient l'heure du repas. Chacun met sa contribution au centre d'une natte. Au menu : du riz collant, bien sûr, mais aussi des herbes et des légumes accompagnés de quelques spécialités locales, dont de petites cailles, des sauterelles grillées et une joyeuse fricassée de fourmis rouges grouillantes de vie. Les conversations tournent autour des bienfaits des produits biologiques sur la vie des producteurs et des consommateurs. « Ici, nous n'avons pas peur de manger notre riz, raconte un voisin. Au centre du pays, ils font quatre récoltes par année (alors qu'ailleurs on n'en fait qu'une ou deux), mais les producteurs utilisent tellement de produits chimiques qu'ils préfèrent acheter le riz des autres régions de Thaïlande pour leur propre consommation. »

IIIIIIIIIIIIIIIIIIIIIIIIIIIIIIIIIIIIIIIIIIIIIIIIIIIIIIIIIIIIIIIIIIIIIII

Quelques champs plus loin, Pa Yanchai et son mari regroupent les gerbes de riz au centre de leur lopin de terre pour le battage. Les gerbes sont alors fermement emprisonnées entre deux bâtons liés par une corde et frappées afin d'extraire les grains des tiges. Dans le champ voisin, Dang, Kam et Pan ont troqué leurs bâtons pour la pelle et l'éventail. Ils éventent les grains pour éliminer sommairement les impuretés, avant que le paddy prenne la route du moulin.

▷ Après avoir battu le riz dans un large panier, Dang, muni d'une pelle en bois, projette les grains dans les airs, tandis que Kam et Pan agitent des éventails pour éventer les grains et éliminer sommairement les impuretés du paddy.

À la coopérative de Surin, dans le nord-est du pays. Le moulin à riz grouille de gens qui vont et viennent. On y décortique le paddy pour obtenir les grains de riz bruns ou blancs. Des femmes s'appliquent à sélectionner à la main le riz qui sera ensuite emballé sous vide pour l'exportation. Contre les murs de l'entrepôt sont entassées les boîtes de divers clients : Claro en Suisse, Alter Eco, en France, et Equita au Canada, la marque de Commerce équitable Oxfam-Québec. Le moulin loge également les bureaux du Surin Rice Fund, la coopérative locale. Aujourd'hui, c'est jour de réunion du conseil d'administration, où siège Kanya Onsri.

Souriante et le regard déterminé, cette mère de deux enfants à la fin de la trentaine, et fille d'un *pram* (gardien des traditions), est présidente de l'association de producteurs de son village, qui compte 45 membres. Elle est aussi à l'origine d'un camp de jour qui cherche à valoriser le travail agricole et à promouvoir la transmission des connaissances ancestrales. Ce projet lui tient particulièrement à cœur puisque 25 des 30 jeunes du village y participent.

Au camp, après le travail aux champs, Kyra, une coopérante états-unienne, donne une leçon d'anglais aux jeunes du village. À la fin de la leçon, lorsque les enfants apprennent que je parle le français, ils manifestent aussitôt le désir d'en apprendre quelques mots. Kyra, qui parle parfaitement le thaï, en profite pour demander des cours de khmer, la langue familière dans cette région à la lisière du Cambodge. « La leçon aura lieu ce soir chez Kanya », leur annonce Kyra. À 19 h 30, tout ce beau monde, plus quelques parents, est réuni. « Bonjour, *good morning, gin kao* » ; leur volonté d'apprendre semble sans limites. Lorsque je leur demande quelle phrase ils souhaitent connaître, Kyra me traduit leur réponse en riant : « Va prendre ton bain ! » « Mais... je me suis douché ! », dis-je, l'air surpris. « Il ne faut surtout pas te sentir visé ajoute-t-elle rapidement, se laver en fin de journée est une habitude incontournable ici. Pour eux, inviter l'étranger à prendre son bain est une façon de bien l'accueillir. » Après les explications de Kyra, tout le monde rit allègrement.

Tôt le lendemain matin, une camionnette s'arrête devant la maison de Kanya. Des femmes s'y entassent avec leurs paniers. « Tous les samedis, nous allons au marché vert de la ville de Surin pour vendre nos surplus agricoles », précise Kanya. De maison en maison, la camionnette se remplit de victuailles, à en déborder sur le toit. « Cette famille ne vend même pas de riz à la coopérative. Elle tire tous ses revenus du marché vert », m'indique Kanya.

Au marché, des clients attendaient l'arrivée de la camionnette. Avant même que les étals soient déployés, on négocie déjà les prix. Fruits, légumes, poissons, grenouilles, arachides glacées, riz frais cuit dans du bambou, bananes frites – on a l'embarras du choix. Une cliente me dit sans

☟ Kanya Onsri avec les jeunes du camp de jour. ☟ Smeuan Rabeunam, père de Kanya et *pram*.

⌂ Sélection manuelle des grains de riz au moulin de la coopérative de Surin.

hésitation: « Ces bananes sont meilleures et moins chères que celles des autres marchés. »

Au retour, il y a de la joie dans la camionnette. Chacun fait le bilan des ventes du jour: 10 $, 25 $, 40 $. Kanya me rappelle que certains font jusqu'à 100 $ en un samedi, ce qui est énorme, considérant qu'un manœuvre gagne 4 $ par jour. Ce marché vert est devenu un complément essentiel à l'agriculture d'exportation. Elle continue: « Ça nous permet non seulement d'augmenter nos revenus, mais surtout d'avoir des entrées d'argent de semaine en semaine. L'argent provenant de la vente du riz sert pour des achats importants, pour rénover nos maisons, etc. Celui provenant du marché vert sert à couvrir nos besoins hebdomadaires. » L'une des femmes saute de la camionnette à la première maison de campagne rencontrée, d'où elle revient rapidement, une bouteille d'alcool de riz sous le bras. La bouteille ne fera pas deux fois le tour du groupe. Dans un vacarme de Khmers, les rires fusent de toute part, révélant des gencives noircies aux noix de bétel. À l'extérieur, la campagne est brossée de chaude lumière. Les paysans, une faucille sur l'épaule, reviennent de leurs champs. Le moment est délicieux.

Le commerce équitable n'a pas seulement transformé les bases matérielles de la vie de Kanya et d'autres petits producteurs thaïlandais. La participation démocratique inhérente à l'organisation paysanne a été et reste un moteur de transformation sociale. « En général, en Thaïlande, les femmes s'occupent des tâches ménagères, mais chez moi ce n'est pas comme ça. Celles et ceux qui ont des idées doivent pouvoir participer aux réunions et s'impliquer! » me dit Kanya. Puis, portant une carapace de tortue, une grande tige de canne à sucre et quelques offrandes, elle et son père se dirigent lentement vers le grenier où est stockée une partie de la récolte annuelle. Elle m'explique la célébration: « C'est l'une des dernières cérémonies pour s'excuser auprès de Mae Phosop d'avoir pris son riz, et pour lui demander d'accompagner ce riz partout où il ira... même au Québec! »

1. Song Ausisa ensemence sa terre.
2. Jeunes pousses de riz.
3. Repiquage du riz.
4. Pa Yanchai attache ses gerbes de riz...
5. ...puis son mari les transporte.
6. Phakphum Inpaen en pleine récolte.
7. Kam Pa lors du battage.
8. Contrôle de qualité au moulin de Surin.

▷ En haut : Pa Yanchai prend une pause bien méritée.
▷ En bas : Ce paddy sera semé pour lancer un nouveau cycle de culture.

le coton

Monade de la tendresse du royaume végétal, le coton s'est mondialisé avant l'humain, préparant peut-être son avènement. L'usage du coton à des fins d'habillement est assurément l'une des premières conquêtes de l'homme. Si l'Inde fut le centre de diffusion du coton vers la Chine et le Moyen-Orient, la connaissance et sans doute la culture du cotonnier remontent à l'aube de différentes civilisations à divers endroits de la planète, comme l'atteste la découverte de fragments de tissus de coton vieux de plus de 7000 ans dans la vallée de Tehuacán, au Mexique. Dans la Grèce antique, Hérodote s'étonnait de la qualité des vêtements portés par les Indiens, faits d'une « laine plus belle et plus douce que celle des moutons ». Cette douceur serait-elle la raison de la préférence universelle des hommes pour cette fibre aux origines mystérieuses ? De l'Inde à la Mésopotamie jusqu'aux colonies du Nouveau Monde, le coton devint, et reste jusqu'à nos jours, la principale fibre textile au monde.

En Afrique, le coton était présent bien avant les contacts avec les Arabes ou les Européens, comme en témoignent les Dogons ou les Soninkés. «Dans la mythologie dogon, Nomo, un ancêtre mythique, crache des fils de coton. Ces fils sont séparés entre ses dents, ses mâchoires inférieure et supérieure formant un métier à tisser. Le tissu, c'est la parole, la parole-étoffe», raconte Boubacar Doumbia, artiste malien du célèbre groupe Kasobané, qui donna toutes ses lettres de noblesse à l'art du bogolan, créant des œuvres contemporaines inspirées d'une technique ancestrale : la teinture du coton avec de l'argile.

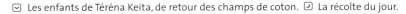

Dans la région de Kita, à quelques centaines de kilomètres au nord-ouest de Bamako, la capitale du Mali, le paysage est ocre et sablonneux, digne des zones arides sud-sahariennes. À Djidian, des maisons en pisé et quelques petits commerces bordent la route de terre battue, et une grande antenne surplombe le village. «C'était pour les téléphones portables, mais on a volé les panneaux solaires, me raconte monsieur le maire. À côté, ce sont les bâtiments pour la génératrice, qui fournit quelques heures d'électricité... habituellement à tous les soirs!» Le Mali est au 173e rang sur 177 pays pour son indice de développement humain, mais le pays n'en est pas moins riche en traditions et en culture.

Dans ses champs, à quelques kilomètres du village, Téréna Keita récolte le coton avec ses enfants. Le soleil est de plomb et la chaleur accablante. «J'ai deux hectares de coton, dont je récolte près de deux tonnes», m'explique-t-il en ramassant une à une les petites boules blanches sur les frêles arbustes. «L'an passé, j'ai vendu pour 280 000 francs de coton, mais mon crédit pour les intrants était de 225 000 francs. Il ne m'est resté que 55 000 francs (125 $) à la fin de la récolte.» Le coton est souvent le seul moyen pour ces producteurs d'obtenir des fertilisants pour l'ensemble de leur production agricole. Téréna cultive également le maïs, les arachides, le sorgho et le mil, principalement pour sa subsistance.

Tout le coton malien est commercialisé par le biais de la Compagnie malienne pour le Développement des Textiles (CMDT). Créée en 1974, la CMDT se dit présente, avec 4000 employés, dans 6345 villages et hameaux, où vivent 3 700 000 personnes, soit 28% de la population du pays. Le coton a longtemps été une force économique du Mali, mais les fluctuations et surtout les baisses des cours mondiaux, et les demandes incessantes de privatisation de la part du Fonds monétaire international (FMI) ont grandement fragilisé la société d'État. En 2003, les producteurs récoltaient 620 000 tonnes de coton, alors qu'en 2006-2007, ils n'en récoltaient que 240 000.

Les enfants de Téréna Keita, de retour des champs de coton. La récolte du jour.

⌃ Téréna Keita récolte son coton, dans la campagne malienne.

Le secteur cotonnier malien vit présentement une crise majeure.

Bien que les coûts de production du coton africain soient inférieurs à ceux du coton états-unien, celui-ci s'impose dans le marché mondial grâce aux subventions dont bénéficient les producteurs des États-Unis, évaluées à plus de quatre milliards de dollars. Avec ces subventions, le coton états-unien rapporte à ses producteurs de 90 à 140 % de plus que les cours mondiaux. Le Brésil a porté plainte contre ces subventions et a obtenu une victoire anodine, puisque le *dumping* états-unien est toujours de mise. L'échec des négociations de la Conférence ministérielle de l'Organisation mondiale du Commerce (cycle de Doha), en 2008, dû à la détermination des pays riches à maintenir leurs subventions, a plongé les agriculteurs du Sud dans l'incertitude.

La charrette bien remplie, il est temps de prendre le chemin de la maison, où les deux épouses de Téréna s'affairent à préparer le repas du soir. La maison de terre est faite de trois chambres adjacentes. Deux greniers, incontournables icônes de la campagne malienne, occupent la cour centrale, et sous l'un d'eux une chèvre broute quelques feuilles. Un petit entrepôt vient compléter le paysage. Deux vaches paissent à l'extérieur des murs qui délimitent la propriété. Cetou, sa deuxième épouse, transporte un seau d'eau tiré d'un puits communautaire, à quelques mètres de la maison et Kanimba, sa première épouse, apporte la pâte de maïs et la sauce aux arachides. En guise de dessert, on m'offre un lait chaud et sucré que je partage avec les 12 enfants de Téréna. Sa fille aînée, Sayou, allaite son bébé, tandis que ses jeunes frères fabriquent, avec quelques bouts de broche, une magnifique voiture. Le soleil couché, la soirée se termine à la lanterne. Ce soir, l'électricité n'est pas au rendez-vous.

La région de Kita fut la première, au Mali, à exporter du coton équitable. En novembre 2003, une alliance entre Max Havelaar France, Dagris, et la CMDT permettait de débuter l'exportation du coton équitable vers l'Europe. En 2004, la FLO officialisait la certification du coton, sa première filière non alimentaire. En France, plus de 20 grandes marques se lancèrent dans les vêtements équitables, à grand renfort promotionnel.

La filière malienne équitable s'est développée rapidement, passant de quatre coopératives en 2003 à 72 en 2007. La production de coton équitable est, quant à elle, passée de 400 à 5000 tonnes. « Les primes équitables et le différentiel de prix ont ajouté 450 millions de francs (1,1 million de dollars) aux revenus des producteurs en 2005-2006 », précise Sékou Amadou Thiéro, responsable du commerce équitable à la CMDT. « Ces fonds ont permis la réalisation de plusieurs projets sociaux comme la construction de puits, d'écoles, de dispensaires, d'entrepôts, etc. »

À quelques kilomètres de Djidian, Dougourakoroba et Dougourakoroni sont parmi les premiers villages à avoir fait le pari de l'équitable. Les classes construites avec les primes équitables ont permis aux enfants d'éviter bien des heures de marche, soir et matin. « Nos salles sont maintenant bien construites ; les enfants ne sont plus sur la terre battue ; nous avons plus de locaux et chaque niveau a sa salle de classe », me raconte Soulale Sekou Aba, le directeur de l'école de Dougourakoroni, qui compte 133 élèves, dont 61 filles.

À Batimakana, les producteurs sont fiers de me faire visiter leur magasin de stockage des pesticides, des fertilisants, des produits vivriers et du coton. Derrière le magasin, un dispensaire est en construction. « On voudrait bien le compléter, mais on attend encore le paiement des primes équitables de la récolte de l'an passé », précise le président de la coopérative de Batimakana. Il semble que même le commerce équitable n'échappe pas à la crise du coton malien. À la CMDT, Sékou Amadou Thiéro ne cache pas son inquiétude : « Malheureusement, après tant d'espoirs soulevés au tout début, les commandes ont plafonné rapidement. En ce moment, nous n'avons toujours pas vendu un seul kilo de la récolte de l'an passé. Le coton est au port de Dakar et tant qu'il n'est pas exporté, nous ne sommes pas payés en totalité. Les 30 nouvelles coopératives certifiées n'ont toujours pas vu la couleur des primes équitables. Les producteurs n'ont pas perdu espoir, mais ils sont inquiets. » Le coton de

⊡ Kadiatou, élève de l'école primaire de Dougourakoroba. ⊡ Classe de Dougourakoroni construite avec les primes équitables. ⊡ Classe en construction à Batimakana.

⌃ Le coton équitable est récolté par de nombreux petits producteurs, au sein de 28 organisations paysannes, dans sept pays.

la saison 2008 ne sera pas certifié équitable, faute de demande.

À l'école de Batimakana, même réalité : les murs en briques sont construits, mais le toit temporaire laisse entrer les rayons du soleil et l'eau de pluie. « Nous avons reçu beaucoup de délégations ici, mais aujourd'hui, ce que nous attendons, c'est l'argent de nos primes », me rappelle le président de la coopérative avec un regard accusateur. À Djidian, Téréna fait le même constat : « Les primes n'ont pas été payées et en plus, nous n'avons pas reçu le paiement du coton avant juin, alors que la récolte était terminée depuis plusieurs mois. Nous sommes passés de 75 membres en 2006-2007 à seulement 25 en 2007-2008. »

L E COTON EST UNE PLANTE DE L'ORDRE DES MALVACÉES, dont les variétés les plus connues sont le *gossypium arboreum* et le *gossypium herbaceum*, présents en Inde, le *gossypium badanense*, présent au Pérou et en Égypte, et le plus célèbre *gossypium hirsutum*, originaire d'Amérique du Sud, qui assure plus de 90 % de la production mondiale. Les graines comptent pour 55 à 65 % du poids total du coton récolté (coton graine), selon les variétés. La fibre (coton fibre) équivaut à 85 % de la valeur marchande de ce même coton. Des graines, on extrait de l'huile végétale pour la cuisson, et on produit des aliments pour le bétail.

La culture du coton est des plus polluantes. Occupant à peine 2,4 % des terres arables, le coton absorbe 11 % des pesticides et 25 % des insecticides produits au monde. En Inde et aux États-Unis, 50 % des pesticides agricoles sont destinés à la production cotonnière. La résistance progressive des nuisibles à ces substances a fini par augmenter la fréquence des pulvérisations, exposant davantage l'homme et l'environnement à des dangers multiples. Le coton transgénique, dont le tristement célèbre « coton BT », du géant de l'agroalimentaire Monsanto, gagne de larges zones de production (66 % de la production en Inde et 93 % aux États-Unis), malgré de nombreuses critiques.

Environ 100 millions de familles vivent du coton, dans 70 pays, mais la production mondiale de coton est l'affaire de trois pays : la Chine, l'Inde et les États-Unis, qui ensemble en totalisent 67 %. La Chine, bien qu'elle soit le premier pays producteur, est aussi un importateur majeur et consomme 45 % du coton de la planète.

Dans l'ouest de l'Afrique, les coûts de production (0,66 $ le kilo) sont deux fois moins élevés qu'aux États-Unis, mais les subventions aux agriculteurs états-uniens leur permettent tout de même de *dumper* à moindres coûts les trois quarts de leur production sur les marchés internationaux, influençant artificiellement à la baisse les cours mondiaux. Depuis 1990, les cours du coton ont baissé de 70 %, avec des crises importantes en 2001-2002 et en 2008-2009 qui ont mis en péril bien des industries cotonnières, dont celle du Mali. Lancée en 2004, la filière du coton équitable a connu un rapide succès. En 2008, elle fut l'une des productions équitables à plus forte croissance, avec une augmentation de 94 % des ventes, pour totaliser 27 millions d'items : t-shirts, bas, draps, serviettes ou jeans équitables, vendus de par le monde. Près des trois quarts de ces ventes ont été réalisées en Grande-Bretagne, où ce marché est passé de seulement 500 000 items en 2006 à 9,3 millions en 2007, et à un rutilant 20 millions d'items en 2008.

le coton en chiffres

COMMERCE CONVENTIONNEL

Production mondiale : 72 504 406 tonnes
Commerce mondial : 11 329 000 000 $

PRINCIPAUX PAYS PRODUCTEURS

Chine	31,6 %
Inde	22,7 %
États-Unis	12,3 %
Pakistan	8 %
Brésil	5,4 %
Mali (23e)	0,4 %

COMMERCE ÉQUITABLE

Année de certification : 2004
Importations mondiales : 27 573 000 items
Ventes au détail : 261 910 000 $
Croissance de 2007 à 2008 : 94 %

ORGANISATIONS CERTIFIÉES

28 organisations de petits producteurs, dans sept pays.

ORIGINE DES ORGANISATIONS CERTIFIÉES

Inde	50 %
Mali	14 %
Sénégal	14 %

PRINCIPAUX PAYS IMPORTATEURS

	Importations (items)	Croissance (2007 à 2008)
Grande-Bretagne	20 200 000	112 %
France	4 000 000	33 %
Suisse	900 000	-13 %
Allemagne	800 000	n.d.
Finlande	500 000	n.d.

PRIX ET PRIMES

Prix équitable : 0,54 à 0,76 $/kg
Prime équitable : 0,07 $/ kg
Prime biologique : 0,10 à 0,15 $/kg
Proportion de coton biologique : 8 %

⌐ La récolte a été bonne pour la famille d'Yvette Sessé. Ce coton graine, composé des fibres et des semences du cotonnier, sera acheminé à l'usine, où les graines en seront extraites puis transformées en huile végétale et en nourriture animale.

Au bureau du Mouvement biologique malien (MOBIOM) à Bougouni, dans la région sud, la mise en marché du coton est également le défi du moment. De 174 producteurs en 2002, à la première phase du projet, ils sont aujourd'hui 11 000 à produire 2000 tonnes de coton biologique et équitable. Le directeur du MOBIOM décrit ainsi la situation : « Au début, il a fallu se battre pour montrer qu'on pouvait faire du coton sans produits chimiques, mais avec l'augmentation des coûts des intrants et la baisse de productivité, le coton biologique est devenu une bonne alternative à la production conventionnelle. »

À Sibirila, les récoltes de riz, de maïs, de coton, d'arachides et de sésame s'activent dans tous les champs. La région est reconnue pour la richesse de ses terres agricoles. Dans le petit village, plusieurs hommes et quelques femmes se sont réunis pour une rencontre avec un spécialiste européen venu évaluer la filière biologique du coton malien. Parmi eux, un seul représente les producteurs de coton conventionnel. « Avant, il y avait 140 producteurs conventionnels et aujourd'hui nous ne sommes plus que 21, annonce-t-il. Le coût des intrants est de 100 000 à 150 000 francs par hectare. Dans le temps, certains faisaient deux tonnes de coton à l'hectare, mais aujourd'hui, on a du mal à faire une tonne. La CMDT fournit les semences, et la variété choisie pour le coton conventionnel compte moins de graines, donc on est perdants. À

160 francs le kilo ou même à 200 francs, le prix de 2008, ce n'est pas profitable. »

Pour le plus volubile des producteurs biologiques, Nahoum Samaké, il fut un temps où le coton conventionnel était synonyme de prospérité : « J'ai déjà cultivé neuf hectares de coton et récolté 12 tonnes ! J'avais même acheté une moto d'un million de francs (2500 $) à ce moment-là, mais les temps ont changé. La dernière année, j'avais réduit mes champs de coton à trois hectares et j'ai quand même perdu 200 000 francs (500 $). J'ai dû vendre un bœuf et une vache pour rembourser mes dettes. L'année suivante, je me suis mis à cultiver de manière biologique. » En 2007-2008 le coton bio-équitable était payé 326 francs, plus 34 francs de prime équitable par kilo, le double du prix conventionnel. « Maintenant, je fais des profits, dit Nahoum, et j'ai pu avoir ma quatrième épouse... C'est ma femme bio-équitable », lance-t-il en riant, avec la complicité de ses compatriotes producteurs. « Tu aurais mieux fait de t'occuper des trois autres », rétorque d'un ton acide Barakali Jara, une productrice également membre du MOBIOM.

« Avant, les femmes n'avaient pas le droit de cultiver le coton à cause des produits chimiques, mais avec le coton bio, plusieurs s'y sont mises. Nous avons débuté avec seulement un quart d'hectare par personne, ou en groupes de dix sur un demi-hectare. De toutes petites productions », raconte Barakali. Yvette Sessé, trésorière du Conseil d'administration du MOBIOM, cultive

☑ Salle d'alphabétisation de la coopérative de Yanfolina. ☑ Nahoom Samaké, ses quatre épouses et ses 21 enfants. ☑ Yvette Sessé à Yanfolina.

⌒ En plus du coton, les paysans maliens récoltent le riz, le mil, les arachides et le maïs, que Maimouna Jara vanne pour le repas du soir.

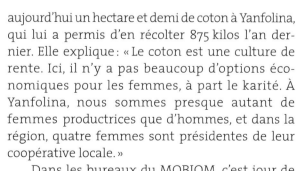

aujourd'hui un hectare et demi de coton à Yanfolina, qui lui a permis d'en récolter 875 kilos l'an dernier. Elle explique : « Le coton est une culture de rente. Ici, il n'y a pas beaucoup d'options économiques pour les femmes, à part le karité. À Yanfolina, nous sommes presque autant de femmes productrices que d'hommes, et dans la région, quatre femmes sont présidentes de leur coopérative locale. »

Dans les bureaux du MOBIOM, c'est jour de rencontre pour le conseil d'administration. Yvette est assise parmi ses compatriotes producteurs, les dirigeants du MOBIOM, coopérants et autres experts venus conseiller l'association. Le directeur du MOBIOM, de retour d'une foire européenne, présente quelques faits inquiétants : « Le coton biologique et équitable indien est bien moins cher en ce moment que celui du Mali ; nous devrons être plus compétitifs. Aujourd'hui, la responsabilité directe du MOBIOM s'arrête à l'usine d'égrenage. Depuis toujours, l'exclusivité de la vente du coton revient à la CMDT, mais avec la privatisation, cela va changer, nous aurons plus de liberté, mais aussi plus de responsabilités pour l'exportation de notre coton. Nous devons nous diversifier et cela veut aussi dire initier plus de transformation locale de notre coton. » Le MOBIOM, profitant de la production de ses membres, offre aussi le sésame, l'arachide et le karité, tous biologiques et équitables.

L'USINE DE LA COMPAGNIE MALIENNE des Textiles (COMATEX), à Ségou, compte 1400 employés. En 1993, 80 % des parts ont été vendues à des Chinois. Malgré cela, en 2009 elle a dû demander le soutien de l'État malien, actionnaire à 20 %, pour contrer « une insuffisance de compétitivité par rapport aux produits chinois ». Zhang Ouyi, le directeur général, m'y accueille dans un français impeccable et m'explique que seulement 10 % du coton malien est transformé au pays. Quant au coton équitable, « nous l'avons déjà filé, me dit-il, nous n'en avons eu que pour quelques heures ! ».

⌃ Filage industriel chez Comatex, au Mali.

« En Afrique, je ne peux pas commander directement du fil de coton équitable. Je dois passer par des intermédiaires européens », explique Marc-Henri Faure, de la coopérative FibrEthik, qui importe son coton équitable de l'Inde, premier producteur mondial, où l'image du Mahatma Gandhi au rouet marqua les âmes. « En Inde, je peux acheter le coton brut, en fil, en tissu ou confectionné en polo, explique-t-il. Je travaille principalement avec Agrocel au Gujarat et Chetna Organics en Andhra Pradesh, l'un des États les plus touchés par les suicides. » Le grand nombre de suicides de paysans indiens incapables de faire face à leurs dettes dues, entre autres, à l'achat de semences, intrants et pesticides pour la production de coton BT de Monsanto, a été qualifié « d'épidémie du coton OGM ». L'affaire a ému les médias et même le prince Charles a dénoncé « l'échec de nombreuses variétés d'OGM ». Pour Marc-Henri, « le rendement du coton biologique est légèrement plus bas, mais son prix d'exportation est bien plus avantageux et donc plus rentable pour les producteurs ».

« Notre confection se fait par une petite entreprise familiale de Calcutta, Raj Laksmi, mais la certification formelle de la FLO s'arrête aux organisations de producteurs », explique Marc-Henri. Lancée par Max Havelaar France en 2004, la certification équitable du coton a donné lieu à certains débats. D'autres initiatives solidaires militaient déjà contre les « ateliers de misère ». Or, Max Havelaar-FLO certifie essentiellement les petits producteurs de la matière première au sein de leurs organisations démocratiques. Les autres intermédiaires (égrainage, filature, tissage, confection) ne sont qu'« agréés » par la FLO et doivent suivre les normes de l'Organisation internationale du Travail.

L'Inde compte pour la moitié des 28 organisations de producteurs de coton certifiées par la FLO en 2008. De plus, le nombre d'entreprises indiennes de transformation agréées est cinq fois plus élevé que celui des organisations de producteurs. Au Mali, il n'y a que quatre organisations de producteurs certifiés et COMATEX est la seule entreprise de transformation agréée.

Lancée par Max Havelaar France en 2004,
la certification équitable du coton a donné lieu à certains débats.
D'autres initiatives solidaires militaient déjà
contre les « ateliers de misère ».

▷ Bintou Traoré file la fibre de coton, à Ségou.

À Ségou, Boubacar Doumbia peint méthodiquement de grandes étoffes de coton. Son atelier, N'domo, se trouve dans un bâtiment d'architecture traditionnelle aux murs de banco qui rappelle la célèbre mosquée de Djenné. « Ce coton est filé par des femmes de Ségou et tissé dans de petits ateliers de la région », me dit Boubacar, comme s'il s'agissait d'une évidence. Pour bien des experts, le bogolan malien est l'un des arts les plus distinctifs du pays. Ce coton fait le tour du monde grâce au langage universel de l'art. Malheureusement, ceux qui pratiquent cet art, aussi splendide soit-il, ne peuvent utiliser tout le coton produit dans les campagnes du pays. Le coton malien, même biologique et équitable, semble encore et toujours souffrir de la concurrence mondiale.

▷ Le soleil est essentiel pour donner tout leur éclat aux étoffes de coton peintes par les artistes de l'atelier N'Domo, à Ségou, avec des teintures naturelles végétales à base d'argile, d'écorce et de feuilles.

1. Capsule de coton.
2. Yvette Sessé en pleine récolte.
3. Charrette remplie de coton.
4. Dans un atelier de Ségou, les bobines de fil s'alignent...
5. Métier à tisser dans un atelier de Ségou.
6. Fibre de coton de Comatex.
7. Tissu imprimé de Comatex.

▷ En haut : Vannage du riz par Awa Samake, à Sibirila.
▷ En bas : La capsule du cotonnier et ses célèbres filaments blancs sont à la base de près de la moitié de la production mondiale de fibres textiles.

la banane

D ans *El papa verde*, l'un des romans de *Trilogía de la república de la banana*, le Guatémaltèque Miguel Ángel Asturias, prix Nobel de littérature en 1967, décrit un monde impitoyable où des paysans sont dépouillés par un monopole qui ne recule devant rien ni personne pour s'installer en maître absolu. Ce pouvoir économique aura son visage politique et son lot de coups de force et de massacres. Dans l'histoire des grands monopoles fruitiers, les saveurs et les décors peuvent changer selon les époques, et les compagnies changer de nom au gré des fusions et des stratégies publicitaires, mais c'est toujours la même injustice qui frappe paysans et travailleurs. Des romans de Miguel Ángel Asturias, revenons à la triste réalité : en 2007, une multinationale du commerce de la banane payait des paramilitaires pour poursuivre des syndicalistes! Qu'à cela ne tienne! Elle a été condamnée par le gouvernement de son pays à payer une « lourde » amende – 25 millions de dollars –, en échange de laquelle la justice de ce grand État renonça à enquêter sur ses crimes de lèse-humanité.

||||||||||||||||||||||||||||||||||||||||||||||||||||||||||||||||||||||||||||||||||||||

Il est à peine six heures du matin à El Guabo, la capitale de la banane, située dans le sud de l'Équateur, et déjà des centaines de travailleurs sont à la croisée des routes principales pour attendre les camions qui les emmèneront aux plantations. Je suis dans l'un des fiefs de Noboa, un groupe privé présent dans les transports, les mines, les banques, les assurances, et qui assure 35 % des exportations de bananes du pays. Noboa est l'un des cinq oligopoles de la banane, avec les États-Uniennes Dole, Chiquita, Del Monte et l'Européenne Fyffes qui, ensemble, se réservent 85 % des exportations mondiales, un marché de près de six milliards de dollars. L'Équateur est le premier exportateur mondial de ce fruit, avec près du tiers du marché (plus de 194 000 hectares y sont consacrés à la culture de la banane). Fait à souligner : seulement 4 % des recettes de vente de la banane conventionnelle demeurent dans les pays producteurs.

À peine suis-je sorti de la ville que les bananeraies envahissent le paysage. Partout, on retrouve l'incontournable variété cavendish, qui accapare 99 % du commerce mondial – malgré le millier de variétés de bananes –, et ce, même si bien des scientifiques ont sonné l'alarme sur les risques majeurs d'épidémie d'une telle monoculture. La quasi-éradication de la variété gros Michel par un champignon dans les années 1960 semble être bien oubliée.

Après une heure de route, j'arrive à la petite plantation de Vincente Matute, l'un des 450 membres de l'Association des petits producteurs de bananes El Guabo. Quelques travailleurs collent des boîtes, d'autres préparent les savons aux bassins de lavage. Fabian, le fils de Vincente, ajuste les chaînes sur les rails pour le transport des régimes. Vincente regarde le tout sans donner de consignes – chacun sait ce qu'il doit faire. « Cette plantation est le travail d'une vie », me raconte celui qui soigne ces terres depuis 30 ans. « Je vis heureux avec mes quatre hectares. À quoi bon en avoir dix sans pouvoir les entretenir ? », philosophe-t-il en marchant au milieu d'un tableau vert, jaune et rouge. Ces fruitiers, parfois hauts de dix mètres, ne cherchent pas vraiment à nous tromper : le bananier n'est pas un arbre, il ne contient aucune matière ligneuse, mais il est l'une des plus grandes herbes au monde. « Un bananier contient 90 % d'eau », m'indique Vincente en pointant un jet de son essentiel système d'irrigation qui fait gicler de l'eau à 360 degrés.

☑ Les régimes sont taillés en mains de quatre à sept bananes, qui reposent ensuite dans les bassins de lavage. ☑ Vincente Matute, membre fondateur d'El Guabo.

⌃ Fabian Matute souhaite poursuivre le travail de son père dans la bananeraie, qui produit 350 boîtes de bananes par semaine en haute saison.

Pablo Mera arrive d'un pas vif avec un sac en bandoulière et une échelle, qu'il dépose délicatement à côté d'un large régime coiffé d'un sac de plastique. Il y monte, sort une chaîne de son sac, attache le régime, le coupe et le laisse descendre doucement. Plus bas, un autre travailleur reçoit les fruits sur un coussin qu'il porte sur l'épaule. Pablo coupe alors toutes les feuilles en un éclair. « On ne coupe pas la plante mère », m'annonce Vincente. Elle contribue à la croissance de ses filles, qui l'entourent en permanence. » Ces bananes ne contiennent point de semences. Leur culture continuelle se fait par rhizome, sous terre. Il faut six à sept mois pour produire des fleurs et un autre trois à quatre mois pour la maturation des fruits.

« Ici, on n'utilise aucun herbicide ni nématicide. Les agronomes de l'Association ne nous poussent pas à utiliser des produits dont on n'a pas besoin », me fait savoir Vincente. Or, les grandes plantations de bananes exigent 30 kilos de pesticides par hectare annuellement, dix fois plus que dans les cultures intensives des pays industrialisés du Nord. Les problèmes de santé liés à l'utilisation massive de pesticides ont d'ailleurs poussé 24 000 anciens travailleurs de l'industrie bananière d'Amérique latine à entamer des poursuites contre Dole, Chiquita et quelques compagnies pétrochimiques, un litige impliquant le nématicide Nemagon (DBCP), qui peut causer la stérilité, des malformations congénitales et des problèmes aux reins et au foie. Banni par l'Agence de protection de l'environnement des États-Unis depuis 1977, ce produit est toujours employé dans certaines plantations.

Vincente continue : « En basse saison, je récolte 120 boîtes, mais en haute saison, c'est plus de 350 boîtes par semaine. Avec les prix actuels, on ne devient pas riches, mais on a de quoi se défendre. » En 30 ans, Vincente a connu plus d'une crise : « Avant l'association, les intermédiaires locaux qui achetaient nos bananes n'étaient pas des exportateurs. C'était des exploiteurs ! Je me souviens parfaitement de notre première rencontre avec des représentants d'une organisation européenne. Nous étions assis sous un arbre. Nous avons ri, nous avons pleuré. À la fin, ils nous ont offert dix fois plus que le prix local, se rappelle-t-il. Certains n'y ont pas cru. Moi, j'ai osé y croire et nous avons formé la première association de petits producteurs de la région. »

L ES DICTONS POPULAIRES AURONT BEAU évoquer les pommes et les oranges, il demeure que c'est un autre fruit qui vole la vedette. L'ineffable banane, avec ses 85 millions de tonnes produites annuellement, est le fruit le plus populaire au monde et la denrée alimentaire la plus importante après les trois céréales de base (riz, blé, maïs). Certains horticulteurs avancent même que l'offrande en forme de sourire, issue de l'herbacée du genre *musa*, pourrait avoir été le premier fruit dans l'évolution du règne végétal.

Les origines de sa culture par l'homme, vieille de 10 000 ans, se situeraient quelque part dans le chapelet de grandes îles de l'Indonésie. Mais après avoir été considérée comme un fruit défendu au Moyen Âge, tant par les chrétiens que les musulmans, la banane aurait suivi les migrations humaines vers l'Afrique – d'où lui vient son nom, qui signifie « doigt arabe » en langue bantoue –, puis vers le Nouveau Monde.

Les avancées technologiques dans le domaine des transports (comme le chemin de fer et le fret maritime réfrigéré) ont permis au plus grand nombre de profiter de ses vertus nutritives, comme son haut taux de glucides et de potassium, et son absence de matières grasses. Mais le prix à payer pour cette internationalisation a été, hélas, élevé pour ceux qui se trouvent aux premiers échelons de la filière. En s'accaparant le contrôle de la commercialisation et d'une partie de la production, quelques grands monopoles occidentaux ont historiquement fait main basse sur les profits du commerce de la banane, en imposant à la main-d'œuvre des conditions de travail qui ont fait la triste réputation des « républiques de bananes ». Encore aujourd'hui, les histoires d'exploitation d'enfants, de gestion environnementale catastrophique ou encore d'intimidation violente contre les syndicats résonnent autour du fruit qui, incurvé vers le bas, ne fait plus sourire.

Les années 1990 verront l'émergence d'un ras-le-bol salutaire, avec le réveil de certains gouvernements régionaux, l'union de pays producteurs, la reprise de terres agricoles au profit des travailleurs ou encore l'imposition de taxes à l'exportation – un ensemble de bouleversements qui mettront la table pour une véritable guerre de la banane entre les producteurs et les oligarches. Une conférence mondiale, organisée par l'Union internationale des travailleurs de l'alimentaire, conviera, en 1998, les différents intervenants à trouver un terrain d'entente. Elle accouchera d'une *Charte internationale de la banane,* un an seulement après l'arrivée en scène d'une filière équitable pour ce fruit. La démarche arrivant à point nommé, la banane est aujourd'hui le premier produit, en termes de poids, de la filière équitable, avec près de 300 000 tonnes vendues en 2008.

la banane en chiffres

COMMERCE CONVENTIONNEL

Production mondiale : 85 855 856 tonnes
Commerce mondial : 5 799 000 000 $

PRINCIPAUX PAYS PRODUCTEURS

Inde	26 %
Chine	9 %
Philippines	9 %
Brésil	8,5 %
Équateur	7,5 %

COMMERCE ÉQUITABLE

Année de certification : 1999
Importations mondiales : 299 205 tonnes
Ventes au détail : 660 720 000 $
Croissance de 2007 à 2008 : 28 %

ORGANISATIONS CERTIFIÉES

28 organisations de petits producteurs et 35 organisations avec des travailleurs salariés, dans neuf pays.

ORIGINE DES ORGANISATIONS CERTIFIÉES

République dominicaine	36 %
Colombie	30 %
Équateur	11 %

PRINCIPAUX PAYS IMPORTATEURS

	Importations (t)	Croissance (2007 à 2008)
Grande-Bretagne	189 413	32 %
Suisse	28 019	-1 %
Allemagne	12 432	-9 %
États-Unis	11 292	244 %
Autriche	10 572	51 %

PRIX ET PRIMES

Prix équitable : 6,75 à 9,25 $ la boîte de 18,14 kg
Prime équitable : 1 $/boîte
Prime biologique : 1,50 à 2,30 $/boîte
Proportion de bananes biologiques : 30 %

◨ Thelmo Japon met en boîtes ses bananes biologiques et équitables dans les petites installations collectives de l'association Muyuyacu, l'une des 15 organisations paysannes regroupées au sein d'El Guabo.

Les premiers pas ont été difficiles, mais le 27 novembre 1997, l'Association des petits producteurs de bananes El Guabo était officiellement reconnue. Il a fallu que ses membres apprennent les rouages du commerce mondial, qu'ils répondent aux exigences de qualité des marchés du Nord, tout en étant en compétition avec des géants. Un autre écueil vint s'ajouter à ces difficultés initiales : le phénomène El Niño. À cause de cette perturbation climatique qui, en 1997, a affecté plus de 25 000 hectares de bananeraies dans tout le pays (13 % de la superficie totale de cette culture), les exportations d'El Guabo ont même dû être interrompues.

Coopérant avec les organisations néerlandaises Stichting Nederlandse Vrijwilligers (SNV) et Solidaridad, El Guabo reprit ses exportations vers l'Europe en octobre 1998. « Ce fut l'épreuve du feu », raconte Wilson Navarrete, producteur et dirigeant d'El Guabo. Épreuve réussie, puisqu'au début de 1999, El Guabo acheminait un conteneur par semaine et triplait son exportation six mois plus tard. Mais le transport, contrôlé par les grands groupes bananiers, demeurait un défi. En 2000, El Guabo trouva un transporteur fiable et abordable, mais qui lui demandait de fournir 20 000 boîtes de bananes par envoi, cinq fois plus que son marché équitable. Les bas prix du marché conventionnel obligèrent alors El Guabo à subventionner ses exportations avec son marché équitable et poussèrent les producteurs à développer une nouvelle alternative : l'agriculture biologique. En 2003, le défi était relevé. El Guabo exportait 10 000 boîtes de bananes équitables, 8000 de bananes biologiques et seulement 3000 de bananes conventionnelles.

« Aujourd'hui, nous exportons plus de 40 000 boîtes par semaine de bananes certifiées équitables pratiquement à 100 % », m'indique Lianne Zoeteweij, la directrice générale d'El Guabo, lors de ma visite au port Puerto Bolivar, l'un des plus importants du pays. Même en ce temps de faible production, quatre millions de boîtes de bananes y sont exportées chaque semaine. Jour et nuit, des bateaux y remplissent leurs cales et repartent pour un séjour d'une à trois semaines vers la Russie, l'Europe occidentale, le Moyen-Orient ou les États-Unis.

« Les États-Unis deviendront bientôt notre deuxième marché, lorsque le partenariat avec Dole sera établi. Il nous reste quelques détails à régler, mais dans quelques semaines, nos bananes équitables importées par Dole seront

⌂ Au port Puerto Bolivar, c'est jour d'embarquement pour les bananes d'El Guabo qui quitteront les côtes équatoriennes pour un périple d'une à trois semaines vers l'Europe, les États-Unis et les autres marchés équitables.

distribuées dans les Sam's Club (une filière de Walmart) de l'ouest des États-Unis », m'explique Lianne. Lorsque je lui demande si elle est à l'aise avec le fait de travailler avec de telles compagnies, elle me répond : « Si nous sommes traités de manière juste, si les règles de la certification équitable sont respectées, c'est bon pour nos membres. C'est un nouveau marché dont nous avons besoin. »

D ANS LES BUREAUX D'EL GUABO, en Équateur, j'ai croisé les représentants de Dole, en Éthiopie ceux de Nestlé, et en Argentine j'ai pu assister à l'embarquement de 50 000 bouteilles de vin équitable en direction des Sam's Club, aux États-Unis. Des géants parmi les géants, dont plusieurs questionnent l'association au commerce équitable. «En Amérique du Nord, plusieurs multinationales ont été poussées par les consommateurs et des organisations militantes à offrir des produits équitables», rappelle Rob Clarke, directeur général de Transfair Canada, l'organisation responsable de la certification équitable au pays.

◨ Les boîtes de bananes d'El Guabo, entreposées avant leur embarquement.

Sur le terrain, toutes les organisations de producteurs rencontrées ont eu les mêmes propos : «Avec nous, ces compagnies respectent pleinement les critères du commerce équitable.» Pour Rob Clarke, «Les multinationales n'ont aucunement changé les standards de la FLO. Toutes les entreprises qui importent des produits équitables doivent respecter les mêmes règles. Notre travail n'est pas de certifier des compagnies, mais des produits.» La distinction est importante. Si, pour un produit donné, une compagnie suit les règles de certification équitable, celle-ci peut utiliser le *label* de la FLO sur l'emballage de ce produit – un *label* qui garantit alors «l'équité» du produit sans prendre position sur l'historique social ou «l'équité» de toutes les pratiques de l'entreprise.

«Notre rôle est de donner aux producteurs du Sud un meilleur accès aux marchés du Nord», précise Rob Clarke. L'accès au marché est souvent le nerf de la guerre ; or les multinationales ont le pouvoir de déplacer de gigantesques volumes. Pour le café, 50 % du volume des organisations certifiées par la FLO sont exportés avec le *label* équitable, pour les fleurs, c'est à peine plus de 25 %, pour le thé, seulement 15 %, et pour les ballons de sport, un maigre 3,7 % des items produits. Il y a donc une grande place à l'expansion de l'équitable, autant chez les multinationales que chez les distributeurs de produits 100 % équitables. «Lorsqu'une entreprise conventionnelle débute avec un faible pourcentage de produits certifiés par rapport à l'ensemble de son offre, nous lui demandons d'augmenter continuellement ses importations équitables. Le commerce équitable doit être un engagement à long terme», conclut Rob Clarke. Le débat demeure donc, pour bien des acteurs de l'équitable, entre d'un côté créer une alternative au marché conventionnel, et de l'autre réformer le système de l'intérieur !

«En Amérique du Nord, plusieurs multinationales ont été poussées par les consommateurs et des organisations militantes à offrir des produits équitables.»

Le vendredi est un jour de récolte pour les membres de l'Association de La Florida, en Équateur, une région agroforestière sans monoculture. Sur des terres pentues, de grands arbres indigènes dépassent les bananiers épars cultivés sans irrigation. Plusieurs producteurs cultivent également des cacaoyers. Des chevaux chargés de boîtes de bananes transitent lentement dans les sentiers, croisant de petites rivières. « Tu ne verras pas de production plus artisanale », m'annonce Edgar, l'un des techniciens d'El Guabo.

Dans les installations collectives des 23 membres de La Florida, Luis Heras coupe avec agilité de petites bananes sur un régime attaché à un bambou. La région de La Florida compte quelques variétés de bananiers. Luis m'instruit : « Avec un régime de cavendish, on peut remplir une boîte de 18 kilos ; pour les petites, on a besoin de quatre régimes et les boîtes ne pèsent que 12 kilos. » Le prix de ces bananes équitables et biologiques est de 7,25 $ la boîte pour les grosses, et de 8,40 $ la boîte pour les petites. Les mêmes boîtes se vendent de 0,80 $ à 3 $ sur les marchés locaux. « Avant El Guabo, il n'y avait pas d'acheteurs pour nos bananes. Je travaillais comme manœuvre à 60 $ par semaine. Aujourd'hui, je gagne au moins 150 $ par semaine avec mes bananes », m'indique Luis.

En 2008, le chiffre d'affaires d'El Guabo a dépassé les 20 millions de dollars, triplant celui de 2003. Pour la vente de bananes, le revenu moyen de 29 000 $ par membre est de loin le meilleur que j'ai vu dans tous mes périples équitables, mais pour les plus petits producteurs, la situation est quand même difficile.

Luis Gamboa et son fils Denny entretiennent 8000 plants de bananes et des cacaoyers sur 12 hectares de terre. « La fertilisation trimestrielle avec du compost de fumier coûte 500 $, dit Luis. Avec 50 boîtes par semaine, il nous reste bien peu. » Victor Samaniego, un voisin, compte dix hectares de cacao et de bananiers. « En haute saison, je peux faire 75 à 80 boîtes de bananes, mais en ce moment, je n'en fais que 25. La boîte biologique est payée 7,25 $, mais 2,20 $ sont déduits pour le coût du carton et des étiquettes, et je dois payer 15 $ pour le transport des boîtes. Que reste-t-il ? », se demande Victor. « Mes deux garçons travaillent avec moi, mais avec seulement 25 boîtes, je ne peux plus leur payer les 60 $ par semaine que gagne un manœuvre. Il faut qu'ils travaillent ailleurs », précise-t-il.

« Nous devons mieux encadrer certains membres pour améliorer leur production et ainsi réduire les coûts », m'indique Lianne dans les bureaux de l'Association. « Pour ceux qui produisent moins de 50 boîtes par semaine, la culture de la banane est difficilement rentable, ajoute-t-elle, mais avec l'aide de la prime équitable, nous allons

⊡ Miguel Merchan transporte ses boîtes de bananes vers les installations collectives de son association. ⊡ Luis Gamboa et son fils, Denny. ⊡ Petites bananes biologiques et équitables destinées au marché européen.

⌃ Luis Heras, nouveau membre de l'Association de La Florida.

développer des programmes pour soutenir le travail de ces membres. » La prime équitable par boîte de bananes est de 1 $. Pour El Guabo, qui exporte 2,2 millions de boîtes annuellement, les sommes en jeu sont colossales. « Vingt pour cent de la prime vont aux 15 associations locales. Nous avons une clinique avec un médecin et une infirmière (qui ont fait plus de 5000 consultations l'an dernier), et nous prenons en charge les salaires de 17 professeurs dans des écoles de la région, m'informe la directrice. De plus, El Guabo paie les primes d'assurance santé de tous ses membres et contribue aux organisations de travailleurs. Chaque travailleur dans les plantations de nos membres reçoit aussi une boîte de denrées de base à tous les mois. »

Une *rana* se repose sur une feuille de bananier, dans la plantation biologique de Guillermo Limones, membre d'El Guabo.

⌃ Rosendo Pujol retire quelques fleurs au bout de ses fruits. ⌃ Doni Varga en pleine récolte. ⌐ Coupe des mains de bananes. ⌐ Préparation à la mise en boîtes pour l'exportation. ⌄ L'immense bananeraie biologique de Finca 6, qui s'étend sur 700 hectares, est subdivisée en 250 lots, un pour chacune des familles membres de cette coopérative équitable de République dominicaine.

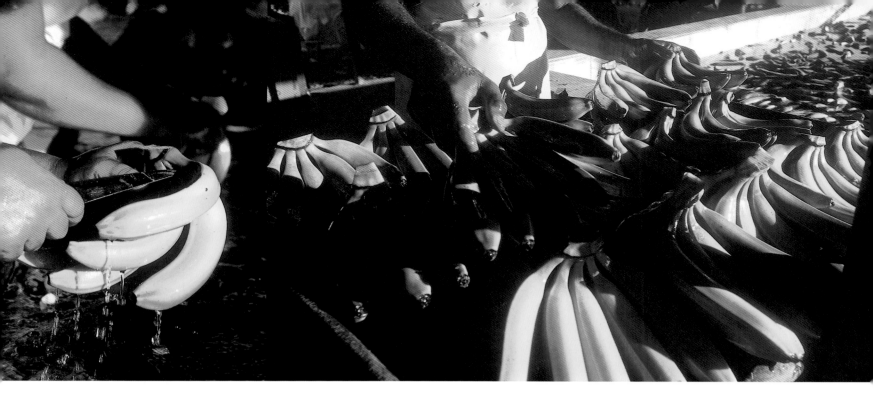

En République dominicaine, l'ampleur de l'organisation Finca 6 n'est certes pas aussi importante que celle d'El Guabo, mais son histoire est passionnante. Au début des années 1990, 250 familles vivaient dans des conditions précaires dans les montagnes de la Loma del Curro, non loin de la frontière haïtienne. Elles pratiquaient une agriculture sur brûlis et transformaient en charbon les forêts d'un futur parc national. « Nous ne voulions pas vraiment faire ça, mais nous n'avions pas le choix », raconte Angel Custodio, l'un des membres fondateurs de l'organisation. Puis, une plantation de 700 hectares à l'abandon, près de la ville d'Azua changea la donne. Débuta alors un bras de fer avec le gouvernement : « Nous avons occupé ces terres pour convaincre le gouvernement de nous écouter », dit Elia, le président de l'organisation. Chaque famille obtint alors un lopin de deux hectares. On y construisit des routes, une école, une église, une petite clinique médicale et une modeste maison par famille. En 1996, une opportunité les poussa à se dédier à la banane – biologique et équitable de surcroît. En 1998, Finca 6 obtint sa certification et aujourd'hui, chaque semaine, six conteneurs de bananes biologiques et équitables quittent les installations de l'organisation vers les mers de l'Atlantique.

Décidément, la douce, nourrissante et joyeuse banane, photo parfaite sur la tête de Carmen Miranda depuis la scène des années 1940 et pour toujours, méritait d'être associée à une histoire heureuse dans la vie de celles et ceux qui la cultivent. Les consommateurs des pays importateurs auront, eux, le choix entre un fruit sain marqué par un souci de justice et un produit conventionnel porteur de résidus chimiques qui pourront se fixer pour de bon dans leurs tissus adipeux. Dans le marché mondialisé où nous vivons, tout bien porte en lui non seulement les résidus des intrants utilisés dans sa confection, mais aussi et surtout, les marques des relations de production qui sont à son origine.

Il est à souhaiter que les consommateurs puissent ressentir, avec la douceur des fruits qui les restaureront, le goût inégalable de la solidarité et de la justice.

1. Luis Gamboa dans sa plantation.
2. Régime de bananes cavendish.
3. Mesure de la taille des bananes.
4. Vérification du taux de maturation.
5. Brossage pour éviter les cochenilles.
6. Leon Segundo pèse de petites bananes.
7. Lavage des mains de bananes.
8. Embarquement des boîtes d'El Guabo.

▷ Laura Ines et Luis Coyago Sagbay, membres d'El Guabo.

le karité

Nommer pour aimer, les Africains l'ont bien compris. En mandingue, le mot «karité» signifie tout bellement « vie ». En wolof, il se traduit par « arbre à beurre ». Une logique empirique a présidé à l'appellation de cet arbre qui a nourri et embelli des générations d'humains à travers les siècles. Selon les Yorubas, le karité peut même aider les dieux à tromper la mort. Lorsque Shango, leur dieu de la foudre et du tonnerre, las de ses échecs et de l'incompréhension des siens, décida de quitter ce monde, c'est sous un karité qu'il s'est assis pour attendre que les éléments qui lui sont soumis viennent secouer la Terre au point de l'engloutir. Serait-ce grâce à cet arbre de jouvence que Shango a pu réapparaître, au-delà des mers et de ses dimensions cosmiques, dans d'autres cultures, pour consoler ses enfants réduits au malheur des champs du Brésil et de Cuba ?

Nom d'un arbre ! Faisant usage de notre liberté dénominative, nous pourrions désigner ce karité « arbre du temps et de la patience », car il lui faut au moins 15 à 25 ans pour produire ses premiers fruits et 50 ans pour commencer une fougueuse jeunesse qui s'étalera jusqu'à l'accomplissement de son premier siècle. Suivront encore deux autres siècles, durant lesquels nous pourrions l'appeler « arbre de la sagesse et de la connaissance », car ses 20 kilos de fruits produits annuellement réclameront la force du travail humain et le savoir traditionnel pour accomplir toute leur bienfaisance. On en tirera seulement six kilos d'amandes pour n'obtenir finalement que deux kilos et demi du précieux beurre de karité. Cette hypothétique nomination amoureuse pourrait se poursuivre et nous l'appellerions alors « arbre de l'omniprésence », car c'est dans le ventre de la mère que le petit d'homme a son premier contact avec le karité, dont le beurre est utilisé par les femmes enceintes pour enduire leur corps, assouplir leur peau et raffermir leurs muscles abdominaux, parois de la demeure de notre préexistence. Le karité, puissant désinfectant, servira ensuite à faire cicatriser le cordon ombilical. Il continuera à reconstituer les corps sous forme d'aliment, les caressera sous forme de pommade, les lavera sous forme de savon. On le retrouve aussi à l'intérieur des maisons sous forme d'objets lourds de leur signification, tel le bandiagra des Dogons, si long à sculpter au ciseau, pyrogravé par d'envoûtants forgerons, portant dans son corps végétal l'inscription de troublantes cosmogonies. Et si la grâce de la vieillesse nous est concédée, il sera encore là pour soulager l'inéluctable rappel de notre « éphémérité » venant de nos jointures et de nos muscles fatigués.

Nommer pour posséder ? Non. L'explorateur écossais Mungo Park n'a pas été le « découvreur » du karité lors de ses aventures à la fin du XVIIIe siècle. L'injuste hommage qu'on lui fit en nommant le karité *butyrospermum parkii* fut corrigé en *vitellaria paradoxa*. À l'instar des savants européens de la Renaissance, qui n'ont appris des Grecs que grâce à leurs prédécesseurs arabes, Park avait sans doute eu vent du karité par les écrits de géographes et voyageurs tels Al-Umari ou Ibn Battuta, quatre siècles avant ses explorations précoloniales, mais ces grands savants arabes n'ont pas non plus été les « découvreurs » du karité. Il se peut que sa « découverte » ait été un bel exploit d'Oya, l'épouse-sœur de Shango. Nul homme ne pourra l'interroger pour en avoir le cœur net, mais ce qui est sûr et certain, c'est que le karité a été découvert par une femme.

E lle était douce et belle comme Alice, souriante comme Zénabou, forte comme Sara et sage comme Kayon, ces autres femmes que je vois marcher d'un pas rapide dans cette campagne de la « Terre des hommes intègres ». La matinée du Burkina Faso est douce en ce mois d'août, période de l'hivernage et des travaux champêtres.

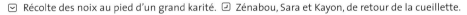
☑ Récolte des noix au pied d'un grand karité. ☑ Zénabou, Sara et Kayon, de retour de la cueillette.

⌂ Après la récolte, les noix de karité sont étendues pour sécher au soleil.

En bordure de la route de terre battue, nous croisons des champs de maïs, de mil et de coton. J'aperçois ici et là quelques baobabs, des nérés et surtout des karités, êtres fiers régnant au beau milieu des champs. « Depuis toujours, nous avons appris qu'il faut protéger le karité. Ce serait impensable d'en couper un pour cultiver la terre ou pour faire du bois pour la cuisson », m'instruit Jamal, l'un des animateurs de l'Union des Groupements de Productrices de Produits de Karité des provinces de la Sissili et du Ziro, ou plus prosaïquement l'Union de Léo, du nom de la ville du sud du Burkina où elle a ses bureaux. L'Union de Léo regroupe 3000 productrices organisées en 67 associations.

La saison des récoltes, commencée dès avril, tire à sa fin. « Pour le karité de l'Union, certifié biologique, nous devons nous rendre en brousse. Les arbres qui se trouvent près des champs sont en contact avec des produits chimiques », m'explique Jamal. Malgré la chaleur qui monte au fur et à mesure, les femmes ne ralentissent pas. Le boubou de Kayon arbore le slogan de la marche de l'Union en 2009 : « Protégeons l'arbre à karité, l'or des femmes ». De la Guinée-Bissau jusqu'en Éthiopie, où l'on retrouve le karité, la récolte et la

transformation locale de son fruit, également appelé karité, sont l'affaire des femmes. Traditions et besoins essentiels se confondent. Pour ces femmes, le karité est souvent leur seul revenu pour subvenir aux besoins de la famille.

Nous avons franchi les cinq premiers kilomètres de la journée. Alice et Sara nous invitent à pénétrer la forêt, où elles s'avancent avec la même célérité. Nous suivons, confiants, les maîtresses de ces lieux pour y trouver un grand arbre encore gorgé de petits fruits verts de la grosseur d'une pommette. « Seuls les fruits au sol seront récoltés. On ne monte jamais dans l'arbre pour ne pas l'endommager », explique Alice. Elle ramasse un fruit bien vert qu'elle me fait goûter. Sa pulpe sucrée est particulièrement délicieuse. Quelques initiatives ont été développées pour en faire de la confiture, mais l'intérêt du karité réside surtout dans ses amandes et le beurre qu'on en tire pour ses vertus cosmétiques, curatives et culinaires. Les fruits au sol sont ramassés et dépulpés grossièrement sur le champ. Après une heure de récolte, les cuves sont remplies et nous reprenons la route vers le village de Tabou avec notre quatuor, portant, cette fois-ci, quelques kilos de noix sur la tête.

Le jour même, Alice ébouillante ses noix pour en arrêter la germination. Elle les étend ensuite au soleil. Le soir, les noix seront ramassées et étendues de nouveau le matin suivant. Ce processus sera reproduit pendant 8 à 12 jours, jusqu'à ce que les noix soient convenablement sèches. Dans tout le village, ici et là, des femmes concassent des noix sèches au pilon. Sous un karité, Catherine et sa fille battent la mesure, intensifiant leur cadence pour fracasser les dernières noix. Le mortier est incliné pour dégager les amandes et les écailles. Elles s'agenouillent ensuite pour trier les amandes. Comme pour le riz et le mil, Catherine passera ensuite au vannage, laissant tomber les amandes de haut pour que le vent élimine poussières et autres résidus.

Le lendemain, je renoue avec Alice, qui, assise à l'ombre de sa demeure en pisé, broie des amandes de karité préalablement lavées. Bien que la récolte du karité soit saisonnière, sa transformation s'étale sur toute l'année, sans hâte, tel un petit sablier qui ne souhaite laisser tomber son dernier grain. Après une heure au pilon, Alice va chercher quelques braises à l'intérieur pour lancer la torréfaction de ses amandes. Remuant constamment, elle ne prend que quelques secondes pour essuyer son visage ruisselant. Après 45 minutes, les amandes sont bien brunes. Une fois refroidies, elles seront apportées au moulin du village pour être transformées en une pâte lisse ressemblant à s'y méprendre à du chocolat fondu.

Le lendemain, une douzaine de femmes du groupement de Tabou se retrouvent chez Kayon, où elles se sont donné rendez-vous pour le barattage. Alice arrive avec son grand bol de pâte, accompagnée de Zénabou, qui porte un large récipient de terre cuite. Elles s'installent à l'ombre d'un arbre. Zénabou enlève quelques bracelets et se met à mélanger doucement la pâte pour qu'elle soit bien homogène. Six femmes se relaient bientôt pour battre vigoureusement la matière visqueuse, pendant que les autres qui les encouragent, chantent et battent le rythme. Plus de 30 minutes se sont écoulées quand, en sueur, elles m'annoncent que la pâte est maintenant prête pour le premier lavage. Un simple bol d'eau et, comme par magie, la pâte brune perd toute sa couleur. À six reprises, l'émulsion blanche est transférée dans un nouveau récipient et l'eau brunie est rejetée. À la fin, une boule d'un blanc immaculé est déposée dans une marmite d'acier pour la cuisson.

Des braises et quelques bouts de bois sont placés sous la marmite et l'émulsion se dissout en une huile jaune cuivrée, comme celle de l'olive ou du coton. Les résidus noirs flottant à la surface sont enlevés, alors qu'au fond d'autres particules plus lourdes se déposent. Il faudra attendre une journée pour que l'huile soit enfin décantée, filtrée et conditionnée. Le lendemain, dans une cuve d'eau fraîche, Alice tourne délicatement un petit bout de bois pour que l'huile se cristallise. L'une des femmes en prend alors une cuillerée qu'elle dépose dans un bol d'eau, pour qu'elle fige. « C'est la mesure qu'on utilise pour les boules que l'on vend au marché », m'annonce-t-elle. C'est la dernière étape d'un marathon débuté il y a trois jours. Au total, il aura fallu passer à travers 20 étapes, à partir de la récolte, pour obtenir du beurre. En moyenne, et en additionnant chaque étape, un seul kilo de beurre demande plus de six heures de travail par productrice, ce à quoi il faut ajouter celui de la vente au marché.

⊡ Alice Nignan broie des amandes de karité.

Aux frontières du territoire subsaharien, une large bande du continent africain dépend des largesses d'un grand arbre robuste. À la fois rempart contre l'avancée du désert et nourrice des populations rurales, de la Guinée-Bissau jusqu'en Éthiopie, le karité tient du sacré. La légende veut que sa coupe malveillante vaille à son responsable des augures de malheur. Si le sage *vitellaria para-doxa* pouvait parler, il serait en mesure de raconter le passage des siècles, lui qui atteint sa maturité autour de 50 ans et qui a une lon-gévité de 300 ans ! Ce n'est qu'après 15 à 25 ans de lente croissance qu'il donne ses premiers fruits, dont la pulpe ressemble à celle de la figue ou de la datte, et dont la noix dissimule une matière grasse aux applications innombrables.

Utilisé soit pour la cuisson des aliments, en Afrique, soit pour les soins corporels, le beurre extrait de l'amande de karité est un baume aux mille vertus : hydratant épidermique, écran solaire, tonifiant capillaire, antibiotique externe, décongestionnant, anti-inflammatoire musculaire, etc. Les neuf dixièmes de la produc-tion mondiale sont consommés localement. Le Nigeria, avec plus de la moitié de cette production, ne figure même pas parmi la liste des principaux pays exportateurs, dont le Burkina Faso occupe le premier rang, avec 26 % des exportations mondiales. L'industrie chocolatière a trouvé une autre qualité fort estimable, en termes commerciaux, au beurre de karité ; à un prix assurément avantageux, il est un parfait succédané au beurre de cacao – un marché qui représente 95 % des exportations. Le karité résiduel est utilisé en pharmacologie et en cosmétologie.

La croissance commerciale du karité, mais aussi la protection de la ressource sont affectées par quel-ques difficultés : malgré des essais persistants, l'arbre ne semble pas se plier de bonne grâce à la culture encadrée, en plus d'être convoité sur le terrain pour son bois par les populations démunies et d'être victime des feux de brousse, surtout d'origine humaine.

À un stade encore marginal, la filière équitable offre probablement la solution la plus sensée à cette problématique. D'une part, en rémunérant sur place les Africaines, responsables traditionnelles de l'ex-ploitation et de la transformation, on s'assure une meilleure qualité du produit (la transformation en sol étranger fait appel à des solvants chimiques qui détériorent les qualités médicinales du beurre) ; et d'autre part, en contribuant au mieux-être économique des communautés, celles-ci sont plus enclines à protéger la ressource à long terme.

le karité en chiffres

COMMERCE CONVENTIONNEL

Commerce mondial (noix) : 784 676 tonnes

PRINCIPAUX PAYS PRODUCTEURS

Nigeria	53 %
Mali	23 %
Burkina Faso	9 %
Ghana	8 %
Côte-d'Ivoire	4 %

COMMERCE ÉQUITABLE

Année de certification : 2006
Importations mondiales (beurre) : 18 tonnes

ORGANISATION CERTIFIÉE

Une organisation de petits producteurs.

ORIGINE DE L'ORGANISATION CERTIFIÉE

Burkina Faso

PRINCIPAUX PAYS IMPORTATEURS

	Importations(t)
Canada	9
France	9

PRIX ET PRIMES

Prix équitable : 3929 $/t
Prime équitable : 275 $/t

Récolte des fruits dans un parc à karité de la commune de Siby, au Mali, où la coopérative Cooprokasi est en voie d'obtenir sa certification de la FLO.

⌃ Au marché de Lon, Adjara Diasso frit des beignets de mil dans l'huile de karité.

||||||||||||||||||||||||||||||||||||||||||||||||||||||||||||||||||||||

L e vendredi après-midi, au village de Lon, à dix kilomètres de Tabou, tous se donnent rendez-vous au marché. Les femmes ont de toutes petites échoppes où elles proposent, dans de grands plats bien remplis, des tubercules de manioc, du gombo ou des soumbalas, fèves de néré noircies par la fermentation. Ces derniers ingrédients sont incontournables dans la préparation des sauces qui accompagnent le tô, pâte de farine de mil qui est la base alimentaire des familles de la région. Les Peuls, qui vivent autour du village avec leurs troupeaux, négocient leur lait frais ou caillé. Des petits commerçants vendent des peignes, des piles, des lampes de poche, des mi-roirs et autres peccadilles apportées de la ville, tandis que d'autres font le négoce d'une multi-tude de cachets de contrebande provenant du Ghana, censés soigner tous les maux.

Des femmes du village vendent également des beignets de mil frits dans l'huile de karité, d'autres offrent leurs boules de beurre de karité à 25 francs. Il leur faut vendre 20 boules au mar-ché, l'équivalent d'un kilo de beurre, pour gagner 500 francs (1 $). « Les bonnes journées, certaines arrivent à vendre pour 500 francs, mais souvent elles atteignent à peine 100 francs (0,20 $), sans jamais faire de réels profits », me raconte Safoura, la trésorière du groupement des productrices de karité du village de Lon. « Souvent, au mois d'avril ou de mai, les réserves de grains sont bien réduites, continue-t-elle. Le karité et les fèves de néré

◔ Les marchés africains sont des carrefours de commerce et de culture où la vie s'exprime en couleurs et en arômes.

deviennent alors leur seule monnaie d'échange pour nourrir leur famille. Lorsqu'elles doivent acheter du mil, elles viennent au marché pour vendre les amandes de karité aux petits marchands, qui eux les revendront aux marchands se dirigeant vers Ouagadougou. »

Elles se font payer 200 francs le bol de plus de 2,5 kilos d'amandes, une mesure qui, transformée, permet d'obtenir environ un kilo de beurre. À l'Union, la même assiette est payée 500 francs, plus du double. Pour le beurre, le prix atteint 1200 francs, encore plus du double du prix obtenu au marché.

« Les femmes qui font partie de l'Union ont un bien meilleur prix et elles peuvent vendre leur karité d'un seul coup, ce qui leur permet de voir les bénéfices », m'explique Safoura. Bien entendu, des revenus modestes, même doublés ou triplés demeurent modestes. La vente de leur karité à l'Union apporte à ces femmes un revenu annuel d'environ 100 $. « Il y a quelques années, nous pouvions espérer atteindre une moyenne annuelle de 150 $, mais nous avons intégré plus de membres et les commandes ne sont pas encore au rendez-vous », explique Abou, l'affable directeur de l'Union.

||||||||||||||||||||||||||||||||||||||||||||||||||||||||||||||||||||||||||||||||||||

Aux bureaux de l'Union, dans la petite usine de transformation de Léo, au sud du pays, pas un jour ne passe sans que Nana, la présidente et Abibata, la responsable de la qualité, viennent saluer les employés et productrices au travail. « L'Union est issue de groupements de productrices agricoles qui s'organisèrent au début des années 1990 », m'explique Abibata, souriante et vêtue d'un magnifique boubou. « En 1997, les gens du CECI (Centre d'étude et de coopération internationale, une organisation canadienne de développement international) ont entrepris de soutenir les femmes productrices de karité de la région. Ils ont d'abord priorisé l'amélioration de la qualité du beurre en travaillant sur des techniques de transformation. Ensuite, ils ont soutenu notre développement organisationnel. Notre Union fut officiellement reconnue en 2001 », précise-t-elle.

« Avant l'Union, on ne pouvait faire de grandes quantités de beurre. C'était trop de travail », explique Abibata. Aujourd'hui, à Léo, la transformation de l'amande en beurre se fait de manière collective. Ici, un moulin pour broyer les amandes, là, des fours pour la torréfaction et surtout des cuves pour le barattage, où des dizaines de femmes besognent. Durant la visite, j'aperçois, dans l'un des bâtiments, ce qui me semble être une véritable incongruité dans cette région du Sahel. « Oui, oui, c'est bien une presse à sirop d'érable ! », me confirme Abou. Praxède Lévesque, propriétaire de la compagnie Delapointe, qui importe et distribue le karité de l'Union au Canada, et qui est également acéricultrice, a fait traverser cette presse outre-atlantique. « Le système de filtration de cette machine nous a permis d'améliorer la qualité de notre beurre », précise Abou. « En travaillant de manière collective et avec quelques infrastructures, nous avons non seulement amélioré sa qualité, mais nous avons réduit à 1 h 30 le temps de transformation moyen par kilo », ajoute-t-il. À la fin de 2009, 18 centres de transformation locaux seront pleinement fonctionnels dans l'ensemble de l'Union.

« Grâce au travail collectif, je peux produire 400 voire 500 kilos de beurre annuellement », déclare fièrement Abibata. « Avant, je ne pouvais pas acheter les fournitures scolaires des enfants ou même les vêtir. Aujourd'hui, cela n'est plus un problème, et je peux même m'acheter de beaux vêtements. Le karité, c'est vraiment le mari des veuves et le père des orphelins », me lance cette mère de cinq enfants dont le mari est décédé en 2003. Encore et toujours, le karité est, à point nommé, « l'or des femmes ».

⊡ Les petites infrastructures de l'Union de Léo, dont les fours de torréfaction, permettent de réduire le temps de transformation du beurre de karité.
⊡ Abibata Ido, productrice de karité et responsable de la qualité au sein du conseil d'administration de l'Union de Léo.

« LA FORCE DE NOTRE UNION RÉSIDE DANS LA SIMILITUDE DE NOS MEMBRES, qui sont tous des femmes paysannes. Notre présidente ne se promène pas dans un quatre-quatre climatisé ; elle roule en vélo et baratte son beurre comme les autres », explique Abou, le directeur de l'Union de Léo. « Nous avons 3000 productrices et plus de 1000 femmes attendent d'intégrer l'Union. »

⌃ Geke Konata et Adama Kamara, membres de Cooprokasi, conditionnent le beurre de karité pour son exportation outre-mer.

« La solidarité envers les femmes africaines a un impact direct sur le niveau de vie de toute la famille », explique Roch Harvey du CECI, qui, depuis 1997, s'investit dans la filière karité au Burkina Faso. « Nous avons élargi notre programme au Mali (en 2001), au Niger (en 2004), en Guinée (en 2005) et bientôt nous serons au Ghana. » Les programmes du CECI touchent au renforcement organisationnel, à la production et à l'amélioration de la qualité du beurre, à la commercialisation et à la gestion de la ressource.

À Siby, au Mali, le CECI soutient la coopérative Cooprokasi, qui regroupe 800 productrices provenant de 21 villages, entre autres, pour la protection des parcs à karité, une initiative considérée par le Fonds pour l'Environnement mondial (FEM) comme un « modèle de réussite ». De plus, 14 productrices de Siby se sont porté candidates aux élections des conseils communaux d'avril 2009. L'augmentation des revenus des femmes a permis de rehausser leur image, leur statut et leur position au sein de la famille et de la communauté tout entière.

« C'est pour les femmes productrices que j'ai choisi de continuer cette aventure », raconte Praxède Lévesque, propriétaire de Karité Delapointe, qui distribue le beurre de l'Union de Léo au Canada. En 2000 et 2001, Daniel La Pointe, son mari, coopérant pour le CECI, eut comme mandat de développer les ventes du karité d'organisations burkinabés auprès de clients internationaux. Il démarcha de nombreux acheteurs, mais l'offre importante de karité et les besoins des productrices les motivèrent, lui et sa femme, à développer eux-mêmes la distribution au Canada. « Nous en avons importé une demi-tonne en 2002, continue Praxède. En 2007, lors du décès de Daniel (dans un accident de voiture), nous en importions une tonne. J'ai décidé de poursuivre malgré la tragédie, car nous avions créé trop d'espoir, je ne pouvais abandonner ces femmes. » En 2008, les importations atteignirent 9 tonnes, puis 18 tonnes en 2009. Karité Delapointe offre des pommades, des laits corporels, des exfoliants, des baumes pour les lèvres et autres savons, en plus d'offrir le beurre brut pour d'autres marques de cosmétiques.

Dans des milliers de points de vente, les produits de Karité Delapointe ou ceux de l'entreprise française l'Occitane, principal client de l'Union, rejoignent les consommatrices du Nord, complétant une chaîne de solidarité toute féminine qui débute dans les campagnes burkinabé, malienne et nigérienne. « Bon pour vous, bon pour elles » est le slogan du CECI pour sa campagne sur le karité. Si les productrices y gagnent en dignité, les consommatrices, elles, découvrent un produit unique aux multiples vertus.

« Bon pour vous, bon pour elles » est le slogan du CECI
pour sa campagne sur le karité.

⌃ Siton Koné, vice-présidente de Cooprokasi, en compagnie de deux autres productrices.

Les 20 étapes de la production du beurre de karité :

1. Récolte des fruits.
2. Dépulpage des fruits.
3. Ébouillantage des noix.
4. Séchage des noix.
5. Concassage des noix.
6. Premier tri des amandes.
7. Lavage des amandes.
8. Séchage des amandes.
9. Deuxième tri des amandes.
10. Broyage manuel des amandes.
11. Torréfaction des amandes.
12. Broyage mécanique des amandes.
13. Barattage de la pâte.
14. Lavage de la pâte.
15. Récupération de l'émulsion.
16. Cuisson de l'émulsion.
17. Décantation de l'huile.
18. Filtration de l'huile.
19. Cristallisation de l'huile.
20. Conditionnement du beurre.

▷ Dans la commune de Siby, Nantene Konaté ramasse ses noix de karité avant que ne tombe l'humidité. Bien sèches, elles se conserveront plusieurs mois.

Miguel-Angel Mayorga regroupe des gerbes de quinoa fraîchement coupé dans la vallée d'Ancoyo, sur l'Altiplano bolivien.

le quinoa

L'Inca suprême de Tawantinsuyo commen-
çait lui-même les semailles du quinoa à
l'aide d'une houe en or. C'était le début
d'une fête célébrée plusieurs jours durant dans
tout l'Empire inca. Régnant sur plus de 100 millions de sujets à leur apogée, les Incas s'étaient im-
posés moins par la force des armes que par la sécurité alimentaire et la splendeur qu'ils offraient à
ceux qui acceptaient de rendre culte au dieu Inti, le
soleil, celui-là même qui avait envoyé le premier
empereur, Manco Capac, sorti tout droit du lac
Titicaca, pour enseigner l'agriculture aux survi-
vants du Grand Déluge. Et c'était à ce même dieu
Inti qu'ils offraient, à la fin des récoltes, dans une
fontaine en or massif, des graines de quinoa.

Du haut des airs, l'Altiplano bolivien, qui fit
jadis partie du territoire des Incas, ressemble à un
désert entouré des blancs sommets de la cordil-
lère des Andes. Dans la partie méridionale de ce

181

vaste plateau, les plaines jaunes se transforment en de grands lacs d'un blanc immaculé : ce sont les salars de Coipasa et de Uyuni. À 3550 mètres au-dessus du niveau de la mer, ces étendues de sel sont de magnifiques rappels des forces de Mère Nature, qui a repoussé vers le ciel ces lits océaniques d'un autre temps. Les terres qui bordent ces lacs salins sont le grenier du quinoa real, la variété de quinoa la plus prisée.

La « mère de tous les grains » des Incas, pilier de leur civilisation, était vénérée et intégrée à nombre de rituels. Cette force culturelle explique en partie son bannissement par les colonisateurs espagnols, qui iront jusqu'à en interdire les plantations. Le quinoa fut ainsi circonscrit aux grandes hauteurs, ce qui a sans doute contribué à une perte de sa diversité génétique. Dénommé « bouffe d'Indien » par les maîtres chrétiens du Nouveau Monde, le quinoa sera supplanté par d'autres aliments, jusqu'à n'être plus qu'un vestige culturel.

Du sommet des collines qui bordent Salinas, on peut distinguer à l'horizon le salar de Uyuni et le majestueux sommet du volcan Thunupa, qui culmine à 5000 mètres. Cette petite ville de l'Altiplano bolivien est connue comme la capitale mondiale du quinoa. Tout autour, sur les flancs des collines volcaniques, les champs de quinoa sont divisés par de petits murs de pierres formant une mosaïque disparate. Selon Max Uhle, le doyen des américanistes, ces terres sont cultivées par les peuples andins depuis plus de 5000 ans. À l'époque, les familles autochtones avaient pérennisé un système de production agricole traditionnel, pratiquant une gestion rationnelle des sols, avec de longues jachères de quatre à huit ans et un contrôle naturel des nuisibles. Le quinoa n'était pas une monoculture. Les paysans préparaient à la sueur de leur front un hectare de terre, voire moins, pour sa culture. Sur les terrasses cultivées des montagnes poussaient aussi des variétés locales de pommes de terre et d'autres cultures d'altitude. Les troupeaux de lamas, quant à eux, apportaient, outre la viande, le fumier nécessaire à la fertilisation des sols.

☑ Célébration de la Fête de la mer à Salinas, la capitale mondiale du quinoa. ☑ La mécanisation de l'agriculture au village d'Ancoyo.

Du quinoa à perte de vue, dans la vallée d'Ancoyo.

Tout près de Salinas, la vallée d'Ancoyo est peinte de rouge, de jaune orangé et d'ocre. Du haut de la vallée, Fisher García Mollo, futur agronome, m'explique l'évolution récente de la culture du quinoa : « Ces terres ont commencé à être cultivées avec l'arrivée des tracteurs. Avant, c'était principalement des pâturages pour les lamas, les alpagas et les vigognes. À présent, le quinoa prend tant de place que nous avons dû délimiter les cultures pour qu'il reste quand même aux animaux de quoi paître. »

En Bolivie, l'actuelle revalorisation du quinoa a commencé avec la « révolution verte ». Il y eut d'abord le constat que l'alimentation des Boliviens s'était dangereusement appauvrie. Des instituts de recherche se sont alors lancés dans l'étude du quinoa, son patrimoine génétique fut répertorié et sa production, stimulée. D'autres marchés ont découvert le quinoa et ses frontières agricoles ont été repoussées pour répondre à une croissante demande des États-Unis et de l'Europe. À la bonne intention d'améliorer la diète quotidienne des Boliviens, ladite révolution verte a ajouté son lot de « solutions », faites de fertilisants, d'engrais chimiques et de mécanisation. L'intensification des cultures des plaines, labourées par des tracteurs, contribua à l'érosion des sols déjà peu fertiles. L'un des buts affichés de la modernisation agricole des années 1960 était l'augmentation de la productivité. Or, dans les années 1940, une famille pouvait espérer récolter entre 1500 et 2000 kilos de quinoa à l'hectare, alors que quelques décennies après la révolution verte, la production à l'hectare atteint à peine 650 kilos en moyenne.

le quinoa

Le quinoa (*CHENOPODIUM QUINOA*), n'est pas une vraie céréale, puisqu'il n'appartient pas à la famille des graminées, étant plutôt un proche parent de la betterave ou des épinards. D'une rare adaptabilité, il s'est répandu dans différents climats, supportant gelées et sécheresses et poussant abondamment sur des sols salins. Au XIXᵉ siècle, Alexander von Humboldt, un naturaliste allemand, constata son omniprésence depuis les savanes de Bogotá jusqu'au sud du Chili.

Le quinoa est riche en protéines et en sels minéraux et ne contient pas de gluten. Sa caractéristique la plus singulière est qu'il possède tous les acides aminés essentiels à l'alimentation humaine. C'est l'aliment le plus proche du lait maternel. Pour le docteur Duane Johnson, de l'université du Colorado, si l'humain se voyait obligé de ne consommer qu'un seul aliment, le quinoa serait le plus indiqué.

Le docteur Johnson et sa collègue Sarah Ward ont breveté les plants masculins stériles de la variété traditionnelle du quinoa bolivien, l'apelawa, ce qui a provoqué une véritable commotion chez les producteurs boliviens, dont les protestations ont été entendues jusqu'à l'ONU. Quatre ans plus tard, le controversé brevet a dû être abandonné.

La production mondiale de quinoa, qui avoisine les 60 000 tonnes, est l'affaire de deux pays, la Bolivie et le Pérou, qui en récoltent plus de 95 %. De 2003 à 2006, les exportations boliviennes ont plus que triplé. Les propriétés nutritives du quinoa ont contribué à sa récente popularité en Occident, et l'augmentation de sa production, y compris pour le marché équitable, a créé des bouleversements importants dans les zones productrices – un défi pour les acteurs d'un mouvement social qui se veut soucieux de la justice, de l'autosuffisance alimentaire et du respect de l'environnement.

le quinoa en chiffres

COMMERCE CONVENTIONNEL

Production mondiale : 59 115 tonnes
Commerce mondial : 9 296 000 $

PRINCIPAUX PAYS PRODUCTEURS

Pérou	53 %
Bolivie	44 %
Équateur	1 %

COMMERCE ÉQUITABLE

Année de certification : 2004
Importations mondiales : 552 tonnes
Ventes au détail : 4 320 000 $

ORGANISATIONS CERTIFIÉES

Quatre organisations de petits producteurs, dans deux pays.

ORIGINE DES ORGANISATIONS CERTIFIÉES

Bolivie	75 %
Équateur	25 %

PRINCIPAUX PAYS IMPORTATEURS

	Importations (t)
France	370
Grande-Bretagne	135
Australie/Nouvelle-Zélande	7
Suisse	7
Canada	6

PRIX ET PRIMES

Prix équitable : 711 $/t
Prime équitable : 85 $/t
Prime biologique : 150 $/t
Proportion de quinoa biologique : 82 %

⌃ Contrairement à la croyance populaire, le quinoa n'est pas une vraie céréale...

⌃ Ciprian Beliz Mayorga, président de l'Acroproquirc. ⌃ Une vigogne dans un champ de quinoa, près du village d'Irpani. ⌃ Un jeune lama et sa mère.
⌃ Valério Silvestre et ses lamas, au pied du volcan Thunupa.

|||||||||||||||||||||||||||||||||||||||||||||||||||||||||||||

Au village d'Irpani, situé au pied du volcan Thunupa, le changement de culture est visible. Ici et là, on aperçoit quelques parcelles sur les flancs du volcan, mais ce sont les basses terres de la vallée qui, elles, regorgent de champs aux couleurs de l'arc-en-ciel. « Cette année nous avons cultivé le côté sud de la vallée et labouré les terres du côté nord pour les prochaines semences », m'explique Valério Silvestre en tentant d'attraper une de ses brebis. Dans la région, les jachères ne durent souvent pas plus d'un an. Les labours, entre janvier et mars, permettent à la terre d'absorber un peu d'humidité jusqu'aux semences de septembre, mais ils la rendent également très vulnérable à l'érosion hydrique et éolienne.

Valério se dirige tranquillement vers un enclos de pierre, où il garde 60 lamas. Il ajoute : « J'en avais davantage, mais à cause du manque de pâturages, j'ai dû réduire mon troupeau. Il y a bien moins de pluie en hiver et les lamas n'ont que des branches à manger. » Les 60 lamas et 120 moutons de Valério semblent composer la totalité de la population d'Irpani. « Les gens vont arriver sous peu. La récolte va bientôt commencer ! », me dit-il. Les sécheresses et les inondations, le sous-emploi de la main-d'œuvre, les revenus agricoles anémiques, l'accès difficile à l'éducation, la parcellisation des terres, l'érosion des sols, l'attrait de la vie urbaine, les facteurs qui expliquent l'exode des populations locales sont multiples. Le phénomène est endémique.

|||||||||||||||||||||||||||||||||||||||||||||||||||||||||||||

Pour Ciprian Beliz Mayorga, président de l'Acroproquirc, c'est le niveau de vie précaire qui a poussé les gens à quitter la région. Dans son village d'Ancoyo, des 36 familles résidentes, seulement huit y vivent à temps plein. À Sebingal, à seulement quelques kilomètres de Salinas, le constat est encore plus désolant : seulement deux familles résident au village. Même l'électricité ne s'y est pas arrêtée. L'église, les maisons traditionnelles et le petit champ de quinoa offrent une image bucolique, mais en y regardant de plus près, on voit que plusieurs toits de chaume s'écroulent et que même les murs en pisé ont commencé à s'affaisser ici et là. De toute évidence, il y a bien longtemps que le terrain de basket-ball de l'école du village n'a pas vu de ballon ou d'enfant !

« Je suis resté 20 ans à La Paz, où j'étais chauffeur de taxi, mais aujourd'hui, mon quinoa est bien plus rentable », me raconte Ciprian. D'abord secrétaire, puis vice-président et aujourd'hui président de l'Acroproquirc, il croit que le quinoa a beaucoup d'avenir et qu'il peut revitaliser la région : « Présentement, notre principal projet social est d'améliorer la fertilité des terres avec du fumier de lama et de mouton. Après un épandage, nous pouvons voir les résultats sur trois récoltes. Nous devons poursuivre le travail de développement et trouver des alliés pour lancer d'autres projets porteurs. »

Le village de Sebingal, avec sa petite église d'inspiration coloniale.

Empaquetage du quinoa pour la marque canadienne GoGo Quinoa. ⊡ L'usine de l'ANAPQUI à Challapata.

L'Acroproquirc est l'une des huit organisations membres de l'Association nationale des producteurs de quinoa (ANAPQUI). « Avant l'existence de l'ANAPQUI, les producteurs échangeaient leur quinoa pour des produits de base. Ils étaient totalement dépendants des commerçants », me raconte Miguel Choque dans les bureaux de l'ANAPQUI à La Paz. « À nos débuts, tous les producteurs de quinoa du pays étaient considérés membres de l'ANAPQUI, mais au milieu des années 1990, nous avons commencé à fidéliser nos membres et leur nombre a radicalement baissé. Nous représentons aujourd'hui 1500 producteurs, tous du sud de l'Altiplano. » La grande majorité des exportations de l'ANAPQUI est destinée aux marchés solidaires. L'organisation a obtenu sa certification biologique en 1992, et équitable en 2005. Il continue : « Nous avons plus d'une douzaine de clients en Europe et en Amérique du Nord. En 2008, nous avons exporté 1800 tonnes de quinoa, soit environ 25 % des exportations du pays. »

Une faible proportion du quinoa commercialisé par l'ANAPQUI est transformée en farine, en flocons ou même en quinoa soufflé, mais la grande majorité (70 %) est exportée sous forme de grains. « En 1997, nous avons construit notre propre usine pour le conditionnement du quinoa », rappelle Miguel. Située à Challapata, l'usine de l'ANAPQUI réalise une étape importante de la commercialisation, soit la « désaponisation ». Le grain de quinoa comporte de la saponine, un glycoside légèrement toxique et amer. Dans l'usine, on enlève d'abord mécaniquement l'enveloppe des grains, pour ensuite les faire tremper et ainsi éliminer la saponine. Puis, les grains sont de nouveau séchés et triés avant l'emballage.

Les fins de semaine, Challapata se transforme en grand marché à ciel ouvert. À la foire, on retrouve des fruits, des grains, des animaux, des feuilles de coca, des instruments agraires et même des tracteurs. Ceux-ci sont de seconde main pour la plupart et arrivent par bateaux de fermes européennes ou états-uniennes. La foire de Challapata tient également lieu de Bourse du quinoa. On y fixe les prix pour le quinoa non conditionné vendu directement par les producteurs. En 2008, dès avril, au début de la récolte, les prix avaient déjà augmenté de 50 %, mais à la fin de la récolte, ils étaient de 190 % supérieurs à ceux de 2007. Avec des prix trois fois plus élevés, bien que la récolte de 2008 fût de 40 % inférieure à celles des années précédentes, les producteurs ont obtenu de meilleurs revenus. « En 2007, le prix d'exportation était de 1200 $ la tonne ; il est maintenant de 3200 $, précise Miguel. Pour nos membres, le prix est de 110 $ le quintal (46 kilos), alors que le prix minimum garanti du commerce équitable est de 40 $. »

En 2003, c'était au tour de l'Acroproquirc de faire construire sa propre usine de conditionnement, dans le village d'Irpani. Ciprian Beliz Mayorga, son président, a été l'un des grands promoteurs de la mise en place de cette usine. « Vendre du quinoa lavé (prêt à la consommation) rapporte davantage et on crée des emplois locaux pour conserver nos gens dans la région, dit-il. Cette année, nous avons terminé la période de probation pour la certification biologique et nous avons 15 nouveaux membres. Nous sommes prêts pour une bonne saison. Maintenant que le quinoa obtient de bons prix, les gens reviennent pour réclamer leurs terres ! Cinq familles sont de retour cette année. Elles ont semé en septembre et devraient revenir sous peu pour récolter. »

De retour dans la vallée d'Ancoyo, Fisher me fait visiter ses champs de quinoa real en compagnie de deux autres étudiants en agronomie de l'université d'Oruro. De très grandes pousses d'un rouge écarlate le dépassent d'une tête. « Ces terres sont jeunes et la production y est très, très bonne », lance-t-il avec fierté. De plant en plant, il regarde attentivement les grains pour s'assurer de leur bonne maturation, et surtout qu'il n'y a pas de champignons ou de larves nuisibles. « Tous mes champs sont cultivés de manière biologique, dit-il. Ça exige plus de travail, mais les résultats en valent la peine. Il faut nous voir durant le mois de novembre, la nuit, avec nos lanternes, recueillir les papillons avant qu'ils pondent leurs œufs. » Plus loin, ses

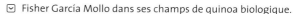
Fisher García Mollo dans ses champs de quinoa biologique.

LE QUINOA RESTE UN PRODUIT PEU CONNU EN DEHORS DES PAYS ANDINS, qui le cultivent depuis des millénaires. C'est grâce au marché biologique et équitable (82 % du quinoa équitable est également biologique) qu'il jouit présentement d'une certaine célébrité. En 1997, lors de mes premières conférences pour faire connaître la situation des caféiculteurs de l'UCIRI et l'alternative équitable, il n'y avait, au Québec, ni quinoa, ni épices, ni vin équitable. En fait, un seul produit, le café, était disponible dans quelques points de vente seulement. Aujourd'hui, les points de vente et les produits se comptent par milliers et le commerce équitable devient même la norme dans certains pays (en Suisse, 50 % des fleurs et des bananes vendues sont équitables).

Il y avait aussi, en 1997, quelques initiatives d'artisanat équitable avec, bien entendu, une extraordinaire variété de paniers tressés, de poteries, de broderies et autres textiles, de sculptures, de bijoux et de produits en cuir. Aujourd'hui, les 50 boutiques Dix Mille Villages au Canada offrent à elles seules 2000 produits différents.

En 2008, la FLO a certifié plus de 6000 produits distribués par 2700 compagnies licenciées pour l'utilisation de son *label*. Le millet et le quinoa sont des produits singuliers, en comparaison avec les têtes d'affiche que sont le café, le thé, le cacao ou encore la banane. Au total, la FLO a déterminé des prix et primes équitables pour près de 100 produits, qui se regroupent en 18 filières, principalement alimentaires, sauf pour les ballons de sport, le coton et les fleurs.

La commercialisation de certains de ces produits se fait indéniablement pour des motifs économiques, mais d'autres sont d'abord lancés pour des raisons politiques ou de solidarité envers des États fragiles, tel Haïti, ou non reconnus, comme la Palestine, d'où proviennent plusieurs marques d'huile d'olive équitable, comme Zeitouna, promue au Canada par l'Aide médicale pour la Palestine. La culture de l'olivier date de 3000 ans dans cette région et représente la principale source de revenus pour 25 % de la population cisjordanienne.

Dans les années à venir, la FLO souhaite poursuivre sa diversification et sa croissance pour que les organisations certifiées puissent augmenter leurs exportations et que le commerce équitable rejoigne plus de groupes de producteurs, plus de catégories de produits et plus de pays. La WFTO, quant à elle, prévoit la création d'un *label* pour les produits artisanaux qui pourra augmenter substantiellement leur disponibilité auprès des consommateurs solidaires.

FILIÈRES DE LA FLO, EN 2008

Produit	Associations de petits producteurs	Organisations de travailleurs salariés	Total	Importations (t/* 1000 Items)	Croissance (2007 à 2008)	Ventes totales
Café	291	0	291	65 808	14 %	1 784 230 000 $
Banane	28	35	63	299 205	28 %	660 720 000 $
Thé	31	43	74	11 467	112 %	294 640 000 $
Cacao	30	0	30	10 299	n.d.	275 300 000 $
Coton	28	0	28	*27 573	94 %	261 910 000 $
Sucre de canne	15	0	15	56 990	n.d.	257 440 000 $
Fleurs	0	46	46	*311 000	31 %	255 950 000 $
Jus de fruits	14	1	15	28 219	11 %	101 190 000 $
Fruit frais/légumes	25	53	78	26 424	1 %	98 210 000 $
Vin	4	23	27	*8980	57 %	71 430 000 $
Miel	19	0	19	2055	22 %	29 760 000 $
Riz	15	0	15	4685	11 %	28 270 000 $
Karité (noix et huile)	16	0	16	775	n.d.	20 830 000 $
Fruits séchés	6	0	6	712	n.d.	17 860 000 $
Épices	14	0	14	197	n.d.	6 100 000 $
Ballons de sport	0	4	4	*141	2 %	4 320 000 $
Quinoa	4	0	4	552	n.d.	4 320 000 $
Autres	1	0	1	n.d.	n.d.	135 420 000 $
Total	**541**	**205**	**746**			**4 308 050 000 $**

collègues ont une parcelle expérimentale avec diverses variétés, dont la pisankalla, l'une des plus recherchées.

De retour à la maison, nous retrouvons Carmen, la mère de Fisher, debout avec ses bottes dans un grand mortier, qui écrase les grains de quinoa pour éliminer l'écosse riche en saponine. Elle recueille ensuite ces grains et les laisse tomber délicatement pour que les poussières d'écorces volent au vent. Ce soir, on servira une soupe de quinoa au repas.

Les grandes qualités nutritives du quinoa expliquent largement l'intérêt grandissant qu'il suscite dans l'hémisphère Nord. Selon l'Académie des sciences des États-Unis, le quinoa est l'un des meilleurs aliments d'origine végétale pour l'espèce humaine. En effet, la recherche scientifique contemporaine prouve que le quinoa possède tous les acides aminés, et ce, dans les proportions adéquates pour être assimilés par l'organisme humain ; un phénomène unique parmi les aliments d'origine végétale. En outre, le quinoa est riche en minéraux, dont le phosphore, le magnésium, le potassium et le calcium. La NASA l'a même inclus parmi les aliments à emporter lors des voyages spatiaux de longue durée.

Les Incas, adorateurs du Soleil, organisaient leurs calendriers agricoles les yeux tournés vers les astres. Leur science astronomique leur a permis de prévoir les éclipses et le passage des comètes. L'un des 13 Incas, dans un moment d'extrême clairvoyance, a sans doute deviné qu'un jour le grain sacré de quinoa emprunterait des voies spatiales dans les bagages des astronautes de notre temps afin de mieux contempler, de là-haut, Inti dans toute sa plénitude.

1. Grains de quinoa.
2. Plants de quinoa.
3. Brigida Silvestre, cultivatrice, en pleine récolte.
4. Miguel-Angel Mayorga récolte son quinoa.
5. Séchage des grains à l'usine de l'ANAPQUI.
6. Sacs de pâtes de quinoa de Coronilla.
7. Quinoa soufflé au chocolat, à l'usine de Coronilla.
8. Pâtes et grains de quinoa transformés de Coronilla.

▷ En haut : Eugenia Apaza emmène paître les moutons de sa famille sur l'Altiplano bolivien.
▷ En bas : Benita Calane Ayabide à Salinas, lors de la Fête de la mer qui commémore la perte de la province d'Atacama au profit du Chili, en 1879, qui a privé les Boliviens de leur unique accès à la mer.

le Vin

Comme en témoignent les feuilles de vigne fossilisées de près de 60 millions d'années retrouvées en Champagne, en France, l'esprit du vin a très longtemps attendu les hommes. La vocation de ces terres à la sublime ivresse viendrait donc du paléocène ! Des grains de raisins ont bien été recueillis dans des cavernes préhistoriques, mais la fermentation du fruit pour la production du vin a vraisemblablement commencé il y a 7000 ans, peu après la découverte de l'agriculture. Tout naturellement, le vin devint divin. En Mésopotamie, il était réservé aux prêtres et aux rois. Les Égyptiens l'attribuèrent à Osiris, les Grecs à Dionysos, et les Romains à Bacchus. Les Perses, eux, selon une de leurs légendes, l'attribuèrent à une princesse abandonnée par un roi qui voulut s'empoisonner avec les résidus d'un pot de raisins fermentés. Au lieu de trouver la mort, la belle retrouva le plaisir dans les bras de son souverain, qui la récompensa en volupté pour avoir découvert une telle merveille.

Toujours lié à la Foi et aux Passions, le vin n'aura cure de la Justice, mais il est néanmoins aisé de le reconnaître dans la quête de l'Équilibre. Selon Hérodote, les Perses s'enivraient au vin pour faire des choix capitaux, mais c'est au lendemain de la cuite que ces hommes responsables vérifiaient si leurs décisions avaient été justes.

Le vin égaye, mais peut aussi égarer l'homme et le mener à la colère. L'Empire romain allait tomber sous le poids de ses excès, mais pas la viticulture, aidée qu'elle fut par les monastères. Le christianisme, plus que toute autre religion, sacralisa le vin. Les vignobles furent mis sous la protection de saint Vincent, dont la vénération traversa nécessairement les océans, car les *conquistadors* espagnols empoignèrent la lance au nom de Dieu et les nouveaux sujets durent dorénavant manger le corps du Christ et boire son sang sous les espèces du pain et du vin. Pour la pérennisation de la foi chrétienne, les vignes poursuivirent la progression de la colonisation espagnole. En 1543, Salta accueillit les premières vignes argentines, mais c'est à Santiago del Estero que les jésuites, dès 1557, firent du vin à satiété. En 1561, des vignes provenant du Chili se multiplièrent sur le sol argentin de Mendoza, puis à Misiones et à Santa Fe. Décidément, les noms ne nous trompent pas : la Foi avait sur quoi s'appuyer et les calices vides ne mettraient pas en danger le salut des âmes.

||||||||||||||||||||||||||||||||||||||||||||||||||||||||||||||||||||||||||||||||||||||||||||||

Dans la banlieue de Mendoza, au nord de l'Argentine, le soleil se lève sur les vignes centenaires de Francisco Farina. C'est une matinée fraîche d'automne ; avril n'en est qu'à ses premiers jours, mais dans le vignoble, c'est la fin d'une année de labeur. « En deux jours, 12 mois de travail prennent la route des caves », soupire Francisco. Le vert est encore intense, mais quelques feuilles tournent au jaune ou au rouge, à l'ombre des oliviers. Au loin, les Andes sont majestueuses. La petite bourgade de Lunlunta est reconnue pour la qualité de ses raisins. « Notre climat privilégié, avec une grande amplitude thermique journalière, est parfait pour le raisin ! Nos vins ont ce petit goût épicé unique », explique Francisco au milieu de ses cinq hectares de malbec, cépage emblématique du terroir argentin.

⊡ Récolte de malbec. ⊡ La récolte d'Anthonio Camani et Oracio Arce a été bonne... ⊡ Francisco Farina dans ses vignes centenaires de la bourgade de Lunlunta.

⌃ Les vendanges au pied des Andes, en Argentine.

L'introduction du malbec en Argentine suivit des chemins tortueux. En 1849, le coup d'État du 18 Brumaire de Louis Bonaparte poussa l'agronome républicain français Michel Aimé Pouget à l'exil. Il se rendit d'abord au Chili, où il introduisit des techniques agricoles et de nouvelles espèces végétales, puis, en 1852, Sarmiento, futur président argentin, l'invita à créer un immense jardin botanique à Mendoza. En 1853, Pouget s'y installa avec différents cépages, plants et boutures de vignes... et les premières colonies d'abeilles italiennes. Celui qui deviendrait Miguel Amado Pouget restera à jamais lié à l'histoire du malbec argentin. C'est en Argentine que ce cépage a pu révéler ses meilleures qualités. Aujourd'hui, plus de la moitié des terres consacrées au malbec se trouvent en Argentine !

« Ne laissez pas un raisin sur les vignes et pas de feuilles dans vos paniers. Ces raisins sont destinés aux vins "réserve"», lance Francisco aux cueilleurs. Francisco est membre de Viña de la Solidaridad (Viñasol), une organisation de producteurs, fondée en 2005, qui compte 19 membres. « Plusieurs producteurs ont été sollicités, mais peu voulaient participer à cause de la mauvaise réputation qu'ont ici les coopératives », explique Francisco. Pourtant, les petits producteurs argentins avaient tout intérêt à travailler collectivement. Entre 1990 et 2000, les deux tiers des petits vignobles du pays ont disparu ; ils ont été rachetés, fusionnés, transformés. Eduardo Bertona, président de Viñasol, raconte cette époque : « J'ai coupé 40 % de mes vignes par manque de marché, j'ai même fait du vin blanc à partir de mon malbec pour le marché national. Si, en janvier, je n'avais pas d'acheteurs pour mon raisin, j'angoissais. À la fondation de Viñasol, la promesse d'un prix minimum garanti m'était inconcevable, mais cette année, j'ai obtenu, pour mes raisins équitables, le double du prix en vigueur dans la région ! »

Fait particulier en commerce équitable, à Viñasol, il y a des producteurs propriétaires et des *contratistas*, travailleurs au statut particulier. Le *contratista*, qui a une longue histoire en Argentine, est le responsable permanent de l'entretien des vignes d'un propriétaire. C'est une sorte de métayer qui perçoit pour son travail une faible allocation mensuelle, mais qui tire ses principaux revenus des vendanges, où il a droit à 15 à 18 % des recettes. Les frais de production, quant à eux, reviennent aux propriétaires.

Antonio et Osvaldo, les *contratistas* d'Eduardo, cumulent à eux deux 80 ans d'expérience ! « La vigne, c'est 12 mois par an », dit Osvaldo, le doyen. Avec 221 jours de travail par hectare, la vigne exige plus de main-d'œuvre que toute autre culture. « Nous devons tailler, attacher, irriguer, fertiliser, soigner et tailler encore... Un seul homme ne peut s'occuper de dix hectares ! » Les deux *contratistas* d'Eduardo sont responsables de six hectares chacun. « Nous sommes tous les trois membres de Viñasol, précise Eduardo. Pour l'instant, tout notre raisin ne peut être vendu équitable, faute de marché, mais la part des *contratistas* bénéficie en priorité des prix supérieurs et de la prime sociale. Cette année, les enfants d'Antonio recevront l'appui de Viñasol. Pour Osvaldo... ce sera pour ses petits-enfants ! »

L es raisins équitables des membres de Viñasol sont achetés par la Bodega Furlotti, agréée par la FLO comme exportatrice. Gabriela Furlotti, l'une des propriétaires, me reçoit dans sa maison ancestrale, aujourd'hui transformée en auberge campagnarde. L'endroit transpire la tradition et la vigne. « Ici, c'était le vignoble de mon grand-père. Ma famille est arrivée d'Italie au début du siècle passé. Mes ancêtres étaient d'abord *contratistas* avant de devenir propriétaires de leur vignoble, et ensuite de leur cave », m'explique-t-elle. Entreprise viticole privée, la Bodega Furlotti fut fondée pour vinifier du raisin équitable. Gabriela continue : « L'équitable n'était, au départ, qu'une opportunité commerciale, mais aujourd'hui, la part sociale prend de plus en plus de place. Nous avons dû faire tout un travail éducatif. Personne ne voulait d'une coopérative. Viñasol est donc une association sans but lucratif. Nous payons directement les membres pour le raisin que nous achetons, qui représente entre 20 et 25 % de leur récolte. Avec la prime équitable, on sent que l'association se consolide. Comme Viñasol est une association de producteurs, ses membres ont aussi pu obtenir cette année une aide gouvernementale de 3000 $ par hectare pour améliorer leur production. »

P our Maria Laura, agronome responsable de la production de Viñasol et également représentante de la FLO en Argentine et au Chili, « sans commerce équitable, les petits producteurs disparaîtraient. » La dynamique agronome court d'un vignoble à l'autre sans jamais manquer de temps pour répondre aux questions des membres. « Regarde ce vignoble, il n'y a qu'un seul hectare, mais il est cajolé comme un jardin », dit-elle en me faisant visiter le vignoble de Miguel et Marta, deux viticulteurs membres de Viñasol, dont la récolte bat son plein. « Des membres comme eux, j'en voudrais des dizaines. C'est pour eux que le commerce équitable existe », lance-t-elle, pour la fierté de Miguel.

⌃ Gerardo Gauthier, *contratista,* travaillant les vignes de Francisco Farina. ⌐ Osvaldo, Antonio, et Eduardo. ⌐ Maria-Laura Bardotti, agronome, et Miguel Borderon, viticulteur propriétaire d'un hectare de malbec. ⌐ Gabriela Furlotti, l'une des propriétaires de la Bodega Furlotti qui vinifie les raisins des membres de Viñasol, avec deux de ses employés.

À L'INSTAR DE BIEN D'AUTRES ALIMENTS ayant accompagné l'homme dans son destin, la genèse de la vinification des fruits de la vigne *(vitis vinifera)* se perd dans le dédale de l'Histoire. Des preuves de l'existence du vin chez les Perses, il y a 7000 ans, en passant par son commerce par les Phéniciens, jusqu'au développement du savoir-faire en Europe latine, c'est un véritable univers de cultivars (cépages, en termes œnologiques) qui s'est disséminé à travers la planète, conditionné par la nature du sol, les particularités climatiques des lieux et l'instinct des généticiens-artisans que sont les viticulteurs. Bien au-delà de la robe rouge, blanche ou rosée, ce sont les subtilités aromatiques et gustatives des différents cépages – cabernet-sauvignon, pinot, chardonnay, riesling, malbec, shiraz, sangiovese, muscat, pour n'en nommer que quelques-uns –, qui ont fait du vin le plus distingué des breuvages. Le vin définit plus que tout autre aliment, dans sa diversité, « l'art de vivre ».

Si cette image de noblesse et d'exclusivité resta longtemps l'apanage de quelques contrées productrices, la deuxième moitié du XXe siècle verra la consécration d'une réelle mondialisation du vin, tant au niveau de son commerce que de sa consommation avec, d'un côté, l'*establishment* des pays de tradition ancestrale – avec la France et l'Italie en tête –, et de l'autre, les nations émergentes du Nouveau Monde, comme les États-Unis, l'Australie, l'Argentine, le Chili et bien d'autres. Un peu partout – même dans un pays comme la Chine, où le vin ne fut pendant longtemps qu'une curiosité occidentale –, on tente sa chance pour produire du vin non plus simplement de consommation locale, mais de qualité suffisante pour l'exportation.

On peut bien comparer les vins sur la base de leurs qualités gustatives, mais il est plus aléatoire de le faire au niveau des conditions socioéconomiques dans lesquelles ils sont produits. L'imaginaire public soupçonne peu l'existence d'une problématique de pauvreté et d'exploitation dans ce domaine. Hélas, dans bien des pays du Sud, où il y a absence de filet de sécurité sociale, la production du vin se fait souvent sur le dos des petits producteurs et d'une main-d'œuvre aisément abusée.

La démarche encore timide du commerce équitable (qui représente environ 0,02 % du marché du vin) réussit à réduire les injustices économiques, notamment en Argentine, au Chili et surtout en Afrique du Sud, où le paiement des salaires en vin a longtemps fait des ravages. Avec l'aide d'organisations non gouvernementales et en ciblant des marchés où la production locale n'entre pas en concurrence, des percées encourageantes ont été réalisées, notamment en Grande-Bretagne et en Belgique (avec une augmentation globale des ventes de 57 % en 2008).

le vin en chiffres

COMMERCE CONVENTIONNEL

Production mondiale : 26 444 731 000 litres
Commerce mondial : 22 422 000 000 $

PRINCIPAUX PAYS PRODUCTEURS

Italie	18 %
France	14 %
États-Unis	9 %
Argentine	6 %
Chine	5 %
Chili (8e)	3 %

COMMERCE ÉQUITABLE

Année de certification : 2003
Importations mondiales : 8 980 000 litres
Ventes au détail : 71 430 000 $
Croissance de 2007 à 2008 : 57 %

ORGANISATIONS CERTIFIÉES

Quatre organisations de petits producteurs, et 23 organisations avec des travailleurs salariés.

ORIGINE DES ORGANISATIONS CERTIFIÉES

Afrique du Sud	44 %
Argentine	30 %
Chili	26 %

PRINCIPAUX PAYS IMPORTATEURS

	Importations (l)	Croissance (2007 à 2008)
Grande-Bretagne	4 411 000	25 %
Suède	1 766 000	87 %
Pays-Bas	689 000	56 %
Belgique	565 000	423 %
Allemagne	557 000	72 %

PRIX ET PRIMES (raisins)

Prix équitable : 0,22 à 0,37 $/kg
Prime équitable : 0,07 $/kg
Prime biologique : 0,07 $/kg
Proportion de raisins biologiques : 35 %

⌃ À la Bodega Furlotti, Luisa Delgado trie les raisins équitables des membres de Viñasol, en Argentine. Viñasol et Sagrada Familia, au Chili, font partie des quatre organisations de petits producteurs de vin équitable certifiées par la FLO. Les 23 autres organisations certifiées par la FLO sont des plantations privées dépendant de main-d'œuvre salariée.

Au Chili, les débuts de la Sociedad Vitivinícola Sagrada Familia font penser à ceux de Viñasol. Les 16 membres fondateurs de l'association totalisent moins de 100 hectares et, comme en Argentine, les coopératives ont laissé d'amers souvenirs dans la région. «Les membres ne voulaient rien savoir d'une coopérative, mais si vous regardez nos statuts, tout y est, sauf le nom», m'explique Raul Navarette, le directeur de la société. Fondée en 1997, la société à capital fermé compte 16 propriétaires égaux, tous petits producteurs de raisins. Raul et Raphael Espinoza Inostroza, président du conseil d'administration, m'accueillent dans la petite ville de Curicó, au cœur de la vallée de Lontué, une riche région fruitière du Chili.

«Dans les débuts de l'organisation, on pouvait à peine répondre par oui ou non lorsqu'on recevait des visiteurs étrangers», me confie Raphael en riant. «Il faut voir d'où l'on vient!» Raphael a commencé sa vie de manœuvre à neuf ans. À 11 ans, il quittait la maison pour travailler à l'extérieur. Il ajoute: «Avec la réforme agraire, mon père a obtenu ce petit lopin de quelques hectares. Il voulait léguer quelque chose à ses enfants pour qu'ils ne dépendent pas d'un patron. Certains se plaignent car nous gagnons peu, mais nous avons quelque chose qui n'a pas de prix: la liberté.»

Nous partons dans sa camionnette pour visiter des membres de l'organisation: Miguel Jesus, Manuel, Domingo et Luis. Ils témoignent: «Dans le temps, nous n'avions même pas de souliers à nous mettre dans les pieds et nous travaillions du lundi... au lundi!» Miguel Jesus n'a que quelques pas à franchir pour passer de sa maison à son vignoble, où se suivent les rangées de raisins blancs et rouges: sauvignon blanc, merlot, cabernet sauvignon, carmenère... Il continue: «Ça fait 30 ans que je cultive cette terre. J'ai toujours travaillé avec mon père. Avant l'association, on devait vendre notre raisin à 0,05 $ le kilo. Un désastre! La veille de la récolte, on ne dormait pas. Aujourd'hui, on sait où vendre notre raisin. Avec l'association, nous sommes tranquilles. De plus, le fonds social est un énorme soulagement. Ma mère est diabétique, mais je sais que si elle a besoin de soins, elle les aura.» Les primes équitables sont bonifiées par les achats d'Oxfam-Wereldwinkles, principal client de la société, qui ajoute 1,50 euro par boîte de vin. Ces fonds permettent à Sagrada Familia d'assumer tous les frais de santé de ses membres, et d'offrir également des bourses d'études. «Je n'ai pu faire que ma quatrième année, mais aujourd'hui nos enfants vont à l'université, certains sont ingénieurs et nous avons même un médecin», lance Miguel Jesus. Raphael ajoute:

◙ Miguel Jesus, l'un des 16 membres fondateurs de Sagrada Familia. ◙ L'agronome Andaur Rojas et l'œnologue Fernando Torres dégustent les vins «réserve» de la société.

⌃ Vendanges de carbernet sauvignon biologique et équitable sur la plantation de José Elias Palma Vallejos, membre de Sagrada Familia.

« Mes deux aînés font des études supérieures, ce qui aurait été impossible uniquement avec mes revenus personnels. » En 2008, 30 étudiants ont reçu l'appui du fonds social de Sagrada Familia.

En ce temps de vendanges, l'agronome Andaur Rojas et l'œnologue Fernando Torres se déplacent de vignoble en vignoble pour s'assurer de la bonne maturation des raisins. Dès leur arrivée au vignoble, ils lancent : « Sois prêt demain, Manuel. Nous viendrons récolter ton merlot. » Ce sera l'entrée officielle de Manuel Campo dans l'organisation. Il est l'un des six nouveaux membres à intégrer Sagrada Familia pour la récolte de 2009. « J'aurai l'assurance de vendre mon raisin à bon prix », se réjouit Manuel. Pour Miguel Jesus, l'évolution de l'organisation est phénoménale : « Au début, on ne vendait que du raisin. Ensuite, on en a vinifié une partie. Aujourd'hui, on doit même intégrer de nouveaux membres ! »

La société loue les services d'une cave, où les raisins, dès leur arrivée, sont broyés et mis dans de grandes cuves. Suivent les différentes étapes de la vinification : macération, pressage, fermentation, clarification, filtrage, embouteillage et parfois, pour les vins « réserve », l'historique barrique de bois. « Ce sont nos propres barriques », s'enorgueillit Andaur.

À notre retour dans les bureaux de la société, Raphael et Raul, le directeur, reçoivent des compatriotes qui ont quatre grandes cuves à vendre. « L'achat de ces cuves est un autre pas vers la réalisation de notre rêve d'avoir notre propre cave », dit Raphael. « En 2008, notre croissance a été de 76 % ! Nous vinifions aujourd'hui 1 300 000 litres de vin par an. Nous en produirons bientôt suffisamment pour justifier cet investissement », précise Raul. Sans le commerce équitable, on n'y serait jamais parvenus. Nous voulons aujourd'hui que d'autres groupes de petits producteurs bénéficient de ce modèle. »

En avril 2009, Sagrada Familia recevait des délégations de plusieurs organisations chiliennes et des représentants de pays importateurs. « Nous étions plus de 90 personnes à ces rencontres », précise le Belge Léo Ghysel, d'Oxfam-Wereldwinkels qui entretient une longue tradition de coopération avec le Chili. Il continue : « Avec la fin du régime de Pinochet, nous avons commencé à travailler au Chili ; ce fut un geste politique de bienvenue à la démocratie. Ce pays a plusieurs produits exportables dans le réseau équitable. Nous avons récemment fait du jus à partir de concentré de pomme chilien mélangé à des jus frais de Belgique. C'est bien prometteur ! Avec un représentant de la FLO dans la région, les perspectives sont encore meilleures. Les gens de Sagrada Familia sont d'excellents ambassadeurs du commerce équitable ; avec eux, pas de décoration de vitrines mais de vraies valeurs équitables. »

La commune de Sagrada Familia est baignée par la rivière Mataquito, où fut tué le résistant mapuche Lautaro. Réduit en esclavage à l'âge de 12 ans, il fut le palefrenier de Pedro de Valdivia, un *conquistador* espagnol. Au contact des Espagnols, Lautaro apprit des techniques de guerre. Après avoir été témoin des meurtres de certains de ses frères mapuches et des mutilations que les hommes de Valdivia infligeaient aux siens, Lautaro prit la fuite, rejoignit les Mapuches et leur apprit que les chevaux n'étaient pas des moitiés de centaures. Il leur enseigna également des stratégies de combat et créa la première cavalerie indigène. Lautaro pris sa revanche sur Pedro de Valdivia lors de la Bataille de Tucapel, en 1553. Quatre ans après, les troupes de Lautaro, fatiguées après l'enivrement rituel lors d'une célébration, furent prises dans une embuscade. Lautaro tomba sous les coups de son bourreau, Francisco de Villagra, mais sa résistance ne fut pas vaine et son exemple inspira les luttes futures des Chiliens pour leur liberté. L'esprit de solidarité qui a animé les combattants mapuches d'hier et les a fait travailler ensemble pour résister et avancer a survécu. Les producteurs de Sagrada Familia sont eux aussi des résistants, dans ce marché viticole chilien où seuls quelques groupes sont hégémoniques. Le fait que leurs vins portent le nom du légendaire Lautaro est, plus qu'un juste hommage, une expression de courage et de créativité.

☑ Vin de Sagrada Familia de marque Lautaro, du nom du légendaire résistant mapuche. ☑ La vigne est liée à l'homme depuis la nuit des temps.

«AGIR ENSEMBLE APPORTE PLUS QUE LA SOMME de nos actions individuelles» pourrait être la devise officielle de la FLO. Cette réflexion, si souvent présente chez celles et ceux qui travaillent dans le commerce équitable, part assurément d'un constat : le réseautage fait partie de la solidarité.

La FLO certifie 750 organisations de producteurs, et la WFTO compte 350 organisations membres, dont les deux tiers sont dans l'hémisphère Sud. En 2008, plus de 450 nouvelles organisations ont demandé leur certification auprès de la FLO. Pour favoriser leur intégration, la FLO a présentement 35 agents de liaison travaillant en permanence dans l'hémisphère Sud. Les débuts des organisations de producteurs ont aussi souvent bénéficié de l'appui d'organisations non gouvernementales liées au développement international, à l'instar de l'appui de la Belge Oxfam-Wereldwinkles à la Chilienne Sagrada Familia.

Coopératives ou autres structures démocratiques, les organisations de petits producteurs peuvent représenter quelques centaines d'artisans ou plus de 10 000 paysans, telle CoopeAgri au Costa Rica. Plusieurs de ces organisations ont aussi fondé des unions ou des fédérations nationales. Dans le berceau génétique du café, en Éthiopie, l'Union des coopératives de caféiculteurs d'Oromia fait la force de 230 000 familles. Au Pérou, la Cocla est constituée de 23 coopératives de producteurs de café et inscrit la «consolidation d'alliances» parmi ses principaux objectifs.

Des coopératives locales aux unions nationales, le monde équitable compte aujourd'hui trois réseaux internationaux de producteurs. En Amérique latine, la Coordinadora Lationoamericana y del Caribe de Pequeños Productores de Comercio Justo (CLAC) rassemble plus de 300 groupes représentant plus de 100 000 familles, en Afrique, African Fairtrade Network, en pleine croissance, regroupe plus de 200 organisations de producteurs dans 24 pays, et en Asie, le Network of Asian Producers (NAP) s'est donné pour mission d'incorporer plus de producteurs asiatiques au commerce équitable.

Ces trois réseaux ont quatre sièges permanents sur le conseil d'administration de la FLO. La nouvelle stratégie globale pour le commerce équitable de l'organisation propose que dans les années à venir, ces réseaux prennent leur place comme acteurs fondamentaux du système, au lieu de simples bénéficiaires du commerce équitable. Une décentralisation salutaire pour le mouvement équitable, ratifiant son engagement pour l'autonomie et le pouvoir de décision des producteurs, deux objectifs fondateurs du mouvement.

« Agir ensemble apporte plus que la somme de nos actions individuelles » pourrait être la devise officielle de la FLO. Cette réflexion, si souvent présente chez celles et ceux qui travaillent dans le commerce équitable, part assurément d'un constat : le réseautage fait partie de la solidarité.

les réseaux équitables dans l'hémisphère Sud

1. Cabernet sauvignon.
2. Richard, un cueilleur, lors des vendanges chez Francisco Farina.
3. Malbec argentin.
4. Tri manuel à la Bodega Furlotti.
5. Marc Weis, œnologue suisse, déguste ses vins « réserve ».
6. Embarquement des vins à la Bodega Furlotti.
7. Vin biologique de la Bodega Furlotti, fait avec les raisins de Viñasol.

SOLUNA

ORGANIC
malbec

VINO TINTO

▷ Marc Weis, responsable de la vinification du malbec des membres de Viñasol à la Bodega Furlotti.

le guarana

« A vant le temps, il y avait le Noçoquém, une forêt sacrée habitée par trois divinités : la déesse Onhiámuáçabê et ses frères. Ces derniers ne voulaient pas qu'elle se marie, mais tous les animaux rêvaient d'Onhiámuáçabê. Un jour, le serpent frôla une de ses jambes et elle tomba aussitôt enceinte. L'enfant naquit beau et sain. Jaloux, ses oncles ordonnèrent au singe de tuer l'enfant. Onhiámuáçabê récupéra le cadavre de son fils et planta son œil droit dans la terre, duquel naquit le guarana. L'enfant ressuscita quelque temps après. Pendant qu'elle lavait son corps tout sale de terre, sa mère lui dit : "Tes oncles ont commandité ta mort par jalousie. Ils voulaient que tu sois un misérable, mais tu seras le plus grand. Tu seras vénéré par tous et l'on viendra de très loin juste pour te célébrer." Cet enfant fut le premier Satéré-Mawé », raconte Perpétua, sage et

211

cuisinière de l'expédition qui m'emmène en terre amazonienne. Le *Juruena* a quitté le port de Parintins, au Brésil, à destination du territoire démarqué des Indiens Satéré-Mawé, où près de 10 000 âmes se distribuent dans une centaine de villages sur 788 000 hectares de forêts et de rivières. Le bateau avance paisiblement dans l'immensité verte. De fleuve en fleuve, devant mes yeux, défilent des îles vouées à disparaître lors des prochaines crues, des oiseaux multicolores et d'autres bateaux dont les voyageurs, politesse amazonienne oblige, nous saluent et nous sourient invariablement. De temps à autre, des botos – dauphins d'eau douce – apparaissent à la surface de l'eau, comme pour nous inviter dans leur univers mystérieux.

C'est le premier voyage pour l'achat du guarana de la récolte de 2008. Obadias Garcia, leader des Satéré-Mawé et principal organisateur du commerce équitable du guarana rassemble tout l'équipage. Un *çapó*, breuvage sacré des Satéré-Mawé, commence à circuler. Éducateur inlassable, Obadias sait qu'il faut revenir sans cesse sur les principes et les objectifs de ce qu'il nomme le Projet Guarana : « Le commerce équitable ne se réduit pas à de meilleurs prix. C'est une question de justice sociale, de santé, d'éducation, de culture, de souveraineté alimentaire et d'écologie. Le commerce équitable est une politique intégrale. »

Pendant des siècles, le guarana fut le produit le plus important de l'économie satéré-mawé, utilisé dans les échanges avec les peuples des Amériques précolombiennes. « Il y a déjà des écrits relatant la présence des ancêtres des Satéré-Mawé vendant du guarana au Mexique en 1550 ! » rappelle Obadias. Au cours des dernières décennies, la croissance constante des boissons gazeuses à base de guarana (en 2008, près de trois milliards de litres de boissons à saveur de guarana ont été consommés au Brésil) a donné lieu au développement d'une agriculture intensive dans d'autres régions du pays et à une constante dépréciation du guarana. « Dans le temps, tout mon peuple produisait du guarana en quantité. À présent, 70 % des champs sont à l'abandon », dit Obadias. Pour les Satéré-Mawé, qui s'identifient comme « fils du guarana », bien au-delà de l'aspect économique, ce processus a eu des impacts socioculturels majeurs.

Il y a près de 15 ans, la rencontre du socio-économiste italien Maurizio Fraboni donna à Obadias la chance de stopper un processus de dégradation qui menaçait l'existence même de son peuple. Les deux hommes prirent contact avec CTM Altromercato, la plus importante organisation de commerce équitable de l'Italie. « La première exportation de guarana n'était que de 20 kilos », se souvient Obadias. En France, Guayapi Tropical, une entreprise de commercialisation de

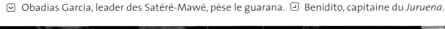
⊡ Obadias Garcia, leader des Satéré-Mawé, pèse le guarana.　⊡ Benidito, capitaine du *Juruena*.

Le *Juruena*, ancré à Guaranatuba, en Amazonie, accueille les Satéré-Mawé venus vendre leur guarana.

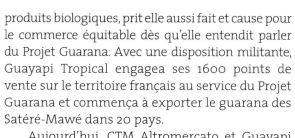

produits biologiques, prit elle aussi fait et cause pour le commerce équitable dès qu'elle entendit parler du Projet Guarana. Avec une disposition militante, Guayapi Tropical engagea ses 1600 points de vente sur le territoire français au service du Projet Guarana et commença à exporter le guarana des Satéré-Mawé dans 20 pays.

Aujourd'hui, CTM Altromercato et Guayapi Tropical absorbent toute la production tribale de guarana, d'environ sept tonnes par an. Pour mieux s'organiser, les chefs des villages ont créé le Conseil général de la tribu des Satéré-Mawé. La

certification biologique de leur agriculture et la mise en place de projets sociaux et écologiques grâce au commerce équitable ont grandement contribué à l'amélioration des conditions de vie de la nation, mais ont surtout renforcé la culture et permis aux Satéré-Mawé de reprendre conscience de leur rôle sur cette planète : celui de protecteurs de la forêt et de la vie. « Sacré commerce équitable ! s'exclame Obadias. Ça ressemble tout à fait à l'économie indienne ; dans les deux cas, il s'agit de protéger les hommes et l'environnement ! »

⌃ Paulo da Costa, producteur de guarana, boit un *çapó,* la boisson sacrée des Satéré-Mawé.

Il fait déjà nuit lorsque nous arrivons à Guaranatuba, le premier village satéré-mawé de la région du fleuve Andirá. Avant d'accrocher nos hamacs, nous saluons le bon *tuxaua** Delcides et sa mère, Dona Iraci, la doyenne et la sage de Guaranatuba. Assise sur son tabouret, Dona Iraci prépare le *çapô* en râpant un bâton de guarana sur une pierre au-dessus d'une calebasse remplie d'eau. Bien plus qu'un breuvage énergétique, nourrissant et médicinal, le *çapô* est pour ces Indiens une boisson sacrée qui, à l'instar de l'eucharistie, célèbre une alliance entre Dieu et les hommes. Cette eau terreuse renvoie à celle qui s'est déposée dans la calebasse mythique où Onhiámuáçabê a lavé son enfant ressuscité. Le *waraná*** est « la source de toute connaissance ».

Le lendemain, dès la première heure, des producteurs arrivent sur le bateau en transportant sur leur dos des sacs de jute remplis de graines de guarana. « À 40 réaux (20 $) le kilo, les Satéré-Mawé sont les guaraniculteurs les mieux payés au monde », rappelle fièrement Obadias. C'est près de dix fois le prix d'un kilo de café. Avec son paiement, chaque producteur reçoit une invitation écrite à la réunion pour la fondation du Consortium des guaraniculteurs satéré-mawé, qui se tiendra bientôt, assortie d'un discours d'Obadias sur l'importance de renforcer leur organisation autonome.

* Chez les Satéré-Mawé, le *tuxaua* est le chef du village.
** Guarana, en langue satéré-mawé.

En offrant de meilleurs prix au guarana biologique et équitable des Satéré-Mawé, le Projet Guarana a enclenché un processus de valorisation agricole dans toute la région. En moins de cinq ans, le guarana des Caboclos – métis descendant d'Européens blancs et d'Indiens – qui cultivent le guarana en périphérie du territoire des Satéré-Mawé, a connu une valorisation de près de 600 %, ce qui a dérangé certains acteurs commerciaux et suscité de la convoitise. Le Projet Guarana a subi des attaques diffamatoires dans certains médias à scandale, et même des poursuites non fondées, semant le doute et la zizanie au sein de la nation satéré-mawé.

Chez Dona Iraci, un producteur attend Obadias. Il a des questions sur le commerce équitable et veut en avoir le cœur net. Pour que rien ne lui échappe, il fait venir sa fille aînée, qui maîtrise parfaitement le portugais et la langue satéré-mawé. Muni d'un prospectus de Guayapi Tropical détaillant les prix, Obadias lui explique patiemment les coûts de transport, les divers impôts et le salaire payé à chaque collaborateur : « Le commerce équitable est une chaîne solidaire où chacun a son rôle. Nous n'avons pas de clients, mais des partenaires et des alliés. » Les discussions se prolongent jusqu'à l'heure du midi. Dans le bateau, Perpétua, la sage, nous attend avec un poisson *tucunaré,* du riz, des haricots de plage et l'incontournable farine jaune de manioc. Tout cela accompagné de jus de fruits au choix : buriti, açai ou cupuaçu.

▷ Pour préparer le *çapô,* Dona Iraci râpe rituellement un bâton fait de graines de guarana torréfiées, pilées et séchées.

⌃ Retour vers Guaranatuba avec la récolte de guarana. ⌄ Paulo da Costa transporte un lourd panier de fruits de guarana.
▷ Récolte des grappes de fruits de guarana.

||||||||||||||||||||||||||||||||||||||||||||||||||||||||||||||||||||||||||||||||

Très tôt le lendemain, Paulo da Costa, un culti-vateur de l'endroit, nous invite à la cueillette dans des champs éloignés du village. Nous mettons quelques minutes, en petit bateau, pour arriver près de ses champs où, sous des arbres fruitiers, des abeilles sans dard s'agitent à l'entrée de leurs ruches. La multiplication de ces ruches est un élément important du Projet, puisque les abeilles assurent la pollinisation non seulement du guarana, mais de 90 % de la forêt amazonienne !

Paulo da Costa nous invite ensuite à prendre le « sentier de l'iguane », au bout duquel nous trouvons ses premiers plants de guarana. Seulement 135 des 390 arbustes de cette parcelle sont vraiment productifs. « La plupart de mes arbustes sont encore très jeunes. Et puis, j'avais bien nettoyé le champ, mais il a trop plu et les herbes ont repoussé avec vigueur, justifie-t-il. L'an passé, j'ai récolté 89 kilos de guarana, mais cette année, je suis tout juste rendu à 20 kilos. » Nous sommes loin des petits producteurs de café équitable, dont les modestes récoltes atteignent tout de même une demi-tonne.

Paulo songe à cultiver un nouveau champ de 150 plants. « Dans cinq ans, ils regorgeront de fruits », dit-il, confiant. Conformément au protocole de production satéré-mawé, il devra cueillir ses nouveaux plants dans la forêt vierge, où le guarana adulte prend la forme d'une liane qui fait son tapis de pousses au pied de l'arbre auquel elle s'agrippe.

▷ L'intrigant fruit du guarana, avec sa graine noire entourée d'une pulpe blanche, ressemble à un œil humain.

Dans un village voisin, nous demandons à Elivaldo, un autre producteur, de nous montrer une liane mère. Il accepte de nous guider, et après un peu plus d'une heure dans son petit bateau, nous arrivons à un abri de chasseur, à l'entrée d'un sentier. Nous avons quelques heures de marche à faire avant d'arriver à la liane et nous nous arrêtons pour reprendre des forces avant de partir. Elivaldo se met à ramasser des tiges et des fibres végétales avec lesquelles il improvise des arcs et des flèches. « Quand les fourmis *tocandeiras* meurent, elles se transforment en ces fibres qui nous servent de cordes pour construire nos huttes », dit-il, parfaitement à l'aise avec la poésie de ses mythes. Une fois restaurés, nous pénétrons dans la jungle d'un pas rapide.

Jour et nuit, la forêt chante. Selon mes compagnons, le gazouillis que nous entendons durant notre incursion tient à notre présence. Assimilant les chants à des paroles de la langue satéré-mawé, Obadias et Elivaldo comprennent la question permanente des oiseaux: « Qui êtes-vous? Qui êtes-vous? » Je suis émerveillé au milieu d'une biodiversité qui me surprend chaque seconde. « Cours! Cours! » crient soudainement mes amis. Sans me poser de questions, je suis leurs consignes jusqu'à ce qu'ils m'arrêtent. « Tu étais en plein territoire des fourmis *taocas* », m'informe Elivaldo. Trop tard! Quelques-unes se sont déjà insinuées sous mes vêtements et me font payer le prix de mon intrusion.

Après trois heures de marche, nous apercevons les premiers plants sauvages de guarana. Leur présence signale l'existence certaine d'une liane mère dans les environs. En effet, quelques minutes après, Elivaldo identifie un arbre sur lequel s'appuie la prolifique liane, qu'Obadias embrasse, comme par dévotion. Il est particulièrement heureux de se faire photographier à côté d'une liane mère: « En presque 15 ans de Projet Guarana, c'est bien la première fois que ça m'arrive! »

Au retour, Obadias m'invite à prendre un autre sentier. Il veut me faire voir un arbre tout à fait spécial appelé *sapopema*. Le majestueux géant de la forêt s'impose devant nos yeux comme un être doué de raison et de volonté. Ses racines aériennes érigent des murs végétaux aux quatre points cardinaux pour soutenir une longue et lourde masse plantée dans un sol peu profond. Son équilibre est une question de forces conjuguées, de collaboration amoureuse et fraternelle. Cet arbre envoie un message aux peuples de la forêt. Dans l'univers du guarana, certains ont déjà commencé à le saisir.

⊡ Obadias Garcia, à côté d'une liane mère de guarana.

L<small>E GUARANA</small> *(PAULLINIA CUPANA SORBILIS)* <small>EST UNE LIANE</small> de la famille des sapindacées, dont le berceau génétique se trouve entre les rivières Tapajós et Madeira, en Amazonie brésilienne, territoire ancestral des Indiens Satéré-Mawé. Riche en différents alcaloïdes, tanins, sels minéraux, vitamines et oligoéléments, le guarana est un puissant stimulant et aphrodisiaque employé également à des fins médicinales pour ses propriétés antidiarrhéiques et antinévralgiques. On lui a aussi récemment découvert des propriétés anticarcinogéniques.

Depuis des millénaires, les Satéré-Mawé torréfient les graines de guarana dans des fours en argile. Elles sont ensuite pilées et transformées en bâton. Rituellement râpé dans une calebasse remplie d'eau, ce bâton est à la base de leur boisson sacrée, le *çapó*.

Aujourd'hui, le guarana entre dans la composition de maintes boissons rafraîchissantes et produits énergisants. Au Brésil seulement, les boissons gazeuses à saveur de guarana occupent 22,6 % du marché national, avec trois milliards de litres consommés annuellement, et la conquête mondiale du guarana semble bien enclenchée, surtout dans le domaine des boissons énergisantes, dont l'industrie est en pleine explosion, avec une croissance de 50 % depuis 2002! Cinq cents nouvelles marques ont été lancées, seulement au cours de l'année 2007.

Pourtant, bien que le guarana soit la plante à plus haute teneur en caféine, sa production dans l'ensemble du territoire du Brésil, le seul pays à le cultiver commercialement, n'atteint même pas 4000 tonnes, une quantité dérisoire si on la compare aux sept millions de tonnes et plus de café produites mondialement. Selon un agronome brésilien spécialiste en la matière : « C'est un fait bien connu que la production annuelle de guarana ne peut même pas fournir le minimum de caféine requis par la loi pour les boissons à "saveur de guarana" vendues au pays. »

Le guarana biologique et équitable (certifié par Ecocert et la WFTO, mais pas encore reconnu par la FLO, qui étudie la question) est principalement distribué par Guayapi Tropical en France et dans 20 autres pays, et CTM Altromercato en Italie. Au Canada, la compagnie de produits équitables Nitro Gène distribue depuis 2008 du guarana en poudre et des barres de chocolat au guarana, et développe de nouveaux produits prometteurs.

Riche en différents alcaloïdes, tanins, sels minéraux, vitamines et oligoéléments, le guarana est un puissant stimulant et aphrodisiaque employé également à des fins médicinales pour ses propriétés antidiarrhéiques et antinévralgiques.

La Société des peuples pour l'écodéveloppement de l'Amazonie (SAPOPEMA) est le fruit de l'union entre les producteurs de guarana satéré-mawé, des associations et coopératives de Caboclos et une petite entreprise familiale de commerce de produits amazoniens. Pour que la réussite économique des Satéré-Mawé s'étende à des producteurs non indiens capables d'offrir un guarana biologique de haute qualité, la SAPOPEMA souhaite bâtir un solide mouvement de valorisation d'une production agricole respectueuse de l'environnement en Amazonie.

Plus loin dans notre périple, nous visitons José Francisco Marques, le plus grand producteur individuel de guarana biologique de Maués et véritable porte-parole non officiel de la SAPOPEMA auprès des guaraniculteurs locaux. «La situation des Caboclos était plus que semblable à celle des Indiens, dit-il. Il n'y avait aucune différence! Un monopole a cherché à faire baisser les prix du guarana. Les producteurs n'étaient jamais reconnus comme des interlocuteurs.» José Francisco Marques a été à l'origine de deux associations locales de producteurs.

Le lendemain, Adeilson Gomes de Souza, alias Dedeco, président d'une association, nous fait visiter son champ de guarana. Il insiste sur l'importance de l'organisation : «Nous avons 170 membres à l'association, dont 95 sont certifiés biologiques.» Pour Dedeco, l'organisation a donné une autre place sociale aux producteurs de guarana : «Avant, nous étions soumis aux intermédiaires et devions subir des humiliations. Maintenant, nous sommes des partenaires économiques. En soutenant le processus de certification, le gouvernement fédéral nous a attribué des titres de propriété. Cela change la donne, surtout maintenant que les vents sont favorables au guarana.» Obadias ajoute : «La SAPOPEMA n'en est qu'à ses débuts, mais notre objectif est d'en faire une réelle alternative économique pour valoriser le mode de vie des habitants de la forêt amazonienne, et donc préserver la forêt elle-même.»

Le leader indien allait poursuivre son voyage d'achat du guarana en appelant à chaque rencontre une présence massive à la réunion de fondation du Consortium des guaraniculteurs satéré-mawé, une étape décisive pour freiner les attaques de leurs ennemis. Ses efforts ont été

▽ Fofinha et son paresseux, son animal de compagnie. ▽ Pêche au filet, près du village de Coatá. ▽ Cuisson de la farine de manioc, un élément incontournable de la cuisine brésilienne.

Le grand fleuve Andirá, à Guaranatuba.

couronnés de succès. Le 19 décembre 2008, réunis en assemblée sur l'île Michiles, une centaine de producteurs ont officiellement créé leur Consortium.

D'autres batailles se présenteront à l'avenir. « Nous sommes dans un long processus pour faire reconnaître le territoire satéré-mawé comme berceau génétique du guarana, dit Obadias. Nous aurons notre appellation d'origine contrôlée : le *waraná*. » À l'instar de leurs héros mythiques, les Satéré-Mawé devront affronter les futurs défis courageusement et en sortir toujours plus forts et plus sages.

1. Le fruit du guarana.
2. Paulo da Costa récolte ses fruits.
3. José Francisco Marques et ses fils égrainent les fruits.
4. Graines de guarana.
5. Delcides, le *tuxaua,* torréfie les graines de guarana.
6. Bâtons traditionnels de guarana.
7. Extrait de guarana pour le Guaranito de CTM Altromercato.
8. Graines de guarana pour l'exportation.
9. Poudre de guarana de la SAPOPEMA.

▷ Paulo da Costa, qui égraine les fruits de guarana avec ses petits-enfants, profite de l'occasion pour leur transmettre ses connaissances ancestrales et ses valeurs. Les jeunes Satéré-Mawé sont impliqués dans les activités de tous les jours, un complément à leur enseignement régulier qui se fait en langue satéré-mawé.

La globalisation de
l'équitable

« Tout comme la démocratie, qui ne se limite pas à aller voter de temps à autre, la mondialisation de la justice sociale et environnementale n'est pas qu'un discours. Elle exige de passer de la pensée à l'action quotidienne », écrit Laure Waridel dans son livre *Acheter, c'est voter*, publié en 2005. Dix ans auparavant, le hasard voulut que je fasse la connaissance de Laure à l'occasion d'une entrevue pour travailler chez Greenpeace. Nous avons tous les deux obtenu un emploi et une amitié s'est tissée. Lorsque nous avons pris le chemin de la coopérative UCIRI au Mexique, en 1996, le hasard a encore une fois bien fait les choses : nous mettions les pieds dans l'une des coopératives phares du mouvement équitable, avec en son sein Francisco Van der Hoff.

⌃ Sculptures en pierre de rivière noire du Comité Artisanal Haïtien, distribuées dans le réseau de boutiques Dix Mille Villages.

Au retour de ce séjour, plusieurs se sont joints à nous pour lancer la campagne « Un juste café », supportée jusqu'à ce jour par Équiterre. Nous étions de plus en plus nombreux à vouloir nous impliquer pour plus de justice par la voie du commerce équitable, mais au Québec tout restait à faire. Notre premier répertoire de points de vente était mince, très mince, les adresses se comptaient sur les doigts d'une main et tenaient sur une simple carte d'affaires !

Dans les autres régions du Canada, les boutiques Dix Mille Villages constituaient déjà un solide réseau. Aujourd'hui, l'initiative lancée par Edna Ruth Byler, en 1946, et soutenue par le Mennonite Central Committee fait affaire avec plus de 130 groupes d'artisans, dans 35 pays.

Les organisations non gouvernementales de développement international ont toujours joué un rôle prépondérant dans le soutien de l'équitable. À elle seule, la famille Oxfam, dont la maison mère d'Oxford démarra la distribution d'artisanat de réfugiés chinois à Hong-Kong en 1950, compte maintenant de grands réseaux et de solides entreprises d'importation de produits équitables, à l'instar d'Oxfam-Wereldwinkels en Belgique. En avril 2002, les 14 branches d'Oxfam lançaient la vaste campagne de lobbying et de sensibilisation « Pour un commerce équitable », dans le but d'en appeler « aux gouvernements, aux institutions et aux entreprises multinationales pour qu'ils changent les règles, afin que le commerce international fasse partie de la solution à la pauvreté et non du problème. » Equita, la marque de Commerce équitable Oxfam-Québec, compte la plus vaste gamme de produits équitables au pays, avec du riz, des épices et des fruits séchés, aux côtés des café, thé et cacao.

Lors de mes premières conférences, il n'y avait qu'un seul produit équitable, le café, et une seule marque, Bridgehead, alors le bras commercial d'Oxfam Canada, était offerte. Oxfam Canada s'est retirée de l'activité commerciale, mais la marque Bridgehead a été rachetée par des employés et ses cafés sont maintenant nombreux dans la région d'Ottawa. La certification équitable n'était toujours pas arrivée au pays, mais Bob Thompson, premier directeur de Transfair Canada, en 1997, y travaillait avec acharnement.

À cette époque, plusieurs entrepreneurs développaient de petites et moyennes entreprises dédiées à 100 % au commerce équitable. En Nouvelle-Écosse, la compagnie Just Us ! devenait, en 1995, le premier torréfacteur de café 100 % équitable. « Nous croyons fermement qu'il faut prioriser les gens et la planète avant les profits », explique Jeff Moore, son fondateur et directeur général. Just Us !, qui distribue des produits équitables et biologiques, est elle-même une coopérative de travailleurs.

Il en va de même pour La Siembra, à Ottawa, qui fêtait, en 2009, l'anniversaire de sa fondation avec le slogan « Coopérativement équitable depuis 10 ans », et qui se décrit ainsi : « Nous avons choisi de nous identifier à nos partenaires producteurs en optant pour une forme d'entreprise qui intègre les mêmes valeurs de démocratie, d'équité, de solidarité et de transparence qu'ils appliquent au sein de leurs propres coopératives. » Caitlin Peeling, membre travailleuse, explique le cheminement de La Siembra : « Nous avons développé le cacao et le sucre équitables pour offrir des produits différents du café. Nous souhaitions aussi toucher les jeunes, qui représentent le futur. Auprès d'eux, le chocolat est beaucoup plus porteur ! » Cocoa Camino, la marque de commerce de La Siembra, est aujourd'hui la plus importante marque de chocolat équitable au Canada.

Les produits de La Siembra sont également distribués aux États-Unis sous la bannière d'Equal Exchange, une autre coopérative de travailleurs, fondée en 1986. « Notre premier café venait du Nicaragua. En passant par un torréfacteur néerlandais, nous contournions un embargo imposé à ce pays par le gouvernement Reagan. Le geste était politique », raconte Rink Dickinson, l'un des trois fondateurs d'Equal Exchange, qui compte aujourd'hui 80 membres travailleurs. La coopérative est également la principale propriétaire d'Oké USA, qui distribue aux États-Unis les bananes d'El Guabo. Oké USA et El Guabo sont actionnaires d'Agrofair, basée aux Pays-Bas et formée d'un consortium d'organisations, d'entreprises et de groupes de producteurs du Sud spécialisés dans les fruits frais. Avec ses 60 millions d'euros de chiffre d'affaires, Agrofair est la plus grande importatrice de produits 100 % équitables au monde.

« Les organisations offrant des produits 100 % équitables ont été les pionnières du mouvement et encore aujourd'hui, ce sont les plus exigeantes et les plus vigilantes », explique Rob Clarke, actuel directeur de Transfair Canada. Le Canada est le pays qui compte le plus grand nombre d'organisations offrant des produits 100 % équitables parmi ses licenciés. Mais la certification équitable, débutée aux Pays-Bas en 1988, allait marquer l'arrivée des grandes entreprises de l'alimentaire dans ce giron. « À nos

⌃ Rink Dickinson, l'un des fondateurs de la coopérative de travailleurs Equal Exchange, pionnière du mouvement équitable aux États-Unis.

débuts, nos cafés étaient vendus dans les coopératives d'aliments naturels, explique Rink Dickinson. La progression fut très lente dans les marchés conventionnels, mais à la fin des années 1990, avec l'arrivée des multinationales, les choses ont changé. Nous avons toujours voulu cette croissance, mais nous savions que cela apporterait des contradictions dans le système. »

L'arrivée des multinationales dans l'importation et la distribution de produits équitables fut souvent mal reçue. Certains y ont vu un pacte avec le diable, avec des entreprises qui traînent parfois de lourds bilans sociaux et environnementaux et qui sacrifient tout pour les profits immédiats. D'autres ont critiqué l'opportunisme des multinationales qui prennent le train de l'équitable uniquement pour ne pas perdre des parts de marché.

Pour les producteurs du Sud, le besoin de marché justifiait l'arrivée des grands joueurs. Il y a 10 ans, alors que la certification équitable en était à la moitié de son histoire, les coopératives de café certifiées exportaient moins de 10 % de leurs produits dans le marché équitable. Aujourd'hui, elles en exportent 50 %, en moyenne, et de nouveaux groupes de producteurs veulent joindre le mouvement chaque année.

Le Canada est l'un des pays où la vente de produits équitables connaît la plus forte progression, avec une croissance de 67 % entre 2007 et 2008. Même la consommation *per capita*, de près de six dollars, est similaire à celle de la France et se compare à celle des Pays-Bas et de l'Allemagne, pourtant des châteaux forts du mouvement. En Grande-Bretagne, le plus important marché équitable, les consommateurs investissent près de 22 dollars en produits équitables, alors que les champions, les Suisses, dépassent les 33 dollars.

C'est d'ailleurs en Europe que le marché équitable est le plus consolidé. Les vastes réseaux de boutiques spécialisées sont non seulement des points de vente de produits équitables, mais des centres névralgiques d'éducation et de sensibilisation, où de nombreux bénévoles s'impliquent. En 1994, 13 associations nationales de boutiques ont fondé le Network of European Worldshops (NEWS !) représentant plus de 2000 « magasins du monde », soit la moitié de ce marché.

Ces réseaux de boutiques sont souvent associés à des organisations d'importation qui parcourent le monde à la recherche de nouveaux produits, voire de nouveaux groupes de producteurs. CTM Altromercato, en Italie, possède une triple identité – entreprise, mouvement et réseau de boutiques. Intermón Oxfam en Espagne, Tradecraft en Angleterre ou Gepa en Allemagne ont toutes débuté dans le monde de l'artisanat pour devenir des pionnières des produits alimentaires. En 1987, 11 organisations importatrices fondèrent la European Fair Trade Association (EFTA), regroupant certaines des plus anciennes et des plus grandes organisations spécialisées en commerce équitable.

Sous l'acronyme FINE, les quatre grands réseaux équitables (la FLO, la WFTO, le NEWS, et la EFTA) collaborent depuis 1996 pour, entre autres, développer un système de surveillance intégré pour l'ensemble du mouvement équitable et faire du lobbying au niveau international. Basée à Washington, la Fair Trade Federation (FTF), qui regroupe 300 organisations, principalement au Canada et aux États-Unis, vient compléter les grands réseaux équitables des pays consommateurs.

Au Sud, le commerce équitable fait également tourner les têtes. En plus des trois réseaux continentaux liés à la FLO (la CLAC, l'AFN et le NAP), le Brésil développe son propre marché national de commerce équitable, Faces do Brasil, qui regroupe plus de 1000 organisations de producteurs, commerçants et autres partenaires officiels. L'Alternative bolivarienne pour les Amériques (ALBA) se réclame également du commerce équitable et applique plusieurs de ses principes dans les accords commerciaux qui unissent neuf pays des Caraïbes et d'Amérique du Sud.

VENTES AU DÉTAIL DE PRODUITS CERTIFIÉS ÉQUITABLES PAR LA FLO, EN 2008

Pays	Ventes totales	Dépenses totales *per capita*	Croissance (2007 à 2008)
Grande-Bretagne	1 318 700 000 $	21,71 $	43 %
États-Unis	1 134 800 000 $	3,74 $	10 %
France	382 800 000 $	5,99 $	22 %
Allemagne	318 670 000 $	3,89 $	50 %
Suisse	252 800 000 $	33,69 $	7 %
Canada	192 400 000 $	5,84 $	67 %
Suède	109 000 000 $	11,98 $	75 %
Allemagne	97 600 000 $	11,83 $	23 %
Pays-Bas	91 200 000 $	5,54 $	28 %
Finlande	81 600 000 $	15,42 $	57 %
Danemark	76 700 000 $	14,23 $	40 %
Belgique	68 600 000 $	6,44 $	31 %
Italie	61 700 000 $	1,05 $	6 %
Norvège	46 400 000 $	9,88 $	73 %
Irlande	45 100 000 $	10,48 $	29 %
Australie/Nouvelle-Zélande	27 900 000 $	1,20 $	72 %
Japon	14 400 000 $	0,15 $	44 %
Espagne	8 200 000 $	0,15 $	40 %
Luxembourg	6 300 000 $	13,18 $	33 %
FLO	150 000 $	n.d.	n.d.
Total	**4 334 800 000 $**		

La certification équitable de la FLO, qui représente 90 % des ventes de produits équitables, a connu une croissance phénoménale de 1300 % entre 2000 et 2008. En 2009, Starbucks s'est engagée à doubler ses achats de café équitable, ce qui représente seulement 10 % de ses importations, mais près du tiers de l'offre globale de café équitable. De son côté, la Britannique Cadbury vient de lancer sa Dairy Milk équitable, faite de sucre et de cacao certifiés. La compagnie quadruplera ainsi les exportations de cacao équitable du Ghana pour atteindre 20 000 tonnes annuellement, soit le double de tout le cacao équitable exporté en 2008. L'avantage des multinationales est qu'elles ont les ressources financières et les réseaux de distribution pour faire bouger de gigantesques volumes.

« Nous sommes flattés de l'arrivé de Cadbury dans l'équitable, commente Caitlin Peeling de La Siembra, nous la voyons comme une preuve de notre succès ; si l'équitable n'était pas rentable, les grands joueurs ne s'y investiraient pas. Ça démontre aussi l'importance de toujours pousser pour un commerce encore plus équitable. Nous sommes conduits par la mission du commerce équitable, non par la seule certification de nos produits. »

Lancés en 2009, les produits de cuisine Camino (cacao en poudre, pépites de chocolat, chocolat de cuisson et cassonade intégrale) sont non seulement faits de cacao et de sucre produits de manière équitable et biologique, mais toute leur transformation est réalisée dans divers pays d'Amérique latine. « Nous allons toujours encourager la transformation en pays d'origine par les producteurs, pour leur assurer un maximum de la valeur ajoutée, insiste Caitlin. Le commerce équitable s'insère dans une préoccupation plus large, celle d'une consommation plus responsable, plus éthique, plus respectueuse des communautés, de l'environnement et des générations futures. »

Dans le plus large marché de la « consommation responsable » et de la « responsabilité sociale », plusieurs lancent leurs *labels,* codes d'éthique, fondations, œuvres de charité et autres initiatives pour faire valoir certains engagements sociaux ou environnementaux. On ne peut faire autrement que de constater l'actuelle abondance de produits « verts », « éthiques », « biologiques », « écologiques », des épithètes miracles que l'on peut coller sur les bouteilles de détergent comme sur le dépliant explicatif d'un fonds d'investissement. Il ne s'agit pas d'une simple mode, mais d'une réelle

☑ Equita, la marque de Commerce équitable Oxfam-Québec, compte la plus vaste gamme de produits certifiés équitables au pays : café, riz, épices, fruits séchés et autres barres de chocolat sont distribués dans les boutiques spécialisées, ainsi que dans les grandes surfaces.

Expression sportive de la globalisation, le soccer (ou football), ne connaît pas de frontières. Fascination ancienne, le ballon de cuir enflé, joué des pieds, est présent dès l'Antiquité grecque et chinoise. Le Moyen Âge européen connaîtra ses versions antécédentes à l'ère du football, qui ne tarderont pas à réapparaître dans les territoires conquis, rebaptisés Amériques... où les peuples originaires avaient déjà leur propre jeu de pelote.

Les yeux brillants des enfants devant les ballons de baudruche ne réfléchissent-ils pas les étincelles de cette pulsion atavique ? Ce sport, qui fascine les foules de tous les continents, a de bien solides bases historiques ou psychiques. Ses bases économiques seront lancées dès la fin du XIXᵉ siècle, lors de la naissance du « football » pour le monde des affaires en Angleterre – berceau du capitalisme, que nul n'ose en douter. Aux recettes des guichets viendront s'ajouter celles de la publicité et des droits de transmission par les divers médias. La construction de stades et de toutes les infrastructures nécessaires, les produits dérivés et les salaires des professionnels font de ce sport une activité économique majeure. Parfois objet de viles manipulations politiques, le soccer est aussi un terrain d'affirmation symbolique pour les humiliés de ce monde, où les Palestiniens imposent de cuisantes défaites à Israël et les États-Unis tremblent de peur devant le Nigeria.

Ménandre 1ᵉʳ inscrira la capitale de son royaume, Sagala, dans l'histoire du bouddhisme. Cette marque de célébrité lui aurait suffi. Mais l'histoire a transformé ce lieu de sagesse en Sialkot, ville pakistanaise connue pour sa production d'instruments de musique, d'instruments chirurgicaux, de textile et d'articles de sport, dont rien de moins que 70 % des ballons de soccer commercialisés à travers le monde. De petites mains les fabriquent... encore dans des conditions analogues à celles de l'esclavage. Dès 1996, la Confédération internationale des syndicats libres (CISL) dénonça la surexploitation des enfants, et poussa à un accord impliquant divers organismes internationaux et les fournisseurs pakistanais, mais une telle initiative, bien que fort positive, ne parvint pas à enrayer le phénomène. Selon Tim Noonan, de la CISL, « sans régulation sociale du commerce international, la compétition vers le bas restera. »

La mouvance du commerce équitable a voulu apporter une réponse à cette situation intolérable en certifiant des entreprises de ballons pour, entre autres, proscrire le travail des moins de 15 ans. Mais malgré ses efforts, la part de marché des ballons de soccer équitables reste résiduelle, avec 3,7 % de la production de quatre entreprises pakistanaises en 2008. Il faut espérer que le développement de cette filière équitable contribue à une transformation totale de l'actuelle production de ces articles de sport symboles de disparités marquantes entre enfants travailleurs, au Sud, et enfants joueurs au Nord.

⌃ Jason Nelson, chef du bistro Olivieri à Montréal, utilise du riz équitable thaïlandais, des pleurotes biologiques, du filet mignon de chevreau d'un élevage local et l'huile d'olive Zeitouna, solidaire avec la Palestine, pour concocter un plat résolument ancré dans la « consommation responsable ».

tendance de marché. Le commerce équitable s'inscrit certes dans cette dynamique, qui déborde d'ailleurs du cadre Nord-Sud. Une volonté de justice croissante inspire, dans un pôle comme dans l'autre, de plus en plus d'initiatives responsables aux niveaux social et environnemental.

Le consommateur est un élément clé de ce succès. « Consomacteur », « écocitoyen », « alter-consommateur », quel que soit l'adjectif qui le qualifie, il a le pouvoir de poser les gestes qui permettent ces changements. « La révolution actuelle et celles qui suivront s'amorcent dans notre esprit, mais se poursuivent dans chacune de nos actions », persiste et signe Laure Waridel. Les personnes qui refusent les injustices et les disparités du marché conventionnel sont nombreuses. La force du commerce équitable est d'offrir une alternative bien réelle, qui peut s'exprimer à tous les jours par nos choix de consommation, nos achats ou les lieux de commerce que nous privilégions.

Pour les consommateurs, le commerce équitable est également un riche vecteur d'idées nouvelles. Conférences, expositions, publicités sur Internet, études universitaires et programmes scolaires, il est devenu un outil pour sensibiliser les jeunes et les moins jeunes aux enjeux planétaires. Dans les écoles de la province, et particulièrement dans le réseau des Établissements verts Brundtland, la Centrale des syndicats du Québec (CSQ), qui représente, entre autres, les professeurs, a réalisé divers outils d'enseignement sur le commerce équitable, en plus de soutenir les « magasins du monde » en milieu scolaire, inspirée par l'expérience belge qui touche plus de 125 écoles et universités. Il y a des universités équitables et maintenant des villes équitables ! Depuis l'initiative, en 2001, des 4000 habitants de Garstang, en Grande-Bretagne, 650 villes, villages et régions de par le monde, dont Londres, Bruxelles, Rome et San Francisco, respectent au moins cinq des principes fondamentaux établis par la FLO pour augmenter la sensibilisation et la disponibilité des produits équitables. La ville de Québec sera-t-elle la prochaine à embrasser la cause ?

« L'utopie est la vérité de demain », prophétisa Victor Hugo. Les pionniers du commerce équitable se reconnaissent pleinement dans les paroles de cet apôtre de la paix et de la justice sociale. Les rêves poétiques des débuts du commerce équitable ont emprunté un chemin pavé de solidarité, pour devenir aujourd'hui une réalité tangible : 6000 produits certifiés, 125 000 points de vente, cinq milliards de dollars de ventes au détail ; les résultats de l'équitable sont indéniables. Certains pourraient n'y voir que de modestes valeurs face aux chiffres du commerce mondial, mais pour les millions de producteurs et leur famille qui sont à la base du système, cette « modeste » différence apporte des améliorations substantielles dans leurs conditions de vie. De plus, le commerce équitable ne doit pas être évalué qu'en termes de chiffres. Bien malin celui qui pourra quantifier l'espoir, la fierté et la dignité.

Le succès actuel du commerce équitable est d'abord une preuve que le commerce peut sortir les gens de la misère lorsqu'il est fait dans des conditions justes. C'est également la preuve, devant les tenants du libre marché, qu'avec quelques principes de base, il est possible de joindre « commerce » et « équitable ». Ultimement, le but n'est pas d'atteindre 20 ou 50 milliards de dollars de ventes de produits certifiés. L'utopie serait plutôt de transposer ce succès en influence politique afin de transformer le système du commerce conventionnel, pour que celui-ci puisse concrètement bénéficier aux populations du Sud. Que l'alternative d'aujourd'hui devienne la norme de demain.

Les produits que nous achetons sont le fruit du labeur d'hommes et de femmes. Leurs gestes créateurs contribuent à notre confort et à l'amélioration de nos vies. Et pourtant, ces personnes demeurent anonymes, cachées derrière le voile des chiffres et des statistiques, ou celui de la publicité et des emballages. Je souhaite que ce tour du monde équitable vous ait permis de mieux connaître les origines de certains produits qui ponctuent notre quotidien. J'espère qu'avec ce livre, vous aurez pu contempler les visages et les gestes de ces producteurs, pour y reconnaître les aspirations au bonheur et à la liberté qui nous sont communes et qui nous identifient tous comme frères et sœurs de la grande famille humaine.

▶ Alice Nignan, productrice de karité membre de l'Union de Léo, au Burkina Faso.

1. Le chocolat chaud Cocoa Camino, de La Siembra.
2. Le café Just Us!, de Nouvelle-Écosse.
3. L'usine de café d'Equal Exchange, à Boston.
4. Le *label* de certification équitable de Transfair Canada.
5. Les «magasins du monde» en milieu scolaire, promus par la Centrale des syndicats du Québec (CSQ).
6. Les épices Equita d'Oxfam-Québec.
7. Les produits au karité de Delapointe.
8. Fatoumata, volontaire du programme Uniterra du CECI et de l'EUMC.
9. Boutique Dix Mille Villages, rue St-Denis, à Montréal.
10. *Latte* de Ian Clark dans un café Bridgehead, à Ottawa.

remerciements

En premier lieu, j'aimerais remercier chaleureusement tous les hommes, femmes et enfants avec qui j'ai pu partager un moment, une journée de travail, quelques mots, un repas et parfois même un toit. Je leur suis redevable pour leur généreuse hospitalité, ainsi que pour les connaissances et expériences qu'ils ont bien voulu partager avec moi. Un merci tout particulier à ceux et celles qui m'ont donné le privilège de saisir, à l'aide de ma caméra, quelques moments de leur vie.

Merci aux membres de l'UCIRI au Mexique, aux artisans de Prokritee au Bangladesh, aux petits producteurs de café d'Oromia en Éthiopie, aux cacaoculteurs de la CONACADO en République dominicaine, aux membres de CoopeAgri au Costa Rica, aux travailleurs des jardins de thé indiens et aux membres de la SOFA au Sri Lanka, aux travailleurs des serres de Nevado Roses et Agrogana en Équateur, aux riziculteurs thaïlandais de Green Net, aux producteurs de coton maliens de Kita et du MOBIOM, aux membres d'El Guabo en Équateur et à ceux de Finca 6 en République dominicaine, aux productrices de karité de l'Union de Léo au Burkina Faso et à celles de Siby au Mali, aux membres de l'ANAPQUI en Bolivie, aux viticulteurs de Sagrada Familia au Chili et de Viñasol en Argentine, et aux guaraniculteurs satéré-mawé en Amazonie.

Merci à Oxfam-Québec et son équipe d'Equita, à Transfair Canada, au Centre d'étude et de coopération internationale (CECI) et à son programme Uniterra, en collaboration avec l'Entraide universitaire mondiale du Canada (EUMC), au réseau de boutiques Dix Mille Villages, à la Centrale des syndicats du Québec (CSQ), aux cafés Bridgehead, aux coopératives de travailleurs La Siembra, Just US! et Equal Exchange, ainsi qu'à la compagnie Delapointe, pour leur soutien financier et technique dans la réalisation des reportages. Je tiens également à remercier ces organisations pour leur engagement envers le commerce équitable et leur grande contribution pour la réalisation d'un monde plus juste.

Merci à Francisco Van der Hoff pour sa grande sagesse, qu'il sait si bien partager, à Laure Waridel, avec qui cette quête a débuté, et qui est devenue un leader exceptionnel pour le mouvement équitable, à Emerson da Silva et Mathieu Lamarre pour leur essentielle contribution aux textes de cet ouvrage, à Marc-Henri Faure de FibrEthik pour son appui, et à Nitro Gène pour son soutien lors de mon séjour en Amazonie.

Merci à l'équipe d'Équiterre, et à celles de la FLO et de Transfair Canada pour leurs statistiques.

Merci aux amis, collègues, professeurs et organisations diverses qui m'ont conseillé et soutenu au cours de ces 15 années de travail.

À mes parents, merci de m'avoir transmis le goût du voyage et d'avoir semé l'idée que les rêves peuvent devenir réalité. Merci à ma belle-famille d'être toujours présente pour moi, particulièrement auprès des enfants lors de mes nombreux séjours à l'étranger. Merci Aline pour tes innombrables révisions.

À Sophie, ma douce moitié, et à nos trois enfants, Jérémie, Dominic et Justin, merci de trouver un équilibre avec les aléas d'un globe-trotter et d'être des sources d'inspiration intarissables pour une vie trépidante pavée de moments privilégiés.

adresses utiles

Les organisations du commerce équitable

European Fair Trade Association (EFTA) :
www.eftafairtrade.org
Fairtrade Labelling Organizations International (FLO) :
www.fairtrade.net
Fair Trade Federation (FTF) : www.fairtradefederation.org
Network of European World Shops (NEWS) :
www.worldshops.org
World Fair Trade Organization (WFTO) : www.wfto.com

Les initiatives nationales de certification équitable

ALLEMAGNE
TransFair Allemagne : www.transfair.org
AUSTRALIE/NOUVELLE-ZÉLANDE
Fairtrade Association Australia and New Zealand :
www.fta.org.au
AUTRICHE
Fairtrade Austria : www.fairtrade.at
BELGIQUE
Max Havelaar Belgique : www.maxhavelaar.be
CANADA
TransFair Canada : www.transfair.ca
DANEMARK
Fairtrade Mærket : www.fairtrade-maerket.dk
ESPAGNE
Asociación del Sello de Comercio Justo :
www.sellocomerciojusto.org
ÉTATS-UNIS
TransFair États-Unis : www.transfairusa.org
FINLANDE
Reilu Kauppa : www.reilukauppa.fi
FRANCE
Max Havelaar France : www.maxhavelaarfrance.org
GRANDE-BRETAGNE
The Fairtrade Foundation : www.fairtrade.org.uk
IRLANDE
Fairtrade Mark Ireland : www.fairtrade.ie
ITALIE
TransFair Italie : www.fairtradeitalia.it
JAPON
Fairtrade Label : www.fairtrade-jp.org
LUXEMBOURG
TransFair Minka Luxembourg : www.transfair.lu
NORVÈGE
Max Havelaar Norvège : www.fairtrade.no
PAYS-BAS
Stichting Max Havelaar Pays-Bas : www.maxhavelaar.nl
SUÈDE
Rättvisemärkt : www.rattvisemarkt.se
SUISSE
Max Havelaar Suisse : www.maxhavelaar.ch

Le commerce équitable en Amérique du Nord

Bridgehead : www.bridgehead.ca
Centrale des syndicats du Québec (CSQ) : www.csq.qc.net
Centre d'étude et de coopération internationale (CECI) :
www.ceci.ca
Dix Mille Villages : www.tenthousandvillages.ca
Equal Exchange : www.equalexchange.coop
Équiterre : www.equiterre.org
FibreEthik : www.fibrethik.org
Just Us ! : www.justuscoffee.com
Karité Delapointe : www.karitedelapointe.com
La Siembra : www.cocoacamino.com
Nitro Gène : www.nitrogene.ca
Oxfam-Québec et sa marque Equita : www.oxfam.qc.ca et
www.equita.qc.ca

Les réseaux de producteurs

African Fairtrade Network (AFN) : africafairtrade@yahoo.com
Coordinadora Latinoamericana y del Caribe de Pequeños
Productores de Comercio Justo (CLAC) :
www.clac-comerciojusto.org
Network of Asian Producers (NAP) : www.fairtradenap.net

Les organisations de producteurs

Agrogana : alvaro@agrogana.com
Ambootia Tea Group Exports : ambootia@vsnl.com
Association des petits producteurs de bananes El Guabo :
www.asoguabo.com.ec
Association nationale des producteurs de quinoa
(ANAPQUI) : anapqui@entelnet.bo
Compagnie malienne pour le développement des Textiles
(CMDT) : www.cmdt.ml
CoopeAgri : www.coopeagri.co.cr
Coopérative des Productrices de beurre de karité de Siby
(COOPROKASI) : www.maisondukarite.org
Green Net : www.greennet.or.th
Jardin de thé Makaibari : www.makaibari.com
L'Union des coopératives de caféiculteurs d'Oromia (OCFCU) :
www.oromiacoffeeunion.org
La Confederación Nacional de Cacaocultores Dominicanos
(CONACADO) : www.conacado.com.do
Mouvement biologique malien (MOBIOM) :
Siaka.Doumbia@helvetas.org
Nevado Ecuador : www.nevadoroses.com
Prokritee : www.prokritee.com
SAPOPEMA-Consortium des guaraniculteurs satéré-mawé :
http://sites.google.com/site/filhosdowarana/
Small Organic Farmers Association (SOFA) et Biofoods :
www.biofoodslk.com
Sociedad Vitivinícola Sagrada Familia : www.vinoslautaro.cl
Union communale des coopératives de producteurs de coton
de Djidian : solobamadi@Yahoo.fr
Unión de Comunidades Indígenas de la Región del Istmo
(UCIRI) : www.uciri.org
Union des Groupements de Productrices de Produits de
Karité des provinces de la Sissili et du Ziro (Union de Léo) :
www.afriquekarite.com
Viña de la Solidaridad (Viñasol) : www.solunawines.com

⌃ Corvée quotidienne au puits pour Zénabou et Kadio, de Tabou, au Burkina Faso.

Achevé d'imprimé au Canada
sur papier Flo Gloss 200M
Contient 10 % de fibres postconsommation
Certifié Éco-Logo, procédé sans chlore et FSC Recyclé
Fabriqué à partir d'énergie biogaz

Recyclé
Contribue à l'utilisation responsable
des ressources forestières
www.fsc.org   Cert no. SGS-COC-003153
© 1996 Forest Stewardship Council